PHILLIPA ASHLEY writes warm, funny romantic fiction for a variety of world-famous international publishers.

After studying English at Oxford, she worked as a copywriter and journalist. Her first novel, *Decent Exposure*, won the RNA New Writers Award and was made into a TV movie called *12 Men of Christmas* starring Kristin Chenoweth and Josh Hopkins. As Pippa Croft, she also wrote the Oxford Blue series – *The First Time We Met*, *The Second Time I Saw You* and *Third Time Lucky*.

Phillipa lives in a Staffordshire village and has an engineer husband and scientist daughter who indulge her arty whims. She runs a holiday-let business in the Lake District, but a big part of her heart belongs to Cornwall. She visits the county several times a year for 'research purposes', an arduous task that involves sampling cream teas, swimming in wild Cornish coves and following actors around film shoots in a camper van. Her hobbies include watching *Poldark*, Earl Grey tea, Prosecco-tasting and falling off surf boards in front of RNLI lifeguards.

🐦 @PhillipaAshley

A Surprise Christmas Wedding

Phillipa Ashley

avon.

Published by AVON
A division of HarperCollins*Publishers* Ltd
1 London Bridge Street
London SE1 9GF

www.harpercollins.co.uk

A Paperback Original 2020

3

First published in Great Britain by HarperCollins*Publishers* 2020

A catalogue copy of this book is available from the British Library.

ISBN: 978-0-00-837160-9

Typeset in Birka by Palimpsest Book Production Limited, Falkirk, Stirlingshire
Printed and bound in UK by CPI Group (UK) Ltd, Croydon CR0 4YY

MIX
Paper from
responsible sources

FSC C007454

This book is produced from independently certified FSC™ paper to ensure responsible forest management.

For more information visit: www.harpercollins.co.uk/green

For my family, with much love

Prologue

15 September
Porthmellow, Cornwall

'Hold on! I won't be a minute,' Connor said, as he suddenly let go of Lottie's hand.

She frowned. 'Why? Where are you going?'

She reached for him but Connor was already yards away.

He came back and brushed her lips with his. 'You'll find out soon enough. Wait here on the harbour for me. Don't worry, I won't be long, Dotty Lottie.'

'Don't call me that!' Lottie said, trying not to laugh.

Connor's grin was unrepentant as he melted into crowds of holidaymakers thronging the harbourside of Porthmellow, leaving Lottie on the quayside.

She shook her head. Dotty Lottie was what some of the kids had called her at the Lakeland school she and Connor had both attended. He'd been four years above her and as a result they'd barely been aware of each other's presence at the time, only meeting again through their work a few years before. Lottie was an events organiser at a hotel and Connor's insurance firm had been one of their clients. However, she'd once unwisely confessed to him how much she hated the nickname and he'd used it ever since to wind her up and tease her – affectionately, of course.

Puzzling over his mysterious behaviour, Lottie wandered along the harbourside, while she waited for him to return. She was hardly alone, surrounded by hundreds of tourists enjoying the late September heatwave, but she had a curious feeling that she'd been cast adrift, like a cork bobbing in the sea.

Perhaps it was the unfamiliar surroundings, and the fact that she hadn't known they were even coming to Cornwall until forty-eight hours previously, when Connor had parked the car outside a tiny holiday cottage on Porthmellow's quayside.

Lottie could see its jaunty blue facade now, on the opposite side of the harbour, part of a row all painted in bubble-gum colours. The holiday cottage was such a contrast from the stone and slated houses of the Lakeland village where she and Connor lived. Langmere nestled on the shores of Derwentwater, encircled by the heather-clad fells and soaring peaks – equally pretty but with a subtler palette.

It struck her that in many ways, the tight-knit community of Porthmellow, with its houses huddled around the harbour – and the sense that everyone knew each other – reminded her of the Lakeland village she'd grown up in. The locals chattered outside the fish kiosk, just as they did outside the village shop and post office. Sail ropes clanked against masts just as they did on the yachts moored in the lakeside marina. But the contrast delighted her too. While the sea was steely blue topped with whitecaps, the lake's dark surface reflected the fells like a mirror. That morning, she'd woken to the slap of waves on the harbour wall rather than the beck tumbling beside their Lakeland home.

It felt wonderful, but slightly disconcerting to have been whisked almost five hundred miles south at short notice, especially when she'd had no idea of their precise destination. Now she was here, she was keen to embrace every moment.

She breathed in, savouring the tang of sea air and fishing creels, rather than the scent of woodsmoke and fresh rain she was used to.

'Hello!' Connor tapped her shoulder.

Lottie twisted round. 'You made me jump!'

'Guilty conscience.' With a smile, he joined her on the bench and crossed one leg over the other. He seemed extremely pleased with himself and he was grinning broadly.

'You look like a dog with two tails.'

He waggled his eyebrows. 'You should be so lucky.'

She groaned. 'That's a terrifying idea.'

'Terrifying?'

'Weird too. I don't think I could handle it.' She wrinkled her nose but was smiling.

'Or them,' he said, with what was meant to be a sexy grin. 'Come on, let's go back to the cottage.'

'I'm not sure I want to after what you just said . . .'

But of course, she did want to go back to the cottage and knew exactly what he had in mind when they got there. Their unexpected week in Cornwall had certainly amped up the romance in their relationship – if the past couple of days was anything to go by. Although Lottie was now wondering where he'd been and what had happened to make Connor so smugly happy. Whatever it was, she was intrigued at this newly mysterious side to her partner.

He certainly didn't relish surprises normally. His work as an actuary for an insurance company was a job that involved the precise calculation and prediction of risk. And while Lottie's job as an events organiser at a large hotel also involved careful planning, she loved spontaneous things – an impromptu picnic on the fells, a last-minute trip to the theatre – unlike Connor, who preferred to plan in advance. He liked to discuss where they were going, research it in great detail and make sure they were both happy – right down to insisting they both looked at any hotel or resort on Google Earth to make sure there was no rubbish tip next door and you really could walk to that 'charming bistro' in the ten minutes the website claimed. It had to be a joint decision, often involving spreadsheets weighing up the merits of several different options and giving them a score.

Which made it all the more surprising that he'd sprung this week in Cornwall on her. She already had the time off work booked and thought they were going to spend it redecorating the sitting room – after due diligence with relation to paint charts.

However, when she'd come home from work on the Friday,

Connor had informed her to pack her holiday clothes because they were spending a week 'by the seaside' from the very next day.

Lottie had first reconnected with Connor when his company had held a charity ball at the hotel where Lottie worked. He'd volunteered for the firm's community fund-raising team and was helping to organise the event.

They'd recognised each other immediately, because Connor's family had, for a time, lived in the same village as Lottie's. When he walked into the meeting at the hotel, Lottie had thought he was ambitious, efficient and very good-looking. She'd been surprised by the amount of attention he'd paid her. At first, she'd dismissed it as polite flirtation, but at the end of their third meeting, when they were alone having a coffee in the hotel bistro, he'd asked her out.

The rest was history, and she'd allowed herself to be swept away by his charm, his energy and sheer determination to go for what he wanted in life. This, she remembered thinking, must be what a 'whirlwind romance' was. They did happen. A couple of months after they'd met, Lottie had moved out of the house she shared with her sister Steph and her lively two-year-old twin girls, to move in with Connor.

Now, two years later, they were 'partners' and had bought their own cottage in Langmere. The flame of romance was still very much alive, and Lottie had started to envisage a long-term future that included, hopefully in time, a family. For now, she was going to simply enjoy the moment and her surprise visit to Cornwall.

* * *

Over the next few days, they walked the coast path, dined in the harbour restaurants, sunbathed on the beach and swam in secluded coves. Connor made no reference to his mysterious errand, and Lottie wondered if he'd merely gone to buy something for her birthday – she'd be thirty-three in just a few weeks.

Then, on Thursday evening, after dinner on the cottage terrace, Connor whisked her down to the cove next to Porthmellow. It was a mild September evening, still warm enough to wear shorts. They left their shoes on the rocks, and walked barefoot in the frilly edge of the surf. The sun sank lower, tingeing the sky with coral. They kissed, with the sound of the waves breaking on the sand and the gulls crying above them.

Glowing from the sun, Lottie thought she had never been so happy.

In high spirits, she broke away from him and shouted: 'Bet you can't catch me!'

'Bet I can!'

He ran towards her. She dodged him, though both of them were laughing too much to take the chase seriously. She waded into the sea, the surf wetting her calves.

'You'll have to come in to get me! Dare you!'

'You dare to dare Connor,' he said, wading into the water, 'who never turns down a challenge?'

He swept her up in his arms. She shrieked and protested as he carried her out of the surf and set her down in the shallows. Still breathless, he held her face in his hands and kissed her, while the wind tugged at her hair and the surf roared.

'Keep your eyes closed,' he whispered. 'No, don't even think about peeping!'

'OK . . .' She squeezed her lids shut, pulse racing with anticipation while wavelets lapped her ankles with the gentlest of caresses. She felt invincible, as if nothing bad could touch her or ever would.

Grasping her hand, he guided her out of the shallows onto the wet sand and finally she felt soft powder between her toes.

'Wait here,' he ordered, his hands at her elbows, putting her into position. The temptation to steal a look was killing her.

'You can open them now.'

She blinked against the sun but Connor wasn't in front of her. She looked down. He was at her feet, balanced on one knee on the sand.

Her heart rate went into overdrive. 'What's this?'

'What does it look like?' He reached into the pocket of his shorts, wobbling a little on the sand.

'No . . .' Her hand flew to her mouth.

'Yes.' He took her other hand, opened the palm and placed a small blue box in it.

She was shaking. 'You can't.'

'I can and I am. Open it.'

Her fingers trembled as she undid the clasp on the box and the fire of diamonds glittered in the evening sunlight. 'Wh-where did you get this?'

'Here . . .' He looked at her a little sheepishly. 'That little jewellery maker by the shell shop in Porthmellow.'

A gold ring nestled in the box, the stones glinting in the sunlight. 'Y-you mean you decided while we were here?'

'Yes. No. I've wanted to ask you for a while and I was going to ask you and wait until we could choose a ring together but then I saw you admiring the jewellery in their window and I thought, why wait? Why not just got for it? I hope it fits. Have I done the right thing? Though I suppose I ought to actually propose to you, first.'

Lottie was dumbstruck. She hadn't expected this. It had come, literally, out of a clear blue sky.

'OK, I'll just get on with it.' He took a breath. 'Lottie Hargreaves,' he said, gazing up at her. 'Would you do me the honour of becoming my wife?'

What? Words would not come, only emotion: shock, excitement, joy, shock . . . robbing her of breath. He'd kept this secret for a whole week – no, longer than that . . .

'This is so – sudden, Connor.'

'Not that sudden. Not unexpected, surely? We've known each other for years. Plus, I love you. That's all that matters.'

'I love you too . . .'

He laughed. 'Then what else do we need?'

What else? To commit to a lifetime . . .

He searched her face, doubt filling his eyes. 'Have I made a huge mistake?'

'No. Not a mistake. I'm just shocked. I mean I'm flabbergasted. I never expected this.'

'But it's not a "no" as in "no, I don't want to marry you"?'

'No. I mean, yes. Yes, I do want to . . .' The words slipped out before she'd even realised.

His eyes lit up. 'Thank God for that. Would you mind if I got up now? I think I'm kneeling on a sea urchin.'

Laughing though still stunned, Lottie helped him to his feet. It wasn't a sea urchin, only a broken shell that had grazed the skin. He rubbed it and they hugged each other and kissed for what seemed like forever. If he was willing to make a lifetime commitment, she was ready to meet him. Her heart danced like the waves on the sea and her spirit soared like gulls wheeling impossibly high in the sky.

She genuinely wondered if it was possible to burst with happiness.

Connor took out the ring and slipped it on her finger. It fitted perfectly and its fire caught the rays of the setting sun.

Hand in hand, they'd wandered back to their holiday cottage, where Connor produced a bottle of champagne with a beautiful card featuring a painting of the cove where he'd proposed. Lottie wasn't sure if he'd written it before or after she'd said yes but frankly, she didn't care.

It thanked her for accepting his proposal and said she'd 'made him the happiest man alive'.

They took the glasses upstairs, but even after they'd made love, she couldn't sleep for excitement, allowing herself to imagine the future stretching on forever with Connor, imagining children . . . grandchildren.

The next day, on the long journey north, all she could think about was how excited Steph would be when she found out her four-year-old twins were going to be bridesmaids. It was too momentous a piece of news to be delivered by phone, she thought, driving home while Connor dozed in the passenger seat. It had to be in person, preferably with Connor by her side.

She'd get him to come with her the following evening after work, make a big occasion of it, maybe get a taxi so they could all have a bottle of champagne. Yes, that's how she'd break the news. She knew Steph would be as thrilled as she was.

It was past eleven when she got home. Connor had driven the last few hours and gone straight to bed, saying he was knackered and had an early start. Lottie woke just as he was on his way out of the kitchen the next morning. She immediately noticed the overnight bag at his feet.

'Not running away, are you?' she said, putting her arms around him.

'Running away?' he said sharply.

'I was joking.'

'Oh. No . . . but I'm afraid I do have to go away to the Edinburgh office.'

'Edinburgh?'

Disappointed, she let go of him. This business trip was news to her. 'What? Now?'

'Unfortunately I'll probably have to stay for a couple of days.' He grimaced. 'I've got a big project on. I had a message on the way home from Cornwall saying it was all going tits up. I need to spend the next few days kicking arses up in the Scottish branch.'

Lottie couldn't hide her dismay. 'Arghh. I was hoping we could go round to Steph's to announce our news. I thought we could make a proper thing of it, maybe get a cab so we can take a bottle of champagne.'

'Can we hang fire until I get back? I'll probably be stuck in the office until Thursday.'

'Thursday? You want me to wait until Thursday to tell Steph our news? I'll burst!'

'Well . . .' He sat down, a serious expression on his face. 'It might be a good idea to hold on for a while anyway before we start shouting about it. Steph's hardly had the happiest experiences with men, has she?'

'No . . . but that won't stop her from being happy for us, Connor.'

'Even so, perhaps we should curb a little of our enthusiasm. Be slightly more tactful?'

She frowned. 'Tactful?'

He patted her hand. 'Sensitive, then.'

'If you really think so . . .' Lottie said, slightly hurt that Connor had misjudged Steph, but unwilling to cause a scene when he was about to leave.

Connor smiled and picked up his phone. 'I'll see you later in the week.'

'OK.' With a quick kiss, he left.

Lottie consoled herself with the reminder that it was only a few days, after all, and she'd rather wait until the weekend when he was able to relax and fully enjoy the moment.

However, she spent the entire drive to work still disappointed he'd rushed off and wondering exactly what he'd meant about being 'tactful'. Granted Steph had had a few disastrous encounters with guys. The twins' father was a guy she'd met on holiday in Ibiza and he'd given Steph a fake phone number so she'd never even been able to track him down to tell him about his daughters. Even so, Lottie was certain Steph would have been overjoyed to hear about her engagement.

Lottie had been the first person Steph had called to reveal she was pregnant; the one she shared all her news with, good and bad, big and small. Steph was the rock of Lottie's life, now their parents lived in New Zealand. She was the woman she wanted to talk to now more than she ever had before: her big sister and her closest friend.

Telling herself Thursday would soon come around, Lottie threw herself into her work, even though her fingers itched to dial Steph's number. She also couldn't help planning her wedding in her head. It would probably be at the village church overlooking the lake with the reception at the hotel she worked for. She knew a local designer whose dresses she loved. She smiled to herself, thinking what a thrill it would be to ask the seamstress to make her a bespoke bridal gown.

Now she'd had chance to think about it, it was probably not the worst thing that Connor had persuaded her to delay announcing their engagement by a few days. If she timed it right, they could catch their parents on Zoom before they went to work, and after the twins were in bed, make a proper 'party' of it even if not everyone could be there.

Buoyed by making plans for the wedding in her head, Lottie managed to get through the days. Connor was busy in the evenings and they only managed a quick text exchange but by Thursday Lottie was growing as excited as a kid on Christmas Eve. Connor messaged to say he'd be home from Scotland very late, so not to wait up if she was too tired.

But Lottie very much did want to wait up. She put some fizz on ice and sat in the sitting room, in heels and a slinky dress, waiting for him. She heard his BMW crunch onto the driveway, the security light flicked on and she flew into the kitchen, grabbed the champagne and flung back the door, ready for a romantic reunion – and the start of the celebrations.

Yet there was something about Connor that made her pause in the doorway, and stopped the cry of 'Surprise!' in her throat. Even from metres away, she could see that something was wrong. His shoulders were slumped; his face was pale. He looked a broken man.

His first words when he reached the door were: 'I'm sorry. I've done something unforgivable.'

Five seconds later, Lottie's world started to unravel.

Chapter One

4 November, the following year
Langmere, Lake District

'Morning, Lottie. How's it going? Found yourself a nice young man, yet?'

Lottie rolled her eyes. One of the village's senior residents asked her this very question every time he saw her, often in front of everyone in the post office. It was now a running joke between Irina and her husband, Jan.

'Not yet, Irina,' she said. 'Still waiting . . .'

'I would keep away from them all. Especially the nice ones – they're the most dangerous.' Irina raised her voice. 'I don't have a problem fending off the young ones any more.'

'Eh? What's that?' Jan asked, walking out of the storeroom with a carton of Kendal Mint Cake. Originally from Poland, he and Irina had been running the post office for over a decade now and were both stalwarts of the village.

'Is it your day off?' Irina asked Lottie. 'Doing some Christmas shopping?'

'No, I'm on my way back to Firholme from dropping the twins at school. Steph has a hospital appointment today.'

Irina frowned in sympathy. 'How's she doing? I bet she'll be glad when that's over.'

'She's OK. It's been very tough for her.'

'Those gorgeous little girls of hers are such angels. Good job she has you to help her out, what with your parents living on the other side of the world.'

Amused at the idea of Myra and Jodie as 'angels', Lottie smiled. 'I'm definitely glad I live so close.'

'Here you go, have these for the girls.' Irina reached for a bag of Milky Way Magic Stars and pushed them under the screen.

Lottie smiled. 'Thanks, you're very kind but let me pay for them.'

'No way. It's only a little treat!'

'In that case, thank you.' Lottie popped some coins in the mountain rescue box.

The doorbell dinged and an elderly man with a stick walked in. Wilf Carman was over ninety and had piloted a glider into Normandy as part of the D-day landings, as he never ceased to remind everyone, not that Lottie minded.

He waved his stick. 'Hello, young lady! I still remember when you were Dotty Lottie.'

'Morning, Mr Carman.' Lottie smiled, but did wish he wouldn't use her school nickname every time he saw her. He'd been caretaker at the school when she'd first started at the village primary. Out of the corner of her eye, she saw Irina stifling a giggle behind the post office screen.

'Have you found a nice young man, yet?' he said.

'Not yet, Mr Carman. Why? Are you offering?'

He let out a cackle. 'If I was sixty years younger. I cut quite a dash in my RAF uniform, you know.'

After listening to him reminisce for a few minutes, and then begin to tell Irina the latest news about a branch of his family who lived in Cornwall, Lottie had to excuse herself as she needed to get back to work.

She walked towards her car, parked on the small car park by the lakeside café. Ducks and geese waddled around, picking at scraps. Woodsmoke spiralled out of the chimneys of the village, where the stone and slate-roofed cottages huddled around the pub and church looked as if they were straight from a Beatrix Potter tale.

Lottie drove out of the village, past the café, mountain equipment shop, gallery and pub until the houses gave way to the open fellside, edged with dry-stone walls. The Herdwick sheep had been brought down off the fellside to the lower fields now and were gathered in fields near the farms. They munched away as she drove past, their winter fleeces shaggy and marked crimson to make them easier to identify. Lottie had often thought they were the punk rockers of the sheep world and her nieces delighted in finding the most colourful.

It was a crisp November morning, with the sheen of frost still lying on the grass and bracken. The road out of Langmere twisted and turned for over a mile until the entrance to the Firholme estate appeared, marked by two huge stone pillars topped with two creatures that had once been griffins but whose faces were now weathered away and covered with orange lichen.

After passing the 'Welcome to Firholme' sign and the visitor car parks, the big house itself came into view.

Lottie never ceased to be impressed by how beautiful it was, and how spectacular the setting. In fact, everything about the Firholme estate had been designed to make a statement, to impress and wow visitors. The house had been built at the turn of the twentieth century as a 'gentleman's residence'. Its original owner had made his money from cotton mills, and every aspect, from the elaborate oak panelling and stone fireplaces to the grand staircase, was designed to impress guests and business associates with his 'self-made' wealth.

It was set in the middle of a large estate whose grounds stretched from the shore of Derwentwater right up to the high open fellsides, with gardens, outbuildings, cottages and woodland in between.

Lottie continued beyond the visitor car park and turned down a small track marked 'Private' until she reached a pair of semidetached cottages, situated a few hundred yards below the house and screened by a small stand of trees.

Back in the day, they'd been deliberately built well out of sight of the main house so its owners would never have had to see their workers' humble cottages. That suited Lottie because it gave her privacy from the visitors and some demarcation between her working day and home life.

Each cottage had a postage-stamp front garden bordered by a low beech hedge with its own gate. She left the car outside the one called 'The Bothy', noting there was no sign of the muddy pick-up truck owned by her new neighbour. Jay Calder, Firholme's newly recruited estates manager, had only moved in a week or so before.

Lottie had seen him standing beside his pick-up when she'd popped back to her cottage in the middle of the morning. He'd been unloading his possessions and had no one with him apart from a friendly black Labrador. She'd introduced herself, and when she'd asked him if he needed anything, or any help, he'd politely but firmly muttered, 'Thanks for the offer, but I am fine.'

She'd walked back to work, with a sense even at this early stage that Jay wasn't going to be the most sociable of neighbours. That was his business, of course, but she was unable to shake his image from her mind. Somehow, she'd expected a homely older man, not a good-looking guy around her own age. She could only wish him good luck if he didn't want to be noticed. With his handsome face and physique, in a small community like Firholme, which was fascinated by any newcomer, he'd have a hard time *not* attracting attention.

Lottie went inside, changed into her suit, slicked on some lip gloss and hurried up to Firholme House where she'd arranged to meet her boss for a 'quick chat'. Knowing Shayla Kendrick, Lottie knew it would be anything but quick, and definitely not just a 'chat'.

'Now, what Firholme really needs is a big juicy, *lavish* wedding that we can slap on the website and shout about on social media. The bigger, the better! We need a showpiece!'

Lottie's boss threw her arms out like a diva on the last note of an aria. Shayla Lambert was clearly inspired by the grand setting of the ballroom of Firholme House. It was at least the fifth time that week Shayla had uttered this line in one form or another. She'd rescued the estate from near bankruptcy and was dedicated to turn it into a must-visit destination for events and weddings.

'Well, the Valentine's Week wedding fair will give us a huge boost,' Lottie replied. 'And I've secured several features in the bridal magazines from now right through to late spring.'

Shayla gave her an encouraging smile. 'And that's all good . . .'

'Plus, we have the festive season coming up,' Lottie pointed out. 'The Edwardian Christmas evening will bring in lots of visitors and some may book other events. There's a team-building day in the grounds and at least three big company Christmas parties.'

'I know. I know you've worked very hard so far and I can't believe how fast you organised that autumn antiques fair last month or how you managed to persuade all those performers and stallholders to take part in the Edwardian night.'

'Most of them were contacts from when I worked at the Lakeland Hotel,' Lottie said. 'With a little persuasion, most were happy to add an extra date to their schedules – even if it is a new event at an untried venue.'

'I knew you'd pull a rabbit out of a hat. That's why I was so keen to poach you, but we *do* need as many showcase events as we can to make up for the start to the year.'

'We're definitely getting lots of enquiries . . .' Lottie said, thinking of how long the nights had become, and how often she woke to autumn fog shrouding the view that Firholme was famous for.

Shayla smiled. 'What you've achieved so far is great . . .' Lottie waited for the 'but' . . .

'If we *could* get a truly amazing wedding before Christmas, it would be such a showcase for Firholme, not to mention the revenue would help see us through. We really need to persuade people to come back in their droves.'

Lottie nodded in all the right places. Shayla was a dynamic and exciting boss to work for, if a little overoptimistic at times. Despite this, the fact remained: it was Lottie's job to get the wedding calendar filling up, although she thought there wasn't a cat in hell's chance of securing one with Christmas only seven weeks away.

'We should definitely set up a photo shoot with all our bridal suppliers. We can show couples that Firholme is a fantastic place for a wedding whatever the season,' Lottie said, keeping the conversation positive. 'And that nowhere could be more romantic or spectacular for their big day.'

'It's incredible, isn't it?' Shayla said with a sigh of awe. 'Even if I do say so myself.'

Despite the huge challenge ahead, the gloss of owning Firholme clearly hadn't worn off for Shayla and Lottie didn't blame her. Steps led up to the grand vestibule where double doors opened onto a drawing room, morning room and a ballroom complete with chandelier and three sets of double doors out onto the terrace. Even on this autumn day, the lake glittered in the valley, its surface reflecting the fells rising up on either side, with dark forests giving way to hills, which were still russet with bracken.

While it didn't operate as a hotel, the ten bedrooms were perfect for accommodating wedding guests, parties and conferences. The numerous smaller rooms, hidden away at the rear of the building, were used as extra kitchens, and for storage and services. It always amused Lottie that the moment you opened a grand door onto a 'working' part of the house, the lavish wall coverings and parquet floors were replaced by the grey plaster and flagstones the servants would have been accustomed to.

Over the years, Firholme had been through various incarnations, including serving as a nursing home and a rather run-down hotel, until Shayla had bought it that summer and injected a load of cash to turn it into a prestige events and wedding venue.

It gave Lottie a good feeling to think that the house now provided jobs for twenty full- and part-time staff and many seasonal workers, plus accommodation for key staff like herself. She also liked to think about how Shayla, a self-made woman, now owned it and was determined to help her justify the investment and hard work that had been poured into restoring it.

Lottie had helped Shayla plan how the space would be used for weddings. Guests would gather for champagne on the terrace if it was warm or the drawing room on cold or wet days. The brides would enter via the vestibule with its elaborate oak staircase, before walking up the 'aisle' in the ballroom for the ceremony itself. Later, the space could be transformed for the reception and party.

Shayla raised her eyes to the chandelier hanging from the high ceiling in the ballroom. 'I do think a photo shoot is a great idea. We could even make it a video,' she said.

'Even better. I'll set it up right away,' Lottie said enthusiastically. 'I've also been thinking about the Christmas decorations for the house and working on a colour scheme.'

'Really? Great minds think alike . . .' Shayla cut in. 'So have I! I'm very excited about . . .' She opened her large handbag and pulled out a grey object. 'This! I thought we could have a minimalist theme throughout Firholme this Christmas. Everyone's doing understated chic these days. Well, what do you think?'

'Um. It's definitely very . . . understated,' Lottie began, thinking the bauble in Shayla's hand looked the same colour as the old long johns her grandad kept to clean his shed windows. She couldn't visualise the drab decorations adorning the Christmas trees of Firholme.

'Exactly what I thought.' Shayla clapped her hands together. 'Now, take a look at these samples I ordered from the web.' She handed Lottie a black snowflake decoration. 'They do a complete range in steel, charcoal, gunmetal and if we do think we need a bit of bling, they do a new line of pewter tinsel . . .'

'Pewter tinsel?' Lottie said. 'That's um, different.'

'Yes. I can't wait to see them on the Christmas trees. How lucky are we to have our own Christmas tree plantation? It was the icing on the cake when I bought the place, a valuable source of revenue at a quiet time of year. And how lovely to tell couples we have our own home-grown trees and greenery for their winter weddings.'

'We'd need to get the Christmas trees and decorations in place earlier than planned if we want a photo shoot,' Lottie said. 'I've already arranged to meet Jay Calder up at the plantation this morning to talk about the Christmas tree sales opening day so I'll ask him about the trees for the house at the same time.'

'Great.' Shayla smiled. 'Have you had much contact with him yet? I expect you two will be chatting over the garden fence already.'

'We've said hello a couple of times and I've seen him out walking with his dog, but that's all.' She smiled. 'I expect he's still settling in. He doesn't know us yet.'

Lottie was being charitable. Jay had given her the briefest of nods and a polite but brief response to her attempt at conversation.

She'd also received an equally brief reply to her email requesting a meeting about the Christmas tree centre. She'd heard music through the wall and the dog – Trevor – barking from time to time, but there had been no sign of visitors. If he wanted his privacy, she respected that. She guarded her own private life just as keenly after all that had happened to her over the past year.

'I think he likes to keep himself to himself,' Lottie said.

'I'm sure you can draw him out of his shell. He comes with very good references. We were lucky to lure him away from Greythwaite Hall.'

'I hadn't realised he'd been working in such a big estate.' Lottie was impressed. Greythwaite Hall was a large stately home in the northern Lake District with far bigger acreage than Firholme; Jay must surely have been earning more there.

'Yes, quite a coup to get him – you too, of course,' Shayla added quickly. 'I'm gathering a great team around me. I never thought we'd find anyone suitable for estates manager, and they don't tend to move around once they've got a place they like, but Jay said he wanted a fresh challenge and, of course, we were able to offer on-site accommodation. I think he'd been renting a little flat in a town and was desperate to live in the countryside again.'

'I can see why Firholme would appeal to him,' Lottie said, thinking of the rugged, tousle-haired guy she'd glimpsed around the site or striding off towards the high fells, with his dog at his side. Generally when she'd seen Jay, he'd had his head down, giving off every signal that he didn't want company or to engage in small talk. 'I get the impression he's quite shy though,' she added, to dampen down Shayla's expectations of being able to turn him into a party animal overnight.

'If anyone can draw him out, you will.' Shayla's eyes glinted. 'Let's face it, it wouldn't be a hardship. He's so fit . . . in every sense of the word.' She sighed. 'Fifteen years too young for me though, quite apart from the fact I'm his boss.'

Lottie had to smile. It wasn't the most professional way to talk about a new colleague, but Lottie had known Shayla for years as a friend, even before she'd come to work for her. Despite their age difference, Lottie and Shayla had hit it off when they'd first met properly, at a local tourism awards ceremony. Lottie had been training as a junior events manager at a hotel in the South Lakes and Shayla had been running a rival hotel in the same area.

Lottie had admired Shayla's drive and Shayla had taken her under her wing and mentored her informally over the years. They'd become friends and, finally, Shayla had headhunted Lottie from her previous job at the hotel to be the events manager for Firholme.

After her split from Connor, Lottie had been equally keen for a fresh start. She'd relished the chance to throw her energy into kick-starting Firholme, to leave old associations behind and have something to take her mind off her heartache and worries about Steph.

'Oh, hang on.' Shayla broke off to answer a call. She pointed at the phone, pulled a face and mouthed. 'Sorry. It's. The. Mayor.'

Lottie nodded and scribbled a note on a Firholme leaflet in her bag.

Sorting out trees with Jay. Back in half an hour. I've borrowed the decorations.

Shayla gave her an 'OK' sign and returned to her conversation. Lottie knew that she'd be ages talking to the mayor of the local town, a couple of miles from the Firholme estate. He had 'verbal diarrhoea' according to Shayla, and having arranged a recent civic awards evening for him at Firholme, Lottie was inclined to agree.

He got on well with Shayla, however, and had put a lot of valuable business their way. Shayla drew people to her like a

26

moth to a flame. She had a way of persuading people to go the extra mile – and then some – for her.

Lottie scooted out of Firholme House so she could change from her suit and heels into something more suitable for a freezing forest. Her breath misted the air the moment she stepped out of the door, and she was glad it took only two minutes to dash across the courtyard from where the offices were located to the Bothy. When she'd been offered the job at Firholme, accommodation on the estate had been a massive bonus, and every morning, she'd opened her curtains onto magnificent views of Derwentwater and the fells.

Well, maybe not quite *every* morning, because it did tend to rain a bit, as Lottie was keen to point out to guests, with a wry smile. On this early November morning, however, the highest fell tops, soaring three thousand feet above the lake, were covered with snow. At Firholme, frost spiked the grass and glistened in the morning sun.

Back in the day, Firholme's courtyard would have been alive with servants and estate workers, hurrying around the stables, laundry and brewhouse, or to and from the kitchen and vegetable garden. In recent years, one side of the single-storey buildings had been turned into offices, an information centre and refreshment kiosk. The other side of the courtyard overlooked the lake, so that had been converted into a smart café and shop with a terrace that made the most of the view.

In the summer it would be packed with visitors but today it was quiet apart from a few walkers with their dogs. All of the walkers were cossetted in down coats and woolly hats, cradling hot drinks, while their dogs lay at their feet, most with their own little jackets.

Through the steamy windows of the café itself, Lottie glimpsed the less hardy souls hunkered down with hot chocolates and Cumbrian breakfasts. From the start of November, the aroma of mince pies, cinnamon lattes and mulled wine had drifted tantalisingly into the offices while Lottie and the rest of the Firholme staff were trying to work.

The Bothy was typical of an estate worker's cottage, with grey stone walls and a slated roof spotted in yellow lichen. Its windows and door had been painted a subtle pale green, which gave it a cheerful air. The modest gardens were separated front and back by a low hedge and a garden gate, painted in the same green. To the rear of both cottages, there was a small coppice of trees with a rough path that eventually led down to the lake.

Lottie opened the door to the scent of the previous evening's woodsmoke. The cottage had central heating but she also enjoyed lighting a fire in the sitting room on cool evenings, which could happen any time in these northern mountain climes. To the rear of the cottage was a small dining kitchen, while upstairs there was a bedroom, bathroom and a box room, which was crammed with possessions left over from her life with Connor.

All those hopes and dreams from two years together seemed so far away, and the plans she'd allowed herself to make on that magical week in Cornwall were as cold as the ashes in the hearth.

She changed from her suit into jeans and jumper and

hunted for her bobble hat. Since October, when it had been unearthed from her chest of drawers, the hat was usually shoved in the pocket of her coat, or hung on a peg in the hall of her tiny cottage. However, it was nowhere to be found and she didn't have time to waste, so she ran upstairs to get her new one from her bedroom.

She had to stand on a little folding stool, a gift from her nieces, to reach the top cupboard of the wardrobe, but the red hat was there, tucked away at the rear of the cupboard. 'Hurrah!' she said, pulling it out.

As she stepped down, hat in hand, a scarf and a card fluttered onto the carpet.

She gave a little intake of breath when she picked it up. She hadn't even known she'd brought it with her when she moved to Firholme, but it must have been wrapped in a scarf or tucked inside some clothes. She obviously hadn't been able to throw it out.

She picked it up. The front was a watercolour of the cove in Cornwall, with gulls scudding across wet sand, reflecting the sky at sunset. The rear had a simple message in neat, restrained handwriting, so even and level, it could almost have been written with the aid of a ruler.

The message wasn't restrained; it was heartfelt.

Lottie,
Thank you for saying yes,
You've made me the happiest man alive,
All my love forever,
Connor xx

Lottie sat down on the bed, before reading the card again. Over a year later, those words still had the power to cut the ground from under her feet, and leave her turning over bad memories in a fruitless quest to understand how their relationship had turned from blissful to disastrous so suddenly.

Even though she should have thrown the card in the bin, it was impossible not to recall those heady times and wonder if they'd all been a deluded dream.

Chapter Two

'*I'm sorry. I've done something unforgivable.*'

Connor's words, on the doorstep that dark September night, rushed back to her, along with all the memories of the misery that followed in the hours and months afterwards. They were like dust and litter she'd swept out of the door, now blowing back in her face on an ill wind.

She'd never forget Connor's face; so white and drawn that her first fear was that he was ill or his sister or mother were. He looked up at her and said two words: 'I'm sorry.'

'Sorry about what?'

He threw his keys on the table. 'I've done something unforgivable.'

Her stomach turned over. 'What do you mean? Have you had an accident?' He must have run someone over, she thought . . . a child . . . 'Oh my God, sit down.'

'No. I – I . . . There's no way of saying this that can excuse me or soften the blow, but I care for you too much to live a lie, or make you live a lie.' Lottie's skin had prickled with unease, with dismay at that word. *'Care?'*

'I care a lot for you. I'm very fond of you but . . . you tried to warn me when I asked you at the beach.'

'What do you mean? I tried to warn you?'

'You said it was unexpected – out of the blue – and you're right. When we came home, even before – walking in here and realising what marriage truly means: a lifetime of commitment. You deserve nothing less, Lottie, and I should never have let myself be carried along by the idea of it.'

She couldn't believe he was passing the responsibility for his cruel act to her. What had happened to him during these few days away? What had changed his mind?

'I can't inflict myself on you, Lottie. It isn't fair. God knows, it's killing me to be the one to hurt you like this but it's better I do it now, before things go too far. I'm sorry, truly I am, and I realise there's no coming back from this. I'll pack my bags.'

'But why? Why have you changed your mind?'

'It's for the best,' he said wearily. 'There's no other reason. Best I end it now before everyone knows.'

'Is there someone else? Did you meet someone in Scotland?'

'No!' His tone changed to something like anger, though Lottie later realised it was guilt. 'I just . . . can't make the commitment you need. The commitment you deserve. This time away has made me realise that. I've woken up to reality and the reality is that I'm not the man you need and I should never have led you to believe I was. I got carried away . . .'

'B-but you can't just change your mind. I don't understand.'

He set his mouth in a hard line. 'I'm very sorry, Lottie, but I have to leave. It'll be simpler that way. Less painful in the long run. You deserve way better than me.'

That was it. He moved out that night, leaving Lottie feeling like a vase that had been hurled onto a marble floor, the pieces scattered far and wide.

For many many months, she'd wasted her nights trying to pinpoint the exact moment when Connor had decided he didn't want to marry her after all.

It couldn't have been the evening they'd shared champagne and spent a glorious night in bed . . .

Was it on the way home? Some point along the journey, when the green fields of the West Country gave way to the suburbs and factories? Was that when the magic of a holiday proposal melted into the reality of a lifetime of commitment? Connor had obviously calculated the cost of keeping their relationship going for a lifetime, with responsibilities, a family, and it outweighed the benefits.

Lottie had combed through every moment, searching for the exact point when her dreams were shattered, but all she had were Connor's bland statements. Platitudes, words he'd obviously been rehearsing for hours – days – they were such a contrast from his heartfelt declaration on the beach.

The next morning, she had dragged herself off the bed, dried her eyes and gone to work. She longed to call Steph but her sister would be busy taking the girls to school and then at work herself. It would have to wait until later.

Somehow, she managed to get through a meeting about a forthcoming conference and had a few minutes to grab a coffee. She took it outside into the hotel grounds when Steph's name flashed up on her screen. For a second, she wondered if Connor had already told her about the engagement, even though he'd seemed so hesitant . . . but he'd never do that.

Then she wondered why Steph was calling in the middle of the school morning.

'Hello, hon . . . sorry to call you at work.' Steph sounded strange, distant.

'Steph? Where are you?' she asked. 'Out in the playground?'

'Playground? No – I'm not in the playground. I wish.' There was a long pause. 'I'm outside the surgery and I have some news. And I'm sorry, hon, but it's not good.'

'Oh my God. Is it one of the girls?'

'No. No, thank God. No . . .'

Lottie remembered the silence as much as her sister's words. It was heavy and ominous, and the hairs on the back of her neck stood on end.

'Hon, I don't know how to say this because I haven't even had time to take it in myself. It's not the twins; it's me. The GP's really worried. She thinks I might have cervical cancer and—' Lottie heard the wobble in Steph's voice. 'I'm trying to stay positive but I can't lie. W-what if I never see my beautiful girls grow up?'

Reeling from the shock, Lottie had had to tell her boss she was feeling unwell and needed to leave. She'd driven to Steph's, scraping her car on a dry-stone wall along the way, but she hadn't cared. It turned out Steph had been having worrying symptoms for a while but hid her fears from Lottie, thinking everything would be OK. She'd tried to comfort Steph, had broken the news to their parents, before collecting the girls from school, pretending all was well.

She'd held her greatest fears back, stemmed her tears and bottled her emotions for Steph's sake and to reassure the twins. All she wanted was to fling herself on Connor, be held and soothed and let everything out.

That was what partners were for: to be there in sickness and in health, for better and for worse.

The last thing Steph needed to deal with was Lottie's ruined love life, so she kept her heartbreak secret and lied, saying she'd told Connor she was staying the night with Steph – not that she could face the thought of their empty house anyway.

There was no way she intended to tell Connor about Steph either – what if he thought she was trying to play the sympathy card? She was too proud for that. He'd severed their connection so brutally and suddenly, she felt he had no right to any part of her life.

She told Steph, and everyone else including her parents, who had enough to worry about with Steph and their granddaughters, that she and Connor had mutually decided to split up. Connor was happy to go along with it. So while Steph had been going through her treatment, Lottie bottled up her own pain, telling herself it was a pinprick next to the avalanche of worry Steph was dealing with. She wept secretly in the dark of the night, and every tear she shed made her feel guilty.

Now, looking down at Connor's card, she remembered the previous Christmas when she'd promised Steph she'd look after the girls, if the worst happened.

It had been a mixed blessing to stay so local to home after

her split with Connor. They'd sold their little house and Lottie had stayed with Steph. Although her place was small for the four of them now the twins were bigger, at least it meant she could lend a hand with the childcare while Steph was going through months of gruelling radiotherapy and chemotherapy.

The treatment had left her sister mentally and physically exhausted and she'd had to take sick leave from her job as a teaching assistant. To help even more, Lottie had taken several weeks off after leaving her job at the hotel in early August and before starting at Firholme in September.

When Steph had first called her with the news she'd been sent by her GP for a biopsy after some worrying symptoms, Lottie had hoped that it would be a false alarm and that the problem would be quickly solved. The opposite had been true. It had taken almost two months of scans and biopsies for Steph to be properly diagnosed and nearly two more for her treatment to start.

Now, six months after Steph's treatment had ended, things were looking brighter. Lottie was settled in her new job at Firholme, and Steph was back at work as a teaching assistant although she was often exhausted and had to have regular check-ups at the hospital. The treatment had also brought on an early menopause with its mood swings and tiredness, on top of the ever-present fear of the cancer returning. Despite all this, Lottie was amazed by her sister's determination to make the most of every moment for the sake of her twin daughters.

Likewise, Lottie had decided to make a fresh start and had

jumped at Shayla's offer of the Firholme job. It was still close to Steph's house and she'd immediately been made to feel welcome. She loved her new role, and when Connor left Cumbria, gradually she'd begun to heal from the split.

Lottie glanced at his card one more time, and a new resolve filled her veins. That day, when Connor had walked out and Steph had called about her cancer, had been the worst day of her life but she *had* to look to the future and hope. She'd pull out all the stops to make sure that Firholme stayed in business and that this Christmas would be the best ever for Steph and the twins.

She took the card downstairs and threw it in the kitchen bin, like she should have done a year ago.

Chapter Three

With fresh determination, Lottie laced up her boots, pulled the red bobble hat over her curls and headed off towards the Christmas tree plantation. Her mood soon lifted once she was out in the fresh air, surrounded by the fells.

Even though she was used to hill walking, she was breathing a little more heavily by the time she'd climbed the slope to the forest gate. Her nose twitched at the scent of pine needles in the crisp air.

Jay was talking to two of the estate workers, their hi-vis outfits shining like beacons against the dark forest. Chainsaws and visors lay at their feet. She guessed that Jay's dog, Trevor, was at home, safely kept away from the working area.

Lottie hung back while he finished his conversation, quietly observing him. He was also fully kitted up in sturdy boots, cargo pants and an olive 'Firholme' sweatshirt. So far, so mundane, but as for the man in the uniform, he was anything but mundane.

The forest workers picked up the chainsaws and left, so Lottie walked up to him.

'Hello. Sorry, I'm a bit late,' she said, struck by how the earthy tones of his clothes suited his colouring: brown hair, bronzed skin and hazel eyes. 'I needed to change out of my heels into something a bit more practical.' She lifted her sturdy boot, dragging her attention from Jay's rugged physique.

He smiled briefly. 'No rush. I needed to talk to those guys. We're off to cut some big spruces later for a delivery to Keswick. The council and some of the hotels are ready to put their trees up.'

'Wow. That's early,' Lottie said. 'And in fact, that's what I came to talk to you about, as well as the plans for the Christmas tree launch. Did you get my email about the reindeer?' she asked, referring to her plans to have real live reindeer at the tree sales opening weekend.

'The reindeer? Oh . . . yeah. Thanks.'

Oh dear, Lottie thought. He didn't seem very enthusiastic.

'They live at a farm just down the valley. I thought it would be a great way of attracting families on the opening day,' she said. 'Are you OK to liaise directly with the reindeer farmer on all the logistics of getting them up to Firholme? Unless,' she added, 'you're too busy and want me to do it.'

'Thanks for the offer, but I'll sort it.'

Lottie had booked the visit by the deer the moment she'd started work at Firholme, knowing they'd be the perfect way of starting the Christmas tree sales season with a bang. Maybe Jay was just allergic to Rudolph or something.

He pushed his hair out of his eyes. 'You said you wanted to talk about trees for the house?'

'Yes. I was hoping we could have some a bit earlier than planned.'

'I don't see why not. Any particular variety or size?'

'I don't know . . . I'm no expert on trees,' she said with a smile. 'I was thinking you'd help me out with that.'

He seemed to relax and he gave a brief smile in return. 'Yes, I can certainly help you with the trees.' He frowned at her. 'But before we go into the woods, you'd better put this on.' He handed her a yellow safety helmet. 'Can't have a breach of health and safety. Shayla would have my guts for garters.'

Lottie was amused. It was unlikely Shayla would tell Jay off; generally she was fairly laid-back, though she could be magnificently assertive when she needed to be.

'I doubt it,' she said, putting the oversized helmet on her head with a grimace. It would flatten her hair and she had a client meeting after lunch. 'Even so, I'd better stick to the rules.'

She noted he didn't smile at her joke. Hmm, she wondered how he'd go down with his team if he was this strait-laced. His predecessor, Graham, had been not only efficient but also very popular. 'So, how many trees do you need for the house and public areas?' he asked, getting straight the point.

'Five for various locations inside and out, but I was hoping you'd advise me on the size and type for each place.' She was struck by an idea that might engage him more. 'On that note, can I ask your opinion on these?'

She pulled the drab bauble and black snowflake that Shayla

had given her from her pockets. 'What do you think of these? We were thinking of having a futuristic minimalist theme in the house this year.'

His brow wrinkled. 'What's that when it's at home?'

'Geometric shapes. Cones, plain baubles, pyramids. All in muted tones of pewter, charcoal and er . . . black.' Lottie sighed. 'In every room.'

He raised an eyebrow. 'Whose idea was that?'

'Shayla's,' Lottie said, unwilling to criticise her boss, yet rather hoping Jay would share her lack of enthusiasm for the downbeat décor. 'Personally, I prefer to pile on every decoration I've collected over the years on my tree, but that's not the same as decorating an Edwardian mansion for the festive season. Shayla wants Firholme to look its spectacular best, especially as we want to do a wedding shoot and put the pictures up on the website.'

He took the grey pyramid decoration from Lottie and rested it in his hand. 'It's er . . . very *grey*.'

His palm was dusty but it was 'clean' dirt, as Lottie's gran might have said. Lottie had never quite worked out what it meant but she presumed it was appropriate in Jay's case. He obviously hadn't realised he had pine needles in his hair or a mossy streak above his cheekbone, though she guessed he was probably far too busy chopping down trees to be looking in mirrors.

'What do you really think? This range of decorations costs a fortune and I think we need more colour even if it's only accent touches like blues or purples.'

He shrugged. 'I don't think anything. I don't put up a tree.'

Lottie couldn't hide her surprise. 'You don't put up a tree? But you manage the Christmas tree plantation. You can't not have one yourself.'

'I can and I do. *Not* have one, I mean. I've had my fill of the green stuff by the big day, anyway and . . . I got over the excitement of Christmas a while ago,' he said briskly, then finally managed a twitch of the lips. 'Anyway, Trevor would only try and eat the decorations. Now, shall we go and look at the type of trees you might want for the house? We have several varieties ready this year, or . . .' he added thoughtfully, 'you could even have a different one in each room?'

'Hmm. Good idea. Maybe I can hint to Shayla that some varieties of tree would look better with a different theme? Blind her with science?'

'It's worth a try.'

Lottie was still unable to believe Jay didn't bother with a tree, but she took the hint that he didn't want to discuss it further.

Jay led the way into the plantation area where the trees were grown. 'You can have a Nordmann fir or a Norway spruce,' he said. 'Here's a Norway,' he said, leading her to a classic triangular-shaped tree like the ones seen in thousands of homes every year.

He picked up a branch with its long cones hanging down.

Lottie inhaled the rich, sweet scent. 'I love the smell,' she said, realising she'd passed countless trees before but allowed them to become part of the background. 'How long do they take to grow?'

'Around twelve years for a Nordmann and eight for the

spruce . . . which means these trees were planted when I was still at school.'

'No way!' Lottie laughed.

'Hmm. I am pretty weather-beaten.' He rubbed his chin, which she thought had just the right amount of stubble. 'Note to self. Use more sunscreen and moisturiser.'

She was taken aback by the glimmer of humour that appeared to have burst through. 'No, you look great. I mean . . .' she said, backpedalling furiously even though she sensed he was winding her up. 'I didn't mean to be so um – personal.'

'Oh, so you'd thought I was much older than that?'

She was almost convinced he was teasing her, but erred on the side of caution, in case. She smiled. 'Actually, I thought you were around my age,' she said, which was true.

'I'm thirty-five, which I'm sure is older that you,' he said.

'Not much. I'm thirty-four,' she said, wondering if she'd really offended him.

'I was only joking when I said I was weather-beaten, although to be fair –' he ran his hand over his curls, which unlike her own, were allowed to grow untamed '– I am a bit of a scruff. Good job I'm not in a customer-facing job like yours.'

Lottie was amused. 'I'd have called you rugged rather than scruffy,' she said warily.

Jay raised a rather bushy eyebrow. 'Rugged? You mean like Scafell Pike or Helvellyn? Spiky and dangerous if tackled in the wrong conditions?'

She felt as if she'd made another faux pas. 'Stop it. I'm not digging a deeper hole for myself.' Or revealing any more glimpses into the fact that she found him attractive.

In fact, it struck her that he was the first man she'd looked twice at since Connor had left. Chatting to him now, she felt they'd already crossed a line from the friendliness of colleagues into something a little less professional.

'You're fine as you are. Now, shall we look at some more trees?' she said worried that she'd let on she fancied him even a little bit. She pushed up her jacket sleeve to check her watch. 'Because the morning's rushing by.'

'Let's get busy, then,' said Jay. 'I'll mark this tree and we'll move on.'

The next twenty minutes was taken up entirely by talk of tree varieties. By the end of it, Lottie had selected five specimens, with guidance from Jay. He might not enjoy Christmas, but he obviously had a deep passion for nature and the great outdoors.

He identified the chosen trees with tape as they walked through the Christmas plantation with its regimented rows of firs, to the more established 'natural' woodland, which was also part of the Firholme estate. Here, there were a great variety of species, including oaks and silver birch, most of which were completely stripped of foliage. Some of the beeches clung to withered copper leaves but by and large the wood was a latticework of spiky branches against the blue sky.

'My niece, Myra, asked me if the trees were "skellingtons" at Halloween,' Lottie said, when they stopped at the edge of the forest.

He stared up at the tree. 'Skeletons. That's a good description. Some people find it sad to see bare branches but actually I like them. You know the leaves will be back soon and it's all part of the process. It's essential that the leaf litter provides a habitat and food for lots of insects and fungi.'

'All part of the circle of life?' Lottie said archly.

Jay smiled. 'Like in the *Lion King*, yeah.'

'The twins loved that film. Especially the belching warthogs.'

'That's my favourite part too.'

'Really?'

Jay smiled, and Lottie's opinion of him rose a little higher. Perhaps his initial gruffness was merely because he was so new to Firholme and needed to find his feet. 'Not really. I'm more of a thriller fan myself. I'm not sure I can remember the last time I went to see an animated film. Must have been when Ben and I were at school.'

'Ben?' Lottie picked up on the name, wondering if Jay was referring to a partner.

'My brother.' Jay's smile evaporated instantly. 'But I should shut up. I must be keeping you from your work.'

'This *is* part of my work,' Lottie said, detecting a sharp change in the atmosphere between them.

'Even so, I'll walk you back through the woods. With the storm we had last week, there are a lot of fallen trees and branches. That's one of our main jobs at the moment, clearing up the debris to make the grounds safe.'

Lottie was about to tell him that she'd be fine and knew her way around Firholme even better than him, but he'd already started walking off down the forest track. She caught up with him, wondering what had caused the abrupt downturn in his mood when out of the corner of her eye, she caught a glimpse of russet dashing up a tree.

'Shh. Hang on a moment!' Jay touched her sleeve, indicating she should hold back.

Lottie was shocked at his touch but froze anyway. 'What?' she mouthed.

'Red squirrel.' He lifted his hand slowly to point at an oak a few metres away.

She followed the direction of his finger but could see nothing among the leaf litter, bracken and twigs. Suddenly, there was a rustle and a flash of red as a furry tail appeared and the creature dashed from behind a trunk towards the woods. It stopped halfway to another tree and dug at the ground, found an acorn and started to nibble it.

It was a magical moment, seeing a wild animal in its natural habitat, especially one as cute as a red squirrel. They were quite rare now, and had been pushed into smaller pockets of the Lakes by the greys.

She and Jay stood very close together, neither moving in case they disturbed the squirrel, its fluffy tail quivering in the shaft of sunlight. The squirrel found another nut, popped it in its mouth and then raced off again, over the ground and up a tree.

'It's great to know they're thriving here at Firholme,' Jay said, when it became clear the squirrel was gone. Lottie moved away and they continued walking back to the house. 'They love eating the spruce cones, you know.'

She was pleased that he shared her excitement. 'Firholme is one heck of an office.'

He nodded enthusiastically. 'I worked in an office after I left college. I'd trained as an accountant and I'm not knocking it as a career, but I pretty much hated it from the start. I'd worked a vacation job with a tree surgeon and I'd enjoyed that a lot more, so I went back to uni and retrained in landscape management. I worked for the forestry commission in the Highlands of Scotland and Kielder Forest before I came back to the Lakes. They had red squirrels there too.'

His animated expression made it clear that the squirrel had lifted his mood again.

'They're beautiful creatures,' Lottie said. 'I only hope they won't be driven out by the greys.'

'Or chased away by Trevor. I have to keep him on the lead when I'm walking through here. He goes mad if he gets a sniff of squirrel.'

'I can imagine,' Lottie said, having seen Trevor hurtling out of Jay's cottage on his way for a walk. 'Occasionally they come onto the feeders outside the cottage but I've never seen any here in the woods,' she said, still with a glow of excitement from the squirrel encounter.

Her glow might also have to do with the fact that she'd enjoyed sharing the moment with someone who loved their surroundings as much as she did.

They emerged from the plantation and reached the top of the estate. The sun had come out and the courtyard of build-ings and estate stretched out below them. The lake ploughed a shining furrow through the valley, reflecting snow-topped mountains.

Without a word, they both stopped to admire the spectacular view. 'Not too shabby, is it?' Jay said. 'But you must be used to it?'

'Actually, it still takes my breath away and I've lived in the Lakes all my life.'

He pushed a hand through his tousled hair. It was naturally curly, verging on unruly, and brushing the nape of his neck. 'Look, I'm sorry if I sounded grouchy back there for a while. Don't get me wrong, I love my job and I'm happy to help other people celebrate . . . It's only that I don't feel like joining in all the jollity at the moment.'

'Christmas can be a tough time,' Lottie said, guessing he found it very awkward to reveal any hint of his personal problems. 'I didn't feel much like partying myself, last year.'

His beautiful eyes darkened. 'Why was that?' he asked softly.

'Oh . . .' She already regretted mentioning a time that she'd hoped to put behind her. Not forget: that was impossible. It was still too raw.

She didn't know Jay and he was probably the last person who'd enjoy listening to her troubles.

So why did she suddenly feel like pouring out everything to him?

Chapter Four

With a mountain of things on her to-do list, Lottie really should have been getting back to the office, but Jay's tone was so gentle and encouraging, she felt she had to tell him what had happened the previous Christmas – or at least part of it.

She took a mental breath. 'Last Christmas, my sister was seriously ill,' she said. 'She'd just been diagnosed with cervical cancer and was waiting for treatment. She's also a single mum to my twin nieces.'

'That must have been very hard to deal with.' He paused by an old fallen tree, which people had been using as a makeshift bench, judging by the worn surface.

'It was but . . . I'm sure you don't have time for this. I've kept you long enough as it is.'

'I'm not too busy to listen, so why don't you sit down here for a minute and tell me about it?'

He sat down himself, giving Lottie no excuse. She joined

him, although his unexpected empathy had the power almost to bring her to tears, the last thing she wanted when he was a virtual stranger. 'Last Christmas was . . . very hard. Neither of us felt like celebrating but we had little Myra and Jodie to think about so we did our best. Our parents live and work in New Zealand and they couldn't get any flights until the New Year so they couldn't be there and even when they did come over to help, they had to go back to their jobs eventually.'

He frowned in sympathy. 'My God, that is tough. I'm so sorry you went through this.'

'Thanks. It was hard but we had no choice but to try and get through it. Before Steph started her treatment, we went for the whole Christmas to the max thing. You could barely move for decorations and presents.' Lottie had crunched her credit card to spoil her sister and the twins, and her parents, relatives and friends had also gone a bit mad. Still, she had no regrets.

'You must have been out of your mind with worry,' he said softly.

'It was hard but a hundred times harder for Steph than me.'

'How's she doing now?'

'She's OK. She has to have regular checks and the treatment had lots of after-effects but we try to stay positive. Touch wood,' Lottie said, flattening her palm on the log's surface. 'One thing's for sure, this Christmas has got to be better than last.'

He let the silence hang for a second, as if he didn't know how to reply. Perhaps he felt uncomfortable at Lottie's unexpected display of emotion. Many people couldn't deal with illness and if they'd never had a close family member affected, it was impossible to imagine how they might feel. Or perhaps he didn't even *want* to imagine.

There was no time for any more conversation because Lottie's phone buzzed with a text from Shayla, asking her to return urgently to the house to meet some potential clients.

'I really have to go. Thanks for the tree. For everything,' she said.

'No problem.'

Lottie nodded and scooted off to the Bothy to change again. While she scrubbed her nails, removed a spruce twig from her hair and redid her lipstick, she thought about her conversation with Jay. He'd avoided revealing anything about why he didn't celebrate the season and had allowed her to do all the talking. Lottie thought about the reindeer, Santa's grotto, families converging on the Christmas tree centre. Not only was Christmas the busiest time of year for Jay, he also obviously loathed it. It was the perfect storm for him.

She didn't regret telling him about Steph, even though she didn't talk about it much at work.

However, she'd held back the other reason that the previous Christmas had been so tough: that she'd been dealing with her own heartache over Connor but had had to force her problems into the background in the light of her sister's far more serious situation.

It had been all she could do to function at work and all her energy and cheerfulness went into supporting Steph, the girls and her parents.

Yet it had hurt; it had hurt like hell and she had loved Connor. She'd thought he loved her. Perhaps she was simply hopeless at judging any man's feelings? Jay had seemed empathetic and he'd revealed a little more about himself . . . but she wasn't under any illusions.

It was too soon to even think of any guy romantically – especially one who'd only just moved in next door and worked with her. Better not to even start anything, and that meant flirting too.

When she went into the outer office, she looked through the glass windows and saw Shayla walking around her own office, phone at her ear. Originally from north London, Shayla herself had worked as a hotel receptionist until her grandpa had left her a small inheritance that she'd invested in a tiny boutique bed and breakfast.

Her battle to do it up on a shoestring and make it pay had featured on a TV series. Her success and personality had led to more media work, enabling her to invest in more properties, including Firholme. Before Shayla took over, it had been a rather dated hotel. She'd bought it in early spring and spent several months – and a serious amount of money – restoring the main house and converting the outbuildings to a café and shop.

It had reopened in early September just after Lottie had joined, and Shayla intended to make it a must-visit destination and events venue that visitors and locals returned to in all seasons of the year.

Lottie would love to own – or at least be in charge – of a place like Firholme, and was hoping her role as events manager might be expanded if Firholme could thrive – but that was dependent on her doing a great job and bringing in more business.

Shayla waved at Lottie to enter the office. As Lottie closed the door as quietly as she could, Shayla wound down her call.

A few minutes later, they walked up to the house together. Lottie decided to dive straight in with her concerns about the decorations.

'Shayla, I've just been to the Christmas centre with Jay. While we were choosing the trees for the house, I had a thought about the décor. What about keeping the minimal tones but adding a different accent colour in each room? It would look really striking and help show potential couples we can match any wedding theme.' Lottie went in with the clincher. 'Plus, it would save money. Some of those uber cool monotone decs are very pricey.'

'Hmm. I think you're right . . . I'd been wondering about the colours myself and agree we could do with something a bit more, er, cheerful.'

Buoyed by her boss's response, Lottie outlined her ideas on a walk-through of the main ground-floor rooms. Shayla seemed enthused and happy to let her deal with the styling. Should she message Jay and tell him that the grey was out, and colour back in? It wasn't part of his job. Was she simply looking for a reason to text him?

How did he really feel about having listened to her problems?

Next, they headed upstairs where Shayla wanted to get Lottie's opinion on a possible makeover for some of the rooms in the spring. The view from the main bridal suite was stunning, with a magnificent window overlooking the lake and mountains. Lottie couldn't help thinking what a romantic setting it would be to spend a first night as a married couple . . . and a pang of sharp regret took her by surprise. She could have been spending her wedding night here.

'Lottie?'

She turned around to find Shayla standing by the huge sleigh bed.

'You like the idea for the new rooms?'

'Yes . . . yes.' Lottie smiled. 'I think they'll look superb.'

'Great. Shall we go back to the office for coffee?'

Shaking off her memories for the second time that morning, Lottie walked with Shayla down the stairs into the vestibule. Voices reached them and the front door opened.

A tall woman, about Lottie's own age, walked through, followed by one of the admin assistants, Thorsten, a Norwegian student on a gap year.

'Hello, Shayla, Lottie . . . This is Ms Sinclair.'

'Hi there. Please call me Keegan,' the woman said, her voice, with its Aussie twang, echoed around the hallway.

'Ms Sinclair and her partner are looking at wedding venues and dropped by on the off chance. I explained that you'd have preferred to have met them yourself . . .' Thorsten said, his eyes flicking nervously from Lottie to Shayla.

'I made him bring us straight up!' Keegan declared. 'I couldn't wait! I'm with my fiancé actually but I've no idea where he's disappeared to.'

'I think he was looking at the view,' said Thorsten.

'He's always going AWOL.' Laughing, Keegan flicked her jet-black hair over her shoulder. She was wearing a camel maxi coat with a faux fur collar, and would have given Kim Kardashian a run for her money in the glamour stakes, Lottie thought. 'I'd better round him up.'

Neither Lottie nor Shayla had yet had a chance to get a word in before the door opened and a man walked in.

In an instant, Lottie found herself physically unable to speak.

It couldn't be him . . . and yet here he was, in a smart reefer coat and scarf, his hair styled in a trendy cut and every bit as good-looking as she remembered. No, scrub that. He was *far* better-looking than she remembered.

At the sound of his footsteps, Keegan swung round. 'Oh, there you are, baby!' She seized his arm and beamed. 'This is my fiancé, Connor. We're absolutely desperate to get married at Firholme and the sooner the better!'

Chapter Five

Lottie stared at Connor, and he gawped back. She must have held her breath because when she finally came to her senses, it rushed out in a whoosh.

Shock and anger bubbled up. How could Connor, of all people, have turned up at Firholme with his fiancée? How could he do that to her?

All of this, however, seemed to have been missed by everyone else in the room, as Keegan sang the praises of the house.

'Wow. This place is even more amazing than you said it was, Connor. Your website really doesn't do it justice, you know!' She directed this at Shayla.

Lottie had had a big input into the redesign of the new site, but that was the least of her worries.

'It's incredible.' Keegan planted a smacker on Connor's cheek that reverberated around the room. 'No wonder your mum always wanted you to get married here.'

Avoiding Lottie's eye, Connor found his tongue. 'Hold on. They might not have a vacancy, Keegan,' he said. 'Not at short notice. You know we're in a hurry.'

'Oh, don't be so defeatist! If you don't ask, you don't get.'

'Yes but . . . Firholme must be booked up years in advance,' he said.

Shayla exchanged a puzzled glance with Lottie before jumping in. 'If you want to hold your wedding here at Firholme, you've found the right person.' She practically thrust Lottie to the fore with one look. 'Lottie Hargreaves is our events and wedding coordinator. I'm sure she can help you sort out a date.' Shayla beamed at Lottie, obviously willing her to speak to their new potential customers.

'Well. Um. I think we do have some weekends in early March,' Lottie said.

'March!' Keegan exclaimed. 'Oh no. That's way too late. We want to get married as soon as possible. Next week wouldn't be too early!'

'Next week!' Despite her best efforts, Lottie's squeak of horror escaped.

'Keegan's joking,' Connor said, with the weakest of smiles. 'We were thinking more like next month. If possible, but I know it's a tall order.'

'It *has* to be before Christmas,' Keegan said firmly. 'That's what you said, baby.' She turned to Lottie. 'It's a surprise for Connor's mum. She's been very poorly and we want to give her the best Christmas present ever,' she said to Lottie and Shayla.

'Your mum?' Lottie was unable to keep the shock from her voice. 'How poorly? Is she OK now?'

'She had a stroke a few months ago but she's recovering,' Connor said, seeming more crestfallen by the second. 'We thought that a surprise wedding at Firholme would cheer her up. We'll totally understand if it's not possible.' His expression gave Lottie no doubt that he wanted her to bail him out.

However, that wasn't in Lottie's power and Shayla dived in, shooting Lottie a very puzzled glance. 'Don't worry. I'm sure we can fit it in,' she said.

'Great,' said Keegan, shooting Lottie a forensic glare. 'Do you two know each other?' she said to Lottie.

'I was wondering the same myself,' Shayla said, smiling.

'Yes. We used to live in the same village,' Lottie said, still reeling from the fact that Fiona had had a stroke. 'Didn't we, Connor?'

'Yes . . . um . . . we did.' Connor was obviously trying to pick up on the clues she was attempting to send him. She was sure he hadn't told Keegan about their relationship so he certainly hadn't mentioned they'd been engaged, or that he'd called it off three days after his proposal.

'I didn't realise Lottie worked here,' he said.

'I only started here in early September.' Lottie was finding coherent speech almost impossible to come by.

'Oh. I'd no idea,' Connor repeated, adding limply, 'what a coincidence.'

Keegan clearly wasn't ready let them off the hook. 'Wow. You guys grew up in the same village?'

'Keswick is more of a town,' Connor stated, as if that made all the difference. 'And my parents moved to Cockermouth when I was a teenager.'

Keegan's perfectly arched eyebrows shot up. 'Yet you still recognised each other instantly?' She reminded Lottie of a smiling assassin.

'We had some . . . er . . . contact afterwards,' Lottie replied. 'Connor's firm used to hold functions at the hotel I was working at.'

'But it was ages ago,' Connor added quickly.

His deft reaction jolted Lottie, but she hid her shock that he was so very keen to deny their relationship. She didn't want anyone to know how close they'd been either and wasn't going to volunteer the information. It would be far less messy and far less painful and besides, Connor surely wouldn't dream of getting married at Firholme now he'd found out who'd be organising the wedding. Certainly not by Christmas and hopefully not ever.

However, Keegan had other ideas. 'Babe, it's so lovely that you know Lottie and that she's going to be our wedding planner.' She flashed a smile at Lottie. 'It's fate! We're obviously meant to get married here. It's an amazing venue and we can really push the boat out.'

Shayla was grinning widely at the prospect of a lucrative wedding. 'I think you absolutely *are* meant to have your wedding here,' she declared. 'Don't you agree, Lottie?' she added firmly.

Lottie snapped out of her shock. 'Oh, yes. *Absolutely*,' she said, not wanting to face the ramifications of having to organise Connor's wedding.

Shayla ploughed on. 'And in fact, I have some wonderful news. We do have a Saturday available for the weekend before Christmas. How does Saturday nineteenth sound?'

Keegan squealed in delight. 'What? You are kidding me!'

'No,' said Shayla. 'So, you really *are* meant to be married at Firholme.'

Keegan smacked a kiss on Connor's mouth. 'That settles it then, doesn't it, Connor? It's fate!'

'It seems like it . . .' Connor said mechanically.

'Let's not waste a moment more then,' Shayla said. 'Would you like Lottie to give you both a tour of Firholme House so we can set the ball rolling immediately? Funnily enough, we were just discussing the Christmas tree and decorations for the ballroom where we hold our wedding ceremonies and receptions. Of course, we can tailor those to your wedding colour scheme.'

'We hadn't got around to choosing colours yet,' Connor muttered. 'We hadn't even got a confirmed date or venue until a few minutes ago.'

Keegan laughed at him. 'But we do *now*, babe, and I've already been thinking about the theme a lot. We'd love to have a tour and the sooner we nail down all the details, the better.'

'I'll leave Lottie to show you round, then, as she's our expert, aren't you?' Lottie felt a little nudge on the elbow. 'I'm sure you have a lot of catching up to do as you and Connor are old friends.'

Shayla must be wondering why Lottie herself wasn't gushing about Firholme like Shayla was, but she was still paralysed by the shock of Connor walking in and wanting to get married.

'*Lottie?*' Shayla's tone was laden with a hint that she should show more enthusiasm.

'Of course, I'd be delighted to show you round,' she said,

as brightly as she could. 'It's a shame the decorations aren't up, but as Shayla mentioned, that means we can discuss your own scheme and have it ready for your special day.'

She was fighting to keep the slightest trace of irony from her voice, terrified that Keegan would think she was being sarcastic – or worse, that Connor would. He was handling the situation by saying as little as possible, but Keegan was the opposite, raving about the architecture, the furnishings, the possibilities for photo opportunities.

It was agony for Lottie to have to extol Firholme's virtues when she longed to claim it was a terrible place to get married; that it was draughty, had mice and the catering wasn't up to scratch – and most of all that the events manager was incompetent and was wishing her bridal couple would vanish with a puff of smoke.

Instead she had to run through her sales patter of how marvellous it was, with its grand ballroom being perfect for the ceremony; the drawing room ideal for the pre-drinks; and suite of first-floor bedrooms wonderful for the bridal couple and their guests.

She threw open the double doors to the ballroom so that Keegan could walk in ahead.

'Oh. My. God. What an incredible space!' Keegan wandered into the centre of the room and turned in a circle, taking in the parquet floor, the walls and up to the wood-panelled ceiling with its ornate carvings and chandelier. 'That ceiling. The panelling. Is this all original?'

'Yes, we restored it back to its original state from 1906 when it was built . . .'

'It's awesome.' Keegan turned. 'Isn't it, Connor?'

'It's undeniably impressive,' he muttered, wandering towards the window, shoulders hunched and hands in his pockets.

'No wonder your mother loves this place so much.' Keegan returned her attention to the room, arching her neck to stare at the chandelier. 'It's every bit as gorgeous as you said.'

'I'd forgotten how grand it was.' Connor followed Keegan's gaze. 'Mum liked to bring us for afternoon tea when it was a hotel and we were younger. She hasn't been able to visit since she was ill and it was being refurbished, but I know she wants to.'

Keegan looked around in wonder. 'She's going to freak out when she walks in here to find we're actually getting married.'

'You can say that again . . .' Momentarily, Connor caught Lottie's eye behind Keegan's back and mouthed, 'Sorry.'

Lottie glanced away, unable to respond. Sorry for what? Turning up out of the blue? Not knowing she worked there? Proposing to her, then saying he wasn't sure that his love was strong enough to make a lifelong commitment? Finding someone he *did* love enough within a matter of months?

No matter how professional she tried to remain, the regrets and 'what-ifs' whirled around her head. It didn't matter how many times she told herself she was better off without him and it wasn't meant to be, it still hurt.

However, she had no time to gather her thoughts properly because Keegan had swooped on a small dais in the bay window. The sun had come out and the view over the gardens to the lake and snow-topped fells was to die for. How could Keegan *not* fall headlong in love with the place?

'Is this it?' Keegan was almost breathless with wonder. 'Where we actually make our vows?'

'Yes. This is where the registrar will conduct the ceremony,' Lottie said. 'We hold the wedding service in here and in the winter months we serve drinks in the drawing room while this space is rearranged for the reception.' She glanced out of the window at the sun glinting off the lake. 'In summer, we do drinks on the terrace; obviously, that's not possible in December . . . But you can still have a wide choice of menus, or any kind of reception format – sit-down or buffet. As casual or formal as you wish.' She reeled off the patter, still feeling as if someone else was saying the words.

'Oh, I want a formal sit-down. I want silver service, little place names, a top table, speeches – the whole traditional English shebang.' Keegan called to Connor who was at the window, with his back to them. 'That's what your mum's always dreamed of, isn't it, Connor? I know my folks will go nuts for it too.'

Connor's face seemed to have turned pale under his tan. 'Is there time to get them over here?' he asked. 'You know how busy the flights from Oz are at this time of year. Would it be better to delay things a while?'

'They'll get here,' Keegan declared. 'If I have to fly them all out first class.'

Lottie stopped her jaw from unhinging again. She was used to wealthy clients at Firholme, but Keegan was taking it to another level – she hadn't even asked how much it would all cost.

'I'm sure it won't come to that,' Connor said hurriedly. 'I

was only thinking through the logistics. Christmas itself is less than eight weeks away. What about all the legal stuff? The licence?'

Joining him, Keegan stroked his arm. 'We've gone through all that, baby. Now we have a venue and date we can book the registrar. I'm sure they're not busy this time of year, are they, Lottie?'

'Probably not,' Lottie said. 'But I can help you with all of that.'

'There you are, Connor,' Keegan said triumphantly. 'Lottie will take care of everything for us. Aren't we lucky? Now, I need to touch up my lipstick if you'll show me the way to the washroom?'

Flicking her hair over her shoulder, Keegan swept off to the cloakroom, leaving Lottie and Connor alone.

The silence was painful before Connor spoke. 'Keegan's joking about the first-class flights.'

What? Those were his first words after unexpectedly re-appearing in her life after over a year?

'It's up to you,' Lottie said tightly. 'I totally understand that Keegan would want her family to be at her wedding.'

'Yes, but there's no way we'd fly them here first class,' Connor insisted. 'Business class maybe.'

'Connor, you really don't have to apologise or explain anything,' Lottie said, wishing she hadn't been left alone with him. 'I'll do anything I can to make sure you have a happy day and that your mum has a wonderful Christmas surprise. I'm so sorry she's been ill. I wish I'd known.' Lottie just stopped herself from putting her hand on his arm in comfort. With her own mother living so far away, Lottie's relationship with Fiona had probably been closer than it might normally have been. 'I wish I'd known. I would have gone to see her or sent some flowers and a card. Poor Fiona.'

'She understood why you didn't . . .' Connor glanced away guiltily. 'Why I hadn't told you. In the circumstances, she knew it would have been really awkward for you.'

Really awkward for *Connor*, she thought, but stayed tight-lipped. Her natural sympathy for him and his parents trumped any bitter feelings towards him. However, she'd resolved to take control of the situation they'd both found themselves in.

'How close we once were is irrelevant now,' she said, although she felt that her relationship with Connor was all too relevant, given the hurt and anger she still felt.

'True . . . and I apologise. I never should have turned up without making an appointment, but Keegan was all for haring up here the moment I happened to say that Mum loved Firholme. She said we could look round, have a coffee and then when she mentioned about possibly getting married to that guy on reception, he said he would find someone to show us round – the wedding events manager, he said; he didn't use your name or I would have twigged.'

'You still wouldn't have been able to stop Keegan from getting married here, though, would you?'

'No . . . I suppose not. When she gets her teeth into an idea, it's very hard to stop her.'

It was on the tip of Lottie's tongue to say 'I can imagine' but she stopped herself. Henceforth, she had to be scrupulously professional with her 'bridal couple' and that meant being enthusiastic and welcoming. She was finding it almost impossible with Connor, however.

'Jeez, Lottie. I'm so sorry for landing here like this unannounced. It's unforgivable. I'd never want to hurt you; you must understand that?'

But you did *hurt me, Connor,* she thought. *You're still doing it now.* Words dried in her throat. She'd finally got her life back on track, but now he'd ripped the dressing from a still-healing wound. The pain was sharper than she'd ever imagined it could be – because she *hadn't* imagined it, she'd half hoped she'd never have to see him again because it was easier for her. She didn't think she could bleed again at a look or touch from Connor; now she knew she could.

'I can tell Keegan we can't hold the wedding here if you really want me to,' he said, but with a look as if he'd rather have his fingernails pulled out.

'No!' she said quickly. 'No, you absolutely mustn't change your plans because of us.' How could she confess to Shayla that she'd been the cause of cancelling her first wedding at Firholme? The business really needed the revenue, and Keegan was clearly hoping to make it a lavish affair.

'OK, I won't then . . . and I am sorry.' He touched her arm, leaving his fingers there long enough for her to feel a familiar tingle of pleasure at his touch, which she had missed so much in the early days. How could it still have the power to affect her?

Subtly, she moved away a little. 'Let's stick to the practicalities.'

'OK. If you're absolutely sure. Perhaps it would be less

complicated if we didn't get into the details of our past relationship? Maybe it would be easier to let Keegan think we were just friends?' His voice lifted hopefully.

Even though Lottie had been thinking the exact same thing, it stung to hear him ask her to deny how close they'd been. Was that another sign that she still had feelings for him? She didn't want to feel anything: she wanted to be numb – at least for this particular wedding. How would she summon up the joy and excitement she normally felt for her bridal couples?

'Of course,' she said, forcing herself into professional mode, even though her emotions were in turmoil. 'There's no reason for anyone to make the connection between us. I didn't know anyone at Firholme before I started, though I can't guarantee that no one will work out we were together . . . you know what it's like in a small community.'

'That's a risk I'm prepared to take.'

'What about your dad and your family and friends?' she said. 'Won't you have to tell them the wedding is here?'

'Yes, but we might keep the venue a secret as long as we can, even from my dad. I can't trust him not to let something slip to Mum. He's terrible at keeping secrets –' he smiled briefly '– as you know.'

She nodded. Derrick Moran had once blurted out that Connor had arranged a trip to Paris for her birthday, spoiling the surprise. Connor had been far more annoyed than Lottie, who really hadn't minded. Derrick could be opinionated but he loved his family and had always been kind to Lottie.

'OK, but there's a chance they *might* realise once you finally reveal the venue. Some of them might know I work here.'

Shayla had wanted photos of key team members on the website but the photographer hadn't had time to take official photos yet, Lottie thought ruefully, otherwise Connor would have realised she worked at Firholme and would have put off Keegan.

'I doubt it. Besides I've lost touch with most of the old crew while I've been in Australia. After we split up, I wanted to make a completely fresh start. Once the wedding is over, I'll come clean if I have to, though Keegan still won't need to know um . . . how close we were. That's my problem to resolve,' he said firmly, as if Keegan was a workplace issue to be tackled.

'Well, if you're sure Keegan won't feel . . .' Lottie paused to choose her words carefully. 'That she's been kept in the dark if the truth comes out eventually.'

'I prefer to call it being diplomatic. I'd rather we didn't have to deal with it at all.' He clammed up, as voices could be heard in the corridor. It was Keegan, returning from the ladies' restrooms, gushing over the elaborate Edwardian fixtures, presumably to one of the housekeeping staff.

'Unfortunately, we're going to have to, whether we like it or not,' Connor said hastily.

'It really isn't a problem,' she muttered, already regretting letting him get under her skin.

'Con-nor!' Keegan's voice penetrated the walls.

'Coming!' He hurried to the door and Lottie followed him. She escorted them both out of the house and down to the office area, answering Keegan's questions about catering, flowers and bedrooms for the bridal party. She'd already texted the café manager who had reserved a quiet seating area in the corner, and had coffee and home-made Cumbrian biscuits waiting.

An hour later, the plans for the wedding were already under way, if not quite 'nailed down'. Lottie gave Keegan her due; she was nothing if not decisive, just as Connor had said. He sat by, agreeing with everything while scrolling through his phone. Lottie suspected that now he'd realised he couldn't put off Keegan from having the wedding at Firholme, he'd decided to give in and hope for a quiet life – from his fiancée and his ex, she thought wryly.

Somehow, she managed to pretend that the wedding was like any other, although she had to avoid meeting Connor's eye too often. She had a long 'to-do' list, but that was part of the job. It was, however, the fastest wedding she'd ever overseen, and she was also worried that Fiona would get wind of the surprise somehow.

She decided to send an email around to all the staff, warning them not to discuss it outside of work. Hopefully, if Fiona *did* find out, it wouldn't be from anyone at Firholme and she'd have done her job. Privately, Lottie was also convinced Fiona might have preferred to be involved in all the excitement of the planning. She loved organising family 'dos' . . . but that wasn't Lottie's problem, so she'd have to go along with it.

She advised Connor and Keegan on the legal admin and saw them out of the café. They climbed into an SUV in the car park and drove out of the grounds.

Still in her dress and jacket, Lottie realised she was shivering. The sun had slipped behind the fells, and the house was now in shade. At this time of year, the sun set well before four and with the clear skies, they were in for a very chilly night. While the temperatures might plummet, it was too early in the year for snow in the valley where Firholme was situated.

Connor's car had been one of the last to leave the car park, as the café emptied of its visitors and the grounds closed for the day. Folding her arms for warmth, Lottie wandered slowly back to her office, where Shayla would be gleeful about getting the pre-Christmas wedding that Lottie had thought impossible.

Shayla might be thrilled but despondency settled on Lottie like the gathering dusk. The day had started so positively. She'd been looking forward to Christmas with Steph and the twins and choosing trees with Jay had been an unexpected pleasure. Yet it had ended with memories resurfacing from a dark time of her life. She was glad that Connor had found someone he loved, even if it was rather quick, but it hurt that he'd edited her out of his life.

She'd found it so much harder to move on from him.

She still cared about him, fancied him, and the 'what might have beens' had resurfaced like creatures from the deep. All of which made her more determined, no matter how hard it was, to make sure that her ex and his fiancée never suspected how hurt she was . . . and that they would have the most amazing wedding *ever*.

Chapter Six

Jay had allowed himself a discreet smile when he'd watched Lottie make her way down the path that skirted the plantation, earlier that day. Perhaps he should have been thinking about trees, but his mind was occupied by how great she looked in her coat and hiking boots. The fresh air had reddened the tip of her nose and brought out a pink glow in her cheeks that only enhanced her pretty face.

Some of his colleagues had already made an effort to be friendly with him in his first week at Firholme but he hadn't felt drawn to anyone until he'd spoken to Lottie that morning. Her love for her family had touched him and he suspected the bond between Lottie and her sister had been strengthened by the ordeal they'd been through.

Jay knew how that connection with a sibling felt. He'd thought his bond with his older brother had been unbreakable, right until the moment Ben had shattered the trust between them. Jay hadn't seen him since the previous Christmas Eve.

As he walked back to the area where his team were clearing the forest, bitter memories battled with the pleasant emotions that had come from being in Lottie's company. He'd have loved to ask her out for a drink, under other circumstances; those circumstances being he'd made a promise to himself never to get seriously entangled with another woman. He already liked her too much to let her down, and far too much to inflict his cynical, hardened self on, so it was kinder to avoid any involvement altogether.

The most useful thing he could do for her was his job – which meant making sure the Christmas trees and greenery were harvested and transported to the house at their naturally spectacular best.

Until public sales opened, he relished the chance to get stuck into the actual essence of his new role: managing the forest. He certainly hadn't taken the job to give orders and watch other people doing the hard graft. Quite the contrary – the more time he spent out of doors in natural surroundings, the better.

With that in mind, he briefed the plantation supervisor as soon as Lottie had left. Kerr Henshall was a Scot in his early forties with a bone-dry sense of humour. He lived just a mile away, in Langmere village with his son.

'OK. I've marked the two Nordmanns and the spruces for the big house. I'd like to make a start on felling them once I have the go-ahead from Lottie . . . from the office,' Jay corrected himself. 'I think we'll do the Nordmanns first and transport them to the house in the truck.'

'I'll get it sorted,' Kerr said confidently.

'I'm sure you could but I'd also like to be involved in felling the trees.'

Kerr frowned. 'We can handle that . . .'

'I know, but I want to make sure these trees are at their very best for the big house.'

'Whatever you say, *boss*.'

Jay guessed that Kerr felt Jay was micromanaging the situation. 'It'll give me an excuse to get out of the office,' he said quickly, keen to keep his deputy onside.

Kerr smiled briefly. He seemed an easy-going guy and good at his job but Jay suspected that his predecessor had been very hands-off with the team. They must be finding it hard to get used to an upstart like himself.

'Shall we get on with the thinning in the Middle Glade?' Kerr said briskly. 'We're ready to take some of the wood down to the sawmill. You'll be wanting to supervise that too, I take it?' Kerr added casually, giving him a knowing look. 'Or will you be away down to the big house again this afternoon?'

Jay groaned inwardly. Kerr had obviously picked up on Jay's keenness to make sure everything was perfect for the offices. Whether he'd also connected that with Jay's chat with Lottie, Jay wasn't sure.

'No, I'll be here to keep an eye on you,' he said, with a smile. 'You're not getting rid of me that easily.'

'OK . . . Oh, and by the way, will you be joining us at the pub on Wednesday? We have a get-together at the local every month if we can.' Kerr grinned. 'Just a pint, a laugh and a meal. It's a good chance for us to relax before the madness of Christmas starts.'

Jay was caught off-guard. 'I um . . . I'm not sure what I'm doing that evening.'

Kerr nodded. 'Well, the invitation's open but if you're otherwise engaged, that's fine. I can see you might have a better offer.'

Jay cringed. So far, during breaks, he was comfortable while the talk had been about sport or nature but he dreaded being drawn into any conversations about his personal life.

'Thanks for letting me know,' he said, trying to keep his reply low-key.

'Lottie usually organises it . . . nice lass . . .' Kerr said. 'But there's no pressure if you don't fancy it.'

Jay searched Kerr's face for any hint that his colleague thought Lottie might be an added attraction for Jay.

Which she was, of course.

'I'll do my best,' he said evenly. 'Thanks for letting me know about it.' Then briskly: 'I'll be off to the High Copse and then I'll join you in the Middle Glade.'

He hurried away, wishing that people wouldn't invite him to things . . . yet also recognising that socialising was a normal part of work – of life. He knew he was already getting a reputation for being standoffish at best and an antisocial weirdo at worst. He was aware he'd become a hermit over the past year, avoiding all contact with people from his past life and his present.

It wasn't good for his mental health – but so far, he hadn't cared.

He loved working in the outdoors. It had been his solace to be surrounded by trees and wildlife, and the fells. It had helped soothe him and put his problems in perspective, not to mention it was physically tiring. Even before he'd moved to Firholme from an estate in the north of the county, he loved to set off for a walk with Trevor after his work shift, taking off into the hills or down by the lake until darkness fell.

Sometimes he was alone, but long summer evenings attracted tourists. Even in autumn, there had been many visitors packing the russet fells, enjoying the autumn colours and the last days before winter arrived.

Now, the throngs had thinned, but the first snows of winter on the peaks still drew the hardy back at the weekends, to marvel at the high tops, covered with white. Jay took off with an ice axe and crampons, hiking above the snow line where only the most intrepid ventured. He usually left Trevor safely tucked up in the cottage. He knew it was risky to walk and scramble alone, but he felt alive when he was up on the crags, looking down on the rest of the world.

He climbed the slope to the copse, an ancient area of woodland above the plantation, full of oak, beech and mountain ash. It was the final wooded area before the ground rose sharply and opened out into heather-clad fells, populated only by the Herdwick sheep. As it wasn't open to the public, it was one of his favourite places to seek peace and solitude. A deer emerged briefly into a clearing and he stopped to watch it vanish into the shadows. Nature helped to clear his mind.

Jay walked on, working through his schedule for the run-up to Christmas in his mind. Tree sales opened on the final weekend in November and closed on the twenty-first of

December, by which time everyone should have bought their tree or they'd have run out of stock.

It was a delicate balancing act. He'd managed a similar scheme in a previous job at a forestry centre and it was a short but incredibly intense period. He doubted he'd get much rest, with sales being open from nine a.m. until eight p.m. every day. The upside meant he'd be exhausted by Christmas Eve and hopefully sleep through it all.

The downside was Trevor having to spend more time inside the cottage, although Jay made time to walk him at lunchtime, no matter how busy he was. The dog was also used to taking his walks in all weathers. He didn't care if it was hailing, blowing a gale and pitch black, he was so excited to be in the outdoors. Firholme was a gourmet location for dogs, with its fellsides, woods and array of delicious doggy smells.

Trevor had also helped keep Jay sane after his split from Nadia. He'd been so relieved when she'd made it clear that she didn't want to take the dog when she'd moved out. It would have been the nail in the coffin for Jay to lose Trevor too, along with everyone else he loved.

Jay strode back into the forest, checking out the areas where the holly grew and looking for mistletoe. He'd suggested harvesting some festive greenery for the house and café to Lottie, and she'd seemed very pleased he'd offered. He felt soothed and calmer since he'd taken the job at Firholme – he supposed he was 'healing' slowly, though he also felt he was a long way from a full recovery.

He was almost at the edge of the forest when a rustle in the leaves stopped him dead. A squirrel scampered across his path and stopped in a pool of sunlight, the rays making its bushy tail seem like a halo.

Jay held his breath, watching as it nibbled an acorn, oblivious to his presence. He thought of Lottie's delight and their shared wonder at seeing the squirrel together. He had a feeling they'd share more than a love of nature, if they got the chance.

His snort of derision at the idea of him sharing anything more with Lottie startled the squirrel and it fled up the trunk of an oak.

Who was he kidding? Even if he overcame every instinct and asked her out, he had absolutely no idea if someone as lively and sociable – and gorgeous – as her was even interested in him.

Chapter Seven

Stars twinkled in the sky as Lottie drove from Firholme to Carnthwaite, a small village at the northern end of Derwentwater where Steph and the twins lived. It was only a few miles away, but on the twisty, narrow roads, it took twenty minutes. There were no streetlights on the road and only a sliver of moon, and occasionally her headlights swept over sheep huddled by farm gates or the white walls of cottages.

She'd lain awake into the small hours the night after Connor had walked back into her life, bringing his fiancée with him. She'd been trying to come to terms with his reappearance and wondering how much to tell her sister. Although Steph's chemo and radiotherapy had finished in the summer, she was still anxiously awaiting a date for a scan and check-up to see if the cancer had been treated successfully. Lottie didn't want to add yet another layer of anxiety but, on the other hand, she knew Steph would probably want her to share such major news.

Carnthwaite was encircled by the heather-clad fells and soaring peaks of Skiddaw and Blencathra. The lights of the houses and pub twinkled in the valley as Lottie descended from Firholme. Fireworks fizzed in the sky, and there was a lingering smell of smoke in the air. The girls were off to an organised event that weekend, so they were happy to stay in on Bonfire Night itself and Steph would be tired anyway after working at the school all day.

Lottie parked outside her sister's semi, in a small close in the heart of the village. The girls were waiting and flew on her as soon as she'd gone into the hall.

'You're pleased to see me, then?' she said, hugging both girls at once. Instantly, her mood lifted and the cares of the day were temporarily forgotten.

Over dinner, she related the story about the red squirrel she and Jay had seen, and told them about the trees they'd chosen for Firholme. Afterwards, Lottie snuggled on the sofa with her nieces in the living room. The girls were as full of beans as a Heinz warehouse, despite being in their pyjamas and meant to be winding down. Lottie had taken the dishes out to the kitchen while Steph had supervised their bath time and they were all now relaxing – or meant to be – in the sitting room.

'Is it *almost* time for Santa to come yet?' Myra asked, clambering onto the sofa next to Lottie. Her damp hair was fluffy and she smelled of strawberry bubble bath.

'Not yet, sweetheart. Let's get Bonfire Night over first. I expect he's busy getting ready,' Lottie answered. 'You know that, though. Christmas Day is still seven weeks away.' And

Connor's wedding only six, she thought, with a lump in her throat and a rising sense of panic.

'Santa won't come if you keep asking when he'll come,' Jodie said, rolling her eyes at her sister. 'Like Mummy says when we're in the car. We won't get there if you keep asking when we'll be there.'

Myra stuck out her tongue. Before Lottie could issue a gentle reminder to 'Be kind', Myra had switched tack. 'Guess what happened at school today?' she said, studiously ignoring her sister.

'Jonas Baxter's brother did a poo in the garden!' Jodie shouted and dissolved into giggles.

Myra squealed in indignation. 'Shut up, Jodie, I wanted to tell Auntie Lottie that!'

'It's my story too!' Jodie cried.

'Girls, girls. You can *both* tell me, one at a time. Myra: doesn't this Jonas have a bathroom?'

'I 'spect so but his dad told him to do it in the garden,' said Myra.

Lottie exchanged an 'eugh' face with Steph.

Jodie shrugged dramatically and held out her hands. 'Well, how d'you expect *me* to know?'

Lottie was struggling to hold in her laughter. Jodie's shrug and eye-roll were exactly like Steph's gestures.

'Jonas's brother is three,' Steph explained. 'Apparently, his dad told him that weeing on the compost was good for it. He was only following orders, I suppose.'

'But why should we do a wee on the compost?' Myra asked then pushed her glasses up her nose. 'What's compost?'

80

'It's a place where you put the dead leaves and grass from your garden and all the insects turn it into a mush that helps the plants grow,' Lottie said. 'I don't know why anyone would wee on it.'

'But . . . that will kill the insects and the hedgehogs sleeping in the leaves!' Myra said.

'Urgh . . .' Jodie poked her tongue out.

Steph laughed. 'I'm not sure it's the best way of looking after your garden. I'd stick to the bathroom, I think.'

Steph and Lottie exchanged amused glances.

Later, after listening patiently to more details of the twins' day at school, Lottie helped get them to bed and stayed to read them a bedtime story, while her sister had a short break.

The twins were a joy but a handful. They were the result of a holiday romance in Spain. Steph had always had problems with her periods and hadn't realised she was pregnant for a few months. Lottie would never forget the shock on her face when she'd revealed she was carrying twins. The father hadn't left Steph his number and all attempts to track him down on social media had failed so she'd decided to carry on alone. It was bad timing as their parents had only moved to New Zealand a year previously. Lottie was sure they'd have come home if Steph had said she really needed them, but her sister was adamant she could manage alone.

Identical in looks, each had her own distinct personality. Jodie was a bit of a comedian, fond of imitating her mum and giggling at the daftest things. Myra took things more seriously and often came out with some deep questions that Lottie found hard to answer. She was probably more like Lottie than Steph.

When Lottie came downstairs, Steph had her feet up on the sofa and her eyes closed. Even though Steph was tired, Lottie was pleased to see her sister looking a little more like herself. She'd been off work for months, although she'd very recently returned to her role as a teaching assistant at the twins' school.

After loading the dishwasher, Lottie did a quick tidy of the kitchen and made two coffees. When she went into the sitting room, Steph seemed to be coming round.

She blinked and rubbed her eyes. 'Sorry, I nodded off.'

'That's why I came to help. To give you a break.'

She swung her legs off the sofa to make room for Lottie. 'Thanks. They're hyper today. I'm amazed they went to bed at all.'

Lottie handed her a mug and sat down herself. 'They're shattered. Jodie was already dozing off while I finished the story. Myra made it to the end but she's snuggled down now.'

'No more mentions of Jonas Baxter?' Steph asked.

'Not after the first few minutes.'

'Good . . .' Steph sipped her coffee. 'So, tell me more about this Jay.'

'What do you mean?'

'The new gardener bloke who showed you his squirrel.'

Lottie sputtered her coffee. 'It was *a* squirrel, not his squirrel and he only moved in a week ago. I know next to nothing about him.' She smiled. 'He has a lovely Labrador though.'

'A lovely Labrador?' Steph raised an eyebrow.

'He's called Trevor, and he's very friendly,' Lottie said, recalling how Jay had had to call Trevor back when the dog had run into Lottie's garden a couple of times, obviously seeking a fuss. Jay was firm but also very gentle with Trevor. He clearly loved animals of all kinds. She thought back to that short time in the forest. She'd been enjoying Jay's company and the feeling had seemed to be mutual. Funny, she'd half expected him to text her later that day – but now?

Falling for Jay wasn't some miracle cure for a broken heart plus she had no idea if he was even single. And now Connor had come back into her life . . .

'I saw Connor yesterday,' she said, wary of Steph's reaction.

Steph frowned. 'As in Connor, your cowardly ex?'

Lottie winced at Steph's description of him. Though she herself thought he was a quitter at the time, Steph didn't know about Connor's proposal or that he'd broken her heart so badly. Thank God, she'd never told her sister. Steph thought Connor had simply decided to leave; as did their parents. As did everyone they knew. It would only have added to Steph's problems when she needed to focus on getting well.

'Yes. He turned up at Firholme out of the blue.'

Steph snorted in derision. 'What for? To grovel and beg you to come back?'

'No. Why would he do that?' Lottie asked.

'Because he realises how amazing you are? He's an idiot but you're better off without him.'

It was hard to fool Steph and Lottie suspected that her sister hadn't bought the story that Lottie had been OK with the break-up. She was touched by her loyalty but her heart sank. This was going to be even harder than she'd expected. 'He didn't even know I was working there. And, he brought his fiancée.'

Steph splashed coffee on her lap. 'Sodding hell!' She grabbed a tissue to mop it while Lottie fetched some kitchen roll.

'Connor brought his *fiancée* to Firholme?' She dabbed at her jeans with the paper towel. 'Why would he do that?'

'Because he wants to get married there. Or rather she – Keegan – does.'

'No way! That would be excruciating. I presume he called it all off once he realised you organise the weddings?'

'No. They're going ahead.'

'You cannot be serious?! You can't possibly agree to plan his wedding!'

'I didn't want to, but I've no choice. Connor was as shocked as I was when he walked in and found out I'm in charge of the weddings. He'd no idea I was working there . . .' Lottie left out exactly why. 'He went abroad after we split up and met this Australian woman through work.'

Steph shook her head in disbelief. 'Poor woman. When are they doing the dirty deed?'

'The week before Christmas.'

'Jesus, Lottie. Why the hurry? Is she pregnant?'

'I don't think so. They came in on the off chance and Shayla was ecstatic to have a booking before Christmas. We can't afford to turn down the revenue and to be fair, Connor did try to put Keegan off . . . but she thinks Firholme is "a-mazing" and I don't blame her.'

'Even so, why didn't Connor make an excuse and find another venue? It's cruel to rub your nose in things like this.'

Lottie sighed. 'He's not rubbing my nose in it. I got over the break-up ages ago . . .'

Steph raised an eyebrow. 'Mm . . .'

'I really am OK with it,' she said, recalling how her skin tingled and her heart skipped a beat when Connor had touched her. 'Even if I could have persuaded them to go elsewhere, I still wouldn't have. This is my first wedding and they're spending a lot of money that Firholme desperately needs. Plus . . . the main reason they want to get married in a hurry is that Connor's mum has been ill. She had a stroke earlier this year.'

'That's awful,' said Steph. 'I liked Fiona. More than Connor, to be honest.'

'You never said that before.'

'I didn't want to upset you, but I can say it now. How's his mum doing?'

'Connor says she's recovering, but that the whole family has had a huge scare and they want to surprise her with a Christmas wedding. He said she's always wanted to see one of their kids married at Firholme.'

Steph blew out a breath. 'Bugger me . . . I suppose I can't argue with that. I know all about wanting to make the most of every day, but it's hard on you, Lottie. Does this Keegan even know you and Connor were together?'

'No, and I don't want her to. We've agreed to keep it a secret.' Again, Lottie thought it was easier to be economical with the truth. Steph would have been furious to know that it was Connor's idea to pretend he'd never been involved with Lottie, even if Lottie had gone along with it willingly enough.

'Lottie, come on, we agreed to be honest with each other. How do you really feel about him?'

Now, that was the question. Lottie would have liked to have felt nothing other than mild surprise and the pleasure of seeing an old friend when he walked in through Firholme's grand front door. But she did very much still feel something and she didn't like some of those feelings.

'I don't want him to be unhappy,' she said, choosing her words carefully. 'Though I'd never have chosen to plan his wedding, that's for sure. It'll be fine now the first meeting is past.'

'Why am I not convinced?'

'I admit I was shocked,' Lottie said, thinking it might be better to offer Steph a nugget of truth to put her off the scent. 'He's still the Connor I knew in one way.'

'Still the Connor you loved?'

Ouch, Steph could be brutal, but she'd hit the nail on the head, thought Lottie. 'Yes . . . only a shinier version. It could be the tan, or the fact that he must have been hitting the gym in Oz. It can't be surfing,' Lottie said with a smile. 'He can't swim very well.'

'Serves the pompous git right,' Steph declared.

'Anyway, he looks really fit and buff and there's a self-confidence about him, a polish . . .' Lottie said, remembering the impact this 'new' Connor had had on her. 'Although the sight of me took the wind out of his sails.'

'I bet it did!' Steph's eyes narrowed. 'I'd like to tell him a few things, if I see him.'

'No, don't, for my sake,' Lottie cried. 'To be honest I'd find it excruciating to have to explain to Shayla why a couple cancelled a huge expensive wedding because of me. I'd rather try and get through it somehow.'

'What's she like, this Keegan?'

'Tall, glamorous, determined – and she seems to adore Connor and Firholme.' And he seemed totally in awe of Keegan, Lottie thought. 'What more can I say? I only met her yesterday,' she said, trying to keep things casual.

'Do you like her though? Does she deserve Connor? And does he deserve her? I hoped you'd say she was Cruella De Vil.'

Lottie laughed. 'Maybe it would have been easier for me if she was vile, but so far, she hasn't done anything to make me hate her or even dislike her.' She sighed. 'Whether I like it or not, Connor's my client now. I need to set aside my personal feelings and you know I really liked his mum. For her sake, and Firholme's, I'm going to make a good job of it – and I don't have long so if I'm not around here quite as much, you know why.'

'Well, I call it shitty luck that he chose Firholme, even if his mum does love it.' Steph reached out and squeezed Lottie's hand. 'You know you can vent to me whenever you like. This isn't going to be easy.'

Tell me about it, thought Lottie.

'No it's not.' She decided to distract Steph for the time being. 'Talking of work, are you still OK with coming to the staff Christmas ball at Firholme? Can your friend have the chidren for the night so you stay over at mine?'

'Yes, it's all sorted. The girls are going to a sleepover at my friend's house and they're so excited. Almost as excited as me. Thank you for inviting me as your plus-one.' Steph gave a mischievous grin. 'You are sure there's no one else you'd rather ask?'

'I'm sure,' Lottie said firmly. 'We deserve a night out like we used to.' She didn't add that she hoped Steph would be well enough to enjoy it.

'I can't wait. I haven't been out on the town for so long. I'm ready to party.' Steph sighed. 'After all who knows what might happen tomorrow?'

Lottie had the following afternoon off so headed into Langmere village to get a few treats for herself and Steph from the deli-cum-coffee shop by the lake. She walked back to her car via the post office where she went in to buy some stamps and choose a Christmas card to send to her parents. She wanted one with a Lakeland scene by a local artist and it would have to be posted soon.

While she browsed, the door was opened and Wilf made his way in, closely followed by Jay, who was carrying a parcel.

'Thank you, young fella,' Wilf said to Jay who'd held the door open for him. The old man moved to the post office counter where Irina was waiting to serve him. He lifted his stick. 'In here again, Dotty Lottie? Anyone would think you were after me, or something.'

Jay immediately caught Lottie's eye. She cringed at the

nickname but answered Wilf good-naturedly. 'Of course. I came in specially in the hope you'd drop by, Mr Carman.'

Wilf laughed. 'Can't keep away, you see,' he said to Jay who was clearly amused. He nodded a hello to her.

'Are you the young fella who took over from Graham at Firholme?' Wilf said to Jay.

Jay managed a smile. 'Yes, that's me.'

'Big shoes to fill. Everyone liked Graham. Still you look like you're no stranger to hard work. I was a strapping chap in my day,' Wilf said.

'Can I help you, Wilf?' Irina piped up.

'Oh, yes. I want some stamps. Mind you I need to win the lottery first, the price of them these days.'

Jay queued behind Wilf while Lottie chose her card. She risked a glance at Jay to find him looking at her. They both exchanged a smile before Lottie took her purchases to the store till where Jan was in charge.

When she left the shop the afternoon sun was sinking in a crimson sky and glinting off the bonnet of Jay's pick-up, which was parked outside.

Jay walked out. 'Hello,' he said. 'Fancy seeing you in there.'

Lottie rolled her eyes. 'It's a small world, as you've gathered. News travelled fast that you're working at Firholme.'

'I realise that. Graham was a very popular man.'

'He'd worked for the Firholme estate for a long time,' Lottie said. 'He wanted to retire when Shayla bought the place but she asked him to stay on until she could recruit someone new.'

'So I heard. Wilf's a character.'

'He's lived here all his life apart from his service in the war and he knows everyone. He was school caretaker when I was a little girl hence the er . . . nickname.'

Jay smirked. 'I've heard worse.'

Lottie rolled her eyes. 'It was OK until I was about seven, but I don't mind. Wilf's a lovely old chap.'

Jay's eyes lit up in amusement and Lottie was encouraged to glimpse this warmer side of him again. She'd already over-heard a conversation between two of Jay's team as they ate bacon butties in the courtyard earlier that morning. The upshot was that he was very competent but a bit distant. She'd also heard some of the office staff admiring the way he looked, but calling him a 'bit of a loner'. Lottie felt it would be good for Jay, and for everyone, if they could get to know him a little better.

'How are you settling in? You and Trevor?' she added, keeping things light.

'OK. I've everything I need,' he said crisply then seemed to soften his words. 'I'm sorry he's run onto your side of the hedge. He's so excitable and he loves people but they don't always love him.'

'I can't think why. He's such a friendly dog.'

'The squirrels don't think so. He tried to chase one into the woods the other day . . . but just let me know if he's making a nuisance of himself.' Jay smiled, obviously relieved that Lottie was one of Trevor's fans, at least. She was struck by how handsome he was, especially when he smiled. She decided to take her chance while he was more relaxed, and perhaps, away from the work environment.

'Glad you're both finding your feet. Will you be coming to the pub night?' she said.

His brow furrowed. 'Oh yes, can you remind me when it is?'

'Next Wednesday, here at the Bull in the village. We walk down together and it's very informal but we have a laugh and the food is pretty good. Of course, you might have other plans for that evening . . .' she said, seeing his discomfort at being put on the spot.

'Plans?' He sounded amazed at the very idea.

'I mean, you might already be going out,' she said carefully.

'Oh, I see what you mean.' They held each other's gaze, and she waited for him to elaborate and come out with an excuse or prior engagement. 'Kerr did mention it but I haven't had chance to check my diary yet.'

'Well, the invitation's there,' Lottie said, certain he was being ironic about checking his diary.

'Thanks. I'd, er, better be getting home to take Trevor out for his walk. See you later, I'm sure.'

With a brief smile, he flicked the unlock button on his truck and then got in and drove away leaving Lottie feeling rebuffed and wondering whether she should have bothered trying to draw him out at all. Perhaps he was genuinely socially awkward – or maybe just plain awkward. He was harder to approach than any forest creature – and just as wary.

The question was should she even try to get close again or steer well clear?

Chapter Eight

On Tuesday, a few days after his conversation with Lottie in the post office, Jay was still thinking about her as he made his way back to the plantation after a walk with Trevor.

Lottie had tried to make him feel welcome at Firholme while still respecting his privacy and he felt a strange empathy with her despite their circumstances being different. He couldn't help but smile at seeing her cringe when the old guy had called her Dotty Lottie. It was tempting to try it himself but he wouldn't dare, of course.

'Trevor! Heel!' Jay called as Trevor romped off along the fellside but his canine pal was having far too much fun, chasing the trails left by dozens of dogs. 'Trevor! Oh, bloody hell . . .'

Trevor padded into the stream and stood there as proud as punch. After a few more splashes, he rolled in the mud at the edge of the beck. His brown coat was now thick with sludge and wisps of bracken.

Jay put his hands on his hips. 'Great. Thank you for that, Trevor. You're going to need more than a rub-down before I can let you back in the cottage.'

Finally, Trevor trotted back, a stick between his teeth. He presented it to Jay and wagged his tail furiously. 'Thanks, mate. I'll treasure it.'

Trevor flopped down in front of Jay.

'There's no point behaving like a saint now, Trev. You may as well go the whole hog. Roll in some fox poo, play in a bog. Go ahead, be my guest.'

The dog cocked his head on one side, then took his cue from Jay who started walking up the fell path. He was soon running ahead, stopping at every rock or tree that smelled interesting. Not for the first time, Jay wished his life was as simple as Trevor's.

He was still a relatively young dog, barely three years old. Jay had already had him for a year when he'd met Nadia. She'd been happy to have him share their flat, which was a massive relief because Trevor had already been abandoned at a rescue centre by one family who couldn't cope with him. He was still boisterous, but with a lot of patience, Jay had managed to curb the worst of his unruly behaviour. Firholme was the perfect home for him, with lots of space for walks literally on the doorstep.

Lottie clearly liked Trevor too, which was a big plus in Jay's book . . . in fact, when it came to Lottie, he could think of an awful lot of plusses.

He'd been feeling guilty about his curt dismissal of her question about him having a Christmas tree and his comments about not feeling like joining in with the celebrations. Not that he blamed Lottie for wanting to make the most of Christmas after what she and her family had been through. No wonder they wanted to celebrate, but he was filled with dread at the coming season.

The prospect of spending Christmas Day with his family knotted his stomach. In fact, he didn't think he could even set foot in his parents' house if his brother was going to be within a mile of the place. He'd flung so many insults the last time he'd seen him, and so many cruel and harsh words. At first, he didn't regret a single one but over the past few months, he was wishing he hadn't reacted so wildly.

Lottie had, however, reminded him that he hadn't been as responsive as she, or some of his co-workers, deserved . . . She and Kerr had both tried to invite him to the pub, after all, and he'd been non-committal so far.

'Trevor!'

Seeing a couple walking along the path towards him, Jay tried to bring his dog to heel. He was surprised to see people on a dull November day in the middle of the week. They weren't dressed like ramblers either. The woman was in a smart pale blue coat and knee-high Uggs, while the guy wore a Barbour.

Clearly, Trevor found their presence far too exciting to ignore and raced towards them like a Grand National winner.

'Trevor! Heel!' Jay shouted, running after him before he decided to give the woman a 'friendly' greeting probably involving a lot of slobber – or worse, tried to jump up. Not everyone liked dogs and there was no excuse for letting one run out of control.

Luckily, Trevor sensed that Jay meant business and he ran back to his side. 'Sorry, boy, but you'll have to go on your lead for a little while. I'm not sure these people will appreciate one of your special greetings.'

The couple had stopped next to a rowan tree, loaded with crimson berries. They didn't appear to have seen Jay yet, because they seemed to be having an argument. He caught snatches of raised voices on the wind.

'Wait . . .' he said in a low voice to Trevor. Crouching down, he stroked the dog's head. The couple were talking animatedly. He thought he saw the woman give the man a push before she walked away from him and away from Jay. The man called after her.

'Keegan!' he shouted. Or something like it. It was an unusual name so caught his attention.

Keegan took a small path down the fellside. It was steep and she almost slipped. Jay was a little worried about her in those furry boots. The fellside was muddy.

'Grow up!' the man shouted and let out a groan of annoyance that made Trevor's ears twitch.

'Stay, boy. I don't think they want company,' he said. Jay certainly didn't want to intrude on their tiff.

The man followed Keegan down the fell, almost losing his own footing. Keegan had made it to a lower path and was marching along. Her partner caught her up so Jay waited a moment to make sure she was happy that he'd followed her. She rounded on him but after a minute or two, she let the man embrace her and after that they strolled back in the direction of Firholme arm in arm.

Jay let Trevor off the lead and continued towards the opposite end of the lake to Firholme. He didn't want to risk bumping into the couple again – or anyone if he could avoid it.

Nonetheless with her talk of how close her family were, Lottie had reminded him that it was a lonely existence. Perhaps it was time to engage with the world again – just not at Christmas, yet he still felt the old Jay, trusting, loving his family, the centre of their gatherings, had gone.

Trevor licked his hand, as if he sensed Jay's worries.

'Trouble is, Trev,' Jay said, stroking the dog's head, 'I'm not sure he'll ever come back.'

Chapter Nine

Five weeks to the wedding

Lottie wasn't normally superstitious, but couldn't help thinking Friday the thirteenth wasn't the best day for Keegan and Connor to give their verdict on the festive décor and finalise the menus and wine list.

She'd been on edge all morning, wondering how they'd react to the ballroom – and how she'd react to being so close to Connor again, while having to bottle up her emotions under a veneer of cheerful professionalism.

By the time she'd spotted their car, she was worked up so much, her stomach was like a ball of twine. However, Connor stayed in the car to take a call, leaving Lottie to escort Keegan up to the ballroom alone. The huge space was now decorated for Christmas, with the tree already festooned in their colour scheme. Lottie had to admit it looked sensational but would Keegan agree?

Keegan had inspected the nine-foot Nordmann fir that Jay had delivered to the ballroom, along with the other trees, the previous day but it was now resplendent in its finery.

'This is wonderful.' She turned to Lottie, beaming. 'It's just how I imagined it. You're very talented.'

Lottie gave a huge inner sigh of relief and smiled. 'Thank you, but I can't claim all the credit. The whole team worked on it.'

'Well, I think it's awesome that it's been decorated especially for us.'

Lottie was delighted that the tree had arrived inside the ballroom, without any mishaps. Beforehand, she'd worked alongside Jay's team and a freelance interior decorator to remove any furniture or objects that might be damaged.

It had been a delicate and time-consuming operation. Worth every moment, though, because Keegan's theme of rich jewel colours looked fabulous. The glass baubles and tinsel in amethyst, sapphire, emerald and ruby were rich and warm, and perfectly in keeping with the dark oak panelling and tapestries.

'I'm pleased you love it.' Lottie actually was happy. No matter who her couple were, she couldn't help be proud of what her colleagues had achieved.

'It's going to match my dress perfectly. I'm wearing a cran-berry velvet cloak over a cream silk dress. I'll show you on my phone, if you like.'

'Lovely!' Lottie determined to show as much enthusiasm as possible. She was good at hiding her true feelings, having had a lot of practice since Steph had been ill, and knew she was going to need all of that skill now.

Keegan whipped out her phone and showed Lottie a picture

of the designer dress. It really was beautiful and she could easily imagine how stunning it would look on Keegan's slender frame.

'It's gorgeous,' Lottie said, not letting her mask slip.

'Thanks. I went to London to choose it. It's being altered for me and the designer is coming up here especially to do a fitting.'

'Fabulous.' Lottie kept smiling. 'That reminds me. Our florist has asked if she can meet you for a chat about your flowers? Obviously, time is of the essence and she'd like to discuss things here at Firholme so you can get the best idea of how the arrangements will look.'

'I can probably come back tomorrow.'

'That's fine. We can all meet together if you like? In the café before it opens?'

'No problem. Connor won't be needed. I want to show the florist my dress and he can't see it before the day, now can he?' She smirked. 'That would be bad luck.'

'Of course.' Lottie realised that with all the subterfuge she was going to be seeing a lot more of her bridal couple than she normally would but at least Connor wouldn't be around the next day.

A moment later, Lottie's spirits lifted when Jay walked in with a large box full of holly and mistletoe, which would be used to create swags and vases of seasonal greenery.

'This is Jay, our estates manager,' she said brightly. 'He's responsible for the tree.'

'Not only me,' Jay said, placing the box on the tiles. 'There's a team of us.'

'Well, congratulations to you all. It looks great,' Keegan said, looking into the box. 'Is that mistletoe? I've not seen any of the English variety for real before. Is it from Firholme?'

'Yes, it's been gathered on the estate. This came from some of the conifers and hawthorn.'

Keegan picked out a bunch from the box and looked up. 'Oh, Connor! There you are. Come over here and see this!'

Connor walked into the ballroom. 'What's "this"?' he asked, joining her.

'Real mistletoe.' She waggled the sprigs, with their plump white berries, above his head. 'We have to try it out.'

'Perhaps not right now,' Connor said lightly, but Lottie could see him cringing. She felt awkward herself.

'Why not?' said Keegan. 'Don't be shy. We are getting married after all.'

'I'll fetch in the rest of the greenery from outside,' Jay muttered and scuttled off.

Lottie had no such escape route. She feigned interest in her phone while Keegan gave Connor a lingering kiss on the lips.

She heaved a sigh of relief, when Jay came back with another box overflowing with prickly holly. She was struck by the difference in their looks. Was it wrong to fancy them both, even if it was in different ways? In his leather jacket and designer jeans, Connor was artfully casual, his dark brown hair cut and gelled into an on-trend style. Jay was untamed, with tousled hair, in faded jeans and Firholme sweatshirt.

Keegan caught her eye and linked her arm through Connor's, forcing a smile from Lottie and leaving her wondering if Keegan had realised she was admiring her fiancé.

Connor probably hadn't realised he had scarlet lipstick around his mouth, which made him look like a clown had done his make-up in the dark. Lottie squashed down the urge to laugh.

After Connor and Keegan admired the holly, Jay said he'd be back later 'when you aren't so busy' and fled once again. She wondered what he wanted to say to her.

'So, Lottie. You said you'd give us a proper tour of the rooms for the bridal party today?' Keegan said.

'No problem,' Lottie said brightly.

'Connor?' Keegan said. 'You're coming with us?'

Connor pulled his mobile from his pocket. 'I need to take this call first. It's Mum.' Lottie detected a 'sorry, not sorry' edge to his tone.

He hurried out of the room but Keegan lowered her voice anyway. 'He doesn't want Fiona to hear anything that might give the game away. We've told her that we're having a special family lunch to celebrate her recovery, at a smart hotel. That's so we can get her here on the day in her party outfit.'

'You don't think anyone will give the game away?' Lottie said, thinking again of how much Fiona might have enjoyed helping with the wedding prep.

Keegan's eyes flashed. 'We've told them we'll never speak to them again if they do.' The she laughed. 'Only joking but I would be very annoyed if it got out, after all the effort we're going to. Connor would be furious too. He may seem easy-going, but under the charm, he's a tough cookie. You should see him in a board meeting.' Keegan blew out a breath. 'He plays hardball, I can tell you.'

'Really?' Lottie said.

The Connor she remembered had been meticulous and ambitious, but he'd never really struck her as a hard-talking high-flyer. Although for all she knew, the new shiny version could have turned into a corporate megastar.

'You have no idea,' Keegan said then laughed again. 'But this is a wedding not a business deal and we're meant to be on a break. Connor's a big softy when it comes to his family – and me. I'm so lucky.'

'I'm sure he's lucky to have you,' said Lottie, through gritted teeth. 'Now, would you like that tour of the guests' rooms?'

Sometimes families celebrating special occasions could take over the house and its ten bedrooms exclusively – and at a price, of course. However, neither Connor nor Keegan had batted an eyelid when Lottie had told them the cost of their wedding package. Given how obsessed he was with figures and planning, she guessed he'd hate all these hasty plans – either that or he'd changed.

Lottie opened the door to the bridal suite and let Keegan walk ahead of her. It was a huge room with high ceilings and a large bay window that overlooked the lake.

'Wow. This is magnificent.' Keegan shook her head in admiration. 'That's a huge bed.'

'It's an original frame from the Edwardian era,' Lottie said, trying to focus to the facts about the bed, not what might happen in it.

Keegan ran her hand over the cover and lay back on it. 'It's gorgeous.' She closed her eyes. 'I always dreamed of spending our first night in a bed like this. Our first *married* night, that is. We've been living together for over six months now.'

Six months? Lottie stifled a gasp. Connor really had wasted no time in accepting the job and moving in with Keegan.

Keegan got off the bed and Lottie opened a door off to the side of the bedroom. The bathroom was reached through a vestibule lined with wardrobes on both sides.

'There's a full en suite and a dressing area, and we'll provide fizz and flowers in your room.'

'And a claw-foot bathtub big enough for two,' Keegan said. 'How romantic.'

'I'm glad you like it.' Lottie's forced smile was beginning to hurt her jaw. 'Would you like to see the other guest rooms now?'

'Yes, please although I could run a bath right now, fill it with bubbles and sink into it. I'm exhausted, with the jet lag and all the excitement and secrecy. We love a nice soak in the tub together.'

'How lovely,' Lottie murmured, unable to avoid picturing Keegan and Connor in the massive tub, toasting each other.

She moved back into the bedroom. 'Now, as part of your package you get the rooms exclusively of course and we deliver a champagne breakfast for the um . . . the day after, and provide flowers for all the guest rooms . . .' She reeled off the list of services and extra touches that were part of the package she'd put together for her first Firholme wedding, trying not to dwell on the idea of Keegan and Connor in the tub. Not that she'd ever been a bath-sharing kind of person – and come to think of it, neither had Connor. Not that their bath in their little house would have accommodated the pair of them at once.

She steered the conversation onto who would be staying in which room, which seemed like safe territory.

'We've plenty of room for your bridal party. The best man, parents and bridesmaids . . .' she realised that unusually, they hadn't been mentioned. 'Are you having any attendants?'

'Just Alicia – Connor's sister,' Keegan said. 'I expect you might remember her?'

'Yes, we've – er – met a few times,' Lottie said.

'You certainly couldn't forget her,' Keegan said. 'Between us, I mainly asked her because I wanted to include her in the main bridal party. None of my friends could get here at such short notice but that's a sacrifice I'm prepared to make.'

Lottie smiled and continued to show Keegan the rooms where her bridesmaid – Connor's sister – could stay over after the wedding party. She couldn't help remembering Alicia. She was definitely a character and never afraid to speak her mind.

After Keegan had inspected the guest rooms, Lottie led the way down the grand staircase.

Keegan ran her hand along the polished handrail. 'My mum's so stoked about the idea of staying here,' she said. 'She's never been to Europe so they're making the wedding part of a longer trip.'

'That sounds exciting,' Lottie said, relieved to be on ground she felt more comfortable with.

Downstairs, Connor had finished his call and was back in the ballroom. He seemed to be lost in thought when Lottie and Keegan walked in. She thanked her lucky stars he hadn't been in the bridal suite when Keegan was relating their bathtub tales.

She made some more notes about the logistics of the day, to double-check she knew where and when everyone was supposed to be at the agreed times and found she'd relaxed a little now; organising was her forte.

'Dad's transporting Mum, but we'll be bringing his wedding suit here because Mum definitely would be suspicious if she spotted him in a suit and tie for a family lunch,' Connor said. 'Dad normally only wears suits under duress.'

'Good idea,' said Lottie, nodding. 'He's far happier in his gardening clothes or cycle jersey, I bet.'

Keegan gave them both a hard stare. 'What do you mean? His cycle jersey?'

Connor's expression contorted.

'I um . . . meant like most fathers. They don't like dressing up and er . . . I know Connor's dad loves cycling. He marshalled one of the races round the lake a while ago. I saw it in the local paper . . .' Lottie babbled.

'Yes, I have mentioned it to you, Keegan. Dad loves his bike.'

'Oh, yes. Maybe you have.' Keegan smiled. 'It will be an even bigger surprise for your mum when she sees him in a formal suit, then.'

'Yes, it will,' said Connor, avoiding Lottie's eye.

Keegan's phone rang. 'It's the dressmaker. I have to take this. I'll be back shortly.'

After she'd gone, Lottie heaved a sigh of relief. 'I'm sorry about that, Connor. The cycling, I mean.'

He sighed. 'Don't be. Keeping two lots of secrets is harder than I thought.'

'I did warn you.'

'It's too late now,' he replied with a sigh. 'Keegan really will be pissed off if I tell her the truth after this length of time.'

'You do know that people might tell her we were together on the day, don't you?'

'Possibly, though I've asked my sister and Dad not to say anything. My best man, Kai, doesn't know anyway and I haven't asked that many friends from round here.'

'You seem to have covered every avenue,' Lottie said.

'I had to. Jesus, how has it come to this?'

'Like you say, it's too late now.' Lottie wondered what Fiona would make of things when she discovered who'd organised Connor's wedding. That would be a very awkward moment, but it was Connor's problem, not hers.

'If someone gossips on the day, then I'll deal with it but the wedding's so close now, I just want to get it done.'

That didn't sound very much like an excited groom to Lottie, but then again, she knew that many grooms – and a few brides – were secretly relieved when the big day finally came and went. No matter how exciting, it could be a very fraught time.

'How's your dad handling keeping the secret?' she said.

Connor pulled a face. 'Stressed out, if I'm honest. He keeps asking me if it wouldn't be better to tell Mum, or at least let her know a day in advance but Keegan's having none of it. She said that after all the planning, it'd be crazy to ruin the surprise and I guess she's right.'

Lottie stayed neutral, even though she was dying to say that Fiona might have enjoyed all the planning and certainly would have wanted to choose a new outfit.

'I'm sure it'll be a lovely surprise,' she said, trying to inject genuine enthusiasm into her voice.

Connor still didn't seem convinced. 'They hadn't met her until a week ago and I could tell Mum was shocked when we announced our engagement.'

Stunned at Connor's frankness, Lottie was in two minds whether to close down the conversation. However, she couldn't resist the chance to find out more, even if the answers might be uncomfortable to hear. 'Keegan's going to be their daughter-in-law and they'll get to know her a lot better . . . So, you two met at work, did you?' she asked.

'Yes. She was my line manager until I was promoted to the same level. We just sort of clicked straightaway.' A smile crept onto his lips but vanished immediately, as if he'd suddenly realised who he was talking to. 'We moved in a few months after and now here we are,' he added briskly, and glanced at his wristwatch. 'I hope Keegan comes back soon. We need to be at the photographer's by noon.'

He strode to the doorway and called loudly. 'Keegan! Can you get a shift on? We're going to be late for the photographer.'

Keegan strolled back in. 'OK. Calm down. I was only refreshing my make-up for the shoot. We're having some engagement shots done,' Keegan said to Lottie, with an eye-roll. 'Haven't had time yet.'

'Surely you can do that at the studio? Come *on*,' he urged, his hand at Keegan's back.

Lottie almost laughed at his haste to be out of her sight. 'Enjoy yourselves!' she called after them.

'Thank youuuu!' Keegan gave a little wave but Connor left without a word.

The room was suddenly silent and empty, leaving Lottie marooned in the centre of it. She let out a huge sigh. In the past half an hour, she'd been through enough emotions to last a lifetime. Disappointment, sadness, amusement, jealousy and yes – relief. Connor was as attractive as ever – handsomer, in fact – and she couldn't be in his presence without remembering the intimacy and pleasure of their physical relationship, no matter how hard she tried.

She'd also glimpsed some of the traits of the 'old' Connor that she'd loved, the little insecurities that once seemed endearing, and she'd warmed at his acknowledgement that she'd been so very close to his family. He was obviously aware that he and Keegan had got together very quickly.

Surely, Connor wouldn't have been railroaded into a wedding by Keegan?

Lottie had to tell herself that every meeting like this was a step forwards and like aversion therapy for a phobia. The more she faced her fears, the less she would fear the next time.

She took a deep breath and walked out of the house to her office. She had the Christmas party to finalise and that was one event that the past couldn't spoil in any way.

Chapter Ten

Four and a bit weeks to the wedding

'Oh hello, Keegan . . . Yes, I've spoken to the florist and it's all in hand . . . Yes, there's still time to change the toast to Australian sparkling wine. Good timing because I was putting in the final order today . . . Yes, we can have personalised jars of pink jelly beans in all the guest rooms . . . oh, a firework display at the end of the party? Hold on, let me get a pen . . . OK, go ahead . . . I'll do my very best and let you know asap.'

Lottie scribbled on notes on her pad, while Keegan reeled off a list of last-minute 'tweaks' to the schedule. In less than two weeks since she'd first met Keegan, Lottie had mobilised a host of wedding suppliers into action. She'd been on the phone several times a day to them to relay her bride's changing plans and thanked her lucky stars she'd developed such good relations with them in her previous role at the hotel.

109

'Fabulous, I'll get all that sorted, so you can relax,' she said brightly before adding the stinger. 'One thing I would suggest though . . . is there anything else you can think of because we're at the stage where we have to give final numbers to the suppliers and we won't be able to change things easily. Yes . . . yes, I'm looking forward to the run-through with the photographer. I'm sure it will all feel a lot more real then too.'

She put down the phone, realising she'd been smiling fit to burst, even though Keegan couldn't actually see her. At least everything should now be in place. The photographer had actually suggested to Lottie that he come along to test out camera angles to get the best shots for the ceremony. He liked to have a run-through with the bride and groom if possible, especially as Firholme was a new venue to him. And so Lottie had suggested the run-through could also serve as an informal rehearsal and give Keegan and Connor a better idea of how things would work on the day. Keegan had been massively excited about the prospect so it was all arranged for the week before the wedding.

Shayla had been working on the other side of the office and came over as Lottie sank back in her chair with a sigh. 'Demanding bride?' she asked. 'Do I need to put a cup of soothing chamomile tea on?'

Lottie threw her a confident smile in case Shayla thought she wasn't on top of the planning. 'Not yet . . . Keegan wants me to arrange a firework display. One of those frameworks to display "Mr & Mrs Moran" in fireworks as a surprise for Connor. I'll phone the pyrotechnic company and see if they can do it at short notice.'

'Good job he's not called Featherstonehaugh,' Shayla said. 'Or it could have cost her.'

She laughed. 'I'm not sure they can build a frame that big.'

'Well, if anyone can sort it, you can, Lottie. You're a star. I get the impression this wedding has been difficult for you.'

'It's only the haste of it that's a challenge but it'll all be sorted.'

'Well, I do appreciate it. The revenue is much needed.' Shayla eyed her. 'How does seasonal hot chocolate from the café sound? With all the works on top of course. You seem a little frazzled.'

'Sounds great. Thanks.'

While Shayla went to fetch the drinks, Lottie sank back in her chair and closed her eyes. No matter how much she tried to convince herself this wedding was as normal as any other, it didn't feel normal at all.

Keegan's requests weren't even that bizarre compared to some of the demands she'd received in her previous job. She'd once commissioned bridesmaids' 'outfits' for two Chihuahuas. It never ceased to amaze her how seemingly mild-mannered brides, grooms and their in-laws turned from nice, civil people into divas and despots as soon as the wedding was booked.

If she was brutally honest with herself, this was one of the more sensible weddings. Keegan was polite and seemed well aware of the issues created by such a last-minute wedding, but it still felt like a trial. Lottie had vastly underestimated how much effort she would require to show genuine enthusiasm for the event, not to mention she had to conduct it like a covert military operation in terms of secrecy.

She could handle keeping the surprise from Fiona, but deceiving Keegan was a big strain. She'd almost slipped up so many times, and let out little clues as to how close she and Connor had been. At any moment, she expected Keegan to have heard about their relationship from someone else and come charging up to Firholme, demanding to know why Lottie and Connor hadn't told her the full story.

Shayla came back into the office with their reusable cups. 'Here you go. Caramel syrup, marshmallows and edible gold stars for us both – because we're more than worth it.' She put the cups on the desk, with a grin.

'Thanks. I needed this.'

Lottie ate some of the cream and marshmallows off the top, thinking she'd need to climb a hill to cancel out the calories. It was a delicious treat, though, and Shayla was a fun boss. She reminded herself how lucky she was to work at Firholme and that Connor's wedding would be over by Christmas, and she could start to move on with her life again.

'Lottie. Do you know if Jay is coming to the team meal at the pub on Wednesday night?' Shayla asked.

'No, I don't,' Lottie replied, after licking cream from her lips, thinking there was more chance of him landing on Mars.

'Hmm. He keeps himself to himself, but it would be lovely if he would join in. It would help the rest of the guys bond with him. Do you think you could persuade him? He seems to talk to you as much as anyone.'

'I – don't know him that well and I have mentioned it but I can ask him if you like.'

'Great. I don't expect the Bull will be very busy but they

still need some notice of numbers for a large party. They're not well staffed this time of year.'

'OK, I'll mention it next time I see him. I can't promise to persuade him, though.'

'OK but if anyone can do it, I'm sure you can.'

Lottie finished her chocolate, convinced that Shayla had vastly overestimated her influence with Jay.

Lottie spent the next few days dealing with more arrangements for the wedding and finalising arrangements for the Edwardian-themed festive evening, which was being held at Firholme on the first Thursday of December. As the first really big public event at Firholme, Lottie hoped it would showcase Firholme to many more people for the coming year and Lottie had worked hard to make it happen. She was also in charge of organising the staff Christmas ball, to which Jay hadn't RSVP'd . . . She reminded herself to broach the subject at the same time as the pub invite.

By four p.m., she had a headache from being hunched over staring at the screen and decided that some fresh air and exercise would be a better treatment than aspirin. She popped home, pulled on her boots and headed past the brightly lit café and outbuildings towards the forest. Her excuse was to see how the Christmas tree sales prep was going, but it would also be an opportunity to have another go at persuading Jay to come to the pub event. She took her phone, intending to take a few pictures and upload them to the Firholme blog and social media.

A large canvas banner had been hung at the entrance to

the estate advertising that sales would be open at the weekend. Firholme's own trees were now all in place, their lights glistening as dusk fell.

Chatter and laughter drifted from the small marquee, bedecked with coloured lights. Around it, the Christmas tree area itself was packed with felled trees, all with tags attached and illuminated by industrial lighting, which had been set up so that the public could access the area safely. Forestry workers in hi-vis gear and Santa hats buzzed around, dragging cut trees into rows, and putting drums of netting in place. It was a much bigger operation than Lottie had imagined. Next to the tent was a wooden hut with Santa's Grotto marked on it.

She'd absolutely have to bring the twins to see it.

Jay was halfway up a stepladder, fixing a speaker in the gable of the tent. He also wore a Santa hat, which made Lottie smile and struck her as incongruous when he didn't enjoy Christmas that much. 'Can you pass me the other end of that cable?' he said. 'And can you get the electrician to double-check that all the lights and the sound system meet safety regs?' he said to Kerr, his second in command. Kerr could come across as rather brusque if you didn't know him, but he had a wicked sense of humour and Lottie got on really well with him. His son was at the same primary school as the twins.

Kerr came to the bottom of the ladder. 'Jay, one of the netting drums isn't working.'

'OK. I'll be down in a minute.'

'Hello, Lottie,' Kerr said with a broad grin. 'Nice to see your smiling face up here again.'

Lottie laughed, although she wasn't quite sure what he was getting at . . .

Seeing how busy Jay was, she decided to leave him to work and started to walk away but he called to her, from the steps. 'I'll be down in a sec.'

'It's OK. I'll let you get on with it.'

'No. Hang on. *Please.*'

Surprised at the insistence in his voice, she lingered at the side of the tent, snapping a couple of photos of the work to show Shayla. The scene was the closest thing she'd seen to Santa's workshop, with Jay as Santa and the workers as his elves.

Jay climbed down the steps and spoke briefly to Kerr before joining Lottie.

'Sorry. Busy time. How can I help you?' He was a little red in the face.

'You can't right at this moment,' she said, feeling guilty for interrupting him. 'I only came up for a look at how things were going. I'm sorry for disturbing your work.'

'Oh. OK.'

'It's looking great. I hadn't realised what a big operation it is. Have you done this before?'

He smiled. 'You could say that. I supervised the Christmas tree sales for a forestry commission site for three years and we sold them at the estate I used to work on. I'm used to it, but every site is different, the trees are different and nature doesn't always behave as we want it to.'

'Human nature can be just as unpredictable. Especially when a wedding is involved.'

He sucked in a breath. 'Give me trees every time.

'You don't have to go.' To her surprise, his voice held genuine regret. 'We may be busy but the guys could do with a break. We can have five minutes. I could show you Santa's grotto.'

'Um . . .'

He winced. 'That sounds weird. I mean, I can show you how the whole thing works if you like while the guys take a break. I can even rustle up a coffee, not that it's up to the standards of a Firholme cappuccino.' There was a glint in his eye as he said it.

Lottie nodded, still amazed but delighted to be asked to stay. 'OK. I can take a quick break too. I can convince Shayla it's work.'

'Great. Take ten, guys!' he shouted to the workers gathered in the tent.

He took her to a large urn set up at the rear of the tent and made two mugs of coffee. Lottie poured milk into hers but he left his black.

'Sugar?' he said, pointing to a catering-sized bag.

'No, thanks.' She hid her amusement as Jay ladled a large teaspoonful into his mug, reflecting he was fit enough not to have to worry about adding sugar. Carrying their drinks, they wandered out of the tent into the floodlit area, and looked back at the scene. The fog had come down, and hung around the trees and lights, lending them an eerie atmosphere. Lottie was glad she'd wrapped up warmly because the damp air held a chill that seeped into your bones.

'Well, it's not Lapland but it's a dry place for the tree sales and we can rotate the team so they can all spend some time indoors during their shift,' Jay said.

Lottie suppressed a shiver. 'I love nature but I don't envy you working out here in all weathers.'

'We're a hardy bunch but it is hard work, helping people carry trees and putting them through the nets. I take my turn and I certainly don't have any trouble sleeping after a day working out here.' He sipped his tea before adding, 'Which I consider to be one of the perks of the job. Would you like to see the grotto?' He smiled. 'Don't get too excited.'

The grotto – a large and elaborate version of a Wendy house – was definitely a 'work in progress' but Lottie could imagine how the pine cabin might look in a few days' time. Wooden figures and animals were lying outside, on their sides or staring up at the sky. It looked like the elves had held a rave with the woodland creatures.

Jay held up his mug in the direction of the cabin. 'Um. We still need to add extra lights and decorations. It'll look a lot more appealing when it's covered in snowmen and er – squirrels.'

Lottie spotted something outside the hut and burst out laughing. It couldn't be a coincidence that a red-cheeked male elf had fallen *so* precisely on top of a blonde elf in a pink skirt.

Jay followed her gaze. 'Oh God. I'm sorry. Some of the guys larking around.' Leaving his mug on the ground, he jogged over to the elves and parted them.

'You've ruined a great romance, there,' Lottie said with mock solemnity.

117

'Well, I don't want hordes of little elves in the spring to rehome.' He added them to a pile of other figures.

'I think that may be even worse,' she said, trying not to giggle at the unholy group of creatures piled up on top of each other outside the grotto.

'Oh.' He laughed. 'I see what you mean. I promise it will all be suitable for a family audience by the time we open.'

'I'm sure it will. I'll bring my nieces to see it.'

'Yes. Definitely do that. It really will look festive, I promise. Would you like to see the tree sales area too? It's almost ready for the public. If you have time,' he added.

Strictly speaking, Lottie should have gone back to the office. She'd promised to call the florist to discuss the final – *final* – arrangements for the wedding. Maybe, she thought wryly, that was why she'd had a headache and decided she needed to get out of the office and come up here.

'Yes,' she said. 'I'd like that.'

The trees were arranged by height and species in mini paddocks divided by wooden fences. They lay together like ranks of sleeping soldiers, and she thought there was something a little melancholy about the felled trees, which had once been growing in the forest. Then she reminded herself of the joy and excitement they would create for hundreds of families for weeks to come.

'So many trees, waiting for their owners . . . It's strange to be here before all the Christmas madness starts.' She picked up a spruce by its tip, inhaling the pine scent. 'I love a fresh tree in the house.'

'Madness is a good word for it,' Jay murmured, then

changed his tone to something more upbeat. 'Would you like a tree for the Bothy?'

Lottie was taken aback. 'I'd love one, of course but . . . can I be very cheeky? Would you mind very much if I gave it to Steph? The twins would adore it. I'll pay, of course. I intended to treat them to one anyway.'

'I'm sure Shayla won't mind me letting you have a free tree.'

Lottie wasn't quite so confident, or at least she didn't want to pre-empt her boss's generosity. 'I'd better ask her, all the same. I don't want to be treated any differently from any of the other staff. It's not fair.'

'Good idea. What about if I suggest that we donate a tree to all the staff? I can't think that she'll object.'

'OK, but whatever she decides, I'll bring Steph and the girls to choose one.'

'I could pop it round to your sister's place in the pick-up, if transport's going to be a problem.'

'That would be brilliant. I was wondering how I'd fit it in my Fiesta and Steph only has a small car too.'

His eyes sparked with pleasure. 'It's a deal then. You let me know a good time.'

'OK. Steph's bringing the girls to the launch to see Santa and the reindeer.'

'It'll be busy . . . but why don't you tell them to come over before the place opens to the public? The reindeer handler will be here with the animals from nine, to settle them in. I can ask her if it's OK but I don't think she'll mind.'

'Really?' Lottie could imagine Myra and Jodie literally dancing for joy.

'They'd get their own special encounter.'

'They won't be able to contain themselves! What a great idea.'

'They sound as if they all need a special treat. I'll phone the farmer now.'

'Thanks.'

Heartened by his enthusiasm, Lottie listened while Jay called the farmer and sorted the visit for the girls.

His broad grin lit up his face and Lottie was brimming with delight too, desperate to tell the girls. Then she saw the time and realised she'd been out of the office for a good twenty minutes. Shayla gave her a lot of leeway but she really ought to be getting back.

'I have to go,' she said.

'Me too.'

Yet they both seemed in no hurry to part, standing by the grotto with empty mugs. She remembered her only legitimate reason for visiting the tree centre. 'Um, Jay? Have you had any more thoughts about coming to the pub this Wednesday night? If you're not doing anything,' she added, giving him an escape clause but hoping he didn't take it.

'I'm not doing anything,' he said slowly, and Lottie could almost hear the cogs whirring. She was held in suspense a moment longer before he went on. 'OK. If it's not too late, I'll be there. Thanks for reminding me.'

'See you around seven in the café foyer, then?' she said.

'Great.'

With that they parted and Lottie made her way through the mist down to the offices. It had started to rain, and with the temperature dropping, it was rapidly turning to sleet. There might be snow by morning, she thought, and then realised her headache had gone. No fog or sleet could dampen her spirits and Jay had taken her out of herself and reminded her there was a life outside work. The pub trip would be a chance to relax with her friends and colleagues, and get completely away from the wedding with all its old associations. Now that Jay was coming, she was looking forward to it even more.

Chapter Eleven

'Oh, hello there!'
        Even though he'd said he was coming, Lottie couldn't hide her surprise when she found Jay already waiting in the café with Shayla and the other live-in staff the following evening. He was chatting to Lukasz, the chef, and seemed relaxed enough, which was a relief as she'd wondered whether she'd pushed him out of his comfort zone against his will.

'S-sorry, I've kept you waiting.' Slightly out of breath, she caught Jay's eye.

'We thought you'd forgotten all about it,' Shayla said with an eyebrow raise that let Lottie know she was teasing.

'Oh, there's no chance of that. I'm late because my sister was on the phone.'

'Everything OK?' Shayla's voice was instantly tinged with concern.

'Yes, she's fine,' said Lottie, crossing mental fingers for luck.

She'd taken a call from Steph, who hadn't been feeling well. It was hard to know if it was anxiety or linked to the after-effects of her treatment – or a worrying new symptom.

'Good.' Unaware of Lottie's concerns, Shayla rubbed her hands together. 'Right. Let's go, shall we?'

Lottie pushed her fears aside and tried to enjoy the evening. With the aid of a torch, they all walked the half-mile down the hill from Firholme to the village. Frost glittered on the road surface in the light of the torch. Despite her sturdy boots, Lottie almost slipped on a patch of black ice on a hairpin bend.

'Whoa!' Jay grabbed her arm just in time to stop her from falling painfully on her bottom. He let go of her arm. 'Are you OK?'

'Yes, thanks,' she said, embarrassed.

'Do you mind falling over *after* we've been to the pub?' Shayla joked, and everyone laughed. 'Please be careful. I don't want my team laid up with broken ankles, do I?'

'You're all heart, boss,' Jay said.

There were no more slip-ups and they made it to the pub, an old whitewashed inn with a slate roof, in the heart of the village. Langmere might be a tiny community but it had managed to hang on to its pub and post office, along with a café and some tourist shops. It was a hive of activity in summer but on a November evening, there were only a handful of cars in the parking area.

More people had gathered in the bar where a fire glowed in the inglenook and the room echoed with banter and laughter. Irina and Jan were enjoying a meal at one of the tables. Wilf Carman was playing dominoes with a couple of his younger mates of around eighty.

'Evening, Dotty!' he called when Lottie walked in.

Jay was obviously amused, but Lottie still felt embarrassed at this reminder of her schoolgirl days. She rolled her eyes and greeted Wilf cheerfully before continuing to the table reserved for them. Some of the workers lived in the village itself while others had driven from further afield. Lottie noticed the level of revelry ramped up even further when Shayla insisted on paying for everyone's meals: hearty pub fare from the Christmas menu.

It wasn't long before Jay was chatting away over a pint of Cumbrian ale to Lottie and their colleagues about the Christmas tree sales. From his relaxed manner, she wondered why he didn't seem more sociable. His reclusiveness seemed to have little to do with disliking his workmates. Lottie was happy that they'd managed to sit next to each other, the soft cotton of his shirt brushing against her arm from time to time.

One by one, people drifted off to the bar or the loo, or to join in a heated conversation around the darts board and she and Jay were left alone at the table.

'Better enjoy my night out. I'm going to be busy for the next four weeks until sales close,' he said, with a rueful smile.

'When's that?' Lottie asked.

'The twenty-second or until we run out of stock.' He paused before adding, 'I saw our red squirrel again today.'

The 'our' wasn't lost on her. 'In the same place?'

'No, up in the High Copse. There were badgers last night at dusk.' He slid her a look of pleasure and longing that made her shiver. 'I wish you could have seen it.'

'Me too,' she said, allowing herself to imagine being alone in the woods with him, but not looking for wildlife. 'I'd love to see badgers at Firholme.' She forced herself back to safer topics. 'I've spotted plenty of foxes around the Bothy but no Mr Brock yet.'

'They have a sett up there. You should come up and take a look.' His voice was animated, before he added more cautiously, 'If you have time.'

'I'd love to but you must be very busy at the moment?'

'Yes. The lights at the sales centre might scare them off anyway.'

Lottie wished she hadn't been so negative. She hadn't meant to scare *him* off inviting her to the woods.

Their orders arrived so everyone returned to the table and tucked in. The atmosphere was light-hearted and Jay seemed to be enjoying the banter as well as the food. After they'd had the main course, she left him talking about football with Thorsten and Kerr, while she went to the ladies.

Shayla was in there too and took the chance for a gossip. 'I knew you'd be able to bring Jay out of himself,' she said, while they washed their hands.

'I didn't do anything special,' she protested, realising that her cosy with Jay must have been witnessed by Shayla. 'I only asked him if he was coming tonight.'

'Well, it worked. It's important that he gets to know the

rest of the staff better. Now can you work your magic and persuade him to come to the Christmas ball?'

'I don't know about that.'

'I have every confidence in you,' Shayla winked and took out her lip gloss. Nothing got past her, Lottie thought ruefully.

Back in the pub, Jay went to play darts in the games room with Kerr. It was now getting on for nine o'clock and a few more people had come into the bar for a late evening drink. Some were in tracksuits, others in shorts and judging by the ruddy complexions and muddy calves, they were a local rugby team who'd been training. Lottie recognised one of the guys who worked for a company who'd held a training day at Firholme. The others were strangers to her. Jay had been in the games room a while but then Lottie saw him re-enter the bar with Kerr.

He'd made it halfway to her table before he stopped dead and stared at the back of one of the rugby players who was ordering a drink at the bar. Jay's body bristled with tension. It was as if there was no one else in the pub apart from him and the man. Sensing something was very wrong, Lottie held her breath. She was sure that Jay was going to approach the man, maybe even grab hold of him but Shayla and the others were talking so only she had noticed.

The rugby player turned around, his eyes widened in shock and his mouth fell open. 'Jay,' he said.

Jay didn't reply. His face was thunderous, eyes blazing with anger. Seconds later, he marched out of the pub as if the Devil was at his heels.

Chapter Twelve

Jay's chest tightened at the icy air rushing into his lungs as he stormed out of the bar. He was halfway across the car park as realisation hit him like a sledgehammer.

Once again, he'd rushed out into the night because of Ben.

Once again, he'd run away from a situation he found overwhelming.

Because of Ben.

'Jay! Wait!'

The voice calling after him was Lottie's.

He swivelled round. Oh Jesus, he'd caused a scene; the exact thing he didn't want to do. Now, people would be asking questions he didn't want to answer. He should be over it by now.

She caught up with him. 'Jay,' she said, a little out of breath. 'Are you OK?'

'Yes . . . not really but it's nothing for you to worry about.'

'It looked serious to me. Are you sure you're all right?'

'Yes. No . . . It was Ben, my brother. I haven't seen him since the start of this year. I'd no idea he'd walk in to the pub tonight. We don't get on,' he added as if that wasn't bloody obvious.

'I'm sorry . . .' He could see that she really meant it. 'Actually, I recognise the big Maori guy he was with at the bar,' Lottie said. 'He plays for a local club, Langmere. They must have had a game against your brother's team.'

'I'd no idea that Ben had joined that club,' he said gruffly, still shaking from the shock of Ben crashing in on what had been a very enjoyable evening. 'He used to play for Kendal but he must have moved up here. Or at least switched teams.'

'I could see you were shocked,' she said gently.

'I was. Gobsmacked.' He threw up his hands in frustration. 'But I shouldn't have reacted like that.'

'It's OK. I hope you didn't mind me coming after you?' she said, holding out his jacket. 'I brought your coat. You're shivering.'

'Am I?' His stomach clenched in guilt and the rush of emotion at Lottie's kindness. 'Thanks . . .' He took his coat, wrestling for some self-control in front of her. 'Ben and I don't have contact any more, and that's my decision. You must think I'm mad, kicking off like that in front of everyone.'

'No. I don't. I um – understand what it feels like when someone you thought had gone from your life turns up out of the blue.'

'Really?'

'Yes,' she said warily. 'But how are you feeling now?'

'Better . . . but I think I should go home.' Their gazes met, and again he felt a powerful pull to her. He wasn't sure what her comment about 'people turning up' meant, but he wasn't convinced she understood how he was feeling. She was surely too gentle and caring to feel the level of anger that he had in those first few seconds after coming face to face with Ben.

Yet he did feel calmer, simply by talking to her and being in her presence. She touched his arm; it felt like balm on a wound.

'I'll come with you if you like . . .'

'I don't want to cut your evening short,' he said, though the prospect of her company on the walk back to Firholme was very appealing. There was something fresh and lovely about her that made him feel soothed and made him want to talk. He felt ashamed for rushing out and derailing her night yet he wanted to be with her. 'If you really don't mind, I'd like that,' he added.

The glow of pleasure in Lottie's eyes calmed him, but only for a second because suddenly, her smile faded and her mouth opened a little wider, a tiny wisp of breath misting the air. It was enough to raise his pulse and alert him that she'd spotted something behind him.

He twisted round and saw Ben cutting a direct path towards him.

'Don't let him upset you.'

Lottie's warning words were lost in the spike of adrenaline. His heart rate took off. He didn't want to speak to Ben. 'I can't handle this,' he said to Lottie. 'I need to walk away now. Let's go.' He started walking away with Lottie but Ben followed them.

'Wait! Jay! Don't go off on one!'

A hand brushed his shoulder. 'I w-want to talk to you.'

Jay shrugged it off. 'Get off me. This is pointless. We've said all we want to say.'

Ben glanced from Lottie to Jay. 'Don't worry, love. I'm not going to cause a scene.'

Jay exploded. He didn't even want his brother breathing the same air as Lottie 'She's not your love, Ben. You patronising git.'

'He's right, I'm not anyone's love,' Lottie burst out. 'And I can speak for myself. I'll go back inside when I'm sure you two aren't going to have a wrestling match out here in the car park. I have no idea what's wrong between you, but for God's sake, don't settle it with your fists.'

Ben glared at her then said, 'Wow. She's a feisty one, bro.'

Jay curled his lip. 'Oh, just piss off, Ben. And by the way, I'm not your bro.'

Her eyes widened and Jay was filled with dismay at the intensity of his reaction.

'Shall we go back to Firholme now?' he said to Lottie, as calmly as he could.

She hesitated then nodded. 'I'll text Shayla and tell her I'm walking home with you.'

'Wait, Jay. I'm sorry for everything,' Ben said, with ragged desperation. 'Mum and Dad are heartbroken over what's happened. They want us to make it up. I wish I could undo the past but I can't. We need to move on.'

'That's a lie about wishing you could undo the past. You don't because without the past, you wouldn't have Seb.' He turned to Lottie again. 'Please can we go? I'm done here.'

Ben's frustration spilled out. 'This is ridiculous, Jay. It's been a year now . . .'

Jay ignored him, throwing up a wall that Ben's pleas bounced off. If he refused to engage, he couldn't be hurt any more.

'OK, Jay. Be like that. Blank me. I tried my best!'

With Ben's words ringing in his ears, Jay focused on Lottie. 'I am so sorry about that. I think we should leave before we have another row.'

She glanced behind. 'Don't worry. Ben's getting into his car.'

Jay nodded, relief flooding him, though at the same time a creeping sense of despair.

'Thanks for bringing my coat out and offering to keep me company. I expect there'll be talk at work about me rushing out and us leaving together. People love to gossip.'

She shrugged, her jaw set determinedly. 'Let them. It'll make a change for me to create some gossip.'

For the first time since Jay had spotted Ben, he smiled. Lottie had shot up even further in his estimation. 'OK. Let's get back and I'll tell you about it.'

After Lottie had sent her text, they spent most of the walk in silence, Jay only speaking from time to time to make sure Lottie was OK as they only had one torch between them and his phone battery had died. After they reached Firholme, he let Lottie into his cottage, dismayed at the mess. Then, again, he hadn't been expecting visitors. Trevor was delighted to have company and gave them a greeting of licks, barks and tail wagging, before settling down.

Jay shifted his guitar and several well-chewed dog toys

from the sofa and swept up a pile of forestry magazines from the chair. 'Sorry. I'm not used to entertaining.'

'Don't worry.' She sat on the sofa, with a look of amusement.

'Trevor's shedding a bit. I should vacuum more often,' he said, seeing dog hair clinging to Lottie's jeans. He felt agitated and restless.

She laughed. 'It's fine.' Trevor lay at her feet with a drool-covered chew between his paws.

Jay took the armchair opposite her. 'He likes you,' he said. 'Sorry, there's dog hair on your jeans.'

'Don't worry. I like dogs.' She smiled at Trevor. 'Why don't you tell me about this business with Ben?'

He looked at her, his tongue frozen for a moment. There was no easy way to say what had happened, or to explain the level of hurt and betrayal he still felt, but he had to tell someone. He took a breath.

'The reason Ben and I don't get on is because he got my partner pregnant and let me believe I was the father.'

'Oh my God. That's awful!'

'It was a one-night stand, they said at the time, but I've since found out they'd been having an affair for a while. It was while I'd been on a training course in Scotland for a couple of weeks. When I got back, I had flu after working out in the cold and I was wiped out for another fortnight.'

'Well, at first, I thought the baby had been conceived before I went away. Nadia told me it was due at the end of the summer. She'd been nervous and stressed, but I put that down to the shock of learning she was going to be a parent. God knows, it was daunting enough for me but I was still ecstatic. Me, a father. It was incredible . . .'

Trevor had found his way next to Jay, and licked his fingers. Maybe the dog could sense he was upset. Lottie didn't say anything, just waited for him to go on. She was a good listener . . . maybe too good, thought Jay, realising that he was pouring out his woes against all his resolve to keep his past quiet.

Too late now.

'Turns out it really was unbelievable because at the six-week scan, the nurse told us the baby was actually ten weeks,' he said. 'Nadia had been twitchy for days before, trying to persuade me I didn't need to come with her. Saying it was so close to Christmas and wasn't I busy at work. Now I know why. She burst into tears after the nurse told us how many weeks the baby was. I didn't realise what the dates meant straightaway but when she started sobbing her heart out, I worked it out. She couldn't hide the truth then, and blurted it out right there in front of the nurse.'

'That must have been a terrible shock.'

'You could say that. It took my breath away. The nurse made a quick exit, saying "we must need time together". I just lost it. I didn't shout or swear; I just walked out. I felt humiliated, and grief-stricken. It wasn't my baby. That life I thought we'd made together. It wasn't anything to do with me. Jeez, I'd already painted the nursery, started reading the parenting books . . . all the clichés.' He shook his head. 'I feel such a fool.'

She leaned forward. 'Why? For being excited about being a father? That's completely understandable. I can understand

133

that . . .' Her words tapered off as if she'd said too much. Jay wondered if her eyes were suspiciously bright. 'You must have felt your world had fallen apart,' she said finally.

'I did, but what followed was probably worse. It also split our family. Mum and Dad were so upset, they wouldn't even speak to Ben at first but when the baby came, they naturally wanted to see their grandson. I can't blame them for that. The problem is they've now shifted their view and want me to be reconciled with Ben, and for me to forgive and forget, but I can never do that.'

'You must be so hurt. It must have been awful to see your family torn apart like that.'

'It was. It still is, but I can't get past it. I see my mum and dad but I refuse to go to any family occasion that Ben's at too, which makes things awkward.'

'No wonder you're dreading Christmas. It's easy to think everyone's having an amazing time, surrounded by all the family. The truth is that almost everyone is struggling with something: bad memories, the tensions simmering. Disappointment.'

'You sound as if you know what I mean.' Jay snapped out of his woes. Here he was, bemoaning his situation and Lottie had been through even worse. 'Last year must have been so difficult for you,' he said.

'It was. We were doing our best to be cheerful for the twins and they had no idea how serious Steph's condition was. Underneath it all, everyone was terrified of losing her. Not just me but my parents. Mum went down with a bad chest infection with all the stress and had to keep away. My dad had a scare with his heart and of course, we didn't dare tell Steph.'

'Leaving you to shoulder the burden.' He focused on her face: the delicate bone structure, the keen blue eyes and the determination behind them. She was strong as steel as well as beautiful.

She shrugged. 'I didn't see it like that. I just had to get on with it day by day.'

Jay wondered if she'd had a partner to help her at the time and if not, why not? 'What about your family? Are they local?'

She laughed. 'Not exactly. They moved to New Zealand before the twins were born, while they were still young enough to get working visas. Steph and I stayed here because of our jobs but it's been hard since she was diagnosed. We do miss each other a lot though.

'We don't have any other siblings. As for friends . . . I found it hard to talk to them about . . .' She faltered. It must be a painful time for her, Jay thought. 'About Steph's illness even to people I'd known for years. Every time I was on the edge of blurting out to someone how I felt, that I was struggling, I stopped myself. I wanted to cope alone. I felt I should and that talking about it would only exhaust me. I didn't have time to talk to people, or the energy to make a scene or cry. It was simpler to just get on with it,' she added quietly.

'It's less complicated, isn't it? Once you tell someone, they start asking you how you are, texting you, and it saps what little energy you have. You have to rake over the bad times again and again, like pulling a plaster from a wound, and feeling the pain afresh. You wish you'd never told them . . .' he said.

'Yes. Yes, *exactly*.' She nodded, and he felt drawn to her by an invisible bond. Even if their circumstances were very different, they were both scarred, and both unwilling to let anyone pierce the shell around them. Except each other, perhaps . . . the irony of that. He'd finally opened up a little to someone and glimpsed a pinprick of light at the end of the tunnel. For the first time in a year, he could imagine growing close to a woman again. He'd been sucked into a spiral of cynicism, which he feared would be impossible to escape.

'Lottie, I want you to know that until I kicked off about Ben, I'd been having a good time at the pub – if I'm honest, a far better time than I'd expected.'

'I'm glad about that.' She smiled. 'It wasn't as awful as you'd feared.'

'Awful? No. It was great. Getting to know the others . . .' *Getting to know you,* he thought. 'Thank you for dragging me out to it.'

'I'm sorry it ended like this.'

'Me too but it's not your fault. It's my problem that I can't forgive Ben but he's right about one thing. It is time I carried on with my own life, instead of being angry about his.'

'Then that's all the more reason you should come to the Christmas ball,' she said. Was that a glimmer of hope in her voice or was he imagining it?

'The ball?' he said, feeling panicky again. 'I don't know . . . I – I'll think about it. I made such a tit of myself tonight that I don't think I can face everyone at work.'

'Just say you were feeling under the weather.'

'Thanks, but I don't think they'll believe it. They *will* ask questions and wind me up.' He shrugged. 'I suppose it's fair enough.'

'You'd be disappointed if they didn't.' She gave a wry smile. 'You shouldn't care what they think, but if you do want to show that there was nothing seriously wrong tonight, then come to the ball.' She smiled encouragingly at him. 'Go on. It might not be half as bad as you think. In fact, you might even enjoy a chance to let your hair down. You can meet Steph too. You won't want to miss that.'

He found it impossible not to smile back. 'I'd like to meet her,' he said, but really meaning he'd like to spend more time with Lottie. 'Do I have to dress up though? Some of the guys have said it's black tie. I am not a tux kind of guy, but you'll have worked that out already.'

'Wear what you like. No one will mind.' Her eyes glittered with mischief. 'You can turn up in your work overalls if you really want to.'

'Oh, I think I can do a bit better than my overalls.' The pleasure he felt seemed to thaw his frozen soul, and it was a warmth Lottie had rekindled. 'If I come,' he added hastily, wary of fully committing and not being able to change his mind.

She looked crestfallen. 'Well, let me know . . .'

'I will. I promise.'

He let her out, but sat up afterwards, restlessly turning over the night's events. He'd missed female company. He'd missed company full stop and until Ben had walked into the pub, he'd felt he'd turned a corner and was ready to make a fresh start.

137

He heard the low drone of conversation on her TV and eventually, the creak of stairs and water running, presumably as she got ready for bed. It was comforting – and frustrating – to think of her on the other side of the wall. So close . . . yet so far.

He had no intention of making it up with Ben, not even for his parents' sake, but Lottie had opened up a view on an alternative path to the one he'd been hellbent on. A path with fresh horizons, and relationships. Tonight had been meant to mark a first step on that – if only Ben hadn't turned up and hurled him back into the shadows.

Chapter Thirteen

Lottie was still turning over what had happened at the pub when she took the chance for a spot of party and Christmas shopping in Kendal on Friday. It was her day off and as there was a training day at the school, Steph and the twins were able to come with her.

Shayla had said she wanted the staff to have a Christmas bash as glamorous as any corporate event, so the dress code was 'fabulous as you dare', which seemed to cover all bases. While black tie wasn't compulsory for the men, she guessed many would want to make an effort especially as many of the team wore uniform to work. Most of the female staff were excited about the excuse to dress up, and while some of the guys grumbled, she knew for a fact that several had had a day out in Manchester to hunt down new clothes. Jay hadn't been one of them, but Lottie couldn't help wondering what he'd be wearing, in the unlikely event he agreed to come.

It was a long drive from the northern Lake District to

Kendal but they decided to take the scenic route. Every turn of the road brought a fresh panorama. The mountain tops were all white with snow, and even the lower fells had a dusting of snow on them. Their drive took them past Thirlmere with its dark pine-covered slopes and over the high pass at Dunmail before Grasmere came into view, with its church and Wordsworth's cottage just outside the village.

A while later, they stopped for coffee in the bustling little town of Ambleside in the heart of the Lakes. Jay had mentioned his parents lived there and found herself imagining which of the cottages straggling up the fellside might be theirs. Finally, they reached Kendal, with the girls fidgeting in the back, desperate to be unleashed on the shops.

Kendal was hardly Oxford Street, but its main street held intriguing shops selling everything from luxury lingerie to pots and pans. The old buildings mostly dated back to the eighteenth century, with coaching inns and cafés tucked away in cobbled alleys.

Steph already had a dress and Lottie had found something in one of the boutiques in town. Steph treated herself to some dangly earrings and they bought some extra decorations that the girls couldn't resist.

With lunch in the town's famous chocolate shop, it had been a fun and relaxing day for everyone, but Steph was looking tired. Lottie didn't like to keep on and on asking how her sister was. She hoped Steph would tell her if she was concerned about anything. However, while the girls were choosing some Christmas chocolate from the display to give to their teacher, she took her chance.

'Are you OK?' she asked.

'Fine.' Steph smiled, then shook her head. 'Except, I'm not really fine.'

Lottie's stomach turned over. 'What's the matter? You haven't had any more symptoms?'

'No. I don't think so but every ache or pain, any tiny thing, makes me think that it's come back. I can't help it and although my Macmillan nurse said it's normal to worry, it doesn't stop me from being terrified if I feel sick or that something's not quite "right" even though I know it's probably only the effects of the treatment. Still, I'll know soon enough.' Steph toyed with her teaspoon. 'I finally had the letter yesterday morning inviting me for an MRI scan to double-check the cancer hasn't spread anywhere else. The scan is December eleventh and then I have an appointment with the gynae-cologist before I can get the all clear.' She heaved a sigh. '*If* I get the all clear.'

'You will. I know you will,' Lottie exclaimed. 'I want to magic all your worries away but you can always tell me anything. If you want to talk, or simply rant and rave or cry, I'm here. You do know that?'

'Hon, of course I do but sometimes I just need to curl in a ball and cry and I don't want to pile my fear onto you every time I have a little wobble. You have a life too, and it makes me happy to see you living it. My nurse said I can phone or email any time too. I don't know what I'd have done without her.'

Lottie rested her hand on Steph's. 'I'll come with you to your scan and appointment.'

'No, please don't. It's a busy time for you.'

141

'Shayla will understand,' Lottie said firmly.

'I'll be fine, honest. If I change my mind, I'll let you know. I won't know anything on the day of the scan, anyway, but I might need some moral support when I go to find out the results.' Steph gave her a stern look. 'Now, please, can we talk about something else? Like this party and whether you and Jay will get together properly?'

'I haven't seen him since Wednesday, not properly,' Lottie said. 'We've both been really busy.'

Steph's ears pricked up. 'Why? What happened on Wednesday?'

'Oh, we just went to the pub with the rest of the Firholme gang,' Lottie said, deciding not to go into the drama of Jay's brother and love life. She suspected that Jay wouldn't want her to share that very personal story even with Steph. They also hadn't spoken more than a few words of greeting since then and she was beginning to wonder if Jay regretted pouring out his heart to her.

'Mummy!' Jodie skipped up to them, interrupting any talk about Jay, which was probably for the best. 'Come and look at this chocolate. It's purple!'

'*Purple* chocolate? Surely not?'

Myra grabbed Lottie's hand. 'It really is. We want to get some for Miss Langley!'

'You go,' Lottie said, 'while I get the bill.'

Steph took the girls to look at the chocolate display, which Lottie knew included some lavender-flavoured treats. Watching them chattering and laughing with Steph, Lottie had a wobbly moment. They were so trusting, so unaware

142

of how fragile life was. Steph was understandably terrified, no matter how much she tried to hide it, and Lottie couldn't work out if she was looking tired because of the worry or because something was actually wrong. Lottie herself was trying to be optimistic but what if Steph's MRI scan wasn't clear and she had to have more treatment – or worse, couldn't have treatment at all?

She went to pay the bill and reminded herself that they'd all got through uncertainty by taking each day as it came, and that today had been a good one. She would focus on the next day when the twins were coming to choose their tree and meet the reindeer.

On Saturday morning, Tigger had nothing on Myra and Lottie as the girls sprang out of the back of the car like demented jack-in-the-boxes. A light dusting of snow had come down overnight, creating a perfect backdrop for the Christmas tree launch, and the visit of the reindeer.

They were literally bouncing up and down when Lottie met them and Steph on the Firholme staff car park.

'What are they on? Red Bull and E numbers?'

Steph shook her head wearily. 'God knows but they were awake at midnight, and four o'clock and six . . . I was hoping for a lie-in after the week I've had but there's no chance of that.'

Lottie did think Steph looked drawn. She really wanted to believe it was down to the twins keeping her awake and not something worse.

'We're going to see the reindeer! We're going to meet the

reindeer!' they shrieked, running around the car park, leaving welly prints in the snow.

'I'm going to hug a baby reindeer,' Myra declared. 'And I'm going to bring him home to live with me.'

'You can't bring him home,' Jodie said. 'Mummy won't let you.'

'The reindeer's mummy won't let you,' Steph said. 'Please calm down, girls.'

Lottie called them over. 'Now, girls. It's very important that we're super gentle and quiet around the reindeer, especially the baby. You don't want them to be scared and upset, do you?'

They both shook their heads solemnly.

'If we're too loud, the reindeer farmer might have to stop our visit,' Steph warned.

Myra's bottom lip wobbled.

'Don't worry,' Lottie said. 'Because I know that you two are going to be the best-behaved, gentlest visitors the reindeer have ever met and they will love you.'

'We will,' Jodie whispered.

Myra nodded. 'We'll be very quiet and very gentle especially with the baby.'

'Good. So, shall we head up to their paddock? We can choose a Christmas tree too, if you're good.'

'Yes!!' The girls erupted into life again. 'We're going to get a treeeeeeee! We're going to meet a babeeeee reindeeerrrrrr!'

'Oh God, I hope we don't cause a stampede,' Steph said, walking beside Lottie to the forest entrance, the twins skipping ahead.

'Jay said the reindeer handlers are very good with children,' Lottie said, highly amused.

'I hope so.'

The Christmas tree centre looked spectacular, as if an invisible hand had sprinkled icing sugar over the fields and roofs of Firholme. Lottie was bubbling, despite the strain of the wedding. Who couldn't be infected with the excitement of two five-year-olds who had snow, Christmas and reindeer to look forward to?

Steph must have caught her mood. 'Feels good, doesn't it?'

'Yes.'

'Thanks for being an awesome sister and friend.' Steph flung her arm around Lottie and gave her a squeeze.

'You're welcome.'

'There they are!' The children hared off across the grass towards the Christmas tree centre where in a small paddock half a dozen reindeer stood munching on hay. The baby was no bigger than a large Labrador. Lottie had to admit, it was incredibly cute.

'Girls. What did I say about being quiet?' The twins slowed and waited for Steph and Lottie to catch up with them.

'There's Jay,' said Lottie.

Steph let out a whistle. 'Wow. That's a sight to cheer up a cold morning. He reminds me of Kit Harington.'

'Really?' Lottie daren't admit the thought had crossed her mind a few times.

'Yes, and with all the snow and trees, it's all very *Game of Thrones* up here this morning.'

Jay joined them, and Lottie was pleased to see he looked

as relaxed as he usually did when he was outdoors and in his element.

She made the introductions before he led them over to the reindeer handler.

'Are they Santa's real reindeer? Myra asked.

'I'm not sure,' he said. 'Shall we ask the lady who looks after them?'

A woman with hair the colour of a peppermint candy cane greeted them by the gate to the reindeer paddock. She had enough ear and nose piercings to set off every airport metal detector this side of Heathrow and the girls stared at her in naked curiosity.

'Hiya,' Jay said. 'This is Cush. She runs the reindeer sanctuary in the valley. Cush, this is Myra and Jodie.'

Unfazed by the twins' stares, Cush grinned. 'Hi there,' she said cheerfully. 'I'm going to let you meet Gary, Jason, Howard and Mark.'

'What the . . .?' Steph whispered to Lottie.

'Take That, I think,' Lottie said, exchanging an amused glance with Jay.

'Not exactly my taste in music,' he said. 'What happened to Robbie?' he added while the girls switched their attention back to the grazing reindeer and the baby.

'He decided to quit the herd,' Cush said. 'Actually, he's a she – Robbie is short for Roberta – and she's back at the reindeer farm.'

'Now, this is little Elvis,' Cush said, pointing to the baby. 'And his mum, Adele.'

'It gets better,' Steph said in delight.

Cush explained where the reindeer normally lived and what they ate, then answered a pile of questions, before asking if the girls would like to stroke one of the larger animals and the baby. The look in the girls' eyes was pure wonder and Lottie had a lump in her throat.

Jay hung around, taking photos with Lottie and Steph's phones.

The twins might happily have stayed all morning but Cush explained that it was almost time for the general public to be allowed in to see them.

While they said a final goodbye, Lottie stood aside with Jay.

'Thanks for sorting out a private visit. The girls have absolutely loved it,' she said. 'Steph's enjoyed it too.'

'You're welcome. I'm glad it lived up to expectations. Would you like to choose a tree before the chaos starts?' he asked. 'I've squared it with Shayla. Every member of staff can have one if they want.'

'OK. As long as you're not too busy.'

'Of course I'm too busy.' He shared a glance. 'But I'm going to make time.'

The five of them wandered through the trees. Myra wanted an eight-foot tree that wouldn't have even fitted through the door of their semi, while Jodie's choice was rejected by Myra as 'too fat' to squeeze into the corner of the lounge. After dozens were rejected as being too bushy, too thin or too big, they eventually agreed on a spruce.

Jay lifted up the chosen tree. 'Do you have a stand for it? It's a lot easier if you can fit them into a proper base.'

'I don't think so,' Steph said.

'We sell them but between us, I have a couple of rejects going spare. They only need a spot of glue on one of the legs,' he said.

'I can do that,' Lottie said.

'If you want to take the stand today, I could come round with the tree after work?' He paused. 'If it's OK with you and Lottie?'

Steph shared a glance with her. 'It's absolutely fine with me and I doubt Lottie has any plans for tonight, do you?'

Lottie winced but she couldn't deny she was more than happy to deliver the tree with Jay. 'It's fine with me,' she said.

Myra looked worried. 'What if someone buys our tree while we're not here?'

'They won't,' Jay said, clearly amused. 'Because we're going to put a big tag on it marked "Sold".'

'Good. No one should touch our tree!' Jodie said, folding her arms.

'No one will, Jodie,' Steph said with an apologetic glance at Jay. 'Thanks so much.'

'Can you keep them out of the tent for a while?' Steph whispered to Lottie. 'I've seen a couple of reindeer decorations for sale. I'd like to get them for them to hang on the tree on Christmas morning.'

The twins were happy to be left with Lottie and Jay. They chased around the felled spruce and fir, playing hide-and-seek for a few minutes before racing back to the adults, pink-cheeked and lively as ever.

'What tree are you having?' Myra asked Jay.

Lottie held her breath.

'The biggest one, of course!' Jodie said.

'I'll have to wait and see if there are any left when we've finished the sales,' Jay said.

Jodie pulled a face. 'You should put a tag on one now.'

'A big one saying "Jay's tree. Do not touch!"' Myra shouted.

He caught Lottie's eye. 'Maybe I will.'

'You need a tree for your children,' Jodie said solemnly.

'I don't have any children yet,' Jay said cheerfully enough though Lottie was instantly on edge.

'Auntie Lottie doesn't have any children either,' Myra chirped up.

'She has us instead. We're her nieces,' Jodie declared before staring up at Jay with her hands on her hips. 'Do you have nieces?'

'No . . .' Jay said. 'I have a nephew though.'

Lottie caught her breath, nursing a faint hope the twins wouldn't pursue this topic.

Jodie folded her arms. 'He needs a tree, then. When he comes to your house, he needs a tree.'

'Girls . . .' Lottie murmured.

'Santa won't know where to leave his presents if you don't have a tree,' Myra said.

Lottie dived in. 'Now, you two, don't get personal.'

'What's personal?' Jodie asked.

'Being nosy! Nosy Jodie!' Myra sang. 'Jodie is nosy. Nosy!'

Jodie looked upset and clutched Lottie's hand. 'I'm not nosy.'

'No, you're not,' Jay said. 'It's OK,' he said to Lottie, with a faint smile.

'You're *not* nosy,' Lottie said, directing this to Myra. 'But I think Jay is very busy and we should let him get on with his work.'

Myra subsided and pushed out her bottom lip. 'Are you going to chop all the trees down?' Jodie asked.

'Not all of them.' Jay didn't seem upset by the girls' interrogation but Lottie thought it had gone far enough. She telegraphed a silent thanks to him.

'Mummy's been a long time in the toilet,' Jodie said.

'She's back now. Look!' Lottie said, with relief. 'Say thanks and goodbye to Jay.'

'Thanks, Jay, Byeeee . . .' the twins trilled in unison and dashed towards their mother.

Lottie hung back. 'Thanks for the tree and the reindeer experience. I never expected the girls to give you the third degree about your personal life.'

'They're only curious,' he said. 'And it was a pleasure to see their faces.'

'See you later, then?'

'Yes, shall I pick you up around seven? Is that too late?' he added hastily.

'No. It's fine.'

He pushed his hands into his pockets. 'Maybe we could go into Keswick after for something to eat.'

Taken aback, Lottie hesitated.

'If you want to,' he added quickly.

'That's a good idea. I'll look forward to it.'

A smile spread across his face. 'Great. Now, I really do have to go. We're almost ready to open the gates. It's officially Christmas at Firholme.'

Fizzing with delight, she watched him walk away, whistling what sounded very much like 'Jingle Bells'.

Chapter Fourteen

Three weeks to the wedding

Jay waved Lottie and her family goodbye before jogging to the sales centre. He hadn't lied when he'd said he was too busy to help them choose a tree but there was no way he was going to miss a chance to spend more time with Lottie. Being able to bring some happiness to her family had been a bonus.

He was relieved that the team had prepared well because there were already a few people queuing up at the entrance, hoping to be first to choose a tree. Some folk liked to have their decorations up before December had even arrived. With the right care, plenty of watering and a cool room, their trees should last right through to twelfth night.

There was no time for a break for him from eleven a.m. right through to six p.m. when the centre closed and he'd had to call Lukasz, the chef at the house, to take Trevor for a walk. Yet, as he buzzed around the site, fixing minor issues and lending a hand with the carrying and netting, he couldn't help thinking of the twins' comments about Sebastian.

It was probably the first time he'd ever acknowledged the baby as his nephew. Hitherto he'd tried to pretend he didn't exist. He now felt ashamed that it had taken two five-year-olds to remind him that no matter the circumstances in which Sebastian had arrived in the world, he was still Jay's flesh and blood, even if not in the way he'd hoped.

After making sure the tree centre was secure, he had time for the quickest shower and change ever, before meeting Lottie in the Firholme car park. He'd loaded the tree into the back of the pick-up earlier so he wasn't covered in mud and pine needles but he was five minutes late.

Lottie was wrapped in a red scarf, hat and gloves and her cheeks were pink in the frosty air. Jay thought she looked fantastic and she also smelled gorgeous, of some delicious floral perfume that reminded him of a trip he'd once made to Provence.

Momentarily, he found himself as tongue-tied as a teenager. 'Um . . . sorry to keep you waiting in this cold weather,' he said before they set off for the village where Steph lived, chatting about the busy day he'd had.

The curtains twitched and two small faces appeared in the front window the moment he pulled onto the driveway of the semi tucked at the end of a small cul-de-sac.

Myra and Jodie were in onesies and just as excited as earlier. Jay had brought his toolkit in case Steph didn't have a suitable saw. With the girls watching from the window, he helped Lottie saw the bottom off the tree while it was on the truck, and trimmed a few of the branches. They carried it inside and fitted it into the stand Lottie had repaired.

The girls were allowed to water it but Steph said dinner was almost ready and it would be too late to stay up and decorate it afterwards.

They protested loudly. 'It'll be even more fun tomorrow,' Jay said. 'And your tree will be all the happier after it's had a rest and a drink of water.'

'Yes, it's been a very long and exciting day,' Lottie said. 'Not only for the tree.'

Jay smiled. Actually, the first day of tree sales had turned out far more fun than he ever expected it to be. He'd been reminded that it might only be a job to him, but it was a highlight of the year for many families.

The girls went upstairs to wash their hands.

'Will you stay for something to eat?' Steph asked.

'Thanks, but we'd planned on going into town for a pub meal,' Lottie said quickly.

Jay felt good at hearing her say it. He was glad he'd found the nerve to ask her out, and the tree delivery had given him an excuse to keep things casual. Even so, he hadn't been that confident she'd say yes. He'd been quite worried that he was overstepping the mark in offering to deliver the tree at all.

'You'd be very welcome. We're having a Christmas pizza night.'

'I don't know . . .' Lottie said. She clearly felt it would be Jay's worst nightmare. He also wondered if Steph was keen to vet him.

'You won't have enough for me,' Jay said.

154

'I can promise you we do. They're pizza bases that I've topped with tomato sauce and I've made extra for the freezer.'

'If you're sure.' He waited for Lottie to give permission. He didn't know the family and he didn't want to intrude.

'Come on,' Steph said. 'Do you know what you've let yourself in for?' she asked. 'The girls can be very . . . inquisitive.'

'Do they take after their mother?' Lottie said, with an ironic eyebrow lift. She was now convinced that Steph's invitation was purely so she could check Jay out.

Steph feigned innocence. 'I've no idea what you mean.'

'Hmm,' Lottie said but Jay seemed OK with the idea.

He smiled. 'Actually, I'm used to kids. I used to run outdoor courses for children. Not as young as the twins, mainly older primary and secondary school.'

'I didn't know that.' Lottie sounded amazed. 'Where was that?'

'In my previous job at Greythwaite Hall. I enjoyed teaching adults and young people. I still have all the certificates. Outdoor pursuits instructor, forestry skills.'

'Wow. That's brilliant. Why don't you suggest we do something like it at Firholme after Christmas?'

'I'd thought about it but . . . life got in the way.' The truth was he didn't know if he could handle being around so many happy families. It was another avenue of enjoyment that he'd shut off because of his bitterness about Ben and Nadia – another door he'd slammed shut. A door that today had encouraged him to open, even if it was only a crack to peer inside at the possibilities. 'With the new job and stuff, I'd put it on the back burner. Do you think Shayla might be interested?'

Lottie nodded enthusiastically and Jay wondered if he'd caught a tiny bit of her zest for making the most of life. 'I'm sure she would,' Lottie said. 'If you have time once Christmas is over, maybe we could run a trial course for February half-term or Easter?'

'That's what I'd wondered.' He nodded, feeling an unaccustomed spark of enthusiasm. 'If you think it's a possibility, I'll definitely work up a plan and send it to her.'

'We need to do all we can to bring in more visitors in the quiet months so I can't see her being anything other than delighted.'

The girls ran back into the room and immediately started their interrogation of Jay.

'Do you know any jokes?' Myra said.

Jay racked his brains. 'How does Good King Wenceslas like his pizza?' he said.

The twins exchanged glances. 'We don't know,' they trilled in unison.

'Deep and crisp and even!' Jay declared, with a big grin.

Jodie wrinkled her nose. 'That's silly.'

'I like pineapples on my pizza,' Myra stated.

Steph, who had been listening at the doorway, walked in. 'I think you just died there, Jay.'

Myra's face fell. 'Jay isn't going to die, is he?'

'No. No. It's only a figure of speech,' Steph said.

'What's a figure of speech?'

'A silly saying. It means nothing.' Steph clapped her hands. 'Look shall we actually eat some pizza? I ought to warn you though, the toppings are somewhat . . . *unusual*.'

'Sounds intriguing,' Jay said.

'That's one way of putting it,' Steph said with a grin. 'Would you mind laying the table, please? Mats, glasses and festive serviettes on the dresser. I'll bring in the cutlery.'

While Steph extracted the pizzas from the oven, Lottie helped Jay set the table. Gales of laughter came from the kitchen and Lottie poked her head around the door.

'You can't look at these,' the girls squealed. 'They have top secret toppings.'

Dissolving into fits of giggles, they made Lottie and Jay wait at the table.

'Why do I have a feeling that this is going to be like no pizza I've ever tried before . . .' Jay said, as Lottie unfolded a serviette.

'Well, you were warned,' Lottie replied, still a little surprised he'd agreed to stay so readily although Steph had hardly given him much option.

Steph and the girls walked out, carrying plates covered in slices of pizza. Myra's almost tipped over onto the carpet but they made it safely to the table. Jodie ran back into the kitchen and came back with a jar of Nutella and a spoon.

'Um. What a feast!' Lottie said when the plates had been put in the middle of the table and the girls were in their seats. 'Pineapple, ham, mushroom – and what are those?' Lottie peered at some of the slices, which were dotted with what looked like albino rabbit droppings, with the mysterious addition of bits of silver foil. The other slices were topped with chocolate gloop and pink bits, on top of the usual cheese.

157

'These are white chocolate snowballs!' Myra said proudly, dumping a slice onto Jay's plate without him asking.

'We tried to pick all the foil off,' said Jodie.

'But watch your teeth,' Steph warned.

Jay poked at the slice with a fork. 'I wondered what the shiny bits were . . .'

'Try one, Auntie Lottie!' Myra thrust the plate under Lottie's nose. She took a slice. 'Oh, yummy.'

'And you can add more Nutella if you want to,' Jodie said, spreading chocolate gloop from a jar onto her pizza.

'Are the pink bits pink marshmallows?' Lottie said.

'No, silly. It's pepperami!' The twins fell about laughing. Myra literally slid off her chair, which made her laugh even more.

'Please, can we eat these pizzas?' Steph sounded frustrated.

Lottie nibbled the end of a slice. 'Mm. Chocolate and spicy sausage. How delicious.'

'It's Mexican and Cumbrian fusion, is it?' Jay said.

'Exactly,' said Steph with a grin. 'Tuck in.'

After the pizzas, the girls quietened down a bit and sat on the sofa reading on their tablets. Lottie kissed them goodbye then she and Jay went to the door.

'Enjoy the rest of your evening,' Steph said. 'Thanks again for all your help with the tree. Sorry about the cuisine.'

'It was eclectic,' Jay said.

Lottie laughed. 'I'd call it experimental.'

'No problem,' Jay said.

'Well, that wasn't quite what I had in mind about having dinner in the pub,' Lottie said as they walked back towards his van. 'Thanks for staying. I'm sure the girls thought it was fun and Steph enjoyed the adult company.'

'Adult?' Jay laughed. 'Not going by my jokes.'

Lottie laughed. 'They still loved having someone new to torment.'

'I enjoyed it too,' Jay said. 'Is there still time for us to go for a drink?' he asked, surprising himself at how much he wanted the answer to be 'yes'.

Lottie smiled. 'It's only half-past eight, so definitely.'

They drove the short distance into the town. Keswick nestled in a bowl that had been scooped out by a glacier in the ice age, leaving a deep valley with its lake. Some of England's highest mountains encircled it, and by the light of the full moon, you could make out the outlines of Blencathra and Skiddaw with snow glowing eerily on their flanks.

Christmas lights twinkled around Keswick's market square when Jay and Lottie walked to one of the town's traditional coaching inns. It was a bitterly cold night, but the windows of several of the pubs and restaurants gleamed as people gathered for early festive celebrations.

A fire blazed in the hearth as Jay ducked his head under the lintel between the bar and lounge. Although it was busy with people, they managed to find a table in a cosy corner. Lottie had a glass of mulled wine, but Jay stuck to an alcohol-free beer as he was driving. She asked him how the first day of sales had gone at the farm and then told him a little more about the twins, and how Steph had done a fantastic job bringing them up.

'I wish Mum and Dad could be here,' she said wistfully. 'We haven't seen them for a year. FaceTime isn't the same.'

Jay sipped his beer. 'Will you see them at Christmas?'

'They're planning to come over again in the spring but it would be so lovely for them to join in all the fun and excitement with the tree and Christmas itself.' She paused. 'Will you be going to see your parents?'

'I – I'm not sure. It's a bit awkward with Ben and Nadia and the baby.'

'Mmm. I can understand that. Have you heard anything from him since the other night in the pub?'

'Not from Ben. My mum called me last night.' He sighed. 'Ben had told her what happened at the pub, of course. She was pretty upset.'

'I'm sorry.'

'Don't be. It's between me and Ben. Only we can sort it out.'

'How old is Seb now?' she asked.

'Six months.' Jay pictured Sebastian. He'd be asleep in his cot, wholly innocent and unsuspecting of the family turmoil surrounding him. Regret and guilt clogged Jay's throat. 'Would you like to see a photo?'

Lottie's lips parted in surprise. God knows, Jay had surprised himself by offering.

'Yes. I'd love to.'

'Mum sends them to me from time to time on WhatsApp. I'm ashamed to say that I've deleted most of them and asked her not to send any more, but I did keep a couple of them. Christ, that all sounds so childish.'

'Not childish. We all do impulsive things when we're hurt and angry,' she said.

'I bet you don't.'

She laughed. 'Of course I do . . . you've no idea.'

He shook his head. 'You'd never pick a fight in a pub with your brother?'

'I don't know what I'd do if Steph had done what Ben has. Not an actual fight, but . . .' She shrugged. 'Who knows? Come on, let's see this photo.'

Scrolling through his messages, he found the latest picture he'd saved. It was of Sebastian on his own, and Jay had felt it was somehow wrong to delete it. He was propped up, gurgling at the camera, clutching a toy brick. Even seeing it again made his stomach tighten, but he also felt he wanted to share it with Lottie. She seemed to understand how he felt, and yet, she wasn't connected with his family.

He handed her the phone. 'Oh, he's gorgeous. What a smile.'

'Yes, he has Nadia's eyes and dark hair . . .' Jay said, thinking of the way he'd fallen instantly for Nadia when he'd met her at a rugby club dinner. She'd been on the committee and had known Ben even then. Perhaps, she even liked him that far back. He shook off the what-ifs that he'd gone over and over in his head.

'Her dad is Jordanian,' he went on, deciding not to say how hard he'd fallen for Nadia, how captivated by her he'd been . . . He'd gone on enough about his ex. 'The smile is Ben's though. He used to get away with murder with Mum and Dad – or anyone – with that smile.'

Jay took a gulp of his beer before realising that it wouldn't make an ounce of difference to how he felt – even if it had had alcohol in it anyway. 'He's a bonny baby. I don't hold anything against him – he's innocent.'

Lottie put the phone on the table. 'He's your nephew,' she said. 'Like you told the twins earlier today.'

'Yes . . . that's the first time I've ever described Seb like that. I guess it's a step forward to acknowledge it.' He smiled. 'But enough of my family dramas. How are you getting on with this last-minute wedding?'

'Oh, it's OK.' She shrugged. 'I've had worse.'

Jay thought she didn't sound very convinced although Lottie seemed to take the events management in her stride generally, and he'd only heard great things about her organisational ability.

Lottie started to tell him some stories about weddings and events she'd organised and the time flew by until it was almost closing time.

It felt strange, but not in a bad way, to think that she would walk into the house next door to him after their night out. He'd thoroughly enjoyed the evening, from the excitement on the twins' faces when he delivered the tree, to the pleasure of Lottie's company. She'd had him laughing out loud at some of her tales.

'Thanks, I enjoyed tonight,' he said on her doorstep.

'Me too.'

He dithered, unsure what to say next or whether to ask her in for coffee. In the end he couldn't think of any way of phrasing the invitation that didn't sound as if coffee wasn't the only thing on offer. 'See you around?' he offered.

Lottie laughed. 'You can hardly avoid it.'

'Oh yes. I mean . . . see you around, but not at Firholme again?'

'Yes . . .' She hesitated. 'You'll come to the ball, then? We do need to know pretty much straightaway. It's a full sit-down Christmas meal, you see.'

The smile on her face alone was worth him saying 'yes' to the invitation.

However, before he could say any more, her phone pinged and she glanced at it. Her smile vanished instantly. 'Sorry, I have to go,' she murmured.

'Anything wrong?' Jay said.

She shook her head. 'No. No. Only the usual stuff to do with this secret wedding. Nothing I can't handle. See you at the Edwardian evening meeting tomorrow. I'd better get some sleep. Early start in the morning.'

'Yes,' Jay said and Lottie left, without pressing him on the ball invitation again.

He stood in the hall for a few moments after closing the door behind her. The text and her reaction to it had bothered him. It was late to receive a text about work business but he guessed that working with bridal couples could be intense. Whatever the message, it had ended her bubbly mood in an instant.

Chapter Fifteen

On Monday morning, Lottie joined Jay, Shayla, Lukasz, and a number of the other key staff for a final meeting about the Edwardian-themed event on the Thursday evening. She was still buzzing about the night out with Jay, but to say that families were complex was an understatement. They came in as many different shapes and sizes as the moods of the lake. She really liked Jay, and thought they were growing close, but he was carrying a lot of baggage.

It could well be a burden too far for her unless he had a change of heart over Ben and his ex . . . Lottie suspected he hadn't got over her yet and wondered if that was the real source of his anger and hurt – was he still in love with Nadia?

At the same time, she'd had a lovely time, and thought he was much more relaxed. Then Connor's mysterious text had floored her.

It had read:

Have to see you. DON'T call me, text.
C

The last person she expected to hear from was Connor – and especially in such a bizarre way. She was at a loss as to what he could have to say to her that Keegan couldn't hear. Unless, of course, he was planning a surprise for his bride, like the fireworks Keegan had ordered for him?

That must be it, although a phone call to the office or an email to her work address would have done the trick.

Should she ignore it completely? No, that wasn't an option, she reminded herself, he was her client and it would be unprofessional to let her personal feelings get in the way of the job.

Ha, she thought to herself, realising she'd already done that. She had to respond soon – but how? Putting it to the back of her mind, she focused her attention on the meeting. She was both excited and nervous about the Edwardian evening. It was the biggest public event they'd held and the estate was banking on the revenue as well as the publicity, so Lottie was determined it would run smoothly.

The house would be lit by candles and firelight, with the tables set with a full Christmas Eve banquet to show how it would have looked in its heyday. Lottie had booked a troupe of Edwardian acrobats and a fire-eater, a brass band and local carol singers. There would be traditional stalls selling roast chestnuts and mulled wine, a traditional fairground organ and carousel.

After the meeting broke up, Lottie was surprised when Jay came up to her on the terrace outside the café instead of heading straight back to the forest centre.

'Hope I didn't keep you up too late?' he said.

'Not at all. I enjoyed myself.' She smiled encouragingly.

Had it been a date? she wondered. She supposed it must have been, but what would happen next? They saw each other nearly every day but they were both so busy – would there be chance for another one?

'Good . . .' he said, hesitating again. 'Would you still like your own tree for the Bothy? I checked it was OK with Shayla this morning before the meeting.'

'A tree? Oh, yes, please, although I gave mine to Steph so I can't really have two free of charge. I'll pay for it.'

'No, there's no need. It's taken care of. I offered to pay for the tree for your family, but Shayla wouldn't hear of it. So, it's on the house – literally.'

'That's lovely,' she said, touched by his gesture. 'If you're sure. That was very kind of you.'

'You're welcome,' he said. 'Oh, and if it isn't too late, I'd definitely like to accept that invitation to the staff ball.'

Lottie resisted punching the air. 'OK. That's great. I'll add you to the list.'

'I'm not too late, am I?'

'Mmm . . . just in the nick of time.' It was another little white lie. She'd actually sent the final numbers only half an hour before but she could send another email adding him. The caterers would forgive her this one time. 'I'll send you the menu straightaway but I'll need it back immediately, if that's all right?'

'That's fine. I'm sorry I messed you around.'

'It's OK.' Her phone buzzed in her hand. From force of

habit, she glanced at it and her mood sank. It was another text from Connor.

Did u get my message?

C x

'I'd um – better get back to work,' Jay said. 'You must be very busy.'

Before she had time to say that she wasn't too busy to talk to him, he was off, striding towards the forest.

Mindful of the slim possibility that Keegan might read Connor's text, she was very careful with her reply.

Message received. Why not phone re the matter we discussed.

Her thumb hovered over the send button. There, that ought to be cryptic enough for Connor to explain away if Keegan did see it. Even as that thought went through her head, Lottie realised once again that she was being sucked in further to a tissue of deception and subterfuge.

Another thought struck her. One that brought a shiver of excitement, followed by guilt and unease. Was Connor playing with her emotions on purpose? Perhaps having Keegan besotted with him wasn't enough and he also didn't want to let go of Lottie herself. Lottie hesitated a moment longer before pressing send. She couldn't really believe Connor still had feelings for her . . . but she couldn't resist finding out either.

Chapter Sixteen

'Come on, mate. Let's do this.' Jay let Trevor out of his car and jogged up the path to the front door of his parents' neat cottage in Ambleside. He and Trevor sheltered in the porch from the lashing rain while the bell rang out in the hall. He could do this.

It was Tuesday and his day off, and he'd decided he should put it to good use and visit his parents.

And here he was.

He'd sat outside the house for a while, working up the courage to go in. There was no sign of Ben visiting, and why would there be when Ben was at work? Even so, he wanted to be sure. Trevor had sat patiently in the footwell, resting his head on the seat, gazing at Jay, as if to say: 'Well, are you going to let me out or not?'

Trevor's tail thumped against the porch at the sound of voices inside the house. Jay's pulse speeded up too.

His mum answered, the 'o' on her face and smile showing

her amazement and pleasure. It must have been a month since he'd seen them and yet they were only half an hour from Firholme.

'Jay, what a lovely surprise. And Trevor too. We're honoured. We didn't expect you. We know how busy you are at this time of year.'

'Hi, Mum.' He kissed her cheek as Trevor shot up the hall, snuffling in delight.

His dad appeared from the kitchen, wearing a flowery apron, a teacloth in his hand. The scent of fruit and baking wafted down the hall, making Jay's mouth water. It was the scent of family Christmases . . . and after all, it was now December.

'Hello, son,' his dad said, wiping suds from his hands with the tea towel. 'To what do we owe this honour?'

'I thought I'd drop by while I could. We've been rushed off our feet with the Christmas tree sales.' He thought of Lottie's face when he'd mentioned the tree. It had lifted him to do something nice for her, however small – he didn't think he'd be here now, if it wasn't for her.

'I bet you are,' his mum said, stroking Trevor.

His dad tutted. 'Always strikes me as ironic that those involved in spreading the festive spirit are too knackered to enjoy it themselves.'

'Everyone wants a tree, Dad.'

'I always get the artificial one out.'

'Oh, bah humbug, Phil!' his mum said. 'We could get a real one from Firholme this year.'

'I'm entitled to a free one,' Jay said, following them into

the lounge where a few early Christmas cards had already been arranged on the mantelpiece.

'Don't you want it?' his mother said.

'Not really. I don't have room in my cottage.'

She eyed him sharply. 'Mm . . . well, if you really don't need it, then yes we'd love to have a tree. Wouldn't we, Phil?'

'Yes.' His father looked doubtful. 'Will it shed loads of needles?'

'Not if you water it regularly,' Jay said.

'Of course, we'll take care of it. It can be your dad's job.' She smiled and even Jay was amused. 'Tea or coffee?'

'Coffee please. Milk and sugar . . . and um, have you made any mince pies yet?'

His mum rolled her eyes. 'You know we have. You must be able to smell them.'

He smiled. 'I can.'

She laughed. 'Some things never change. No matter how many I make, they're always gobbled up before I can blink!'

Jay and his dad shared a look that left them both in no doubt of who ate all the pies. While his dad made a fuss of Trevor, and they talked about work, his mum made the drinks, refusing any help. Jay guessed she was hoping he and his dad might find some time to 'bond'.

She was soon back with a tray of pies, hot drinks and a dog chew for Trevor, who happily settled on the hearth rug. The pie was delicious, with home-made mincemeat and crumbly rich pastry. It seemed to taste better than he even remembered.

It was just like any other visit he'd made, except that the

whole time, he was wondering if or when they were going to bring up the incident in the pub with Ben.

He was midway through the final morsel of pie when his mum said, 'Will you come for Christmas dinner?'

He couldn't be surprised that she'd asked. Christmas Day was less than four weeks away and after all, he'd come round to deal with this very issue.

'I don't know. I can't be here at the same time as Ben and Nadia.'

'That's a shame,' his dad said. 'We had hoped that after so long, you might have reconciled yourself to the idea.'

So long? he thought. *The idea?* Jay forced himself to give a calm answer. All his parents wanted was for their family to be at peace but Jay knew things could never be the same. However, Lottie had reminded him how important family was so he'd come to offer a small olive branch.

Jay put his plate on the coffee table. 'Look, Dad, I'm happy that Seb is doing well. He's a lovely little boy. I've no doubt that Ben and Nadia love him and are a great mum and dad, but I'm not ready to play happy families yet. In time, maybe the situation might improve but there's no point pretending that things can ever be the same.'

'We're not expecting everything to be the same,' his mum said patiently. 'But we were hoping you'd still be able to join us for Christmas dinner? Ben and Nadia are bringing Seb round to open his presents in the evening but we've already discussed the fact that it would be too much to expect us all to sit round the dinner table as usual.'

Jay was wrong-footed that he'd already been 'discussed' by

the rest of the family. 'I don't want to keep them away from you.'

'No . . . but you're on your own, son, and I'm sure they'll be happy to have their own little family celebration as it's their first Christmas together.'

Jay's stomach churned. His dad meant well, but did he realise he was rubbing salt into his wounds by referring to his solitary lifestyle, even if it was partly self-imposed?

His dad patted his shoulder. 'I'm sorry for what Ben did. It was a terrible betrayal but time heals and if you can get through this Christmas, I'm sure things will become easier.'

Jay caught his breath. In the past few weeks, it was true that he'd glimpsed a light ahead and moved towards it. He'd already known he had to get out of a dark hole of bitterness and cynicism and Lottie had helped him take the steps forward. He still thought his dad had no idea of how Ben's actions had destroyed their bond, but he wanted to be kind to his parents and not reject them again.

'Look, as long as it's OK with you both, I'd love to come for Christmas lunch.'

His dad let out a breath. 'Good, because we can't stand the thought of you moping about in that draughty cottage on Christmas Day.'

'I do have Trevor,' he said.

'It's not the same,' his mum said.

'He gives me less trouble than some people!' At the curt remark, his mother's eyes glistened with unshed tears and Jay hated himself. In his own way, he'd caused them as much pain as Ben had although he still didn't know how he could have reacted any differently.

'It's not good for you to shut yourself away. What's done is done and it's time to move on.' His father was obviously frustrated.

'OK, Phil, Jay knows that but it isn't easy, is it?' His mum took his hand. 'It's a big blow to get over. You must understand though, Jay, that we're stuck in the middle and we feel that in some ways, we've lost you both.'

He felt the sting of tears behind his own eyes. His mother understood him better than he'd realised. 'I'll look forward to the day,' he said.

He forced a smile to his face. 'Trevor will too.'

Trevor lifted his head and cocked it on one side.

'We can't wait,' his mum said, brightening up.

He stayed a while longer, talking about Christmas plans and steering clear of anything that might sour the mood.

'Have to go, Mum. I promised Trevor a walk on Latrigg before I go back to Firholme.'

'Isn't it a bit wet?' his father asked.

'We'll be fine. C'mon, Trev. Let's be off.'

He made a swift exit, with an agreement to bring round his parents' tree when he next had a day off. It was strange but the idea of one of 'his' trees in the family home gave him a sense of quiet pride. Small victories, he thought. He'd take anything after the year he'd had.

He walked up the fellside in pouring rain that was turning to sleet, having to cut Trevor's walk short because of the conditions. Despite the shitty weather, his heart was a little lighter. There seemed to be an unwitting conspiracy among everyone he knew to help him 'move on'. His parents, Lottie, even her nieces. All of them kept nudging him back to the 'real world' of family and normality.

He wasn't relishing the idea of Christmas Day. He knew his parents would try to engineer a reconciliation again and that his mother would find it impossible not to regret the lack of family members, her grandson in particular, around the dinner table.

Yet he couldn't reject them. He kept thinking: *What would Lottie do?*

There was no denying he felt much brighter. She'd already had quite an influence on him. It was her reminder of how much family mattered that had prompted him to make a kind of peace with his parents.

She'd also – somehow – not only persuaded him to go to the staff ball, but even succeeded in making him look forward to it.

Chapter Seventeen

Everyone at Firholme, including Lottie, breathed a collective sigh of relief when the rain cleared on the day of the Edwardian evening. It meant that there would probably be a bumper crowd of visitors, keen to get in the festive spirit and hopefully spread the word about how gorgeous Firholme was to keep people returning.

It was also a welcome distraction from Steph's upcoming scan, not to mention Connor and Keegan's wedding.

Darkness fell and soon after headlights wavered on the driveway, as the first visitors started to arrive at the estate. At first it was a trickle of cars, but soon became a torrent of locals, tourists and even a few coach tours. Feeling buoyed by the early signs, Lottie hoped the event would be well received enough to become an annual fixture. Looking around the courtyard, alive with excited visitors, she was confident that it would.

She nodded a hello at Irina and Jan, buying hot chestnuts

from a stall, and smiled as she saw Wilf Carman getting out of a minibus with his mates from the sheltered housing scheme where he lived.

The air was filled with delicious aromas from hot stalls and cabins selling roast chestnuts and mulled wine while a special menu was being served in the café. A local choir were dressed in Edwardian costume, and singing carols, and later, a brass band would play a festive concert in the courtyard. Lottie had also booked a troupe of circus performers. Dressed in period costumes, the jugglers, fire-eater and stilt walker roamed the courtyard, entertaining the crowds.

Bedecked in its festive finery, Firholme House was at the heart of the celebrations, its windows glowing like a beacon, as visitors queued to take a tour. Lottie had helped supervise the preparations and even though she'd seen the house a hundred times, she was entranced by how atmospheric it looked in the flickering candlelight.

Jay and his team had worked incredibly hard, making sure the tree and foliage were in tip top condition. The effect of a lavish country house Christmas was complete, with the dining room laid out for a splendid Christmas Eve dinner, fires burning in the hearths and the tree providing a dramatic centrepiece in the ballroom.

Although Lottie was on call throughout the event, and buzzing about the site to make sure all was well, she'd arranged to meet Steph and the girls who'd come over after school.

Jodie and Myra hurtled up to her, dressed in hats and scarves. Steph followed, smiling but looking knackered. Her coat hung off her slender frame, though her hair was growing thicker now and the gamine style did suit her. Lottie didn't want to show any concern, however, because she didn't want to worry Steph, especially when the twins were so bubbly.

While Steph went to buy hot chocolate, Lottie took charge of the girls – although it was more accurate to say they took charge of her, clutching a hand each.

'Auntie Lottie! Auntie Lottieeee! Will the reindeer be here tonight?' Myra's voice was so hopeful that Lottie wished she *had* arranged for the reindeer to be at Firholme's Edwardian evening.

'Sorry, sweetheart, but I'm afraid not. Jay told me they're busy visiting children in other parts of the Lake District. We can't have them all to ourselves.'

Myra wrinkled her nose in disappointment but then Jodie tugged her sister by the hand. 'Look, there's a lady putting fire in her mouth!'

Shrieking in horror, Myra covered her eyes with her mittens. 'She'll get burnt. I don't like it!'

'Don't worry,' Lottie soothed. 'She won't be hurt. She knows what she's doing.'

Myra peeped through her mittens while Jodie gawped as the woman – who was dressed in an Edwardian circus costume – licked flame from the burning brand.

'I don't recommend you try yourself though,' she said, seeing the fascination in her nieces' eyes.

'*Why?*' the twins chorused together.

Lottie braced herself for a complex discussion about why the fire-eater could shove a flaming stick in her mouth and the kids couldn't. She shuddered to think about it herself. She scanned the crowds, willing Steph to reappear soon but instead, she spotted a different source of distraction. 'Jay!'

Hearing her, he doubled back. The girls started dancing around and quizzing him about the reindeer. Lottie had been about to ask him if he knew the technicalities of fire-eating but there was now no need. Jay was soon explaining exactly where the reindeer had gone – Ulverston Dickensian Fair apparently – and Lottie had been spared.

Steph arrived with a cardboard tray of drinks, which she distributed to Lottie and the girls.

'Sorry I didn't realise you were here or I'd have bought you a hot chocolate,' she told Jay, with a barely concealed glance of delight at Lottie. *Please don't wink at me, Steph,* Lottie prayed silently.

He smiled. 'It's fine, thanks. I just had a coffee. Are you having a good time?'

'Great, thanks.' Steph seemed gleeful. 'I hope *you're* finding time to enjoy yourselves. You *and* Lottie.'

Oh God, Steph was subtle as a brick. 'Oh, look. The brass band are starting up,' Lottie said. 'We can sing some carols.'

'Can you sing?' Myra asked Jay. 'Mummy can't. Auntie Lottie isn't *quite* as bad.'

'Thanks a lot, girls,' Steph said with an eye-roll. 'Actually, Lottie can sing though,' she told Jay, who was clearly trying not to laugh.

'No, I really can't!' Lottie protested.

'Anyone can sing,' Jay said. 'It only takes practice.'

Steph snorted. 'I could practise for a hundred years and still sound like a scalded cat. I'm tone deaf.'

Lottie was saved from having to reply by the band striking up their first carol, a cheery rendition of 'Hark the Herald Angels Sing'. The twins listened for a few minutes, until they begged their mum to take them to the 'living' nativity scene in the old coach house, with its donkey and sheep. Steph had her work cut out making sure the girls didn't spill hot chocolate as they danced off towards the coach house. 'I'll see you later,' she said.

Jay stayed by Lottie's side listening with her.

'It came upon a midnight clear . . .'

The local choir belted out the carol, encouraging the visitors to gather round and join in with them. The brass band reminded Lottie of the Christmas fairs when she and Steph were younger and their parents had lived in the Lakes. Enthused by the atmosphere, she couldn't help but join in the singing, in a quiet voice.

'Good King Wenceslas looked out . . .' the choir sang. *'On the feast of Stephen, when the snow lay round about . . .'*

'Deep and crisp and even, like a Nutella pizza . . .'

Jay's impro version at her side made Lottie burst out in giggles.

A few people gave them funny looks.

'Brightly shone Rudolph's nose that night . . .' Jay sang close to Lottie's ear. 'Through the frost was crue-el. When a reindeer came in sight . . .'

Lottie joined in. 'Gathering winter – er . . . M&Ms?'

They both dissolved into laughter. 'You're a very bad person,' Lottie said when the carol ended.

'So are you for laughing at me.'

She thought he'd never looked so attractive. His smile lit him up from the inside, and it gave her hope that he was more ready for a new relationship than she'd thought.

'It's OK for you,' she said. 'You have a great voice.'

'*Great?* No way. My voice is – was – OK. But I've always been strictly backing vocals.' A wry smile appeared. 'Ben was the lead singer.'

She was intrigued at this new snippet of information. 'Were you both in a band, then?'

'Years back, but don't be too impressed. Ben and I started it when we were in the sixth form. Nothing serious, we never expected to be famous or anything.' He gave a wry smile. 'We enjoyed ourselves, though, and even when I came home from uni we'd get together and do a few gigs in the vacations. Only the back room of the local pub and his rugby club type of thing.'

'Sounds like fun. I'd love to have seen you.'

'It was fun . . .' His smile faded. 'We grew out of it, as you do. I moved away to start my accountant course before I packed that in to retrain in forestry. Are you sure I wasn't too loud?'

'No. Not at all. I'm glad you can sing to drown my caterwauling.'

'Steph's right. You *can* sing,' he shot back.

She laughed, embarrassed at his praise, which she really didn't deserve. 'No way – don't tease me.'

'You're pretty much in tune,' he said, amusing Lottie with his stark honesty. 'Which is a huge plus, I can tell you, and you have a lovely soulful tone. You just need more confidence.'

'Hmm.' Growing uncomfortable at his praise, which she really didn't believe, Lottie turned the subject to Jay's past. 'Did you used to play the guitar too? I noticed it in the cottage.'

'Used to. I haven't picked it up for a year.'

'Did you stop because of the row with your brother?'

'Yes. I don't know why exactly. I've hardly been thinking straight . . . I guess I did associate my music with the old times with Ben.'

'It sounds as if you're punishing yourself,' she said gently. 'I wish you'd start again. It seems a shame to deny yourself something you really love.'

'Maybe.' He shrugged. 'Actually, I thought you'd like to know – though I'm not sure why – that I've decided to go to my parents' place for Christmas dinner.'

'Whew. That sounds very promising.'

'Mum and Dad are pleased but they've arranged for Ben, Nadia and Seb to go over in the morning and leave before I arrive so our paths don't have to cross.' He gave a grim smile. 'Hardly sounds like an overdose of Christmas spirit, does it? Though until a few days ago, I'd decided I was staying at home with Trevor, a microwave meal, the TV unplugged to avoid anything remotely festive.'

She smiled. 'Still feels like major progress to me.'

'Well, I realised it isn't fair to make my parents suffer any more, after the year we've put them through. They seemed so happy I was going for Christmas lunch. Mum nearly cried.'

Lottie had great trouble in not hugging Jay. However, she suspected he'd never been the hugging kind. She contented herself with a smile, and quiet hope that she'd had the tiniest hand in persuading him to be reconciled with his parents, at least.

'Anyway, they're stuck with me and Trevor now and I'm sure he'll be delighted to partake of a turkey dinner, if my mum has her way . . . Oh, someone wants me on the radio. Sorry, I'll have to take this.'

With that he left.

Lottie was kept busy for the next half an hour, dealing with one of Wilf Carman's coach party who'd tripped over a tree stump while having a sneaky vape. It wasn't one of the pensioners but the young warden and the residents had gone into action, looking after the man. Once she'd made sure the warden was OK apart from a bruised knee and she'd failed all attempts to get him to fill in an accident form, she snatched a couple of minutes to grab a hot drink and a pork roll from the hog roast. It was while she was finishing her 'dinner' in front of the carousel ride that Connor appeared.

Her heart sank. 'Connor! What are you doing here?'

'Keegan wanted to come to the event. I could hardly keep her away when the wedding's happening here. I need to see you. We need to have a proper talk about the situation . . .'

'Shh.' Lottie glanced around her. 'I think we've said everything there is to be said about . . .' She was going to say 'about us' but she changed it to: 'about the situation. I don't see why we need to meet face to face.'

'I have to talk to you. Since we met again, I've been thinking about how things ended between us. There's so much I left unsaid. I want to explain.'

'Fine but what if I don't want to hear it?'

'I promise I won't hassle you but can I come round tomorrow?'

'It's my day off,' Lottie said then kicked herself for admitting it. 'I'd planned to see Steph.'

'I thought she worked in a school?'

'She does but I was going later in the day . . .'

'OK, I'll come round mid-morning while Keegan has a trial appointment with the hairdresser,' he said sharply. 'I don't have many opportunities to get away from her.'

Charming, thought Lottie, but realised he wouldn't go away until he'd said his piece. 'If you absolutely can't tell me what you want to say now, I can spare ten minutes tomorrow.'

'Thanks. I owe you.' Connor placed his hand on her arm. 'I'll always regret causing you so much pain.'

'Hello, you two!'

Connor snatched his hand away and sprang apart when Keegan appeared from behind them. 'Discussing plans for the wedding, are you?'

Lottie's mood had been completely dampened. She should have known the evening had been going too well . . . Keegan could hardly have failed to see Connor and her deep in intimate conversation.

While Lottie felt guilty and annoyed at being put in this position, Keegan seemed happy enough and slipped her arm through Connor's. 'Anything I should know about or are you planning a special surprise?' she asked silkily.

'If I was, it wouldn't be a surprise, would it?' Connor replied smoothly.

Keegan pouted. 'I guess I'll have to be patient then.'

Lottie had by now perfected The Smile so well that it set on her face like concrete every time Keegan materialised.

'How are you enjoying the evening?' she asked. 'Have you been in the house yet?'

'Yes, we have. We've just been on the tour. I kept wanting to tell everyone that we were having our wedding there.'

'I don't blame you. Even though I'm biased, I must admit it looks spectacular tonight.'

'It does.' Keegan studied her. 'You know, Lottie, I'm not an easy woman to impress. I have very exacting standards.'

'This is true,' Connor said, smirking, and probably relieved not to have had more of a grilling from Keegan.

'I expect a lot from people,' Keegan droned on. 'In work, in my relationships – and not everyone can live up to those standards.'

'I'm glad we have so far,' Lottie said, itching to escape.

'Good job I did,' Connor said with an edge to his tone that Lottie knew only too well.

'Of course, you did, babe. You swept me off my feet.'

'You said "no" the first time, if I recall,' he muttered.

'Well I had only known you a month.' She gave him a little push on the arm. 'A month! Can you believe it, Lottie?'

Lottie was speechless. She'd guessed the relationship had progressed fast, but a *month* from meeting to a proposal? Her tongue was paralysed but Connor managed to speak.

'Keegan . . .' Connor's smile wobbled while Keegan was hurtling on like an unstoppable Aussie road train.

'I rapidly found out,' she said, 'if Connor wants something, he won't stop until he gets it.'

It was impossible for Lottie to maintain her game face when she remembered Connor's own proposal to her the previous year. That's how she'd felt: swept off her feet; blown away by Connor's romantic gesture, the passion in his voice.

Lottie knew exactly how easy it had been to ignore the little warning voices in the face of Connor's protestations of love and devotion. She felt foolish now – but should she be kinder to herself? She *had* been in love with him. She *had* believed he was in love with her.

He'd probably believed it himself until the cold light of day had dawned on him.

'Keegan. It's *freezing*,' Connor said, his voice rising in desperation. 'We should be getting home *now*. Mum's expecting us to pop round tonight.'

He was clearly mortified and Lottie's own brain was scrabbling for reasons to leave. Her fingers itched for the radio to crackle with an emergency. Even a minor blip would do: a blocked toilet, Wilf Carman's coach tour kicking off after too much mulled wine. She had the distinct feeling that Keegan was marking her territory in terms of Connor – rather like Trevor.

'We have plenty of time, yet, Connor,' Keegan said, before addressing herself to Lottie. 'Did you know Connor told me that he was scared about taking this new job in Australia?' Keegan's tinkly laugh was underpinned by steel. 'He didn't know anyone in Oz, but the opportunity was too good to miss and he'd never forgive himself if he ran away from a challenge.'

'How lovely . . .' Lottie heard herself saying. 'How lovely . . .' She was teetering on the edge of blurting out the truth.

Of shouting 'How lovely . . . Did you know Connor did the exact same thing to me? Did you know I believed him right up until the moment reality hit him and he changed his mind . . .? Do you know how excruciating it is to hear all of this – and think it happened to me too?'

'Connor said he'd never forgive himself if he let the chance for us to be together slip through his fingers,' Keegan steamrollered on.

'Let's not go over the top.' Connor gave a sickly smile. 'You make me sound like a saint.'

She laughed but held on to him. 'No, not a saint, Connor. We both know you're not perfect but you are very single-minded.' She threw a triumphant glance at Lottie. 'Once he's made his mind up, nothing will stand in his way. I think that's why I fell for him at the very start; I recognised his passion to go for what he believes in and *never* go back on his word.'

'Keegan!' Connor snapped. 'I'm sure Lottie's far too busy to hang around listening to our mutual admiration society and I'm sure she's heard a thousand loved-up couples and we're no different. Now, come on. I don't want to end up in a huge queue to get out of this place.'

Practically dragging her away, he left Lottie wondering if Keegan was worried about Connor's actual commitment. Was she sending out a warning to him, that he'd better not change his mind? Keegan wasn't stupid. She might have picked up on the 'signals' between Lottie and Connor and interpreted them as Lottie harbouring a crush on Connor.

She had to face him tomorrow and then hopefully, he'd finally leave her alone.

Chapter Eighteen

When Connor was twenty minutes late Lottie had begun to wonder if he was going to turn up at all. Her hopes were dashed when he rapped at the door.

His first words didn't make her feel any more comfortable about the purpose of his visit.

'Sorry. I had trouble escaping from Keegan.' He pulled a face. 'She was running late for her hair consultation.'

'You'd better come inside.'

'Thanks.' He banged his palms together. 'I've forgotten how bloody cold this place can be. It's forty degrees in Sydney today.'

'You must miss it. Keegan too. When are you meant to be going back to work?'

'January . . . although there's a possibility that we might be able to move back to the UK after this sabbatical's over. She's put in for a transfer to the London office and I'm being headhunted by another insurance company down south.'

'I see,' Lottie said, avoiding any comment that might have sounded like she was glad he'd at least be in the same country as her.

He hugged her. 'Thanks, Lottie. I know this has been hard for you.'

His embrace lasted a little too long for comfort. She didn't want any more reminders of what it had been like when things were good between them, of walks around the lake, and nights by the fire – and Cornwall. She'd tried to avoid looking at him too much before. Now they were alone in her little cottage, and so close, she couldn't avoid focusing on him. Lottie thought again how his life in the sun, his gym habit and on-trend clothes had given him an air of sophistication that had taken his quiet good looks into the realm of handsome.

'I wish I could make it up to you,' he said.

She snapped to her senses. 'I don't need you to make anything up to me.'

'Still . . . I . . .' Seeming lost for words, he glanced around. 'Nice little place you've got here.'

'Yes, it comes with the job.' She was determined to nip any idea she was ready for a cosy chat in the bud.

'Hmm.' He lounged back on the sofa. 'Any chance of a cuppa to warm me up?'

Lottie hesitated, surprised that he wanted to linger any longer than he needed to.

'Tea or coffee?' she said politely, reminding herself he was a client.

'Tea. Builder's with sugar.' He laughed. 'Don't tell Keegan, though. She's got me on a keto diet thingy until the wedding. I'm only supposed to have herbal stuff that tastes like badger's wee.' He threw her a disarming smile.

While making herself a coffee, she quickly made him a drink, squashing the teabag against the side of the cup the way he used to like it. Then she reminded herself that she no longer had to make his tea 'just how he liked it'.

It was surreal to have him enter her life in this intimate setting, turning back the clock to a time that should be long gone. She could barely cope with him on public territory at Firholme, but him violating her home – her new home – in this way, was a step too far. She resolved to get rid of him as quickly as she could.

He'd shed his jacket and was lounging on the settee, one leg crossed over the other, a newspaper spread out on the spare seat, open at the sports pages. A creeping sense of déjà vu sent a chill up her spine. It was exactly as if he'd never moved out.

Tensing up, she held out the mug. 'There's your tea. Now, what's this all about?'

He closed the paper before taking the drink. 'Like I said, I wanted to see you face to face. Thing is . . . I'm not sure I *should* have come here.'

Lottie was even more frustrated. 'You can't talk in riddles like this. You must have wanted something. This is driving me mad. The secrecy and the subterfuge. I'm not cut out for it.'

'You always played everything straight. That's what I liked about you.' Putting down his drink, he moved a little closer to her, and she caught a whiff of his aftershave; a different one from the brand he used to wear. 'I did care . . . I swear I did.' Before she realised, he pushed a tendril of hair off her face. Lottie froze, caught up in a moment that had catapulted her back to another, simpler time. 'I deeply regret the hurt I caused you. You didn't deserve it.'

There was a tenderness in his voice that she'd not heard before, perhaps not even since the moment he'd got down on one knee and proposed. She held her breath, caught between pushing him away and revelling in a moment she'd once longed for. Was he going to say he'd made a huge mistake?

He leaned in closer. 'Lottie, I wish I could . . .'

'Trevor!'

Lottie sprang away from Connor at the sound of Jay's shout from the rear of the house. Seconds later, Trevor dashed into the sitting room, barking. He jumped up at Connor, and knocked him backwards onto the settee.

'Jesus, he's drooling on my jeans!'

'It's only Trevor.' Lottie dived for the dog's collar but Trevor eluded her. His tail thumped wildly against Connor's legs and he shoved his snout into his crotch.

'That's disgusting!' Connor seized a cushion to fend the dog off. 'Get him off me. These are Hugo Boss jeans.'

Lottie could have hugged Trevor. He'd saved her from being lured into who knows what with Connor.

'Trevor doesn't read the fashion mags and he won't hurt you!' She tried to pull Trevor away but he thought Connor was playing a fine old game with the cushion and barked in delight.

'Trevor!' Jay burst into the room, with a wooden box of holly and mistletoe in his arms. 'Come here!'

Trevor was most reluctant to leave Connor but at Jay's command, he slunk back to his owner.

'Sit!' Trevor dropped to the carpet, sinking his nose on his paws, but with his eyes on Connor.

Jay's gaze darted from Lottie to Connor, cowering on the sofa. 'I came round with your Christmas tree and some greenery for the Bothy and Trevor darted round the back of the house. Your back door was open. I'm sorry, he gets over-excited.'

'You can say that again,' Connor snapped. 'Look at my bloody jeans.'

'Oh dear.' Lottie saw a trail of drool glistening on the denim and grabbed a box of tissues from the dresser.

'Sorry,' Jay said as Connor dabbed at his jeans with the tissues. 'I wouldn't have walked in if I'd known you were with a client,' he said to Lottie.

'Client?' Connor laughed sarcastically. 'Lottie and I are old friends.' He threw the tissues on the carpet, sat back down on the sofa and shot Trevor a nasty look.

Trevor's head sank lower onto his paws.

'Of course, I won't intrude.' Jay put the box down on the floor. 'I've left the tree outside for now. I've trimmed and sawn the bottom ready for the stand.'

He was clearly taken aback at Connor being in her sitting room in such a cosy manner. Even though Jay was aware they were acquainted, he must wonder what was going on.

'Thanks,' she said, trying to keep things light. 'That's a

lovely thought. I can't wait to put the tree up. It'll brighten the place up.'

'Right . . .' He aimed another glance at Connor. 'I'd better get back to work, then. Give me a call if you want a hand with the tree.'

Connor picked up the newspaper and started leafing through it again as if Jay didn't exist. Lottie was furious that Jay was being treated like a servant.

'Thanks,' she said, more firmly. 'I know how busy you must be.'

'It was no bother, I needed to come down to the offices anyway,' he said. 'See you later, then. I'll let myself out. Come on, Trevor.'

'Bye,' Connor said, flipping over another page.

Furious with him, Lottie followed Jay to the back door. 'Jay. Connor – Mr Moran – just popped round to talk about the wedding. I think he wants to organise a surprise for Keegan.'

Jay shrugged. 'I'm sorry Trevor jumped on him.'

'He'll live. Trevor was only being friendly, but he's always been wary of dogs.' Damn, Lottie could have bitten out her tongue. 'I mean he seems scared of dogs.'

Jay frowned. 'Right. Well, I'll keep Trevor well away from him in future.'

'Thanks.' She smiled. 'I'll look at my tree as soon as he's gone.'

He nodded, and she realised that he'd probably been expecting her to ask him to bring it in and set it up. Which she would have done if Connor hadn't been there. 'Jay – I've been meaning to say that I'm really pleased you decided to come to the Christmas ball.'

He nodded. 'I decided I'd been a hermit too long. Thanks for making me come.'

Lottie hid a smile at his choice of words. 'I hope I didn't *make* you come.'

'I didn't mean that. I wanted to come . . .'

Wanted to? Past tense? Had seeing Connor in her cottage changed that?

'I really hope you still want to,' she said, aware that Connor might be listening. 'You'll have a great time.'

'I'm sure I will.'

Jay's faint smile was at odds with his words, and in a moment, he was gone, walking determinedly up the path towards the woods.

Lottie shut the door, and leaned against it. It must have looked very off that Connor was in her house, acting as if he owned the place, even if she did know him. Maybe Jay thought she and Connor were closer than they were letting on . . . It could easily appear like that. She'd slipped up with the dog comment too.

Fired up with irritation at herself and Connor, she marched back into the lounge.

Connor had put the box on the coffee table and picked out a sprig. 'A Christmas tree and mistletoe?' he said, with a smirk. 'Wow. And what's this about a Christmas ball? I heard you talking. Are you seeing this woodsman bloke?'

So he *had* been listening at the door? Lottie was fuming. 'He's not a woodsman. He's the estate manager.'

Connor held up his hands. 'Sorry. I didn't mean to touch a raw nerve.'

'It's not a raw nerve and no, I'm not seeing him, not that it's got anything to do with you.'

'OK. Simmer down. I hadn't meant to pry but I did happen to overhear you saying you were really looking forward to going to this do with him.'

'That doesn't mean anything! Everyone's coming. Jay's a colleague and a friend and . . . and someone I can trust,' Lottie exclaimed, mad for him eavesdropping and that she'd let him wind her up. 'Look, Connor, if you've said all you had to, then I think you should leave. Unless there was anything else?'

'Nothing more than I was telling you. These past few weeks have made me realise what I must have put you through. I'd no idea about Steph being ill then. I know that she had cancer . . .'

'How did you find that out?' she said, unsure of his motive in bringing up Steph. Was he trying to assuage his guilt at leaving her – or could the unthinkable be happening and he was trying to get closer to her again?

'Alicia told me. One of her riding students has a kid at Steph's school. She told me when she was diagnosed and all that stuff with her illness must have happened quite soon after we broke up and I wasn't there to support you.'

'It's a bit late to feel guilty now. I coped. I had to, and I don't blame you for not being there. You'd no idea what was going to happen.'

He swallowed. 'You're so strong, Lottie. I'd have fallen to

194

pieces. I was terrified of Mum not making it through and I was ten thousand miles away. Dad wasn't handling it well.'

'It's hard when you're confronted with the prospect that the person you thought would always be there, might not be,' Lottie said.

'I probably didn't deserve you,' Connor murmured. 'That's what Mum said when we split up. If she'd known the real truth, she'd have killed me.'

Lottie's opinion of Fiona went up another notch, but she was also annoyed. Was Connor only here to ease his guilty conscience?

'What I did to you was unforgivable. I lay awake for weeks after I left, raking the reasons over and over, hardly able to face myself every morning for the damage I did.'

'If you were having doubts, why did you ask me to marry you?' Lottie cried. 'Why go for the whole dramatic romantic gesture? All the clichés? The diamond ring, going down on one knee on the beach? Why?'

'If I could answer that . . . I don't know. I was in love, and swept along by the moment.'

'A moment? You bought a ring specially and planned the whole proposal.'

'You said "yes", Lottie. You didn't have to.'

Any words deserted her. She was stunned by his comment. Hurt too – and worse, she knew that, in part, he was right. She'd been caught up in the dizzying romance of it all too. Even at the time, whispers of doubt had niggled her. She should have listened to them.

'I don't want to sound harsh but the moment we walked

through the door of the flat home – back to reality – I suppose I panicked.' He looked at his hands. 'A lifetime is a long time to commit to one person even if you do love them.'

Lottie was briefly speechless. Connor didn't want her. Was it possible that he didn't want her to have anyone else either? She also thought of Keegan's fireworks request and how she wanted to surprise Connor. Keegan seemed devoted to him and Lottie didn't want her to be hurt.

'Connor, I hope you're very sure this time.'

He hesitated then nodded. 'You're right.' He picked up his jacket. 'Never mind, it'll all be over soon,' he muttered and walked out.

She closed the door with a sigh of frustration. She was shocked that, for a moment or two, she'd allowed herself to imagine that the past year hadn't happened, and let the 'what-ifs' creep back into her mind.

In so many ways, the shadow he'd cast over her life was longer than she'd realised.

Even Jay had sensed something was going on between them and she'd hate it if she came across as unprofessional to him, or anyone. What's more, just when she'd had been looking forward to their relationship moving forward, Connor had thrown a spanner in the works. She had to hope Jay hadn't read too much into the situation, and that the ball would be a fresh stage in their relationship – and not another disaster.

Chapter Nineteen

Two weeks to the wedding

On the evening of the ball, Steph was staying over on the sofa bed at the Bothy while the twins were at a school friend's sleepover party. While Steph had been getting dressed in the sitting room, Lottie did her make-up in her bedroom.

She was looking forward to her glamorous night off, but was also a little nervous of how things would go with Jay. Since he'd walked in on her with Connor the previous Friday it had definitely put a dampener on some of her excitement and she was sure it had affected Jay's view of her. Over the past week, her communication with him had been confined to seeing him around the offices from time to time or passing him going in and out of the cottages. She could count the words they'd exchanged on the fingers of one hand.

They'd no real need to interact on a work basis, either, now the Edwardian evening was over. He'd spent all his time at the forest centre, which was natural considering it was peak tree-buying time. She'd been flat-out with the preparations for the ball, which felt as if it had arrived at lightning speed. Even so, she was sure that he had read something into Connor being in the cottage . . . though short of confronting him, she had no way of finding out. She really hoped the ball might be a way of rebuilding the bridges between them. Things had been going so well until Connor had landed back at the Bothy.

She heard the stairs creaking then her sister's voice at the bedroom door.

'What do you think? Not over the top?'

She whipped round, mascara wand in her hand. 'Oh wow! You look amazing. It's new, isn't it? I thought you said you were wearing your LBD. Where did you get that from?'

'There was a Christmas fair at school yesterday and one of the mums was running a designer pre-loved stall.' Steph did a twirl, the sequins on the slinky purple dress shimmering in the lamplight. 'It still had the price tag on it but she said there's no way she'd fit into it.'

Lottie was pleased to see Steph looking brighter, and with a smile on her face glammed up ready for an evening out. Tonight almost felt like it had before Steph had been ill.

'It's completely fabulous and I love the hair.'

'The salon worked wonders with it,' Steph said.

'Your dress looks great with those shoes we got in Kendal.'

Steph lifted the hem to show her silver sandals. 'I don't know how I'm going to dance the night away in them but who cares?'

'You will be OK, won't you?' Lottie asked. 'Don't feel you

have to boogie all night because of me. When you're ready to come home, you will say?'

'Of course I'll say if I need to but at the moment, I'm raring to go . . .' Steph hugged her. 'I just want some normality for one night, even if at midnight, I'll be like Cinderella and everything will go back to the way it really is. No matter what the future holds, I want tonight to be like the old days.'

Lottie felt her eyes prick with tears.

'Do not, repeat, do not cry! You've so much mascara on for a start.'

'I know.' She let Steph go and smiled.

'That's better. Now is there any chance I can borrow that black furry wrap you used to have?' she asked. 'If you still have it.'

'I do have it . . . or at least I don't remember getting rid of it when I moved out of Connor's. It's somewhere in the cubby hole though. I don't think I've unpacked it since I moved here.'

'I can go and hunt for it, while you get dressed.'

'In that dress?' Lottie shook her head.

Steph planted her hands on her hips. 'God, you do sound like Mum.'

'Yeah and you know I'm right. I'll go. My make-up and hair are done and I can get changed afterwards. Neither of us want to be poking round a dusty cupboard in our glad rags. I think I know which box it might be in. You wait here.'

Lottie padded along the landing and opened the cubby hole, which was actually a box room-cum-storage cupboard under the sloping eaves. It wasn't even big enough for a single bed. The naked bulb hanging from the ceiling illuminated the cardboard boxes that had stayed largely undisturbed since she'd moved out of the two-bedroom house she'd shared with Connor the previous year.

Lottie opened the cupboard less and less; really only as the seasons had changed and she'd needed boots and coats.

There was so much stuff she didn't use now. Clothes, tennis rackets – Connor had persuaded her to have lessons but she'd loathed it, hitting the ball everywhere except into the court. Two bodyboards leaned against the wall. They'd bought them back from the Cornish holiday. Lottie had really enjoyed catching the waves but Connor had hated being dumped under water so they'd never used them again. Somewhere in the depths there was a yoghurt maker, a canteen of cutlery and a vintage china tea set from his auntie, which Connor had wanted to throw on the dump. Lottie loved the tea set but there wasn't room in the kitchen and she hadn't yet hosted any afternoon teas.

These mundane items were a reminder of a lifestyle she'd left behind. A couple's life, a life that had been full of cosy plans, some big but many small. Yet wasn't it the small details that knitted people together so closely and made lives so hard to unpick?

Lottie couldn't imagine Keegan bodyboarding even if she was an Aussie . . . but she could imagine her playing tennis, in a chic dress and pristine white trainers . . . Maybe this was another reminder that Keegan and Connor were meant for each other, despite Connor's misgivings.

It was crazy to think he'd been having second thoughts about the wedding because of Lottie. The 'tenderness' he'd shown her before he'd been a git towards Jay must have sprung from guilt. She'd searched her conscience ever since, to see if she'd offered Connor any hint whatsoever that she still had feelings for him. She was sure she hadn't but in future she resolved to try doubly hard not to encourage him one little bit.

His wedding to Keegan had to go ahead and it had to be perfect.

She ducked her head to enter the cupboard. The box with the faux fur stole, of course, was right at the back, but fortunately not underneath any other stuff. Squeezing deeper inside, she opened the lid and saw it on top of the box, along with a black ballgown she'd once worn to a tourism awards ceremony. She'd helped her hotel win a silver hospitality award that night. In fact, she'd first met Shayla at the awards do, which had led to her eventually being offered her current role. Some memories weren't all bad.

She went back to her room and handed the wrap to a delighted Steph, who went downstairs to wait for her.

Lottie could have worn the black ballgown to tonight's party but this was an evening to look to the future so she'd splashed out on a midnight-blue midi-dress spangled with teeny silver stars. It had a high neck and long sleeves and looked good with some velvet heels that would probably be agony within half an hour. The dress had a Gothic air to it that she felt was in keeping with Firholme, so she'd decided on some marcasite chandelier earrings she rarely had the chance to wear.

After adding a slick of lip gloss, and a spritz of perfume,

201

she made her way down the narrow staircase, one hand on the bannister for support.

Steph had been taking a selfie but stopped when she saw Lottie walk in.

'Oh my. You look like a knockout. That dress – the hair. Your eyes. Is this Lottie?'

Glowing with pleasure – and relief – at Steph's reaction, Lottie patted her head. She'd spent ages putting up her hair, securing it with grips and a clip and teasing out just the right number of tendrils to frame her face. Steph probably hadn't noticed when she'd first walked into the bedroom, because she was so caught up in her own finery. Lottie had also been wearing a pink furry dressing gown . . .

'We scrub up pretty well,' Steph said. 'Maybe tonight is the night – with Jay, I mean.'

'Would you mind not matchmaking just yet?' Lottie peered into the mirror and dabbed at a fleck of mascara that had settled on her cheek.

'Why not? You said your evening out went well and you were very cosy at the Edwardian evening.'

'Cosy? We were working.'

'I saw you snuggled up at the carol concert.'

'There were so many people, we couldn't help being close and anyway, I'd no idea you were watching!'

Steph smirked. 'You're so easy to wind up.'

'Argh.' Lottie groaned but laughed too. 'Come on,' she said, 'Let's finish getting ready and grab a few photos.'

After taking some selfies and pictures to WhatsApp their parents and to show the twins the next morning, Lottie grabbed a tiny bag and a large coat. A few large flakes of snow were falling and the grounds were already white. She was glad she had no need to drive home.

Many of the staff had decided to share rooms with the live-in workers and she wondered if the others might end up begging for floors to bunk down on or sleeping in the café, if cars and taxis couldn't make it up the hill to the house. There were worse places to be and the café had squidgy sofas and lots of blankets, so hopefully everyone could be accommodated if need be.

They had to take their wellies even to reach the doors of the big house, and laughed to see the rows of boots abandoned at the entrance to the vestibule. One of the waiting staff who Lottie had hired from a catering company took their coats and they changed into their party shoes.

Steph stared at the vestibule, with its grand staircase. Laughter and chatter echoed to the ceiling two floors up, while people mingled in the hall and spilled out of the drawing room, glasses in hand.

'Wow! This is incredible.'

Lottie agreed, but it wasn't the grand surroundings that had stunned her but the people. The room was full of folk she saw every day but now hardly recognised. Everyone had taken the glamorous dress code to the max. There were gardeners in tuxes, chefs in ballgowns, maintenance men looking like James Bond. Lottie wondered what the mill owner would have thought of all the 'workers' making merry in his home.

It made her glow with pleasure to see her colleagues and

their guests, laughing and gasping in delight as they greeted fellow workers. There was also a lot of fizz being consumed; people were ready to get into the party spirit early and enjoy this particular Christmas to the max. Only one face had eluded her so far.

Steph took two glasses from a waiter and handed one to Lottie. 'Is Jay here yet?' she said, reading Lottie's mind. 'We could have walked up here together.'

'I did think of calling for him but . . . I didn't want to add to the pressure.' Lottie did fear he might have had second thoughts at the last minute. If he did, she hoped it wouldn't be anything to do with Connor's appearance at the cottage. 'He could be here already. There are so many people around, it's hard to tell.'

'Let's see if we can find him. then. Come on, it's party time!'

The ballroom was spectacular, with the round tables laid out for Christmas dinner for the sixty-odd staff and guests, with the tree bedecked in jewel-like finery.

There was still no sign of Jay but Shayla swept up, looking amazing in a full-length silver dress. 'Wow. Fabulous, darlings!' she said. 'You look wonderful, Steph. I'm so glad you're here.'

Steph grinned. 'Not as glad as I am.'

'Oh yes, I see what you mean,' Shayla said, and hugged her.

Lottie smiled. 'You look fantastic too, Shayla.'

She swished her hem. 'Yes, I think I do.'

They all burst out laughing.

'Must circulate! Have a wonderful time. You've both earned it.'

'Oh, he's here.'

Over the rim of her glass, Lottie spotted Jay's curly head above the throng. He was standing by the window, chatting to the head gardener, Thomasina aka Tommy. She'd moved aside to greet someone and Jay was suddenly revealed. With Tommy's attention diverted elsewhere, Jay was temporarily cast adrift. He glanced around him and seemed nervous, sipping at a glass of fizz, one hand in his pocket.

He was positively edible in a dark green velvet jacket and open-neck white shirt and black jeans. A flush of heat rose to Lottie's cheeks.

'Told you.' Steph whispered in her ear. 'It's Kit Harington. The Emmy awards version.'

'Oh God, was I staring?'

'Eyes out on stalks like a gigantic snail,' Steph said.

'Argh.'

'It's normal, Lottie. It's what people do: fancy the pants off each other. You look gorgeous and I bet Jay thinks so too.'

'Shh. Stop it!' Lottie was embarrassed. 'I didn't invite you here so I could go off and drool over some bloke.'

'Hon. Stop worrying about me. We'll be sitting together throughout the dinner and after that? I will be *very* annoyed if you ignore Jay because you feel you have to nursemaid me. You've done more than enough of that to last a lifetime and I'm perfectly capable of chatting to other people.' Steph waggled a glass at her. 'Do I make myself clear?'

Lottie nodded and tried to look angelic. 'Perfectly, bossy big sister.'

'Now, Jay's coming over. I'll stay long enough to be polite and then I'm off to powder my nose, or whatever.'

Trying not to gawp, Lottie waited for Jay to join them, her heart beating a little faster. How could she feel nervous in his presence when she'd spent the past month working with him? She'd seen him almost every day yet this moment felt significant.

'Hello,' he said with a smile.

'Hi, Jay.' Lottie wished she could calm down. How had he acquired the power to zap every nerve ending?

Steph smirked. 'Hi there, Jay. Good to see you again.'

'You too. How's the tree doing?' he asked.

Steph rolled her eyes. 'Still standing. The girls have been squabbling over whose turn it is to water it.'

'That's better than neglecting it.'

'Though they might kill it with kindness,' Lottie added.

'They're sturdy trees. They like plenty of TLC.' He sipped his wine again and caught Lottie's eye. Was she imagining that he seemed to be staring at her? Or was she reading too much into the situation. She longed to stroke the velvet of his jacket – and the skin under it.

How would she get through the evening, if she was in a state before they'd even had dinner? Dare she hope that he'd realised there'd been nothing 'going on' between her and Connor and they could move on?

Some of Lottie's other workmates joined them and soon Jay was part of a small group that included Thorsten and Kerr. He seemed at home and she relaxed too, although every sneaky glance at him sent shivers of desire through her.

206

The dinner gong sounded and everyone peeled off to find their tables. Lottie had done the place settings herself and had placed Jay with Kerr, some of the crew from the forestry team and a couple of guys from the maintenance team.

'I'm surprised you haven't arranged for Jay to sit right next to you,' Steph observed quietly, unfolding her table napkin.

'Maybe that would have been a bit . . . obvious?'

A waiter appeared with a bottle. 'White or red, madam?'

'White, please,' said Steph. 'This is such a treat, Lottie. Thanks for inviting me. Last year I thought I might never go to another Christmas do.'

Steph took a gulp of her wine. Lottie wondered whether she should be having too much alcohol after going so long without it? However, as Steph had pointed out, she didn't need a nursemaid and besides, Lottie was the last person to spoil her fun after all she'd been through.

Chapter Twenty

After dinner, the band started up. Fuelled by the subsidised bar, people were immediately on their feet, and to Lottie's amusement, the most enthusiastic dancers weren't necessarily the ones she'd expected. She was feeling mellower after a couple of glasses but being careful because she still had to organise the raffle which was in aid of the local cottage hospital.

Lottie's last sighting of Steph had been in a group with Shayla, quaffing champagne. She'd been laughing at something Kerr had been saying and they looked like they were thoroughly enjoying themselves.

The band switched to a ballad and people paired up to take to the floor. There were long-standing couples like Lukasz and his partner, but also some intriguing combinations. Two of the female gardeners, who Lottie hadn't even realised were romantically involved, were entwined and Shayla was in the arms of the wine merchant who supplied the estate.

Jay wasn't on the dance floor, to Lottie's relief. She decided to seek him out but hadn't made it far when he zeroed in on her.

'Hello. I've been trying to find you for a while,' he said.

'Me too. Lucky we finally tracked one another down.'

Jay seemed transfixed by her. 'Is it shallow of me to say you look lovely?'

Lottie flushed with pleasure. 'I don't mind . . .' She wondered if she dare pay him a similar compliment, but 'you look like Kit Harington and I'm going weak at the knees' was absolutely not a good idea. 'You decided not to wear the uniform then?' she said as lightly as she could.

'Yeah. I bought this jacket specially. Trevor didn't seem too impressed.' He wrinkled his nose. 'I'll probably never wear it again.'

'Welcome to my world,' said Lottie. 'And Trevor may love you but I don't think he's the best judge of fashion.'

'Maybe not, though I did catch him lying on it the other day.'

She laughed, thinking she wouldn't mind being Trevor, cosying up to Jay in his cottage.

'My Christmas tree is beautiful, by the way,' she said. 'Thanks for bringing it. You must come and have a look, though it's not as grand as the one in here.'

He smiled. 'I'd like that a lot. We've both been so busy over the past few days.'

'Yes. We have.'

She was aware they were dancing around each other, but not actually doing the real thing. Should she ask him? Why did she need to wait for him to make the move?

She went for it. 'Do you want to—'

'Dance?'

They burst out laughing that they'd both asked the question simultaneously.

'I think that settles it,' he said.

A moment later, they were on the dance floor and Jay's hands were resting at her waist. His touch was so light . . .

It felt natural and also extraordinary at the same time, though Lottie couldn't have explained the feeling in words. The two of them barely moved, in fact it was more of a shuffle on the spot. She didn't know if anyone was looking. All she knew was that he smelled gorgeous and when the velvet of his jacket brushed her wrists, her skin tingled.

'This is retro,' he murmured, and Lottie noticed he'd moving a little closer to her and she had no objections. 'It's been a very long time since I went to a do where people danced together – as couples,' he added with a soft emphasis that thrilled her.

She didn't need to reply, simply gave herself to the pleasure of being so close to the warmth of Jay's body. They danced slowly, saying nothing but moving closer all the time, until her face was almost touching his shoulder. She pressed her hands against his back, the velvet smooth beneath her fingertips. She heard his sigh, felt it, even, and wondered if he could sense her heart beating.

A cool current of air made her shiver.

'Are you cold?' he asked, searching her face.

'No. The opposite.'

They were near the French doors, which were open a little

to let some air into the overheated ballroom. The curtains rippled softly in the wind.

'Want to get some air? It might be chilly, but we could stand in the shelter of the doorway.'

She smiled. 'I don't mind about the cold.'

They slipped behind the curtains and the chill embraced her, though it felt exhilarating. An inch of snow coated the terrace but in the immediate shelter of the house, the flag-stones were still bare. Light spilled out from the windows, and the full moon shone through a gap in the clouds, revealing the silvery lake and the hunched black fells above it.

It was beautiful and she didn't want to go back inside, but she shivered again and had to wrap her arms around herself.

'Here.' Jay took off his jacket.

'I'm fine.'

'And I'm happy for an excuse to take it off.'

She laughed. 'OK, then, as a favour to you.' Eyes sparkling with amusement, he slipped it around her shoulders, and cocooned her with the warmth of his body.

'Thank you.' They gazed in silence for a few moments before Lottie murmured, 'I've lived in the Lakes all my life but I still have to pinch myself to believe I work at Firholme.'

'Would you ever move away?' he asked.

'I thought of it once. I almost did but – life got in the way,' she said. 'What about you?'

Jay gazed out at the lake. 'I thought of it too, after last Christmas. I started searching for jobs in Canada, checking if I could make a go of it over there. I wanted to get as far away from all the crap here as possible.'

'Why didn't you?'

He shrugged. 'I don't know. Every time I began to fill in the forms, or press send on an application, something stopped me. I was in limbo, unable to take a step.'

'Maybe it's better you didn't do anything sudden. I'm definitely glad you didn't emigrate.'

He returned his attention to Lottie. 'Me too, and I'm glad you came to work at Firholme. I don't think I'd be at the party tonight if you hadn't encouraged me.'

'Hassled you, more like?'

'I needed a kick up the arse, to be honest.'

She laughed. 'I hadn't intended to do anything quite that drastic.'

'You've helped me to see that my family matter and that I actually used to enjoy Christmas. All the little things that families do together, I might have rolled my eyes and thought they were a bit cheesy but it's still a time for us to get together and have a laugh, and spend time in each other's company: put a brake on all the other madness in our lives.'

'That's true. What happened to Steph focused all our minds, too.'

'I understand. I realise I do actually enjoy opening the silly presents, Mum's baking, Dad's turkey dinner, Ben telling rude jokes at the dinner table. That stuff means more than I realised and while things can't be the same, it's time for me to embrace the new normal.'

This positive sign gave her an even warmer glow. 'I'm happy you made a start.'

He smiled but seemed hesitant too. 'I've been wondering, could this – us – be part of the new normal too?'

His words took her aback. She hadn't been expecting anything so positive from him. 'Yes, I think it could.'

He rested his hand on her cheek and moments later, they were kissing. Lottie gave her answer. She kissed him back. He drew her closer and the kiss deepened. She revelled in the warmth of his mouth, the security of his arms around her and the delicious thrill of desire.

'If this is the new normal,' she said when their lips parted, 'I hope it carries on.'

'Me too, but I don't want things to go too fast. For you, I mean. I haven't been the easiest of people to make friends with. I'm finding it hard to trust people again, even people I should trust. People like you, Lottie.'

Lottie did feel things were happening fast, but that didn't matter. Jay had made a leap forward and she was happier than she'd been for many months. Steph was right about her and Jay: they were both ready to step into the brave new world and find love again.

'Lottie!'

They sprang apart, Lottie's heart thumping. Shayla had whipped the curtains back and disco lights and music spilled out from the ballroom.

'Oh, I'm sorry. Ignore me.'

'Too late for that,' Jay muttered and Lottie stifled a giggle.

'No, it's fine. Jay and I were just getting some fresh air.'

'Very fresh! It's bloody freezing out here. Someone had seen you walk out and I came to see if you'd mind drawing the raffle.'

'Oh, God. Is it that time already?'

'Yes, I can find someone else, if you're busy.'

'No. No, I'm not.'

Jay stayed silent beside her and she hoped he would understand what she meant. Well, what else could she say? *I'm busy having the best kiss ever and finally getting to know Jay intimately so just this once, jog on, boss.'*

'If you're sure.' Shayla let Jay go in ahead and as Lottie passed by, she whispered: 'Nice jacket.'

For the next ten minutes, Lottie had to set aside her magical moment with Jay and concentrate on MC-ing the raffle. She tried to find him in the crowd, but he didn't even appear to be in the room, and he didn't have any winning numbers. Steph also hadn't won anything and Lottie knew her sister had bought several tickets. She wasn't in the room either. Her skin prickled with unease. Come to think of it, Lottie hadn't seen Steph since before she'd danced with Jay.

Chapter Twenty-One

Jay might have been walking on air when he left the ballroom to go to the washrooms. Shayla's appearance had been frustrating to say the least, but it was only a blip. He was sure he could find Lottie later and they could take things from where they'd left off.

Since he'd stumbled upon that guy from the wedding party in Lottie's cottage, he hadn't been able to shake off the sense that she was hiding something – or at least that he was missing a vital aspect of her story. For now, he brushed that feeling aside and enjoyed the memory of their amazing kiss.

As he finished drying his hands he realised he'd left his jacket with Lottie. That was cool. It looked a lot better on her than it had on him, despite her compliments. Still buoyant, he walked back into the vestibule, intending to find Lottie as soon as possible.

'Jayyyy . . .'

The foyer was empty – so where did the groan come from?

215

He soon found out. Steph was slumped on the padded bench at the back, under the stairs that led up to the bedrooms.

'Jayyyy . . .'

She looked pale and her eyes were half-open. Jay's heart sank. He crouched on the tiles and picked up her hand. 'Steph, I'm here. Are you OK?' Clearly, she wasn't but he was hoping it was the champagne, not something more serious, that had caused her to collapse here.

She sparked into life. 'I'm fine. I'm great. I'm wonderful!' She tried to stand but stumbled, grabbing his arm to steady herself. 'Have to go back to the ball. Cinderella needs me.'

'Whoa, careful.' He slipped his arm around her shoulders, now almost certain that she was only suffering from too much party spirit. 'It might be better to sit down again,' he said, gently, helping her back onto the bench.

She was clearly having trouble focusing on his face. 'But Lottie will miss me.'

'I can fetch her if you like?'

'Yes. No.' She put her finger on her lips. 'Shhh.' Her hand slipped and hung loosely by her side.

'Will you be OK for just one minute while I find her?' Jay slowly rose from the bench.

'No! Don't go.' She grabbed his arm and pulled him back.

'I really think I should find Lottie. I promise I won't be more than a few moments.'

'Mm. Okayyyy.' Her word were slurred. 'Ijustwannasay, has anyone ever told you you're a lovely guy?'

'Not often, no,' Jay said and might have been amused under other circumstances. Knowing Steph's medical history, he couldn't help being concerned. Maybe she was on some medication?

'Lottie thinks you're luvverly. She thinks you are Kit Harry ton.'

'Kit Harry . . .' Jay was flummoxed. 'I'm not sure I understand.'

'Kitty Harington.' Steph gave him a little push and tutted at his ignorance. 'You *know*. It's your hair, mainly and all your tools – choppers, stuff like that.'

'Choppers?' Jay was still completely confused.

'The hot one from *Throne of Games* . . . *Game of Stones* . . . oh, sod it. Anyway . . .' Steph poked her finger in his chest. 'She really fancies you. You should snap her up . . . but she's too scared to tell you how much.'

'Too scared?' Jay's intrigue level was now off the scale, but he didn't dare wait any longer to find Lottie.

'Someone broke her heart. Bastard,' Steph declared. 'She deserves someone better. Someone lovely like you. You are a lovely man.'

'Thanks. I'll be back in a sec. You stay here and don't move.' Gently, Jay disentangled Steph's fingers from his, his heart leaping at the prospect of Lottie fancying him although any comparison to Kit Harington was obviously a product of Steph's drunken imagination.

'Wait!' Her fingers closed around his wrist and she gave him a dreamy look. Jay was worried she might slip into unconsciousness.

'Lottie never shuts up about you now . . . Jay this, Jay that.' Steph smiled then shook her head like a child. 'It used to be

217

all Connor. Connor, Connor. On and on about him.' She wagged her finer. 'Not now. Jay, Jay, Jay.'

Jay's intrigue switched to confusion. 'Connor?'

Steph pulled him close to her face. 'You're not like Connor,' she whispered. 'He's a shit. I thought they'd get married one day but he dumped her. You woodendotha'. You're a nice guy.'

Jay's skin prickled with unease. Why would she say Lottie was obsessed with Connor? Was it simply the booze and meds talking or was there more to her relationship with Connor than a passing acquaintance and the wedding?

Steph rested her head on his shoulder. Jay tried to move but she'd flung her arms around him. Her head slid off his shoulder and onto his lap and she closed her eyes.

Jay sat there for a few seconds. Had Lottie been lying to him? The image of Connor, so perfectly at home in Lottie's cottage, reared its head again. He saw it through new eyes and so many things dropped into place – none of them pleasant.

However, his suspicions had to wait. His only priority was to find Lottie and help her get Steph safely home to the Bothy.

Chapter Twenty-Two

'OK, this is the final ticket. It's a green one, number 23. Bumper box of Firholme biscuits!' Lottie held the raffle ticket aloft and one of the Firholme security staff trotted forward to collect his prize.

Her work was done.

She stepped off the dais, eager to find Jay but even keener to track down Steph who she hadn't seen for over half an hour. No matter what Steph had told her, Lottie felt bad about simply abandoning her sister, even if she was desperate to continue the delicious moment on the terrace with Jay.

The DJ had started up the music again, and she was halfway across the dance floor when Shayla met her, an anxious look on her face.

'Lottie! Now, I don't want you to worry.'

Lottie was instantly on the alert. 'Worry about what?'

'It's Steph. I *think* it's only the wine, but you'd better come all the same.'

Lottie let out a groan. 'I should have warned her to go easy but I didn't want to be a killjoy. She's had such a rough time. I should have stayed with her.'

'I'm sure she'll be fine,' Shayla said. 'She's with Jay.'

They hurried out of the ballroom, where everyone was bellowing out The Pogues' 'Fairy Tale of New York'.

'Jay?'

'He found her on the banquette in the vestibule and came to find you but he saw me first. There they are.'

Lottie ran over to where Steph was sprawled over Jay. He had his arm around her. 'Oh my God, what happened?' she asked, kneeling on the tiles by her sister's feet. Steph's eyes were closed and she was snoring, just like she used to when she'd been a child.

'I came out of the gents' and found her here. Actually, she called me over.' He sounded none too pleased which caught Lottie off-guard.

She squatted down so she was at the level of Steph's face. 'Steph?'

Shayla stood nearby. 'Do we need an ambulance?'

'I don't think so.' She rubbed Steph's hands. 'Steph! Can you hear me?'

Her eyes flew open. 'Of course, I can. I'm not bloody deaf!'

'I should have been more careful.' Lottie helped to extricate Steph from Jay and they both propped her upright.

'Don't blame yourself,' Shayla said. 'Steph's been having a wonderful time. She seemed fine less than half an hour ago.'

'I am here, you know . . .' Steph muttered.

'Steph, you've had a bit too much to drink,' Lottie said.

Steph lifted her head and sniggered. 'No shit, Sherlock. Yeah. I'm drunk. Bladdered. Sloshed. Pissed. And I'm glad I'm pissed because at least I know I'm alive.'

'Yes, but maybe we should go home, now.'

'No . . . I wanna stay.'

'I really think we should get you home. It's late.'

'Do you need a hand?' Shayla offered.

'I'll help, if you want me to,' Jay said.

Lottie looked at them both. 'Thanks. I'm sorry about this.'

'It's no problem,' Jay said. 'Shayla, I think we can manage together if you want to go back to the party.'

'I'm not bothered about the party, but I might have to stay and keep order. There's already been an incident between one of the gardeners and the man from the portable toilet firm.'

Suddenly, Kerr appeared and hurried over. 'I've been looking for Steph everywhere. Oh God, is she OK?'

'She's not feeling well,' Lottie said.

Kerr's eyes widened in dismay when he saw the state of Steph. 'She seemed fine half an hour ago. Can I call an ambulance? Help you take her back to the Bothy?'

'She's on medication and she doesn't normally drink. Thanks for the offer but we can manage for now,' Lottie said, grateful for the help but keen to deal with the situation with as few people as possible.

'We're fine, thanks, Kerr,' Jay added.

'I think we should leave Steph to Lottie and Jay,' Shayla said. 'She's in good hands now.'

'OK but call me if you need *anything* and let me know how she is,' Kerr insisted.

'We will,' Lottie said and smiled her gratitude. 'Thanks for offering to help.'

'Come on, she'll be OK.' Shayla ushered him back to the ballroom.

'I feel very sleeeepy,' Steph murmured.

Lottie let out a sigh of relief. 'Time for bed, then.'

'For you . . .' Steph giggled. 'On your own. Not with . . .'

'Think we'd better go now,' Lottie exclaimed.

'Would you mind helping me?' she asked Jay, desperate to move Steph before she passed out again.

'Of course not. Come on.'

He helped Steph to her feet.

'I'll take her,' Lottie said.

'Be careful. She's heavier than you think and she's a dead weight.'

'Oy! You cheeky sod!' Steph shot back, momentarily lucid. 'Maybe you're not so lovely after all.'

'He's trying to help, Steph.'

'He says I'm fat.' She let out a raucous laugh.

'Steph. Shut up, *please*.' Lottie pleaded then tried to laugh off Steph's comments. 'Don't take any notice of her – she doesn't know what she's on about. Whoa!'

Steph had slumped lower. Lottie dived in to support her. Even with her and Jay on either side of her, she was struggling to stay conscious.

Lottie was in despair. 'I'm not sure we'll make it all the way to the Bothy.'

Jay's jaw was set. 'Let's give it a try.'

Somehow, they managed to cajole and half-drag Steph out

of the house. Lottie decided not to bother with the wrap and instead, Jay retrieved his jacket from a chair in the ballroom and helped Steph into it. There was no way she was going to be persuaded into the wellies though so they decided to hope for the best.

While Jay supported Steph, Lottie scrambled into her own boots. Big wet flakes were falling, soaking them within moments of leaving the house. Slipping and slithering, they carried and coaxed Steph across the terrace and down the steps to the cottages. Without Jay, Lottie could never have managed.

Despite her sodden dress and feet, Steph thought it was all a huge laugh.

'You're a keeper,' she kept telling Jay.

'Shh. Steph.' Lottie was mortified.

'A real nice guy . . . not like C—'

'Steph!' Lottie said, dreading what might emerge next from Steph's mouth. Thank God they were now into the garden of the Bothy. Lottie was exhausted, her muscles were aching and her sparkly wrap was a cold wet rag. Jay was right. Taking the weight of a whole person was no mean feat.

Lottie had to let go of Steph to open the door, leaving Jay supporting her. Unexpectedly, she decided to break free of him and lie on the small patch of lawn outside the cottage. 'Oh no, she'll freeze,' Lottie said.

Steph was having a wonderful time, lying in the snow, waving her arms and legs up and down. 'Iman angel. Angellll . . .'

'More like a stranded beetle!' Lottie cried in frustration. 'Come on.'

'Think I'll go sleep now,' said Steph, closing her eyes.

'No. Not here. Oh God, she's soaked and so's your jacket.'

'I don't care about that.' Jay kneeled down in the snow. 'Help me get her sitting up. I'll have to carry her.'

It was hard enough helping her sit up but somehow Lottie and Jay did it. Grunting, he managed to get Steph in his arms and with Lottie's help, hoisted her onto his shoulder, fireman style. He did let slip a few grunts and rude words, but Lottie didn't think Steph was in any fit state to be offended.

He made it through the front door and hallway into Lottie's sitting room. Steph was dumped rather unceremoniously on the sofa but at least it was a soft landing.

She lay back with a dramatic sigh and a beatific smile on her face, oblivious to the fact her clothes were dripping. Lottie wished she hadn't let the fire die down in the sitting room.

'I don't think I can undress her but we could get the jacket off,' Lottie suggested.

Together they pulled off the soaking jacket and removed Steph's silver sandals. Lottie fetched some towels and rubbed her feet and legs dry while Jay went to put the heating on and find the spare duvet from the airing cupboard. While she was upstairs, Lottie changed into her pyjamas and a dressing gown. Passing the cubby hole, she had a thought.

'Oh!' She couldn't stifle her surprise when she found Jay shirtless in the sitting room, rubbing his torso with a large towel. She'd imagined how his body might look but wasn't prepared for the reality. Years of outdoor work, hauling logs and wielding heavy equipment had given him a naturally honed physique. It was impossible not to gawp and the sight of him stirred up the same feelings of desire she'd felt when he'd kissed her, except this time they were undercut by her concern for Steph and unease at her hints about Connor.

He wrapped the bath sheet around his shoulders.

'I brought you this, in case . . . it's the only thing big enough.' She handed over a large knitted poncho that had been a present from her auntie. 'You don't have to wear it. I won't be offended.'

She held it out, expecting Jay to laugh but only being met with a murmured 'Thanks.'

'It was from my auntie. It's miles too big but it will keep you warm until you're back in the cottage. I don't think it would do you any good to walk even that far without your top on,' she said, even though she'd have relished any opportunity to keep him shirtless for as long as possible.

'Thanks.' He pulled the poncho over his head, instantly covering his gorgeous torso with the garish wool.

'I'll sleep down here in the chair in case she's sick.'

'Do you want me to stay?'

She'd have loved his company but didn't want him to hear any more of Steph's ramblings. 'No, thank you. You've done more than enough. Don't you want to get back to the party?'

'Oh, I think I've had enough of it now.'

Steph's lips moved. 'You are a lovely guy, Jay.'

Lottie rolled her eyes. 'I'm sure she'll regret all this tomorrow.'

Steph rambled on. 'A lovely lovely guy and you need someone luverly like our Lottie.'

225

Lottie cringed and judging by Jay's cool expression, he wasn't impressed either.

'Steph. Shut *up*.' She opened the door to usher Jay into the hall. 'Best leave her now. You've done more than enough.'

'Dong Dong Merrily on higheeeee!' Steph caterwauled from the sitting room.

'I'll see you tomorrow probably,' Lottie said. 'It's been a hell of an evening.'

'Yeah . . .' Jay said, turning to the door. 'It sure has.'

With that he walked across the garden into his own cottage.

Lottie shut her door and leaned against it, with a sigh of relief before settling down in the chair and pulling the duvet over herself. The evening hadn't ended how she'd dreamed it might but it could have been far worse: she'd stopped Steph from blabbing about Connor.

Chapter Twenty-Three

Lottie kept watch in a chair until she'd made sure Steph was OK, and finally dragged herself up to bed in the small hours. After a restless night, she got up and made herself some strong coffee and two doorstep slices of toast. The last thing she felt like doing the morning after the party was joining the clear-up group in the ballroom.

Eventually, Steph appeared in the kitchen doorway, wearing Lottie's dressing gown and a face whiter than the cottage loaf.

She leaned against the frame. 'Urghh.'

'Morning,' Lottie said, torn between sympathy and – not.

'Morning.' Steph fumbled her way onto the kitchen stool.

Lottie pushed a large mug of coffee towards her, together with a packet of paracetamol.

'Thanks. I've had two already.' She lifted the mug, sipped and pulled a face. 'That's strong enough to strip paint.'

'I thought it might help. Toast?' Lottie nibbled a slice slathered in butter and home-made apricot jam. It was her failsafe cure for a heavy night, not that she'd had many in the past year.

'Not right now.' Steph grimaced. 'Er, do you mind not crunching that toast quite so loudly?'

Lottie popped the crust in her mouth and munched louder than ever.

Steph looked at her in disgust. 'Do I detect a slight edge to the way you're devouring that innocent crust?'

'Why on earth would I be on edge?'

'I dunno, but you seem a little tetchy.'

'Really?' Lottie picked up her knife and it accidentally-on-purpose slipped onto her plate with a clatter that echoed around the kitchen.

Steph squeezed her eyes shut. 'Oh God. I'm sorry.' After another sip of coffee, during which Lottie remained silent, she said, 'I seem to recall Jay helping you get me home last night. I'm sorry if I was a pain. I'm no party animal these days and I probably shouldn't have had as much fizz as I did.'

'You were ready to celebrate. I can understand that . . .'

'You have that look: the bottled-up one. The one where you're keeping something back from me, while bursting to say it. I call it your pressure cooker look.'

'Pressure cooker?' Lottie buttered the crust of her toast. 'Don't be daft. You're imagining things.'

'I'm not. You've always done it. You're hiding something . . . I know you were when I was ill too. You were really gutted about Connor and yet I was too ill to support you properly.'

Lottie chewed her toast, and raised her eyebrows.

'What exactly did I do then?' Steph asked. 'Last night, I

228

mean. I must have been a bit lairy judging by your face and the way my head is pulsating like something from *Alien* this morning. In fact, it might explode at any moment and a slimy creature of doom will burst out.'

'Can't you remember?' Lottie said, refusing to be diverted by Steph's attempt at humour.

'Not much. I expect I might have been a bit loud . . . I might have fallen over.'

'Yes, you were loud and you fell over.'

Steph put her head in her heads and groaned. 'Anything else?'

Lottie picked her plate up. 'Oh, nothing too disastrous.'

'Nothing *too* disastrous?' She lifted her head. 'Oh my God, what did I say?'

'Like I said, nothing major . . . only that you told Jay he deserved someone "luverly" like me.'

'Oh, sh-sh sugar!' Steph squealed. 'I'm so sorry, Lottie. I can't remember saying that . . . though I did babble on quite a bit. I was muttering all kinds of stuff . . .' She sipped her coffee, avoiding Lottie's eye. 'But I'm sure Jay won't have taken any notice of me.'

Lottie's stomach knotted. 'What kind of stuff?' she said, putting down the plate again.

'Um. I might have mentioned Connor, in passing.'

Lottie's blood ran cold. 'Oh hell. I hope not. I'd thought you were going to at one point but I stopped you in time. When was this?'

'I think it must have been when he came to find me on the sofa thingy outside the ballroom. Sorry, Lottie, but it keeps

229

coming to me in snatches, like a programme that hasn't recorded properly.'

'Oh, Steph. Arghh.' Lottie winced as her own head throbbed – and not due to a hangover but the monumental mess-up.

'Look, don't panic. You can say I'm still on meds and it was the drugs talking.'

'I don't want to tell him any more lies. He has big trust issues as it is.'

Steph gave her a hard stare. 'What do you mean, "trust issues"?'

'He had a bad time with his ex. It's complicated and the main point is I didn't want him to know that Connor and I had been so close.'

Steph sighed. 'I'm sorry, hon, but I thought the secrecy was killing you anyway? Jay would probably have found out you were involved on the wedding day when the rest of Connor's clan turn up. Especially Fiona for a start. Have you thought of that?'

Lottie had – she'd hardly thought of anything else – but hoped in the moment Fiona wouldn't care who was organising the wedding. 'You're right. I should have told him but . . . I didn't want to lose the booking for Firholme and have everyone feeling sorry for me when they knew he was my ex. Plus I'd rather Jay found out when I wanted him to. Connor being my ex, is different to being an old friend.'

Steph heaved a sigh. 'Oh, crap. You're really upset about it, aren't you?'

'It's too late to worry now.'

'But you *are* worried and you're annoyed with me.' Steph's

voice took on a dangerous edge but Lottie was fired up with indignation.

'You knew I wanted to keep it quiet at work. Why couldn't you do this one thing for me?' Lottie couldn't help herself. All the disappointment and worry of the past year – more than a year – poured out in a torrent. 'When you needed me, I came through,' she said.

'And I'm grateful. Bloody grateful,' Steph shot back. 'I'm sorry I interfered in your life but you'd just split up with Connor. I told myself it didn't matter that you were spending so much time around the house with the twins. I convinced myself it would be company. I was selfish and I've thought about it many times since but I wasn't in a fit state to be sensible and thoughtful. I thought I was dying and I'd never see the girls.'

'Oh, Steph! I'm sorry. I shouldn't have taken things out on you—' Emotion bubbled up in Lottie's throat. 'But I can't help being worried about you. I remember . . .' Lottie paused. She would never forget the moment Steph was going in to the clinic for her first round of chemo. Her sister had made her swear that she'd look after the twins if Steph died. She'd made Lottie promise to be their mum. At the memory, tears rose in her eyes.

'I know . . . I'm worried about me. I'm petrified of it coming back! Of having to go through the fear and pain all over again – and never coming out of it at the end. That's probably why I had so much to drink last night. I wanted to blot out the future, forget any of the past crappy year ever happened!'

Steph started to cry, big fat tears rolling down her face.

231

Lottie went to her and held her. The tears didn't last long and Steph was smiling suddenly.

'My God, I bet we look rough . . . and . . . last night was going so well too. I was enjoying myself until everything went suddenly downhill.'

Lottie handed over a roll of kitchen towel so Steph could wipe their eyes.

She blew her nose and sighed. 'You – haven't heard from Kerr since last night, have you?'

'Not yet,' Lottie said, remembering Kerr's concern with a smile. 'But he did ask after you at the time.'

Steph shrieked in horror then held her head. 'Ouch. Bloody hell. You mean he saw me in that state?'

'He was concerned and he'd been trying to find you. He only wanted to help.'

'Oh sh – oh why did I even have any wine at all! I've seen him picking his son up from school and thought he was tasty. He's even better-looking close up and he's funny . . . and kind. But even if he did want to ask me out, he won't now after seeing me spread over the sofa in a drunken stupor.'

'He was worried about you . . . and we told him you haven't been well.'

'That makes it worse! This bloody cancer. What guy would want to take on a woman with twins who might not make it until next bloody Christmas!'

'You will make it,' Lottie said firmly. 'Come here. Big hug.'

After a moment, Lottie released her sister. 'Now get some coffee down you and go back to bed if you need to. I'm sure Kerr will be in touch to see how you are.'

'He doesn't have my number.'

'That's easily solved,' Lottie said. 'I really have to go and see what state the ballroom's in after the party and make sure there's no damage. Help yourself to breakfast. If you can't face toast, there's streaky bacon and some fresh eggs in the fridge.'

'Streaky bacon?' Steph shuddered. 'Yuk.'

'If you want a really big fry-up, I think there's even a spicy Cumberland sausage or two and some juicy black pudding.'

Steph put her hands over her ears. 'Stop torturing me. I can never face fried food again.' She stuck out her tongue in disgust. 'Or alcohol come to that.'

'Yeah, yeah . . . I believe you.'

'Yes. Um. I am sorry I ran my mouth off. I didn't mean to make your life harder. I'll never forget what you did for me and the girls. What you still do. And I hope I haven't caused too much friction with your gorgeous Jay.'

'He's not my Jay.'

'I think he could be.' Steph had a wicked look in her eye so she couldn't be feeling too bad.

'Get some rest and give the girls a huge kiss from me. Tell them I'm looking forward to their nativity play.'

'Oh, no. I just remembered I need to make a donkey and a lobster costume!'

'A lobster? In a nativity play? Good luck with that,' Lottie said, heading for the stairs, leaving Steph to stew in her own juices.

She had a headache and dry mouth herself, partly from partying, but made worse by lying awake half the night. But she had work to do. She picked her way through slush en route to the big house. The leaden skies reflected her mood.

It was bad enough having to deal with and try to hide her own feelings of sadness about the wedding, now she was worrying about Jay's reaction and she'd made Steph feel guilty. Technically, it was no business of Jay's that she'd been engaged to Connor, or even close to him. She'd told no actual lies. However, it felt like a breach of trust not to have mentioned the extent of her connection with him. She had to speak to Jay as soon as it was practical and explain why she'd kept it quiet. Maybe she wouldn't have been so worried about holding back the truth if she hadn't cared about him so much. Their kiss on the terrace had been wonderful; now, she was sure that he felt she'd let him down.

She paused on the steps to the house.

Would it be easier to simply come clean with Jay now? Trouble was, how could she broach the subject when she still wasn't exactly sure *what* Steph had told him about her relationship with Connor? She'd just have to play things by ear and hope for the best.

It was a dreary sight that greeted her when she walked into the ballroom. Most of the food and rubbish had all been cleared away by the caterers, but the floor was littered with silly string and party poppers. The murky daylight wasn't enough to penetrate far so she threw the main light switch. It flickered and then illuminated the room.

She found a broom from the cleaners' cupboard and started to sweep up, while checking that no damage had been done. There was a dirty scuff on the wall behind the celebrant's dais so she made a note to get it painted the next day. Apart from a couple of shattered baubles, the tree was intact and, under the care of Jay's team, should be fresh and well watered for the wedding ceremony. There were a lot of bashed mistletoe sprigs lying around too and when she lifted her boot, she found it sticky with squashed berries. It seemed like a metaphor for the morning after her magical kiss.

Jay walked in with a brush and some bin bags and Lottie braced herself.

'You're here already,' he said.

This wasn't a very promising start.

'I only arrived ten minutes ago.'

His reply was a grunt. He put the bin bags on the buffet table, among the discarded glasses, and cast his eye around the room. 'Some of the greenery has taken a battering but I'll refresh it all again for the wedding.'

'Thanks.' Lottie waited for him to say more but he began gathering up battered mistletoe from the floor. 'How's your sister today?' he asked without turning around.

'A bit sorry for herself but she'll survive.'

He plucked a piece of broken mistletoe from the top of a vase. 'I'm glad she had a good time,' he said, finally facing her.

'Maybe she's wishing she didn't have quite such a good time but thanks again for helping me get her home safely,' Lottie replied, wondering if he was leading in to a comment about Steph.

'No problem.' He dropped the twig in the bag.

She felt naked and stranded. 'Jay. I – some of the things Steph might have said last night. I feel I should explain.'

'You don't have to explain anything. What went on between you and Connor is your business.'

Her spirits sank to her boots. He did know then.

In her heart, she'd expected it and yet she'd clung on to a slim thread of hope that Steph had been mistaken about mentioning Connor.

'I'd prefer it if I could talk to you before anyone else. Connor and I did live together for a while but we decided to split up. These things happen,' she added lightly.

'Like I said, it's your business. I respect your decision.' He picked up a bag of rubbish, as if to signal the conversation was over.

'Oh God, someone turn off the lights!' Shayla said as she walked in wearing dark glasses. She sounded very husky.

Lottie exchanged a look with Jay that signalled any further discussion would have to wait; *if* they ever spoke to each other as more than colleagues again.

Chapter Twenty-Four

With a grim satisfaction, Jay turned up the volume on the music system at the Christmas tree centre. He'd chosen Festive Mix 3 – the one with the floor fillers that normally had even the staff humming along. Probably ones they'd been jigging around to the night before. Some of his team looked like they hadn't been to bed at all.

After helping to clear up the ballroom, he'd headed to the tree centre, churning over what he'd heard about Lottie and Connor.

Helping out Steph and Lottie had stopped him from having any more than the couple of beers and glass of champagne he'd had with dinner. That was, however, the only consolation.

A night that had been fizzing over with promise had turned as flat as the dregs in the discarded flutes. He felt he'd taken one step forward and two back. He'd had a great time with Lottie. She'd looked incredible, felt even more amazing in his arms, and as for that kiss – it sent chills through him even now, in the cold light of day. He'd wanted to whisk her off to his cottage right there and then. It wasn't only physical feelings she'd reawakened, it was hope and trust.

That prospect seemed very remote this morning.

What troubled him was the revelation about Connor. Now when he looked back, he could see the tension between them. It was obvious that Connor and Lottie had been together, and he had dumped her. Now he was engaged to another woman and allowing Lottie to arrange his wedding. Jesus, if there was an Olympic event for being a tosser, Connor would win the gold with a world record.

If Jay had thought that was the end of things, he could have accepted it but there was an elephant in the room he couldn't ignore.

The news they'd been so close threw a new and unpleasant light on the moment he'd found them together in the Bothy. Lottie had seemed guilty and upset. Was that because she was still in love with the man? However much of an arse Connor was, Lottie might still have strong feelings for him, and having to arrange his wedding must have unearthed painful memories, and maybe even made Connor have second thoughts too. As Jay knew all too well, feelings for someone you'd loved and trusted could linger way longer than you expected or wanted. Love wouldn't be dismissed to order, the disappointment – the grief – at the betrayal of a partner was hard to overcome.

His thoughts were interrupted by Kerr slouching into the marquee, holding a large mug of black coffee.

238

'Oh God, not a full day of Slade and the Darkness,' he moaned. 'I had enough of that last night and why does it have to be so bloody loud?'

'It's not loud,' said Jay wryly. 'It's normal volume.'

'If you say so . . . um . . . did you happen to see Lottie this morning?'

Jay frowned. 'I saw her while we were clearing up the ballroom. Why?'

'I wondered how her sister is after last night. I never got her number before she took ill.'

'Oh . . .' Jay was taken aback. He hadn't realised his deputy fancied Steph but he didn't want to mention her cancer in case she hadn't told Kerr so he fudged an answer. 'Um. She's OK, according to Lottie. I think she's er – on some medication and overdid the champagne a bit.'

'Thank God for that. I've been worried. She's a lovely woman.'

Jay almost fainted. This was high praise from Kerr . . . but did he mean Lottie or Steph?

'Well, I'm glad she's OK,' he said, more carefully. Jay could almost see the cogs turning in his mind.

'I'm sure Lottie could tell you more about her sister . . .' Jay said, amused by his deputy's attempts not to seem *too* interested in Steph's wellbeing. 'Why don't you ask her?'

'I might just do that,' Kerr said then added quickly: 'But there's work to be done, even if I feel like I've woken up in a Christmas prison camp where we're doomed to serve a lifetime of festive servitude.'

'Prison? This is the season of goodwill,' Jay said. 'Come on

– smile. The public will be here soon and they're expecting happy people. Where's your Santa hat?'

'Dunno. Must have lost it yesterday,' Kerr growled.

'That's OK, you can have mine.' Jay pulled his hat off and handed it over.

Kerr looked at it in disgust. 'It's too big.'

'You cheeky bugger!' Jay was forced to smile.

Kerr laughed then groaned. 'Ouch, that hurt my head.'

'Serves you right.'

A couple of other workers shuffled into the marquee, looking like they'd spent the night in a badger's hole.

He clapped his hands and felt the collective wince. 'Come on. I know you all partied hard last night and the last thing you feel like is spreading peace and joy but we have a job to do. Drink as much water and coffee as you need to get through the shift, and remember however bad you're feeling, it was self-inflicted.' He added a grin, though he felt even less joyful than the staff. 'It's not the Night of the Living Dead. It's Christmas!'

They trudged off, leaving Jay alone with his thoughts again, none of them pleasant.

The reason Connor looked so at ease in Lottie's cottage was because Connor and Lottie had lived together, shared a home and a bed. The way he'd dismissed Jay was because he was, consciously or otherwise, telling him to back off. Connor still felt that Lottie was his, which meant he might even be having regrets about marrying Keegan.

Did Lottie feel the same about Connor?

He *could* ask her, of course. He knew how he felt, despite

everything. He was in love with Lottie. He should swallow his pride and ask her how she really felt about Connor – and *him*. If only he had the courage . . . The problem was that he'd already fallen hard for Lottie and he wasn't sure he could risk being hurt all over again.

Chapter Twenty-Five

Ten days to the wedding

Setting out the chairs in the ballroom on the Wednesday after the ball, the last thing Lottie felt like facing was a wedding run-through with Keegan and Connor. The subterfuge was killing her. Jay had barely spoken to her since Sunday – and she could hardly blame him after betraying his trust just when she felt they were building something special together.

The photographer, Alok, turned up thirty minutes early to set up so Lottie showed him to the house and asked Thorsten to send up the wedding party when they arrived.

Connor arrived, bang on time, but without Keegan. His quiff was askew, and he was red in the face.

'Keegan's at the hairdresser's having her highlights done or something. I told her it was cutting it fine but she wanted this celebrity stylist woman. Apparently, this woman cut some famous actress's hair for *her* wedding. It was the only day this bloody woman could fit her in.'

'Where's the salon?' Lottie asked.

'Cartmel. It's in a posh hotel. The one with the Michelin star.'

'Wow. That's a long journey to make . . .'

'I told her it was bloody miles away but she set off at six a.m. She should be on her way now. I just hope my sister turns up. She's about as reliable as the weather.'

A few minutes later, as if to prove him wrong, Lottie saw Alicia Moran jump out of a battered Toyota truck outside the house and stride up the steps straight into the vestibule, leaving a trail of mud from her boots. She ran a riding school a couple of miles from Firholme and had clearly come straight from the stables because she was in jodhpurs, boots and a padded jacket that had a strong whiff of horse about it. Although Connor had assured Lottie that Alicia was sworn to secrecy about their previous relationship, Lottie's stomach had been churning for the past hour. Outspoken and funny, Alicia was the life and soul of any family gathering, but diplomacy was definitely not her strong point.

'Hello again! Fancy seeing you here,' she declared, giving Lottie a hug.

'For God's sake, Alicia. Keegan might have seen you,' Connor complained.

'But she hasn't and anyway, I thought you told me she already knows we know Lottie.'

'Only as acquaintances,' Connor said. 'Not on hugging terms.'

'Sorry.' Alicia didn't look sorry at all. 'Where is Keegan anyway?'

'At the hairdressers in Cartmel.'

'Cartmel!' Alicia burst out laughing. 'That's hours away. What's wrong with the local salon in Keswick?'

Connor swore. 'It's her wedding, Alicia, what do you expect?'

'Would you like to meet the photographer?' Lottie said hastily, feeling the tension between Connor and Alicia who didn't get on at the best of times.

When she opened the doors into the ballroom, Alicia's eyes widened like saucers. 'Bloody hell, this is like Buckingham Palace compared to how it used to be. I remember Mum used to bring us for tea sometimes. It's a fantastic setting but I always thought the hotel itself was a bit run-down and fogeyish. Bugger me, but it's like a totally different place now.'

Meanwhile Connor paced the other side of the ballroom, his phone clamped to his ear. His face fell and he let out a groan of frustration. Lottie could tell he was talking to Keegan and imagined she could hear faint squeaks from the mobile.

Lottie knew the photographer from previous weddings they'd worked on together.

'OK. Calm down. I'm sure they can fix it. Don't leave until you're satisfied . . . Tell them we'll sue if you're not happy! OK. OK, nutkin. I'll try and sort it out.'

'Nutkin?' Alicia made a barfing action behind Connor's back.

'OK. I'll sort it. I'll try to delay him.' He held the phone away from his ear. 'Babe, calm down. If you really can't make it, I'll call it off.'

The photographer took Lottie aside. 'I hate to make a fuss

244

but is the bride planning to come? I've got a shoot at the Grasmere hotel and I can't leave it much longer.'

Connor shoved his mobile in his jacket pocket and strode over. 'Keegan's having a bit of a mare at the hairdresser's. Apparently she says the colour makes her look like Marge Simpson and she's got to stay to have it redone.'

Alicia sputtered but Lottie had a horrible vision of Keegan turning apoplectic in the salon and throwing hairbrushes at the stylist.

'Oh no. How frustrating for her. I'm so sorry. She won't be able to make it, then?'

'You're telling me.' He turned to Alok. 'I'm sorry, it's all off, mate, unless you can hang around for an hour or so. I'd appreciate it.'

'I'd love to but I've another appointment in Grasmere. I can't cancel that at this stage.'

'Jesus.' Connor shoved his hands through his hair. 'I suppose it can't be helped. I presume you'll deduct the cost of this run-through from the wedding package?'

'Well I've still had to spend the time here, Mr Moran . . .' Lottie thought Alok was showing admirable restraint.

'You mean, you'll still charge us even though you haven't actually taken any photographs?'

'I'll have to charge something to cover my time and travel costs.'

Connor sneered. 'Clearly, I ought to go into the wedding business instead of insurance. They seem to be a little gold mine.'

Annoyed at his rudeness, Lottie took charge. 'Actually, I

think I have a solution. It's very disappointing that Keegan can't be here but we can still have a quick run-through and check all the camera angles.'

'How?'

'Alicia can stand in for Keegan.'

'What?' She pulled a face. 'No way am I walking up the aisle with my own brother. Eww.'

'What are you?' Connor snapped. 'Twelve?'

Alicia grinned. 'I'll be the vicar.'

'Registrar. We're not in church if you hadn't noticed.'

'Ohh, tetchy.'

Lottie had to stifle her laughter. Despite her tactlessness, Alicia could be very funny.

'Why doesn't Lottie stand in?' Alicia suggested, and Lottie immediately reversed her opinion.

'I'm sure there's no need for that.'

'Er . . .' Connor's jaw dropped so low, it was a wonder it didn't bounce off the parquet floor. 'Perhaps it would be better to cancel after all.'

Lottie squirmed in horror but Alok launched in, understandably keen to get the job done and keep his clients happy. 'Hey. That's a great idea. Shame not to have the Real Deal but Lottie will do nicely as a stand-in.'

Even though it was a good solution, Lottie could have killed him.

In contrast, Alicia was gleeful. 'Great, sorted.' She climbed onto the dais, leaving a trail of mud from her riding boots.

Connor stared at Lottie. 'I'm glad someone's happy,' he said sarcastically. 'And I think this the best we're going to do.'

'I'm not sure Keegan will be happy,' Lottie murmured, while Alok was busy unearthing yet another piece of equipment.

Connor held up his arm. 'Would you mind?' he said.

Lottie's heart was almost too full to reply. So many conflicting emotions fought a battle. Anger, and underlying them, regret. She'd loved him once, looked forward to a moment such as this – for all of a few days. The thought of standing at an altar – well, a registrar's desk – as stand-in for another woman, with Connor, was excruciating.

Alok interrupted them. 'Right, folks. We could do with someone to give you away . . . Hey, Jay!' he called, zeroing in on the open door to the vestibule where Jay was unfolding a stepladder.

Lottie stifled a squeak of dismay. 'I think Jay's probably rather busy . . .'

Alok grinned. 'He won't mind. We only want to borrow him for a minute.'

'You two know each other?' Lottie said, while Connor stood by with a face like thunder.

'Yeah. I've done some jobs at Greythwaite where Jay used to work.' He called to Jay. 'You don't mind, do you? It's an emergency.'

Jay walked in. 'Don't mind what?'

'Escorting Lottie into the room. We need a father-of-the-bride and the bride herself can't be here. I want to check the shots. It'll only take a few minutes.'

Lottie cringed as Jay exchanged a glance with her. 'I'm happy to help but I'm in my work clothes.'

'So's Alicia,' Connor said tartly. 'So, one more won't matter.'

Alicia pursed her lips and Lottie saw her mouth move in a silent swear word, probably because she'd missed out on the chance to get her hands on Jay, as well as being annoyed with Connor.

Lottie stiffened, anticipating a full-on row but Jay provided a distraction.

'I was about to go into the drawing room to water the trees and fix some faulty lights,' he said. 'But that can wait.' Jay rested his ladder on the wall.

'Thank you,' Lottie said. 'It'll only take a few minutes.'

He addressed himself to Lottie alone. 'I really don't mind,' he said. Was that a glint in his eye? 'Though I've no idea what I'm supposed to be doing.'

'All you have to do is wait outside the door with me and when we get the cue, we walk into the room together . . .'

'If everyone's ready, shall we get started?' Alok shouted

Connor moved into place but Alicia was ogling Jay with undisguised lust. Lottie knew exactly how she felt.

'Can you go out and walk in, please?' Alok called, camera in his hand.

Lottie went outside with Jay. 'Thank you,' she said, about to add he didn't have to take it too seriously but it was too late.

He held out his arm. Despite his scruffy jeans, sweatshirt and tousled hair, she found him just as gorgeous as in his tux. The memory of that electrifying kiss, and the disaster that followed came back to her.

His eyes glinted with a look that gave her hope that he'd forgiven her deception about Connor and wanted to move on. 'Ready?'

'As I'll ever be . . .'

She slipped her arm through his.

'Dum-dum-di-dum . . .' Alicia hummed from the ballroom.

Jay shook his head but there was a smile on his face.

'We're not having the "Bridal March",' Connor said. 'We're having "The Arrival of the Queen of Sheba". Keegan thinks it's classier.'

'Really?' Alicia said. 'What about "I Should be So Lucky" by Kylie Minogue?'

'You're so funny, Alicia,' Connor said icily.

Alok snapped away, asking them to pause halfway to the dais where Connor waited.

'OK. Connor, turn and look back at your bride and look gobsmacked at her gorgeousness,' Alok joked, as the shutter clicked endlessly.

Connor didn't look gobsmacked. He had a face like thunder, and Lottie could only think that he seemed jealous . . . jealous that she was with Jay, but how was that possible when he was about to marry Keegan?

Finally, they reached the dais but Jay showed no sign of letting go of Lottie's arm. She didn't know whether to pull it away. She didn't want to.

While Connor had a smile on his face, his expression was stony. 'I think this is where I take over, mate,' he said.

In a moment, Jay let go of her and she was face to face with Connor.

He smiled softly. 'Lottie?' he murmured, holding her gaze. There was a tenderness and intensity behind that look, which threw her back over a year, to the night on the beach when he'd asked her to marry him. The joy and excitement of that moment rushed back and made her stomach flip all over again.

'I think that'll do,' Alok called.

Snapping out of her trance, Lottie stepped away from Connor and swung around to thank Jay but he was already metres away. 'If you don't need me any more, I'll get on with my work,' he muttered.

'I think we're done with you,' Connor cut in. 'Thanks for standing in. You played the part of Keegan's dad well.'

Lottie was sure he'd emphasised the word 'dad'.

'Thanks, Jay,' she called.

'You're welcome,' he said and, with a brief smile, he left. Lottie was assailed by emotions. The feel of Jay's arm through hers, the longing look on his face when they'd waited together outside the ballroom. Then, Connor, staring at her with an intensity that had thrown her back to one heady night when their future had sparkled like a diamond.

The loss had taken her by surprise but so had the look in Jay's eyes.

She had the strangest feeling she'd been standing at a fork in the road: one way lay the past and the other the future, yet she couldn't decide which to choose.

Chapter Twenty-Six

Nine days to the wedding

After the drama of the ball and the wedding run-through, Lottie was relieved to immerse herself in family life, by helping Steph with the nativity costumes. It had taken them several evenings until late to get them ready for the play, which was taking place the week after, at the end of term just days before the wedding. Despite her hectic schedule, Lottie wasn't going to miss the play for the world. She hoped Steph had found the frantic cutting and sewing had helped to take her mind up off the scan she had the next day. Despite all her offers, Steph had insisted that Lottie shouldn't take extra time off come to the actual scan with her and Lottie had had to agree but was adamant she would go with her to get the results.

For a short time, the sewing had helped keep Lottie's thoughts from dwelling on the bizarre wedding 'rehearsal'.

Since she'd walked up the 'aisle' with Jay, she'd seen him in passing, going in and out of the cottage and crossing the stable yard to the offices, but they hadn't spoken.

'Ow!' Lottie cried out.

'Auntie Lottie! You've prickled your finger!' Myra cried, bringing Lottie back to reality.

'Like Sleeping Beauty,' Jodie said. 'There's blood on your finger.'

'Oh. It's only a tiny drop,' Lottie said, sucking her finger where the needle had cut it. She dabbed it with a tissue and resolved to concentrate on the job in hand.

Myra's donkey had proved relatively simple, fashioned from a grey fleecy throw and an Eeyore hat that Myra already had. It turned out that she'd volunteered for the role of donkey precisely *because* of the Eeyore hat. It had seen some action and needed some running repairs.

The lobster was more of a challenge.

'Bloody *Love Actually* has a lot to answer for!' Steph declared, explaining that Jodie had seen a trailer clip of it on the TV and been adamant that no other creature would do.

'She was probably high on poster paint fumes at the time,' Steph had said, frantically googling 'How to make a lobster costume'. 'I'd completely missed the email from the school!'

Steph had managed to get a lobster hat from a dodgy fancy dress site on the Internet. With some fiddling around with a scarlet catsuit from the dance shop and an old pair of gardening gloves and barbecue tongs, they'd managed to fashion some 'claws'.

'While you're at the hospital tomorrow, I'll go into Keswick to try and get some brown tights for Myra,' Lottie said, looking at the costumes hung on the doorframe.

'Thanks, you're a star. If by some miracle, you see any red tissue paper, can you get some?' Steph asked. 'We could make the claws look a bit more realistic.'

'I'll do my best,' Lottie said.

The twins squashed onto the sofa with Lottie. 'Is Jay coming to the nativity play?' Myra asked her.

'I don't think so, darling.'

Steph held up her hands. 'It wasn't my idea!'

'Please ask him, Auntie Lottie!' The squeals hurt her ears.

'He's very busy at the moment,' Lottie insisted, not wanting to have to ask him but also wanting to do anything she could to make the girls happy and Steph's life a little easier.

'Promise you'll ask him!'

'Girls, don't get your hopes up. Jay probably can't leave the Christmas tree centre.'

'Please try . . .' Myra's upturned face, and hopeful eyes, pierced right through Lottie. 'OK, I'll ask him but don't get too excited yet.'

'Will he bring the reindeer?' Jodie asked.

Lottie sighed. Asking two five-year-olds not to get excited was like trying to ask them not to look forward to Christmas too much. As for Jay, after the ball and the rehearsal, she'd no idea how he was going to react – to the invitation or to her.

While Steph was at the hospital, Lottie went into Keswick, on her mission to help with the costume bits and bobs and do some Christmas shopping for the family. They'd agreed with their parents to save their present exchange for when they came over in early spring so there was no rush to post their gifts to them. She still wished they could have celebrated together, but they'd been twice already since Steph had been diagnosed and couldn't afford the sky-high Christmas flights.

It boosted her spirits to see that Christmas had seized the little town with a vengeance, and there were hordes of people filling the shops, pubs and a festive food market that was camped in front of the old town hall. Having found the finishing touches for the costumes, she started her own shopping, ending in Abbott's, a chocolate shop that was sheer confectionery heaven. She loved buying her Christmas gifts from there, and apparently so did half the Lakes as the place was rammed with locals, kids and walkers with backpacks.

She fought her way to the novelty animals display, her basket bulging with truffles, pralines and chocolate liqueurs. There were some cute packs of foiled chocolate reindeer that would make a lovely stocking filler for the twins.

'Ow!' She cried out as someone's wire basket dug into her hip.

'Oh, I'm so sorry!'

'I'm OK—' Lottie inhaled sharply with shock. 'Oh my God, Fiona!'

Fiona's face lit up. 'Lottie. Hello, how lovely to – erm – bump into you.'

Panicking at being caught so unprepared, Lottie embraced Connor's mother with her free hand. 'Gosh. You too.'

'I must apologise about bashing you.' Fiona rolled her eyes. 'I'm still a little clumsy after the Thing.'

254

'The Thing? You mean the stroke?' Lottie said. 'I heard. I'm sorry.'

'Yes, my stroke.' Fiona looked puzzled. 'I call it the Creature from the Black Lagoon as it struck so suddenly from the depths.' She smiled. 'If you already know about it, I'm guessing Alicia told you – or did you hear about it from someone else?'

'Alicia . . .' Lottie scrabbled for a reply, trying to work out at lightning speed what she was meant to know about Fiona and who from. 'Erm . . .' The horror at having to be ready to tell another pack of lies to keep Connor's secret flooded her. Her secret too, since she'd agreed to continue with it.

'Alicia said she'd bumped into you at Firholme when she was walking the dogs?' Fiona said.

'Oh yes, of course. Yes, it must have been then.'

'Excuse *me*!' A woman in a huge Russian fur hat barged past Fiona, squashing her against the Kendal Mint Cake gift boxes.

'How rude,' Lottie said as the woman charged off towards the festive biscuit tower, elbowing everyone out of the way.

'Some people wouldn't recognise Christmas spirit if it bit them on the bottom!' Fiona declared. 'Have you finished your shopping?' she asked, nodding at Lottie's basket.

'I just need to get two packs of milk choc mini reindeers,' Lottie said, before adding, 'For Steph's girls.'

Fiona smiled. 'You mustn't fail in that mission. Shall we pay up and go for a cuppa and a catch-up if you have time, then? It's getting dangerous in here and I'm not great with crowds these days.'

'Yes. I . . .' Lottie started. Under any other circumstances, Lottie would have been desperate to spend time with Fiona, but she was conscious of the danger she'd be in of letting slip anything about the wedding.

'If you're too busy, I honestly won't be offended. Alicia told me you run Firholme these days. How wonderful, I absolutely adore that place.'

'Well, I don't exactly run it. I'm the w— the events manager.'

'Still, sounds like a big job, but I'm sure you have the place ticking over like clockwork.'

'In my dreams,' said Lottie, then deciding it was worth the risk, 'and I'd like to have a quick cuppa. It's been a long time.'

'It has,' Fiona said, her eyes wistful. 'Oh quick, I can see a gap around the reindeer. Tell you what, I'll join the queue while you grab them so we can save more time for our chat.'

Lottie was glad Fiona had suggested the plan, as it gave her a minute or two to marshal her thoughts while she selected the gifts for the girls. With a careful eye on the progress of the queue, she hovered around the display and added two chocolate Santas to her basket to give her an excuse to hold back a while longer. It was obvious Alicia had mentioned they'd met. Maybe Alicia had let it slip then covered her tracks with the dog-walking story.

She braced herself and rejoined Fiona. Soon after, they left the shop and went into a nearby café.

'My treat. It's been so long,' Fiona said, picking up the menu.

'How are you?' Lottie said, reminding herself to tread carefully.

'Oh, I'm on the mend. Much much better than I was.'

Lottie listened as Fiona told her a little more about the

stroke, how shocked she'd been and the long process of recovery. The waitress brought frothy cappuccinos and slices of Cumberland Rum Nicky tart.

'I haven't had this for years,' Lottie said, cutting a morsel off the pastry with her cake fork. The tart smelled divine, filled with juicy dates, ginger and rum and served warm with cream.

'Nor me.' Fiona cut her slice up with a knife. Noticing Lottie's look she explained, 'The stroke affected my left arm. So, this is easier than using a fork, though I've learned to use my other hand for a lot of things.' She rolled her eyes.

They chatted about how busy the town was and Lottie told Fiona about the twins and their play, leaving out the part about Steph's own health problems. She didn't want to darken the mood. Fiona would probably be glad of a happy conversation.

They'd finished their cake when Fiona finally went quiet before speaking up again. 'Lottie, I have to mention this, but did you know that Connor's back?'

'I had . . . heard,' Lottie said, feeling awful. 'On the grapevine.'

'Yes, I – I suppose you know he has a girlfriend, then,' Fiona said. 'Fiancée, actually. I'm sorry.'

'No need to be sorry. We split up well over a year ago now.'

'Hmm. I'm glad you see it like that. You're very generous to him. More generous than he deserves, even if he is my son. It can't have been a happy year for any of us. I heard your sister had been ill from a friend whose grandchildren go to her school. She's back at work now, isn't she? That must be a good sign.'

'We hope so. She's got an MRI today in fact. She didn't want me to go with her though I offered. It ought to be over now, fingers crossed,' Lottie said, holding up her hand.

Fiona gave her a soothing smile. 'That must be worrying. I do understand how you must feel.'

'It is . . . but she's trying to stay positive. We all are.'

'What about your parents? Are they still abroad?'

'Yes, they are.'

'You must miss them.'

'We do. Especially with everything going on with Steph. They both have full-time jobs out there, but we hope they're coming over in the early spring.'

'That's something to look forward to, but I do know how it feels to have family so far away since Connor went to Australia. You might have heard he moved?' Fiona said.

Lottie braced herself for more fibs. It was becoming a habit. 'Um, now you come to mention it, I did,' she said, as casually as she could.

'Connor and Keegan are staying in the village for Christmas. You might even bump into them. I tried to suggest we all go up to Firholme to get a Christmas tree but they didn't seem enthusiastic for some reason. Derrick kept on about them dropping needles everywhere so in the end, I let him get the artificial one down from the loft as usual.'

Lottie felt every response to this stick in her throat. Even though the wedding would be a lovely surprise, she felt she'd have to tie herself in more and more knots so she simply smiled and nodded.

'I've heard how great Firholme looks after the renovations

and I've seen the website photos. I'm determined to visit before Christmas if I can pin down Derrick or Connor and Alicia.'

'You must come . . . if you can't make it before Christmas, then in the New Year when it will be so much more peaceful,' Lottie said hastily then added what she hoped would be the clincher for Fiona to wait. 'I'd have time to give you a personal tour.'

'Oh my. That would be fabulous! I'd love to. Maybe we can meet up properly if you have time? Have lunch together?'

'I'd like that.' Lottie was relieved but still squirmed with guilt.

'Let's not lose touch again because I like to think we became friends, even though I'm Connor's mother. I wanted to call you after you and Connor split up but he convinced me that it would make things worse. I've missed our shopping trips, Sunday lunch . . . Keegan is a lovely girl but it's not the same. Gosh that's so disloyal of me.'

'You'll get to know her better.'

'I hope so. If they stay in the UK and don't go back to Australia. I want them to have an amazing life but I've missed Connor and when they eventually get married one day or have children, I'll miss out on seeing them too.' Fiona fiddled with her spoon nervously, her eyes glinting. 'Keegan says there's the Internet – and they'll also fly me out if that happens – but it's not the same is it? After my scare, I try not to let the family know but I am worried that I'll never see my grand-children grow up.'

Lottie wanted to hug her. 'I'm sure you will,' she said. 'But I also know how you feel. My parents were worried about

Steph not being around for the twins, so I can't imagine how she felt. I agree we need to make the most of every moment.'

'We do! And even if Connor and Keegan stay here and start a family, what about Keegan's parents? They'd be in the same boat as us.' She shook her head. 'All these shows on TV where people emigrate to sunny climes and want to start again. I'd never tell Connor, but I can't watch them any more. There, I'm being silly.'

'Not at all.' She smiled at Fiona. 'I hope they stay in this country, for your sake,' Lottie said. 'Keegan seems to love it here.'

Fiona frowned.

'I mean Keegan sounds as if she loves it here. To come over and stay for so long,' Lottie added. 'Aarghh, is that the time? I'm afraid I do need to go now. I want to call Steph and see if she's finished at the hospital yet and of course, we need to finish the costumes.'

'Of course. OK, it's been wonderful to see you and we'll catch up again soon, I hope?'

'Very soon,' Lottie said, eager to escape before she blurted out the truth to Fiona. She exhaled in relief the moment she was out in the street. Hopefully Fiona would forgive her, and after the wedding was over, Lottie was determined not to lose touch again – no matter what Connor said or did. She'd reached the car when Steph rang, relieved that the scan was done and about to head home. At least, that part of the process was over, Lottie thought, as she drove to her sister's with cake and the rest of the costumes. Now all they had to do was wait for the results.

Chapter Twenty-Seven

Five days to the wedding

On Mondays, the Christmas tree centre was closed so, technically, it was Jay's day off. However, a gale the previous evening had finally brought down a large branch from one of the oaks in the woods, blocking one of the main walking routes.

Needing solace and hoping to stop his churning mind, Jay had decided to clear away the branch. Even as he collected the chain saw from the truck, he couldn't help thinking: was Lottie still in love with Connor Moran or not?

Did she even know herself?

He'd loved the feel of her arm in his and longed to kiss her again the way he had at the ball. His disappointment at finding she and Connor were once together had cooled a little. How could he refuse a chance to get close to her again?

Then, he'd seen the way she looked at Connor in the

wedding run-through. She'd seemed transfixed by the man. Was it simply old memories surfacing or was Lottie falling for her ex all over again?

One thing Jay did know: he'd fallen for *her* and his vows not to let someone get close to him again had been broken.

The last thing he ever wanted was to fall for a woman who was in love with someone else and yet perhaps it was already too late . . .

In one last effort to tame his raging thoughts, he donned his safety gear and started to cut up the wood.

It was a clear day with a bitter wind blowing, but underneath his hoodie and hi-vis, Jay was sweating. He didn't care. What else was he going to do? Mope about in his cottage? Go Christmas shopping? All the 'normal' things that people – families – did at this time of year felt off-limits to him.

Luckily Trevor didn't care about Christmas and Jay had brought him along for company for both of them. He'd scurried about at a safe distance, sending piles of leaves flying into the air but was now sitting proudly on the driver's seat of the truck, gazing over the steering wheel, as if he was in charge of operations, and not Jay.

Jay set the chainsaw in motion and was hard at work when Trevor shot out of the door and past him. He turned off the saw. 'Trevor!' he shouted and pulled off his ear defenders.

Trevor was already 'greeting' Connor on the path nearby. There was no way Jay would have heard him, with the saw going and ear defenders on. Trevor's version of a greeting was to hare around Connor, snuffling at his boots.

Connor backed away. 'Get off me!'

'Trevor. Heel!' he shouted.

Although Jay would have been happy to let Trevor jump all over Connor's designer country clothes, he was aware that not everyone loved dogs.

After a quick sniff at Connor's jeans, Trevor trotted back to Jay. 'Truck, Trev,' he ordered and miraculously, Trevor obeyed, jumping into the seat, sitting upright and watching out of the window like a nosy neighbour.

Connor nodded at the pile of sawn timber. 'That looks like hard work,' he said. 'I used to play here when I was a lad. Climb the trees, walk the fells. It's beautiful.'

'It is . . . but, you should know that this area is cordoned off temporarily until we've cleared the tree,' Jay said, wondering how Connor hadn't seen the warning signs.

'Yes, I saw the cones but I wanted to talk to you.' Connor's tone made it clear he'd thought the rules didn't apply to him.

'Is it about the tree or the decorations for the wedding?' Jay asked.

'No. They're great. Keegan loves them.' Connor scuffed his boot through the fallen leaves. 'Actually, I wanted to discuss the situation with Lottie.'

Jay's stomach flipped. 'Lottie? I don't see what you can have to say about her to me,' he said sharply, then regretted his overreaction.

Connor looked him up and down. 'You like her, don't you?' he said, ignoring Jay's comment. 'I've seen the way you look at each other. I saw your face when you walked her down the aisle last week.'

'That was just work. I was asked to help and I did.'

Connor laughed. 'It didn't look like work to me. You were enjoying it too much.'

Jay's patience was stretched too far. 'OK. I don't know what this is about, mate, and I'm aware you're a guest of Firholme, but I don't think that gives you a right to intrude into my private life, or Lottie's for that matter.'

'I didn't say I had a right but I *am* concerned about her. From your reaction, I'm guessing I've touched a raw nerve and my hunch was right. You're keen on her.' Jay was too annoyed to reply, so Connor jumped into the gap. 'I'm also guessing you've realised that Lottie and I were close.'

'I worked that one out,' Jay said, not wanting to drop Lottie in it. He'd no idea how much Connor knew.

'From Lottie?' Connor asked.

'Like I say, I worked it out but the details are none of my business, and,' he added firmly, 'I don't intend to make them my business either.'

'No need to be so salty,' Connor said. 'I can see I've touched a raw nerve. I don't blame you. Lottie's a lovely girl and I still feel . . . protective of her.'

Jay bit back a very rude word and picked up the chainsaw again. 'Where's this leading? I'm busy.'

'Chopping down trees?' Connor smirked. 'I can see that.'

Some guys, thought Jay wryly, wouldn't risk riling a man with a chainsaw in his hands. However, Connor appeared not to have noticed that fact.

'Look. Why would you have a problem with me and Lottie getting together?'

'No problem. Only I'm not sure you know her like I do.

She's sensitive, she feels deeply, she's very loyal. You may think she's capable, has everything under control – that she's happy but I can see much deeper.'

'Right. Good for you,' Jay said, ready to fire up the chainsaw. He turned his back.

'You're not right for her. You'll only get hurt if you carry on going after her. She's still on the rebound from me. I think that was obvious from what happened the other day at the Bothy.'

'What do you mean?' Jay snapped round.

Connor had a smirk on his face. 'Nothing . . . all I'm saying is that I think Lottie found it hard to let me go. If you know what I mean.'

Jay felt a bit sick. He knew exactly what Connor meant because he'd felt the same way himself and Lottie had looked . . . guilty was the only way of describing it, when he'd walked in on her and Connor. They were standing very close. Might they have been doing more than simply talking?

He wouldn't put anything past Connor.

'Thanks for the tip,' he muttered. 'But you'll forgive me if I don't take your relationship counselling too seriously.'

Connor curled his lip. 'That's a bit rude, considering we're paying your employer a shedload of money to have our wedding here. I'd at least expect some civility from the staff. Man, you are going to regret this.'

Jay lost it. 'Mate, I've regretted a lot of things but telling you you're a massive arse isn't one of them.'

Connor snorted in contempt. 'You do know I could report you to your boss but I'm bigger than that. I'll just leave you with this. Lottie's still in love with me. You might think she's impressed by you and your chainsaw and the whole strong silent thing but she's never really let go of me and—'

Jay pushed his ear defenders down and pulled the cord of the saw, cutting off Connor's tirade. He turned his back and attacked the branch, taking out his indignation on it. The arrogance of Connor. The man relished the prospect of Lottie pining for him and being miserable and yet he seemed to have no intention of ditching his current fiancée and trying to get Lottie back. Jay felt like marching down to Firholme right this minute and telling both Lottie and Keegan what a weak and manipulative little tosser Connor was.

He couldn't do that of course . . .

He turned off the saw.

When he looked round, Connor was gone. Maybe to moan to Shayla, and get him the sack.

Jay didn't care – but oh, shit, if Connor *did* tell tales to Shayla, that meant Lottie could be in trouble. Not to mention that winding Jay up was probably exactly what Connor wanted . . . if only he could be sure how she really felt about Connor – and Jay himself?

'Jeez, what a mess!' His groan brought Trevor running from the truck to his side. Jay pulled his gloves off and crouched down by Trevor, rubbing his back for comfort. Trevor returned the favour by rolling over and let his hind legs flap apart, proudly displaying his bits.

Jay took it as a compliment. 'Thanks for that, Trev. I appreciate the solidarity.'

Jay tickled his chest and Trevor yipped in happiness.

'I really want to be a dog,' he said. 'Humans are either arseholes like Connor or Ben, or I fall in love with them.' Like Nadia. Like Lottie.

After he'd finished working on the branch, he took the wood back to the forest centre then drove Trevor home to the cottage. He didn't know whether to warn Lottie or gamble that Connor wouldn't actually go to Shayla.

Would she be angry that he'd let Connor provoke him and risked her getting into trouble?

He pulled up in front of the cottage, staring at the dark windows of the Bothy.

'Surely, she can't possibly still love a prat like Connor?' he said to Trevor, sitting in the front footwell.

Trevor rested his muzzle on the seat and looked back at Jay.

He ruffled his ears. 'Things must be bad if I'm asking a dog for advice on my love life.'

That was the problem. Jay had no more clue about how Lottie really felt than Trevor did.

He walked home and as he neared the cottage, Lottie was getting out of her car, laden with bags.

'Oh. Hello!' she said. She seemed flustered and dropped two of the bags onto the ground.

Jay picked them up and handed them to her. 'Looks like quite a spree,' he said.

She was pink-cheeked from the cold air, and swathed in a soft scarf that brought out the green in her eyes. His row with Connor brought a fresh pang of guilt, but only in case he got Lottie into trouble. He didn't regret tearing a strip off the man for a moment.

Seeing Lottie now, he felt it was ridiculous that she and Connor might have something going on.

Her smile was wary. 'Thanks.'

He decided to draw her out, hoping to find out more. 'Abbott's. That's my kind of shopping,' he said, seeing the carriers.

'Yes. It's chocolate for the girls, and some stuff for their costumes in the nativity play.'

'They still have those?'

'It's a very loose interpretation. Jodie is the donkey. Myra is playing the role of the lobster.'

'Lobster? I didn't pay much attention in RE but even I don't recall a lobster in the stable. Was there one?'

'There was in *Love Actually*. And in this play there's also a Minion, a Baby Olaf and a kangaroo apparently.' Her smile lit up her eyes and he was filled with relief, but in a moment, she seemed awkward again. 'Um. I know you're too busy and won't be able to come, but I swore to the girls that I'd pass on an invite from them. They'd love you to come to see the play.'

'Me?'

'Yes. It's probably not your scene . . . and it's this Wednesday. I'm sure you're working.'

The words slipped out before he could stop them. Maybe he hadn't wanted to stop them and it was an opportunity to try and find out more about her real feelings for Connor. 'As a matter of fact, I have the afternoon off.'

'Really?'

'Yes.'

'So, you really *want* to come?' Lottie sounded astonished.

'If you're sure it's OK with Steph – and you?'

'It's not up to me.'

This wasn't very encouraging but it was too late to back out now.

'Erm . . . shall we go along together then?' she offered. 'I'll pick you up at one forty-five?'

'OK. Thanks.'

'Bye, then.'

Taking her bags from him, she walked off and let herself into the Bothy.

Jay was none the wiser if she'd wanted him to go along or not. He didn't know if he should have agreed and – much as he liked the girls – a school nativity play ought to have been his idea of hell. However, the temptation to spend more time in Lottie's company, and discover whether Connor's claims were true, was far too tempting.

Chapter Twenty-Eight

Four days to the wedding

With four days to go, wedding fever had seized Firholme. Lottie was like a cat on a hot tin roof, attending to last-minute details, and double- and triple-checking that suppliers and staff knew exactly what they had to do on the day. On Friday morning, the florists would arrive, along with the lighting and electricians to set up ready for the band and DJ. Despite having overseen dozens of weddings, she was aware that there would be snags but it felt vital that this one went without a hitch.

Shayla walked in on Lottie to find her calming down with a few deep breathing exercises.

She dumped her bag on the table. 'What's up? You seem flustered.'

'I am – I was. The wedding car company are having trouble with the vintage Rolls that Keegan wanted. They might have to substitute it with a newer model. I don't know whether to warn her or not.'

'What would you normally do?'

'Call the bride and try to reassure her. We can't switch suppliers at this late stage so I'm afraid she'll have no choice. They'll give her a discount, of course, but I don't think that'll compensate for not having this Silver Ghost she'd set her heart on.'

'That's for the hire car company to sort out,' Shayla said curtly.

'Yes, but I have to break the news as it's part of our package.'

'Anything else I can help with?' Shayla asked.

'There have been a few issues with the boiler and electrics at the big house. With a cold snap forecast, we need to make sure they won't cause problems. We can't have a shivering bride and wedding guests.'

'Maintenance will make it a priority,' Shayla said. 'I'll go and see the supervisor now and impress on him how important it is.'

'Thanks, because with everything going at full blast, we don't want a breakdown.'

'Lottie, please stop worrying. You've put in place contingency plans for every eventuality and I've seen you swing into action to deal with any crisis. Darling, that's why I hired you. You can handle it. I have every confidence in you.'

Lottie nodded gratefully; she knew she was letting the stress get to her more than usual. 'Thanks.' Her phone pinged. 'Sorry, must get back to the florist. Wholesaler's been let down

271

for the wattle flower Keegan wanted in her bouquet for an Australian touch. Oh, and don't forget I need to slip out tomorrow afternoon for the girls' nativity play.'

'I hadn't forgotten. Enjoy yourself and forget about this damn thing for a few hours. It's not life and death.' She smiled. 'Family is what matters and as for the rest? It's just a wedding like any other.'

'I appreciate your faith,' Lottie said, thinking that Shayla had missed the point, although she wasn't to know why. This wasn't a wedding like any other.

First, however, she had the nativity play to look forward to – and now it came with the added complication of Jay.

Chapter Twenty-Nine

Three days to the wedding

The twins' school was tiny but it seemed as if half the village had crammed into the assembly hall. Lottie and Jay stood at the back, leaving the chairs for the parents like Steph and people less able to stand.

She knew he'd never let the girls down – or anyone – after he'd made a promise.

The contrast with Connor was not lost on her, but nonetheless, Jay hadn't suddenly become overcome by festive spirit either. He barely uttered a word on the journey to the school, but she got the feeling he was churning over something in his mind and constantly on the verge of saying it. He was almost impossible to read. She was sure she'd lost his trust after the ball – despite that wonderful kiss – but their walk up the aisle at the run-through had given her fresh hope.

Right up until he'd walked off. She certainly never expected him to agree to come to the play.

Part of her wished she'd never passed on the invitation.

It might have been an unusual nativity play, but no one seemed to care. The sound of children's voices, singing and saying their much-practised lines brought a lump to her throat. The hall seemed to tremble with emotion, and the quiet moments were punctuated by sniffles and the rasp of handbag zips as people fumbled for tissues.

Even though she was bursting with pride, Lottie didn't want to be caught blubbing with Jay at her side and just about held it together. He joined in with the gentle laughter when 'Mary' took 'Baby Jesus' from the cot and almost dropped him onto the hay bale. However, when the Donkey handed over a gift to 'Baby Jesus', she had to wrinkle her nose to stem the tears. By the time the Lobster had sung the first few lines of 'Away in a Manger', the tears were trickling down her cheeks.

She felt Jay press something soft into her clenched fingers.

'It's brand new,' he whispered. 'I brought it just in case.'

Lottie gave in and dabbed at her eyes with his handkerchief. He was a good man, she thought to herself: kind and thoughtful, but she felt he was in turmoil. She was convinced he liked her but was he still in love with Nadia?

The lights dimmed and figures crept onto the darkened stage before the scene was lit up once more. There were wails from the manger and a hand shot up.

The audience gasped as a woman in dark blue robes and scarf gently lifted the new 'Baby Jesus' – now obviously a real

274

infant – from the crib and placed him on the laps of the little girl and boy playing Mary and Joseph.

Standing so close to Jay, Lottie felt him physically stiffen beside her.

She knew immediately that the adult and baby were Nadia and Seb.

Chapter Thirty

With the applause at the end still ringing in her ears, Lottie fought her way through the excited families for mince pies and 'refreshments' in the school canteen.

She fully expected Jay to have escaped to the car but he was waiting just inside the doors.

'Are you OK? I'd no idea that they'd borrowed Seb for the baby.'

'It's OK. I realise you didn't know.'

'She might come into the canteen with Seb. In fact, it's almost guaranteed. We should leave.'

'I don't want to ruin your day, but it's probably best if I wait in the car.'

Even as she spoke, Nadia appeared, still in costume, with Seb in her arms.

Nadia spotted Jay too, if the dismay on her face was anything to go by. Lottie felt sorry for him. This must be his worst nightmare.

Before either of them had time to react, Steph found them, as hyper as the twins. 'How awesome was that?' she cried. 'I know I'm their mum, but weren't the girls amazing?'

Lottie hugged her. 'They were incredible. I couldn't stop crying.'

'I had no idea that the baby was going to be real!' Steph said. 'Did you?' She turned to Jay.

'No, it was a shock.' He smiled. 'The twins are stars.'

Nadia was across the other side of the room chatting to the head, but they were making their way across the room. Would she come over? It seemed unlikely but Lottie was on tenterhooks.

The girls rushed up. 'Mummeeee! Auntieeee Lottieeee?'

Myra grabbed Jay's hand. 'I was the best lobster! I was the best.'

'Oh, shut up, Myra,' Jodie said. 'Don't be such a diva!'

Lottie had never been so grateful for the twins' wild exuberance. Jay had to focus on the children but the head had other ideas. She swept Nadia and Seb in their direction.

'Hello there!' she cried, steering Nadia up to Lottie's group. 'Here's our real-life baby. Wasn't he great?'

Nadia's eyes widened in shock.

Lottie stifled a gasp. How would Jay cope?

Nadia held on to Seb tightly. 'Hello,' she said.

'Hi, Nadia,' Steph said. 'I'd no idea you were going to bring Seb.'

The head smiled broadly. 'It was our big secret, wasn't it, Nadia?' She turned to Lottie and Jay. 'Nadia's on maternity leave from the library service. She organises story times for some of the children and I couldn't resist asking her and Seb to make guest appearances.'

It was then Lottie realised that the head didn't know that Nadia's partner was Jay's brother, and why would she?

Bored with the small talk, Seb tried to wriggle free from Nadia's arms and lunged at Jay's hair.

Nadia looked horrified. 'Seb, no . . .' she said, a frantic edge to her voice but Seb wound his fingers tight in Jay's curls.

'Oh, isn't he gorgeous!' Steph cried.

'He loves your hair,' Myra said.

Trapped by Seb, Jay managed a smile. 'It's OK. He's doing no harm.'

Only Lottie could have spotted the desperate plea in Nadia's eyes as she gently disentangled Seb's chubby fingers from Jay's curls. He stood patiently while she did it.

'Thank you,' Nadia said once Jay was free.

'I'm fine,' he murmured.

Nadia looked relieved. 'You're lucky he hasn't pulled some out by the roots.'

Jay shook his head in wonder at Seb. 'He's strong.'

Seb wasn't impressed and let out a howl of protest.

'I'm sorry, he's very tired,' she said.

'I'm sure he is. He's a gorgeous little boy isn't he?' the head enthused. 'He looks like you, Nadia.'

Lottie winced a little, wondering how Jay felt. She could definitely see a likeness to Jay and wondered if he thought the same. Did that rub salt in his wounds?

Jay couldn't take his eyes off Seb. 'He's grown so . . . big,' he said, then added, 'Maybe he'll be a rugby player.'

Steph shot Jay a curious glance and seemed about to say something but then thought better of it. Lottie guessed that she'd sensed a connection between the two of them.

'It's hard being the star of the show, isn't it, Seb?' The head tried to stroke Seb's cheek but he bawled even louder.

'I'd better take him home.' Nadia had to raise her voice above Seb's screams. 'Bye. Lovely to see you again,' she said. 'And meet you,' she added quickly.

Moments later, she'd left them. The head moved on to other parents and after bombarding Jay with questions about the play and the reindeer, the twins skipped off to say goodbye to their friends.

Jay was putting on a manful effort, smiling and chatting to Steph but Lottie could tell that the experience had shaken him.

Steph was clearly flagging. 'I think I'll get the girls home now,' she said.

'Are you OK?' Lottie asked.

'Yes. Just a bit tired.' She brightened, though Lottie thought it was more of a brave face. 'Did you both enjoy yourselves?'

'It was wonderful,' Lottie said.

'Thank you for coming,' Steph said to Jay. 'It meant a lot to the twins.'

'No problem. It was fun. I'm glad they invited me.'

A short while later, they finally escaped to the haven of the car although Jay was very subdued. Nadia's unexpected appearance had come as a shock to Lottie herself. She'd been wary of taking him, then felt it had brought him out of himself, right up until Seb and Nadia had appeared. At first he'd looked horrified to be confronted with Nadia face to face, but he'd softened quickly and been transfixed by Seb. Lottie found it impossible to ignore the connection that still existed between him and Nadia.

'That was a shock,' she said, when they were finally alone in the car. 'Are you OK?'

'I guess we had to come into contact sometime. It was probably better I didn't know and that I was with so many people . . . and kids are a great distraction from all the crap that grown-ups cause.'

'They are. The girls live for the moment, apart from when they're looking forward to Christmas of course.'

Jay laughed softly but then subsided into silence so Lottie didn't push it.

It was almost dark when they reached Firholme and got out of the car. They stood by the gates to their cottages – so near and yet still separate. In the gathering darkness, the hills were the towering silhouettes of giants, pressing in on them. The wind was blowing straight off the northern fells, chilled by snow, and it seemed to cut through her smart coat.

Jay lingered, seeming at a loss. Lottie rubbed her hands together and shivered.

'Let's not stand out here in the cold any longer,' Jay said. 'Will you come inside for a coffee?'

There was a desperate edge to his tone that moved her. 'That'd be good.'

He let her into the cottage and fed Trevor. She heard the dog's identity tag clanking against his dish in the kitchen and then the kettle boiling. She also noticed a pile of unopened Christmas cards on the coffee table.

Jay walked in with a mug in each hand.

'Thanks,' she said, accepting the drink, warming her palms on it.

He sat next to her on the sofa.

'Aren't you going to open them?' she said, nodding at the cards.

He glanced at them. 'I've been so busy, I haven't got round to it.'

Lottie looked at the fireplace. The bare mantelpiece and house devoid of so much as a holly wreath seemed so sad when the rest of Firholme was bedecked with greenery and colour. She wondered if Jay was thinking that he'd been deprived of having his own family. Was he still in love with Nadia and wishing they were living together as a family, planning their first Christmas together?

'Lottie . . .' he said carefully. 'There's something I need to tell you.'

She tensed. There was a hesitancy in his tone that had her bracing herself for a further bombshell, though goodness knows what it would be. 'Yes?'

'I just want you to know that I don't regret coming today. Not for a moment, despite how it ended.'

She put her mug down. 'Phew. That's a relief. You seemed unsure. Distracted – I wondered if I'd upset you in some way.'

'No . . . I just need to sort myself out sometimes. I'm getting there.' He smiled reticently. 'Slowly but surely . . . and a lot of that is thanks to you.'

'What have I done?'

'You keep giving me a chance. Even when I might not seem as if I appreciate it, I do. You keep making me see that life can be good again, even Christmas . . .'

Lottie went shivery, this time not because of the cold, but because of the way Jay was looking at her: with pleasure – and desire.

She laughed and Jay smiled. Never had he looked more gorgeous, and there was such an intensity in his gaze, such tenderness and need. Never had she wanted him more – wanted anyone more. In a heartbeat, she was in his arms, breathing in the scent of him, woody aftershave, the wool of his sweater under her fingers. He took her face in his and kissed her so softly, it was like a snowflake settling against her skin. He threaded his fingers in her hair and she pressed closer to him.

Trevor burst in, barking.

Lottie broke off the kiss, and Jay groaned. 'Your timing is really bad, Trevor!'

Trevor gave a woof but Lottie laughed. 'Maybe it's good timing . . . this has been lovely but I really ought to go. I have so much to do up at the house. I won't get to bed until late.' She felt bereft in one way, but perhaps it was good that things had gone no further than a kiss at this stage. But what a kiss. Her lips were still tingling.

Jay sighed and let her go. 'I have work too . . .' Yet he sounded regretful.

'We both have a lot to deal with but after Saturday, it'll be over,' she said.

'The wedding?' he said.

'Everything. We'll both have more time soon,' she said, hoping he realised that she wanted Connor to finally be out of her life again, physically and mentally, before she could commit to anything new.

Jay nodded. 'I understand. This probably isn't the ideal moment.'

Lottie left, hoping he did understand, and not minding the icy wind at all. After that amazing kiss, she was full of hope and after this wedding was over, maybe she and Jay could finally make that fresh start Lottie hoped for so much – and never look back.

Chapter Thirty-One

The day before the wedding

Lottie had had a stern word with herself about not imagining what might happen with her and Jay, but it was impossible. That kiss had changed everything and her nights were filled with thoughts of Jay even as the express train of the wedding rolled into Firholme at top speed.

On Friday morning, the headlights of suppliers' vans started sweeping up the drive to Firholme, and began to unload all the paraphernalia needed to create Keegan and Connor's perfect day. The whole thing reminded her of the image of the swan on the lake, gliding along effortlessly, while paddling furiously underneath.

She had several conversations with Keegan, mostly to reassure her that all was well – with the wedding preparations at least. As for Connor . . . she could only hope he was only jealous that Lottie might have moved on from him, rather than having second thoughts about his marriage. She hadn't had a bride jilted yet . . .

Then again, Connor did have a track record . . .

She redoubled her effort to focus on what she could control, throwing herself into work. She was in and out of the house all day, fuelled by coffees – though most of them went cold – ticking off items from a seemingly endless to-do list, making sure everyone knew exactly what was required and had everything in place to do it. Then rechecking and making sure there was a contingency for every eventuality.

As she walked around the site, she imagined the house was as alive as it must ever have been in its heyday, with florists, tradespeople, catering and housekeeping staff buzzing to and fro, just as they would have been for any big showpiece event that Firholme would have hosted.

Lukasz was overseeing the catering but a wedding for eighty was too much for his team to deal with alone, so Lottie had called in extra help from the catering company who'd helped at the ball. After a catch-up to make sure Lucasz was happy, she greeted the floristry team.

The bouquets and corsages would be delivered to the bride's own residence on the morning of the wedding, but all the arrangements for the ballroom and drawing room were arriving today. She watched in delight as the rooms were transformed with seasonal and exotic flowers. Keegan had really pushed the boat out and they'd even managed to find some wattle for her.

The day flew by and Lottie managed to convince Keegan that the replacement vintage car was even more beautiful than the one she'd originally booked. After a final meeting with the team to run through everything one last time, Lottie made it back to the Bothy around eight p.m.

She looked out of the window. It was dark but the moon had peeked between the clouds, lighting up garden and grounds, with trees spreading their spiky fingers. A few snow-flakes were falling, but nothing had settled yet. The weather forecast had said they might be in for a few inches on the high fells but the valleys would escape. The Firholme snow clearers were on duty, ready to clear the paths, just in case of a light fall.

She was eating a ready meal in front of the TV when she heard Trevor barking. She went to the window and lifted the curtain. Beyond the garden gate, a torch beam wavered in the darkness and a shape detached itself and ran to the garden gate. A moment later, she spotted Jay, strolling up to the gate to their cottages. As he did so, the porch lights of both houses clicked on automatically, illuminating him. It was too late to pretend she hadn't seen him so she waved and Jay lifted a hand and smiled broadly. The temptation to run to the door and ask him in was almost overwhelming but she didn't dare. If he came inside . . . well, there was a strong possibility that things would go further than a kiss and she wouldn't get much sleep at all. Reluctantly, she let the curtain drop and contented herself with a message, saying: 'See you in the morning' – as much for her sake as his.

He messaged her back. 'See you tomorrow. Sweet dreams.'

She went to bed early, thinking about Jay as she snuggled down in bed. Her dreams would be sweet indeed . . .

'Aargh!'

Lottie jolted awake. Rather than sweet slumbers, she'd actually been dreaming that someone was trying to break into her cottage. It took a few seconds to realise that her phone was buzzing from the bedside table. Her first thought was that someone must be ill: her parents – or Steph or the girls. With her heart trying to leap out of her chest, she snatched up her phone and saw Connor's name on the screen.

'Connor, what the hell?'

'Lottie. I'm outside. Can you let me in?'

'Outside? Where?' Her sleep-fogged brain was slow to take in the words. 'I can hardly hear you.'

His voice was barely above a whisper. 'Outside your front door.'

'What?'

'Here at Firholme. I can't speak any louder in case I wake someone up. Shit. That bloody dog's barking now. Please let me in.'

Trevor's barks from next door finally got through to Lottie that Connor must be on her doorstep. She grabbed her dressing gown and opened the curtain. Snow was falling on an already thick layer. She could just make out Connor in the darkness. She padded downstairs and opened the door.

'Connor,' she hissed. 'It's past midnight.'

'I know . . . but ple-ease, can I come in now?'

He sounded like one of the girls when they were trying to wheedle their way round Steph and she suspected he'd been drinking, but Lottie didn't have a choice, unless she wanted to risk waking up her neighbours. Trevor had stopped barking

287

but Jay could well be on his way downstairs to see what was going on.

'OK, but only for a minute. Quick,' she said and let Connor in before closing the door behind him. He stood in her hallway. He was wearing his coat, a scarf and smart shoes but they were no match for a Lakeland blizzard. 'What are you doing here? You're soaked and freezing.' He had a definite whiff of booze about him.

'Tell me about it.' He rubbed his face with his hands. 'Jesus, there's no easy way to tell you this. Keegan knows, Lottie. She knows about you and me and she's thrown me out.'

Chapter Thirty-Two

Twelve hours to the wedding

Lottie's heart lurched like a ship hitting the rocks.

Connor continued: 'She's threatened not to go through with the wedding.'

Her hand flew to her mouth. 'Oh my God. Does she mean it?'

'I don't know.' He pushed his hands through his soaking hair. 'What a bloody mess. I wish I'd told her before.'

She was almost too shocked to speak. 'How did she find out?'

'It was Mum who let it slip, actually, though of course it wasn't her fault.'

'What?'

'There was a photo at home. It was my cousin's wedding . . . remember, they had the reception on that big boat on Windermere? I'd forgotten that Mum had a framed group photo on a bookcase on the landing. Keegan went to the bathroom and picked it up. She spotted you in it and asked Mum about it.

'Oh God.' Lottie could picture the scene exactly.

'Mum told Keegan you were an old girlfriend. She didn't realise she'd said anything wrong and she was trying to be tactful as it is. She didn't say we used to live together or anything but it was too late. Keegan managed not to say anything about the wedding, but I could see from her face that she was furious. As soon as she got me on my own, she demanded to know why I hadn't told her before and exactly how close you and I had been. I had to come clean and say we'd only broken up last year, and that we'd lived together.' He sighed. 'That seemed to make her even angrier.'

Lottie squeezed her eyes shut. 'No wonder she was furious. We should never have kept it a secret. I didn't want to for this precise reason!'

She sat on the sofa while Connor paced around, swearing.

'I am so sorry for this. It's been a nightmare keeping it under wraps and now everything's been blown sky-high. I can't see the wedding going ahead tomorrow or any time.'

Lottie was angry with Connor for making her stay quiet about their relationship, angry with herself for letting him come back into her life.

Connor stopped pacing and put his arm around her shoulders.

She shook him off. 'Don't.'

'OK. OK. I was only trying to help.'

'You've done enough. I wish you'd never set foot in Firholme or my life.'

He held up his hands, his eyes full of hurt. How did he even *dare* to look hurt? Lottie thought, anger hardening into determination. 'I should have told Shayla right away,' she said, finally lifting her head. 'I *will* tell her, first thing in the morning.'

'Probably a good idea,' Connor murmured. 'Because Keegan has already sent her an email.'

'What?'

'She said you'd behaved "unprofessionally". Yes, I know it was my fault, and I tried to tell her that we'd had a pact.'

Lottie let out a squeak of horror. 'Connor . . .' she said, reining in the urge to shout.

'That seemed to make her even angrier. She – she – seems to have got some bloody stupid idea that we're still involved. I tried to tell her that's not true until I was blue in the face but she won't believe me. She says we wouldn't have kept our past a secret if there wasn't anything to hide. Maybe she thinks something's been going on since I got back?'

'We both know there isn't but you've lost her trust!' Lottie was horrified. 'We both have.'

'I think you're right – and she kicked me out,' Connor moaned. 'I'd had a couple of whiskies . . . so I couldn't drive and there's no way I could get a cab at this hour out here in the arse end of nowhere – even if they could get through the snow so – I walked.'

'Connor!' Lottie said so loudly, he flinched. 'Do you have any idea of what you've done? Your wedding is tomorrow, you've devastated your bride and you could lose me my job and my professional reputation. You need to own this and

291

sort it out right now. With Keegan and with my boss.' Plus she was convinced he'd had more than a couple of whiskies.

'Now? It's after midnight. I can't do anything now.'

'Well, you can't stay here.' She was horrified at this new twist of events. 'No way, especially after what's happened.'

'Where then? I'm not sure I can make it home in this blizzard.'

'You are *not* staying here for the night,' she repeated, though the sick feeling in her gut was already telling her that every other option was looking impossible.

She thought about saying she'd lend him gloves and a coat then she looked out of the window. The snow was falling more heavily than ever and it was below freezing. There was every likelihood he really wouldn't make it home if she forced him to walk back, especially if he'd been drinking. Maybe she could ask one of the staff to let him share their cottage, but who could she wake up at one a.m. without a lot of explanations. Jay . . . no chance. He and Connor might come to blows.

She ushered him into the lounge, her mind working overtime. 'If Keegan finds out you slept here in my house, then the wedding definitely *will* be off. Look, maybe you could sleep in the café,' she said. 'I can get the key. They have sofas.'

'So, do you – and then neither of us will have go out in a snowstorm.'

She clutched her dressing gown tighter. 'If that's what it takes.'

Water dripped off his coat and trousers, pooling on her carpet. His face was red with the cold and his hair matted with melting snow. It was a wonder he didn't already have hypothermia. 'Won't that cause more fuss than letting me kip in your sitting room for a few hours?' he pleaded. 'All I want is the sofa and a blanket. A hot drink would help too. I swear I'll be gone by first light.'

'If anyone sees you, what will they think?'

'They won't see me. Trust me.'

That was the last thing Lottie was prepared to do. 'Maybe not tonight but you might not be able to get home in the morning.'

'I'll say that someone brought me up here in a Land Rover at first light. I dunno, I'll say they had to drop me off early before everyone else.'

'Your wedding suit isn't here.'

'Well . . . I'll say I decided to wear something more practical and left it behind. The way things are, I probably won't need it. By the looks of the snow, how will anyone get here? How will Keegan and her family make it?' he said. 'If the wedding even happens after this shitstorm.'

'I'll handle the transport even if Keegan has to arrive by tractor. You start thinking of how you're going to get us out of this mess and placate her.'

'Keegan arriving at the wedding in a tractor?' Connor laughed. 'She was bad enough when her first choice of Rolls-Royce wasn't available so there's not a cat in hell's chance of that.'

'That's the least of my worries now.' Lottie's whole focus was on explaining why she'd been the reason behind a lucrative wedding being called off. What if Keegan refused to pay and tried to sue? She'd have to resign.

'OK, I'll do my best to think of something but for now, can I at least have a h-hot drink and maybe get some dry c-clothes?'

Lottie stared at him. What a pathetic, whining individual he was. How had she ever fallen in love with him in the first place? However, realising he genuinely was in danger of hypothermia, she decided she had no choice. 'Go up to the bathroom and get changed. I'll leave some clothes outside the door. God knows what. Do *not* come out until you're ready. I'll make you a coffee.'

She'd no idea what she was going to find Connor to wear. It struck her that she'd had to do the same for Jay. He'd kept the poncho for some reason. Then she had a brainwave. She rooted in the cubby hole and pulled out a large towelling robe with a hood and short sleeves.

'I've left a robe and some socks outside the door,' she said.

A red-faced Connor shuffled into the lounge.

Lottie would have burst out laughing if she hadn't been so annoyed. The towelling robe was designed for getting changed after you'd been surfing or swimming out of doors. It reached down to her ankles but on Connor, it was mid-calf. He might not have looked so peculiar if he hadn't also been wearing fluffy pink socks.

'Do *not* laugh! I will leave right this minute if you so much as titter,' he said.

'Don't tempt me,' Lottie said. 'And don't moan. It's all I could find that was big enough.'

'Really?' He curled his lip. 'If this is your idea of revenge, it's working.'

'It's not, but now you come to mention it . . .' She hardened her tone, catching sight of the clock and seeing it was past one. 'There's your coffee.' She pointed to the mug on the coffee table. 'The duvet's on the sofa and I've asked Alexa to wake you at six forty-five. Then you have to be out of here, without anyone seeing you, or I swear, I will bundle you out into the snow, in the robe and socks.'

She was about to sweep off upstairs when a chilling thought struck her. 'Um . . . who else actually knows you're here?'

'No one yet. I can say I stayed with my best man at his hotel after getting drunk. He'll back me up. Lottie, I appreciate this might be too much to ask but can you do something else for me?'

'What?'

'Tomorrow morning. Would you speak to Keegan for me? Explain that nothing has happened between us – that it's been over for a long time.'

'If you've explained this already, and she won't believe you, why should she believe me?'

'Because you're so genuine, Lottie . . . people trust you. They always have. Like Mum. She said you went for tea together.'

'Well, only because we literally bumped into each other in Abbott's.'

'She was singing your praises as usual. Lottie's looking well, Lottie's done very well to get a job at Firholme, Lottie's hair is lovely – I like how it's grown.

Lottie laughed it off. 'You're pissed, Connor, and your mum never has a bad word to say about anyone.'

'Apart from me.'

'I doubt it.' Lottie hated the way Connor was coming on to her, even if he was drunk.

He rested his fingers on her arm. 'I can't help thinking that this is a big commitment. Can I do it? I – I don't have a great track record.'

'Just because we didn't make it, doesn't mean you can't make a go of things with Keegan. She loves you,' Lottie said, painfully aware of the irony that she was dishing out advice to Connor on marriage and relationships.

He sank onto the sofa and rubbed his face with his hands. 'Do you think she *does* love me? We argue, you know.'

'Doesn't everyone?'

'Jay saw us a few weeks ago. He didn't think I'd spotted him and his dog but I had. We were arguing about the wedding and if we were rushing into this but I do love her.'

'Love isn't about abandoning someone when the going gets tough, when they're ill or hurting. It's about making sacrifices, setting your own dreams aside if need be, to help them through a dark time. It's about not holding on to grudges and bitterness, or thinking "what if" the grass is greener somewhere else.'

She paused for breath.

'Hmm. I can see you're still holding on to a lot of anger . . .' he said.

'No, I'm not angry. I'm indifferent. Our time has gone, Connor. Feelings I had for you and held on to too long. I can't tell you to marry Keegan . . .' and, Lottie thought to herself, she was sure Keegan could do a lot better. Instead she simply said: 'Don't hurt her like you hurt me.'

'You'll talk to her though?' Connor pleaded.

'I can't make any promises.'

She hurried out of the sitting room, closing the door on him. Upstairs, she let out a groan. She'd like to pretend Connor wasn't in her house, shut out the fact he was sleeping on her sofa the night before his wedding to another woman. If he got any sleep, that is. She didn't think she would. As for intervening with Keegan?

Judging by how angry Keegan must be, Lottie thought that was a sure-fire way to make sure the wedding never took place at all.

Chapter Thirty-Three

Six hours to the wedding

'Hey, Trevor, my feet don't need a wash!'

Jay woke to find Trevor poking a wet nose under the duvet and licking his toes.

'OK. I'm getting up. What time is it?' He twisted the digital alarm towards him and groaned. 'Dude, it's not even six a.m!'

Trevor sat by the bed, an expectant look in his eyes. Jay realised he'd have no choice but to exchange his cosy duvet for the cold darkness on the shortest day of the year.

He'd been having a very pleasant dream about Lottie, and what it would feel like to share the warmth of her body. He'd dreamed of waking up to see her hair spread over the pillow and her breathing softly beside him . . .

That kiss the other night had been incredible and made him totally determined to tell her how he felt about her. Just because she'd once loved Connor, didn't mean she was *still* in love with her ex; in fact it was a ridiculous idea.

'I really have been an idiot, haven't I, Trev?'

Trevor stared at him.

Jay grinned. 'Probably best you can't answer that, buddy.'

Feeling as if a weight had been lifted from his mind, he threw off the duvet. 'OK, you win, Trevor!'

Trevor lifted his head, with a look of astonishment, as if Jay had gone mad.

'Early walk, buddy,' he said. 'A quick one because it's cold and we have a lot to do today.'

Today was the day he would draw a line under all the doubts and fears, and put his trust in her, as he should have done weeks ago. Today, when the wedding was over, he would ask if they could start again. Maybe his Christmas could be a happy one after all, with Lottie by his side.

While he pulled on a thick sweater and jeans, Trevor processed the fact that he was actually off for a jaunt and yipped in anticipation. He trotted down the stairs, his tail thumping every newel post as he went. Jay followed, pulling on his coat while Trevor slurped up water from his bowl ready for his outing.

'You won't be so keen to go out when you see all that snow,' Jay told him, lacing up his walking boots.

'Woof!' said Trevor, which Jay knew meant: 'Don't be ridiculous.'

Icy air took Jay's breath away when he stepped outside. It was still dark so he took a torch. The lights were on in the café, and a couple of the other cottages, as people got ready for work. Jay automatically glanced up at Lottie's windows where the curtains were drawn, but lamplight glowed both up and downstairs. He pictured her having a hasty breakfast, ready for the busy day she had in store.

Trevor had left a deep trail of doggy prints in the snow that looked more like a bear had stumbled across the lawn. They led all around the rear of his and Lottie's cottages.

'Come on, Trevor,' he said cheerfully. 'Let's go down to the lake for a change.'

Trevor romped towards the wicket gate in the hedge that led from the rear garden of his own cottage, and down to the lake pathway. He stood by the gate and barked before tearing back to the bird feeder.

'Trevor!' Jay called, as the dog wriggled through a gap in the low box hedge that separated his garden from Lottie's. Jay spotted smaller prints in the snow. A squirrel had clearly visited in the hope of a feed and then tried Lottie's own bird table.

'Leave the squirrel alone, Trev. We don't have time and he won't appreciate you being friendly—'

Out of sight, Trevor's barks became louder and more insistent.

'Oh no. I hope you haven't caught one . . .' Jay stepped over the hedge into Lottie's garden. A moment later he heard a man shouting and stopped dead.

'Can you get him off me!'

Connor was pinned against Lottie's back door by Trevor. 'He's like a wild beast!' he screeched.

'Trevor!' Jay called. 'Come here now!'

300

With a final sniff at Connor's jeans, Trevor slunk back to Jay.

Connor glared at Trevor. 'Thank feck for that.' He took a tentative step away from the door. 'I thought he was going to have me for breakfast.'

'He wouldn't have hurt you. He probably only looking out for Lottie, thinking you were an intruder,' Jay said, as his mind went into overdrive: why would Connor be creeping out of Lottie's house on the dawn of his wedding day. Or had he only just turned up?

Any rational explanation – apart from one – faded when Lottie emerged onto the porch, wearing only a dressing gown. 'Connor,' she said. 'I told you to leave quietly.'

Her face fell when she saw him. 'Jay . . . I didn't expect to see you so early.'

'I was taking Trev for a walk. It's going to be a busy day.' He directed this at Connor, who was smirking now he was safe. 'I thought Trevor had scented a squirrel . . .'

'No, it was Connor. He had to stay the night here because of the snow . . .' Lottie said, clutching her dressing gown tighter. 'I was going to find a way of getting him home. He turned up after midnight,' Lottie added, an edge of desperation in her voice. She looked like she'd been awake all night to Jay, the shadows under her eyes contrasting with her pale face. She threw a desperate glance at Connor, as if wanting him to help her out.

'I had a few too many drinks and ended up here,' Connor said.

Lottie glared at him.

Jay was still in shock at seeing Connor emerge from Lottie's cottage, so cocky and blasé. 'It's your business, but you won't get out in your car,' he said to her alone. No matter what had gone on between her and Connor, Jay could only think of keeping her safe.

'I realise that now. Connor was going out to check how bad it was.'

'If you really want to leave, I'll give you a lift in the truck,' Jay said to Connor.

'Thanks, that would be a great idea, if you don't mind,' Lottie said, glowering at Connor, as if she was angry with him for being caught creeping out of the cottage. 'And the sooner the better. Connor has to get ready for the wedding. I think we're going to need more help with transport for the rest of the bridal party too, if you can.'

Jay hesitated. He didn't give a monkey's if Connor made it to his wedding or not. Privately, he thought Keegan was way better off without him, but that wasn't his business. No matter how broken his trust in Lottie was, no matter what she and Connor might have been up to, he was still prepared to bust a gut to help her.

'I'll sort something out. Let me take Trevor for a quick run and I'll make some calls. I'll meet you back here in twenty minutes?' He forced himself to speak to Connor. 'I'll give you a lift home.'

'How will Keegan get here?' Connor whined, without a word of thanks. 'Lottie mentioned a tractor.' He pulled a face.

Jay restrained the urge to swear. 'We'll think of something.'

'OK. Connor, come back inside!' Lottie snapped.

She vanished inside, leaving Jay to wonder exactly what had gone on in the cottage. Once again, he forced himself to consider the possibility that things weren't as he feared and Lottie was telling the truth. He couldn't imagine that Lottie would want to rekindle her relationship with an arse like Connor – but he wouldn't put anything past the man.

Connor lingered a moment after Lottie had shot back indoors, obviously desperate not to be seen by anyone else. 'Thanks. You know how awkward this could look with Keegan if she found out that I'd – um – spent the night here?' He smirked. 'People do jump to conclusions but you know what it's like. We all do stuff we regret when women are involved. No one's perfect, are they?'

Connor winked and Jay's stomach turned over. Surely, surely, Lottie wouldn't have slept with him? Not after their kiss . . . The guy had to be winding Jay up?

'It's none of my business . . .'

'Thanks all the same. You've got me out of a hole.'

'Don't thank me. I'm doing this for Lottie. No one else. Trevor!'

It was best if he walked away before he told Connor exactly what he thought of him. That would really wake up the Firholme residents. Jay strode off, taking Trevor on a different route than he'd planned. They headed for the lane that led from the estate entrance and out to the public road.

The gritter hadn't been able to reach the public road yet, so it was thick with a layer of as-yet undisturbed snow. Trevor romped ahead, his black head vanishing and reappearing amid the drifts. No matter how often Jay told himself that Connor had been drunk and simply wandered all that way through the snow to Lottie's place uninvited, the worst-case scenario that she had invited Connor to the Bothy and wanted him to stay over still couldn't be magicked away. He tried to force his mind on addressing the immediate problem: transporting Connor home, and then the bridal party back to Firholme.

After a ten-minute outing to enable Trevor to complete his morning 'ablutions', Jay took him home, wiped the snow from his coat and dried him. He then settled him in the kitchen with his breakfast before he headed out again. It was now light and he had to admit, under a blue sky, Firholme resembled Narnia. On any other day, he'd have been uplifted by the sight of the place he loved covered with sparkling snow from fell top to lake shore.

He called his grounds supervisor who was already up and marshalling everyone who lived on site or nearby to help clear the track from the main road. He was still talking as he rapped on the door of the Bothy.

Lottie answered, dressed now, in an oversized sweater and jeans, her hair caught in a ponytail that bobbed up and down as she let him in.

Jay noticed two cereal bowls on the coffee table, alongside two mugs. He heard water running upstairs and assumed Connor was in the bathroom.

'Connor turned up after midnight. Keegan had found out Connor and I used to live together so she threw him out and he ended up here. I didn't want him to stay but he'd have frozen – literally – if I'd turned him away. Who was I going to knock up at that time of night? Shayla? You?

304

How could I explain him coming here? You do believe me, don't you?'

'It's not my business to believe anything . . .' he said, treading carefully. 'You don't have to explain.'

Lottie opened her mouth as if she might apologise but instead, her voice rose. 'Actually, you're absolutely right. I *don't* have to apologise or explain. To anyone. Because I haven't done anything wrong.' She sounded sad and tired. 'It's you, Jay – *you* who have the problem with trust and I can't do a thing about that. Only you can make that shift. Only you.' Her voice was breaking. 'And now, I have to call Shayla and tell her why the bride is threatening to call off the wedding.'

They heard footsteps thudding on the landing.

'Lottie . . .' he began, overwhelmed by her outburst.

'I don't want to talk about it. I have enough to worry about as it is. For now, we need to work together to make sure this wedding goes ahead,' she said desperately. 'For Keegan's sake and for Firholme.'

He nodded, cursing the way he'd handled the situation. He didn't know what to think about Connor any more but one thing was for sure: Lottie was angry and upset with him. The only thing he could do properly was his job. 'I've got a few ideas that might work for transporting everyone,' he said.

'Good. I need to speak to Shayla to try and salvage this mess,' Lottie replied curtly. 'If it is going to happen, we have to make them think it's all under control. It's the only way we'll get through today.'

Moments later, Connor walked into the sitting room. 'I'm ready . . .' he said gloomily as if he was off to the guillotine.

Jay didn't feel the slightest bit sorry for him, but he was determined to get him back home to face the music.

A few minutes later, leaving Lottie to make some calls, he pulled the truck up outside the Bothy. Trevor jumped out and ran to sniff at a bush. Jay went to the door to beckon to Connor to nip out of the house. Even while walking to the truck, Connor's designer jeans and smart boots were soaked.

He slunk down low in his seat so he couldn't be seen.

Jay's insides churned. He didn't know what to believe any more.

Trevor pulled his nose out of a bush and leapt into the truck over Jay's lap and onto Connor, before settling in the footwell.

'Jesus. Does he have to come?' he moaned. 'There's hardly any room for my feet!'

'Yes. Otherwise, he'll be stuck inside the cottage for the whole day because we're so busy with *your* wedding.'

'I'm allergic to dogs.'

Jay gripped the wheel. 'Open the window, then. He can't sit outside.'

Trevor rested his jowls on Connor's jeans and gazed up at him.

Connor swore. 'He's drooling all over my leg!'

'Don't worry. It's because he's decided he likes you,' Jay said, firing up the engine. 'Then again, he's never been the best judge of character.'

Chapter Thirty-Four

The wedding morning

Lottie stepped out of the Bothy into a winter wonderland. Every inch of the landscape that wasn't water was covered in snow, from the top of the mountains to the lake shore. It wasn't so much a blanket as a twenty-tog goose-down duvet of snow, with wispy flakes swirling in the air like feathers. It was the most idyllic backdrop for a Christmas wedding as could be imagined – shame it wasn't going to happen.

She trudged over to Shayla's apartment in the Old Coach House.

Wearing a grim expression, Shayla put a strong cup of coffee in front of her. 'So, you and Connor were close but you decided not to tell me?' she said.

'Yes. He asked me not to although it was my decision to agree. I can understand if you want me to resign,' she said. 'After the wedding is over.'

Shayla shook her head and pressed her lips together. Lottie's stomach turned over. She'd seen that look before on her boss's face. She was angry. Very angry.

'I've messed up, big time,' Lottie said.

'No. You didn't. You made a judgement call in a situation you couldn't win and it was Connor who put you in that situation. You had every right to expect your private life before you came here to remain exactly that: private, but these things have a way of coming out. I'm only disappointed you didn't feel you could trust me enough to tell me.'

Lottie's hopes plummeted. Shayla's disappointment was harder to bear than if she'd been angry. 'It was sheer bad luck that Connor's mum told Keegan we'd been close. I wish she hadn't,' she said. 'That doesn't make any difference to the fact I didn't share the situation with you from the start. I thought I – we – could keep a lid on it and no one would need to know.'

'I understand that . . . but now it's all out.' Shayla pursed her lips but then sighed. 'No use wondering "what if". We're into damage limitation. What have you heard? Is he back? What has the bride said?'

'He texted me to say she won't let him in . . . She doesn't know he spent the night here.'

'That's something, I suppose, but I have to be honest, Lottie, I can't see this wedding going ahead, unless something dramatic happens to turn it around. They're getting married at noon for heaven's sake! We can't force a bride to marry someone; and we shouldn't.'

Yet it *was* partly Lottie's fault, she thought, and she had to

308

try. 'I – I could call Keegan and try to explain. I could go and see her.'

'Wow. That's a big risk.'

'It is, but the way things are, I don't think they can get any worse.'

Shayla thought for a moment. 'What on earth will you say to her?'

'I'm not sure. I don't want to pressure Keegan into marrying Connor, or even persuade her, but I can't bear the thought of her thinking that I – or Firholme by association – is to blame.'

Shayla shook her head. 'Honey, I don't care what she thinks. I may be disappointed that you didn't trust me but you're not going to take the fall for this situation. Not in my eyes, or anyone else's at Firholme.'

But that's what other people *would* think, Lottie wanted to shout: her colleagues, Connor's family, Keegan and her lot – and even Jay. It made her sick to her stomach that after losing Connor and getting over him, he'd overturned her life again and jeopardised her chance of a fresh start.

'Thank you,' she said, her eyes brimming at Shayla's support. 'I could at least call Keegan and see if she'll see me, but I'll have to go straightaway . . .'

After a moment of thought, Shayla said. 'I can take you, if you like.'

'You're so busy here though.'

'Well, I won't have anything to do if there's no wedding, will I?' She leapt up, reminding Lottie of why she was the boss of Firholme. 'Come on, I'll get the Range Rover out of the garage while you phone. At first, I thought it was a terrible

309

idea, but the more I think about it, I realise this is our only hope of salvaging this wedding and our reputation.'

The holiday house that Keegan's family had rented was on the edge of the village, behind large iron gates. Lottie had to buzz the intercom and wait in the cold before they opened to let her inside, an experience that didn't help her nerves.

Shayla sat in the car on the road outside, and Lottie couldn't help thinking whether it was in case her boss thought she needed to make a quick getaway.

She was amazed to have even been allowed admittance at all. After her discussion with Shayla, she'd texted Keegan, asking if she could come round. Ten agonising minutes later, she'd received a curt reply.

Why not?

That could have meant anything. Steeling herself, she trudged up the drive to the house, rapped the knocker and waited. Was she going to get a hearing, or was Keegan going to throw something at her?

Keegan's mother opened the front door. She was tall, bronzed and immaculately coiffed, dressed in silk pyjamas and a cashmere cardigan. 'You'd better come in,' she said wearily. 'Keegan's in her bedroom. This way.'

'Thanks,' said Lottie, relieved at least that Mrs Sinclair hadn't lambasted her as soon as she'd stepped through the door. She wasn't sure what Keegan's parents knew, so she stayed silent as she was shown to Keegan's room.

'She's in there,' Mrs Sinclair said. 'I'll be downstairs while you two talk.' She gave a grim smile. 'Good luck.'

Strangely enough, Lottie didn't feel very lucky when she tapped at the door.

'It's Lottie,' she said.

A few moments later, Keegan called imperiously, 'You'd better come in.'

She was sitting on a stool in front of the dressing table, wearing a silk robe. Her long hair had been swept up into a chignon and she was in full make-up and false eyelashes. Her wedding gown hung on the back of the wardrobe door and her veil was draped over a cheval mirror.

She must have seen Lottie's sideways glance at the dress. 'I – I couldn't bring myself to cancel the hairdresser and beautician,' she said, with a wobble in her voice.

'No . . .' Lottie couldn't help but feel sorry for her and hope that this was a sign Keegan hadn't completely decided against going through with the wedding.

Keegan's eyes glittered and her tone hardened. 'I really thought you were nice,' she said, plunging Lottie's hopes in an instant. 'I thought I could trust you, but I half guessed there was something going on between you and Connor. I just had a feeling and I should have followed my gut.'

'Nothing was going on. Nothing has been, since the day we split up, long before Connor met you,' Lottie said, worried that she might be making the situation worse.

Keegan snorted. 'How can I believe that? I confided in you! You gave me advice and all the time you knew you'd been living together – shared his bed every night – you must have been laughing at me!'

This wasn't the start Lottie had hoped for and her sense

of unfairness at having to put Connor's case forward was growing. 'I can promise you that laughter has been the last thing on my mind,' she said quietly. 'Connor may be no saint, he may have deceived you, but it was all for your sake.'

Keegan pursed her lips. 'He says the same as you, but how can I believe him?'

'Simple. Because it's true. The moment he walked into Firholme, I was so shocked, I could hardly speak. I didn't know what to do or say for the best but you seemed to love Firholme and Connor asked me not to spoil your moment.' Lottie corrected herself, wanting to own her part in the deception. 'I agreed not to say anything but in hindsight, I admit it wasn't the best decision I ever made. I'm sure he feels the same and would make a different one now.'

She kept her fingers crossed, praying Connor wouldn't admit where he'd spent the night. She didn't think Jay would: however angry she was at his lack of trust, she had total faith in his loyalty and discretion.

Keegan gave her a hard stare. 'Do you still love Connor?'

Lottie paused, aware she was steering a very fine line – gossamer thin – between brutal frankness and tact. However, the time for subtlety seemed to have gone.

'No, I don't, and I haven't for a while now – for many months in fact.'

Keegan glared at her. 'Why should I believe you? You've lied for him, after all.'

Lottie decided that her only policy was naked honesty, and hope that Keegan would believe her. 'I'll admit I was very upset when we split up but I came out of the experience knowing I had to put my regrets behind me. I was lucky enough to get the job at Firholme, which might not have happened if I'd stayed with Connor – and also, recently, I've met someone else I care about deeply.'

And someone who didn't trust her – and who she felt would never move on from his trust issues.

Keegan's eyes pierced her. 'Is this the Christmas tree guy?'

Lottie's mouth fell open in surprise. 'Yes. How did you guess?'

She shrugged. 'Like I say, I notice stuff . . . but I couldn't tell if you had a crush on him or were interested in Connor . . . Now I know it was kind of both, but maybe not in the way I'd suspected.'

'Um. Where's Connor now?' Lottie asked.

'With his best man at their hotel. He's hoping I'll call him to say it's all on again.'

Lottie seized her chance. 'I can't tell you to marry Connor. It's your decision, but don't call it off because of me, or something that happened in the past. I don't love him now and I don't want to marry him, but that doesn't mean you shouldn't. It only means he was meant for someone else, not me.' She took a breath. 'If you think that someone is you – and you must have until yesterday – then don't let our past ruin your dream.'

'I was going to put a stop to it when I found out you'd both tricked me all these weeks.'

Lottie winced. She wasn't out of the woods on this, not by a long way. Keegan picked up a hairbrush. 'After I kicked him out, I lay awake half the night before I told Mum and Dad this morning. It was my mother who said I shouldn't do anything hasty and should speak to you. It's been horrible, having my hair done and wondering if the wedding will happen at all.' Her eyes travelled to her dress. 'If I'd ever even wear that dress. It kept mocking me. I felt such a fool.'

'I'm sorry you felt like that. Truly.'

'Like you said, maybe Connor and I need to clear the air and start over . . .' Keegan sighed.

Lottie held her breath. Oh God, had she encouraged Keegan to leave Connor altogether? Personally, she was tempted to say, don't go within a mile of Connor, but she never would. Maybe Connor and Keegan *were* a match made in heaven: like all the couples whose weddings she'd organised, she had no real way of predicting who would celebrate their golden anniversary and who wouldn't last five minutes.

'Erm . . .'

'But it must have taken you some balls to come here,' Keegan said. 'Not that you have any actual balls, but you know what I mean.'

'It was the least I could do, to give you the whole story. Thanks for at least hearing me out.'

'Mmm. Well, I wanted to hear your side of it before I make my final decision. I pride myself on being tough but fair.'

'Thank you,' Lottie said. 'Um. Do you think it would be a good idea to hear Connor out too?'

Keegan sighed. 'I suppose I should at least let him come over so we can talk.'

'Whatever you think best.' Lottie felt that a wrong word now could tip the balance either way. 'I also should be getting back to Firholme now.'

Keegan seemed almost surprised then arched an eyebrow. 'Because you have a wedding to coordinate?'

'Maybe . . .' Lottie said, with a hopeful uplift.

Keegan nodded. 'I'll let you know what I decide after I've spoken to him.'

'OK,' Lottie said, thinking of the logistical operation of getting everyone to Firholme, through the snow at what was increasingly short notice. 'But can it be *quite* soon?' she said.

Keegan picked up her phone, gingerly, careful of her freshly manicured nails. 'I'll call him now and let you have my decision.'

Chapter Thirty-Five

'Well?' Shayla demanded the moment Lottie shut the car door.

Lottie leaned back against the car seat, her eyes closed and a headache starting. 'It's in the lap of the gods, but just in case, we'd better be prepared.'

There was no time to dwell on what might happen. She made some calls and by the time they'd arrived at Firholme, Operation Wedding was back in full swing. The council snow ploughs were too busy clearing the main roads to reach the lane to the estate. Jay and the team had cleared the driveway with the tractor plough and were carving routes to the house and café. He was outside with his staff, in wellies and hi-vis, shovelling away the last few feet of snow from the door of the main house.

Shayla dropped Lottie off in the courtyard. A quick check of her phone again still showed nothing from Keegan. She'd felt hopeful when she left but her optimism was dwindling

316

fast. The sight of all her colleagues making a huge effort, possibly for nothing, wasn't helping.

Jay hurried over to her. 'Is it on?' he asked. Trevor cocked his head on one side, as if to ask the same question.

'The jury's still out.'

He nodded. 'We're going ahead on the assumption it's happening. I've asked my deputy to manage the Christmas tree sales today and we'd have had to clear the access anyway so that's not wasted,' he said curtly.

'That's good . . .' she said.

He looked at her intensely, and she could tell he was struggling for words and still probably stinging from the home truths she'd flung his way. She half-wished her words back now but it was too late.

'I'd better get on with it,' he said and strode off up the drive, with his hands in his pockets and Trevor at his heels.

Lottie felt paralysed with uncertainty.

She thought of all the things she had to do: organise transport for the guests, the bridal party, make sure suppliers were going to turn up, arrange a warm place for people to gather and change, alongside all the usual checks on the flowers, the guest bedrooms, the bridal suite . . . Would that ever be used?

Would Keegan's jelly beans be eaten? Would her firework display light up the sky? They were little things, trivial 'extras' and yet they meant a lot to Keegan.

Lottie felt a lurch of sympathy for her. She didn't want Keegan to be hurt as she had been.

Her phone buzzed and Keegan's text flashed up.

I'm coming.

317

'Thank God for that.' Her shoulders slumped in relief and she started to text Shayla but the phone buzzed again. It was Connor.

Thanks. I do love her, u know. C

'You'd better do,' Lottie murmured.

Another message. Keegan again.

How will I get there?!!!!! ☹

Texting as she walked to Shayla's office, Lottie typed:

Don't worry. It's all sorted. ☺

Another little white lie to Keegan, but Lottie didn't feel bad about this one. Compared to the mountain she'd had to climb to smooth things over with the bride and groom, getting eighty guests, a registrar and all the suppliers to a snow-bound Firholme should be a doddle.

Chapter Thirty-Six

Lottie, Shayla and Jay gathered in the café for a war cabinet. The tractor had already been dispatched to collect some of the staff from the nearby villages and Jay said he'd left his deputy in charge of the Christmas tree centre for any hardy souls who ventured out in the snow.

'The most important thing is obviously to get the bride, groom and their immediate family here safely,' Lottie said, holding a clipboard to write down who was transporting whom. Sometimes, the old-fashioned methods were the best. 'Clearly the vintage Rolls is out of the question and none of the wedding hire company's vehicles can even make it out of their unit.'

'What about the registrar?' Jay asked.

'She called a few minutes ago. She only lives two miles away so she's walking here with her husband,' Shayla said.

'Wow, that's going beyond the call of duty. Without her, there's no wedding.'

Jay picked up a pen and sheet of paper from the desk. 'How many of the guests will I need to arrange transport for?'

'Thirty at least, though we're still working it out. I'm in touch with Connor's best man,' Lottie said. 'He's an Aussie army officer and he's marshalling everyone for me, and letting me know who still needs a lift.' He'd also told Lottie that Connor was panicking and wondering whether to tell his mum what was happening.

'It's a changing situation but so far he knows that half a dozen people who live a distance away have cancelled. That's a shame but in view of the weather, we don't want anyone making dangerous journeys,' she continued. 'There are around twenty people staying in local hotels already so the best man has arranged for as many of those as possible to come in four-wheel drives. He's sent me their names.' She tapped the clipboard. 'We need to tick them off when they get here. We don't want anyone vanishing into a snowdrift . . .'

Shayla laughed. 'I'll find someone to do that. You'll be busy enough as it is, Lottie.'

'Thanks. I also had a message from Connor's sister, Alicia. She's organised a rota among her horsey friends who all seem to have Land Rovers so I think we've covered most of the guests.'

'That's good of her,' Shayla said.

'Yes . . .' Lottie suspected Alicia was relishing the excuse to spend the morning in scruffy gear with her horsey pals, rather than having rows about false eyelashes and manicures.

Jay made a note. 'So that just leaves the bridal party?'

Shayla nodded. 'Yup. I'll collect Keegan and her mum and

dad. She'll have to make do with my car, in the circumstances. How are the groom's family getting here?'

Lottie was on this one. 'His best man has an SUV so he's bringing Connor and his parents. I've warned everyone to allow extra time to get here.'

Jay had been listening carefully. 'I've been sorting out transport in the forestry vehicles for our own staff who live off site. Are the caterers and photographer able to get here?'

'They're used to reaching places with difficult access and in all weathers so they're confident their vehicles can get here,' Lottie said. 'I also organised some hot drinks and a place to change for the guests while they wait for everyone to gather.'

Shayla nodded approvingly. 'Well done, everyone. I suppose no one has thought of how everyone will get home again?'

Jay lifted his phone. 'I've checked the forecast with the national park service. There's no more snow on its way and a mild front coming in by nightfall so hopefully, we should have a thaw by the end of the party.'

Lottie was relieved to hear it. 'Great, otherwise we'll be making up beds in the café.'

'I hope not.' Shayla rubbed her hands together. 'OK. Let's get this show on the road, folks.'

In Lottie's experience, wedding day time operated in a different universe to normal time. Half an hour flew by as if it were five minutes, and in a flash, it was noon, with only two hours to go to the ceremony. Due to the logistics, the guests were already beginning to arrive in an eclectic mix of vehicles.

They were dropped off in front of the café so that they

321

didn't have far to walk. Lottie snapped a few photos of the scene, as a bunch of people in riding gear and wellies exited the drivers' doors, helping people in suits and dresses out of the vehicles.

Alicia climbed out of the muddiest vehicle. Dressed in Hunter's and a padded jacket, she bounded up to Lottie, taking her aside.

A sly smile spread across her face. 'I bet this snow's caused a load of trouble for you but every cloud has a silver lining! I get to wear my "uniform" a bit longer and can put the bridesmaid's dress off until the last minute. I suppose I'd better look happy about it too.'

'I think that would be a very good idea,' Lottie replied with mock sternness.

'Hm. Must go. I need to get changed. Mind you, at least there's no time for me to have my nails painted pink or put any of that gloop on my face!'

Feeling more optimistic than she had done since Connor had turned up at her door, Lottie greeted the guests with a warm smile and showed them into the café. Alicia drove off again, leading her fleet of riding school mates back down the drive.

Soon, the café echoed to the rafters with laughter and chatter as the wedding guests quaffed hot chocolate and mulled wine, while others went to get changed in the washrooms. Now they were safely at Firholme, most of them seemed to think it was a huge adventure, taking photos of the snowy scene and posting pictures and selfies on social media.

Lottie didn't blame them. Apart from the inconvenience of

transporting everyone, you couldn't have dreamed up a more spectacular and idyllic setting for a winter wedding. Plus of course, they also had no idea of the drama that had unfolded overnight ... She tried to picture the scene at Connor's parents' house where his father must be trying to persuade Fiona out for a 'family lunch' in such conditions. Lovely Fiona must have her suspicions.

Shayla set off in good time to collect Keegan and her parents. Lottie was relieved she didn't have to face them again, despite a kind of peace having broken out between them.

Half an hour before the ceremony, all the guests were enjoying their Aussie fizz in the drawing room of Firholme House, where a fire burned brightly in the hearth. Lottie had a few minutes to nip home for a quick change into a smart dress, knee-high boots and her red teddy coat. When she made it to back to the courtyard, Connor and his family were climbing out of the best man's car. The best man, whose name was Kai, was out first, dressed in a dashing uniform, complete with a sword at his side.

Connor exited the passenger door while Kai opened the door for Fiona and stood to attention.

She stepped out, wearing a beautiful green silk suit and wellies, Derrick handing her down from the car like a Victorian lady. Lottie saw her mouth widen in shock and heard her saying: 'How have you kept this a surprise? How?' over and over.

Despite all her drama and stress of the past few weeks, the expression of sheer delight on Fiona's face gave Lottie the warmest glow of pride and happiness. Not needing to feign

323

her broad grin, she hurried to the steps of Firholme House to greet Fiona, while Derrick, Kai and Connor retrieved shoes and coats from the rear of the car.

'Hello Fiona. Welcome to Firholme.'

Dazed, Fiona held up her hands in astonishment. 'Lottie Hargreaves! You dark horse. How on earth did you ever keep this a secret?'

'Honestly, I have no idea,' Lottie said as Fiona kissed her on the cheek. 'I'm sorry I had to stay quiet when we met in town. It was agony. When did you find out about the wedding?'

'Connor told me about an hour and a half ago. He told me to get changed because we were all off to a wedding. He was very emotional, but I expect he was overwhelmed.'

'I bet!' Lottie said, smiling, while thinking it was no wonder Connor had left it until the very last moment to tell his mum.

'I shed a few tears too. He and Keegan wanted to keep this a huge surprise for me after I was ill.' Fiona's eyes were misty. 'I hope it hasn't been too hard on you, my dear. I did let slip that you and Connor had once been close but Keegan didn't seem to take too much notice . . .'

'Not at all,' Lottie said, adding another little lie to her pile. 'I'm delighted I can make their day – and yours – special.'

Fiona hugged her. 'You'll always be a special friend, Lottie; in fact you're part of my family. Please say we'll keep in touch from now on.'

Lottie was losing it herself. 'Of course. Now, don't spoil your lovely make-up. You look wonderful.'

'So, do you, darling. You look very well . . .' Fiona arched an eyebrow. 'Is there a reason for that?'

'Just the fresh air.'

Fiona let her go as Connor and his father approached. 'Let's talk later if we can,' she whispered.

Lottie thought she'd be too busy for a chat, but nodded and smiled at Connor and Kai. 'Welcome to Firholme. Come inside, everyone, and warm yourselves in the café before you head to the main house for champagne. We have hot drinks and a warm fire waiting for you.'

With less than an hour to go, all of the guests had arrived apart from Keegan and her parents. Alicia was using her room in the main house to change out of her jodhpurs and into 'the nightie'.

'I won't have time to put any slap on, naturally,' she said with a smirk.

Leaving Alicia to swipe a glass of fizz, Lottie checked her phone anxiously; Shayla had just left the bride's house, with Keegan and her parents. They should be at Firholme within twenty minutes.

By now the guests were all well away on the champagne and canapés, and Lottie took a few moments to silently congratulate her team and the way they'd worked together against the odds to make Firholme sparkle like the jewel it was. The purples, crimsons and orange floral arrangements offered an exotic foil for the traditional holly, ivy and mistletoe that Jay had provided.

Lottie darted around, making sure everyone was happy, and that the registrar had everything she needed for the ceremony.

'Oh my! What a magnificent tree!' Fiona said, walking into the ballroom. 'And that smell is divine.'

'Our estate manager and his team did all of that,' Lottie said.

'Keegan will be delighted, although I expect she's already seen all of this,' Fiona said in wonder. 'Now I know what all the whispering and phones pinging were all about. I did wonder if this "family lunch" was some kind of celebration but I'd no idea it was a wedding. How Derrick kept it to himself I have no idea. You know what he's like for letting the cat out of the bag.'

Lottie laughed. 'I certainly do.'

Fiona was swept off to chat to a relative. Lottie was filled with relief, at least about the wedding itself. A few hours ago, she was facing disaster but now felt that no matter what she thought of Connor, at least his mother would get to see him married at Firholme. She'd managed to make that happen – anything after the couple left the premises was their own affair. She hoped for everyone's sake that they'd be happy together.

A sharp pang of regret struck her.

All around her, people were laughing, kissing each other, there was a buzz of excitement and anticipation in the air. She was used to the trappings of weddings – flowers, balloons, fireworks – they was part of her job. At the end of the day, though, Connor and Keegan were making a lifelong commitment . . . promising to love and care for each other, hopefully forever. Their future would, with luck, be long and happy and even include a family one day . . .

Never before had Lottie had such a desolate moment at a wedding: the feeling of being on the outside, her face pressed to the window watching other people rejoicing. Never had happiness – the deep and lasting kind that comes from being with someone you love and who loves you deeply – seemed so impossibly remote.

She'd glimpsed a chance that Jay could be the one, but after last night she felt she was further away from him than ever.

Her phone rang and she escaped onto the terrace to take a call from Shayla. 'Hi there. We're all ready for you,' she said.

'Great but we're not ready for you!' Shayla's voice was taut with anxiety. Lottie could hear raised voices in the background. 'We're a mile away but we're not going anywhere. The road's blocked by a delivery van that slid into a wall. I can't turn around either. There are cars behind me. We're completely stuck. I'm outside the car so Keegan and co can't hear me but they're freaking out.'

Lottie groaned. Could anything else possibly go wrong? She spotted Jay at the bottom of the steps and waved to him. He trotted up to her.

'Hang on, we'll come up with something,' she said a few seconds later. 'Jay's here. I'll put him on speaker.'

Shayla explained the problem, with Jay listening intently.

'What are our options?' she said to Jay. 'We can't ask Keegan and her parents to walk through the snow in their wedding gear.'

'Can you collect them in the tractor?' Lottie asked.

Jay scratched his chin. 'Maybe. Where exactly are you?'

'Almost opposite Fellside Farm!'

327

Lottie had a brainwave. 'Isn't there a farm gate around there?'

'Should be,' Jay said, exchanging a glance with her, as if he'd had the same idea.

'Hang on.' Shayla broke off for a few moments and they heard her breathing heavily. 'Yes, there is. About ten yards back.'

'OK. Stay put. I'll bring the tractor over our land and through the field to you. The farmer won't mind.'

Shayla's voice was laced with panic. 'OK but can you be quick? The wedding's in less than an hour.'

'I think you should warn people that the bride might be a bit late,' Jay said to Lottie.

'I agree, especially Connor . . .'

Jay raised his eyebrows. 'You could let him stew?' he said, with satisfaction.

'It's tempting, but for Fiona's sake, I'd better warn them.'

'What state is the cab in?' Lottie said.

'As you'd expect for a vehicle that's been hauling logs through the mud for days. I'll sort that out so don't worry but it will take a bit of time.'

Jay hurried away so Lottie picked up the phone again. When Shayla answered, Lottie could hear Keegan screeching. 'This is an omen! It's someone's way of saying I shouldn't go through with this.'

A stern Aussie voice, which Lottie recognised as Keegan's mother, spoke up. 'Don't be silly, it's just a bit of snow and don't cry – you'll ruin your bloody make-up.'

The next few words were muffled before Shayla came on the line. 'Hello, Lottie, it's all under control, then . . . we have absolutely no need to panic . . .' Shayla said slowly, leaving Lottie in no doubt of the atmosphere in the 'wedding' car.

'It is. Jay's on his way but there might be a short delay. I'll warn the guests if you can reassure Keegan,' Lottie said to Shayla. 'But maybe don't mention the tractor just yet.'

Lottie spoke to Connor, reassuring him Keegan would only be delayed a little longer. Even so, Connor was twitchy. 'Where exactly is she?'

'Jay says it's all in hand. It takes time to prepare the tractor and cab. It's a working vehicle.'

'Tractor!' Connor snorted in horror. 'I can't believe Keegan's going to arrive in a tractor.'

'You're lucky she's coming at all.'

'Yeah . . . Yes. Sorry. I'm a bit stressed.' He nodded. 'Thanks for talking to her. I don't know what you said but it worked. You got me off the hook.'

'Why don't you go back inside and talk to your mum,' Lottie said, keen to steer clear of any friction. She managed a reassuring smile for him. 'This was meant to be her day too, remember?'

'If Keegan ever makes it,' he said gloomily.

'They'll get here. I have every faith in Jay.'

Connor scrutinised her. 'Yes, I can see that.'

'Do you want me to update your guests on the situation?' she asked before Connor said any more about Jay. 'Or do you want to tell them?'

'Me? No, you do it. You'd be so much better. I can hardly speak for nerves as it is.'

'OK. Fine.'

Lottie stood on the dais and addressed those guests still sitting in their seats. 'We may have a little while longer to wait for the bride due to a – um – minor transport malfunction,' she said. 'It's all under control and I can assure you we *will* have a bride. In the meantime, do please return to the drawing room for some more champagne.'

There were a few sighs but most were only too delighted at the prospect of more fizz. Connor was sinking a glass himself and Lottie hoped they wouldn't all be sozzled by the time the actual ceremony took place. She arranged refreshments for the registrar and then retreated to an anteroom to check her phone. Keegan was over an hour late now and Lottie couldn't even get hold of Jay.

Just as she was beginning to wonder if Keegan had changed her mind after all, Lottie received a message from Jay.

Get everyone on the steps of the house ASAP.

Chapter Thirty-Seven

Lottie walked into the drawing room and picked up the mike. 'Ladies and gentlemen, can I have your attention, please? I have some fantastic news. The bride is on her way any time now. Can I please ask you all to either come outside to the steps of the house or keep a lookout from the window of the ballroom for the arrival of the bride?'

Connor hurried over. 'Is everything OK?'

'Yes. Don't worry. She's on her way. I think you should come outside,' she told him.

'Thank God for that.'

Spotting a posy of flowers on a chair, Lottie rescued it and gave it to Alicia, who had a pint in her hand. 'Keegan's on her way,' she said. 'I think it would be a good idea if you waited here in the doorway.'

Sighing, Alicia put down her glass and took the posy and Lottie noticed the Hunter's poking out from the bottom of her bridesmaid's dress.

'No time to change them now,' Alicia declared. 'Look, the queen is here.'

A collective 'oh' rippled through the guests gathered at the windows and on the terrace.

Rushing outside, Lottie almost had to rub her eyes in disbelief. A traditional sleigh driven by Cush and pulled by two reindeer made its way up across the field towards Firholme. Behind it was the tractor driven by Jay carrying Keegan's parents. She whipped out her phone to video the arrival for the twins, wishing they could have come to the wedding and seen it for themselves.

The sleigh drew closer as guests crowded onto the porch steps to take pictures and videos. Keegan was grinning from ear to ear and waving like royalty. The photographer dashed out, snapping pictures of the sleigh and the reindeer in their red harnesses with jingling bells. They looked magnificent against the backdrop of snowy fells, and the lake glittering in the valley below.

Cush brought the deer to a halt a little way from the steps and called: 'Stand back, folks, and if you could dampen down the excitement a little, that would be good.'

She climbed down from the sleigh, leaving Keegan sitting serenely inside, wrapped in her cloak with its furry hood.

'Oh, my word, it's a real-life Snow Queen,' Fiona cried.

'Looks more like the White Witch to me,' Alicia muttered in Lottie's ear. 'I love those gorgeous reindeer though.'

Jay and some of the grounds staff manoeuvred an accessibility ramp into position between the sleigh and the steps and placed a red carpet on it.

Connor appeared to be dumbstruck.

She gave him a gentle nudge. 'Your bride is waiting,' she said.

Snapping into action, he walked down the steps and handed Keegan out of the sleigh, while Cush soothed the reindeer. Meanwhile, Jay helped her parents out of the tractor. Her father stood next to her while her mother spread the cloak out. Dozens of phones were still snapping and videoing, and the photographer was having a field day.

Lottie stood at the top of the steps and clapped her hands. 'Ladies and gentlemen, could you please all make your way back inside to await the entrance of the bride?'

Her announcement had the desired effect and guests made their way back into the house where they were directed into the ballroom to take their seats for the ceremony. Lottie went to help the bridal party. To her relief, Kai had already ushered Connor back inside the house, and Keegan's mum was on her way up the steps too, which left the bride and her father waiting at the bottom.

Lottie was keen to get them out of the cold as soon as possible.

'This is going on the front page of my website!' the photographer said to Lottie. 'Just one more with the sleigh!' he called.

She'd heard that phrase 'just one more' a hundred times before, so she took charge before Keegan and her dad turned blue.

'We're ready to start. Please go back inside,' she said firmly, then turned to Keegan. 'You look amazing.' She was struck

333

by how she'd changed over the past few weeks, from being shocked and hurt that Connor was getting married, to simply being proud that she'd organised a wedding to remember against all the odds.

She saw Keegan and her father safely into the house where Alicia was waiting, as meek as a lamb. Making sure there were no stray guests to be rounded up from outside, Lottie met Jay outside the doors.

'Where's Shayla?' she asked, a little concerned about her boss being stranded.

'She says she'll be along soon because the stranded car is being towed away, but I'll drive down to her in the tractor to make sure,' he said.

'Thanks. For everything. I don't think we will ever top a bride arriving by a sleigh pulled by reindeer.'

'I got lucky and it was all thanks to Cush for agreeing to do it. I'm glad they're happy but . . . I did it for *you*.'

She held her breath.

'I'm not a complete arse. Not all of the time, anyway, but I can see why you're angry with me. I'm probably not the best person for any woman to be with, especially not someone as lovely as you.'

He walked off.

'Wait. Jay.' Lottie was left longing to ask him what he meant, but knowing she could do nothing until this wedding was over.

Darkness had fallen and the speeches were over when Lottie finally snatched a few minutes to herself. She sneaked off to

334

the tiny staff cloakroom, once a butler's pantry, and heaved a huge sigh of relief. Keegan and Connor were married. Her job wasn't done yet; there was the evening party to get through, but with everyone safely inside the house, she hoped nothing major would go wrong.

Exiting the cloakroom she was surprised to find Fiona, holding a glass and gazing up at the grand staircase and entrance hall. Her eyes lit up when she saw Lottie. 'Lottie!'

'Fiona.' Lottie smiled.

'This has been the most amazing experience. I want to thank you. You're very welcome. I'm happy it went so well. Connor had no idea I was the wedding planner when he walked in with Keegan but they wanted the ceremony here for you, and Connor – we both – wanted our former relationship kept private.'

The doors to the gents' opened and Jay strolled out. He was wearing his velvet jacket and jeans, and looking wickedly gorgeous. She wanted to get the conversation over with but Fiona had her back to him, and must have no idea he was there. He waited a few feet away, watching them.

'That must have been very hard for you, my dear,' Fiona said.

'Only at the start. I – I realised that we were never meant for each other.' Lottie trod a very fine line between tact and honesty. Much as she liked Fiona, she couldn't come out and say: I'm glad I never married your son. I'm glad I met someone who would be so much better for me. Or who *could* have been much better, if he'd only learn to let go of the past and let himself be happy again.

335

'That's very diplomatic. I hope Keegan and Connor are meant for each other.'

'I'm sure they are,' Lottie said quickly, hearing the band start up in the ballroom.

'Yes.' Fiona looked wistful. 'Let's keep everything crossed for a happy ending.' She had to raise her voice above the bass line from the ballroom. 'Or a happy beginning. The moment full of optimism, hope, when anything is possible.'

'That's how I try to think of it with every couple.' Lottie gave a wry smile, hoping Jay would leave, but he didn't.

'I hope you've found someone who deserves you.'

Acutely aware that Jay was within hearing distance, Lottie laughed. 'I'm not sure who deserves me.'

'He'd have to be someone pretty special. Someone who appreciates you and knows not to ever let you go.' Fiona hiccupped. 'Whoops. Forgive me. Too much fizz.' She turned and finally caught sight of Jay.

'Is this the Jay who rescued my daughter-in-law and arranged that magnificent entrance?' Fiona waved her glass rather cavalierly in the air; a few drops splashed out. 'Keegan pointed you out earlier but I wanted to thank you personally.'

'It nearly didn't happen,' Lottie said when Jay joined her, standing awkwardly by. 'And I had so many people who all pulled together to make it happen.'

'Well you can relax now. Connor and Keegan are man and wife and the party has only just got going.'

'I hope so,' Lottie said, finally wondering if she dared allow herself the tiniest sip of fizz. Even if her love life was falling apart before it had started – again – she could certainly afford to let out a huge sigh of relief as far as the reception was concerned.

'Go on, have a little glass, both of you. You've earned it.' Fiona summoned a waiter. 'Can you be a love and let us have two glasses of fizz, please, for these amazing people?'

'A tiny one!' Lottie protested.

The waiter held out the silver tray and Lottie took a glass that still had twice as much champagne as she would dare to drink while working.

'Thank you,' Jay said politely, and accepted a glass but didn't drink from it.

'There you are. Cheers!' Fiona raised her glass and Lottie put hers to her lips, just as the lights in the house flickered and everyone was plunged into darkness.

Chapter Thirty-Eight

The band stopped. A few shrieks pierced the air followed by laughter.

'Oh gosh, I never expected that!'

Fiona's shock was mirrored by Lottie, but it was quickly followed by a rush of adrenaline and the need for action. Her eyes tried to adjust to the darkness, but even the clouds had come over, hiding all but the occasional glimpse of the moon shining on the snow. 'The emergency lighting will come on any moment,' she said, switching on her phone torch. 'Fiona, come into the ballroom with me and we'll reassure everyone.'

Jay's deep voice was at her side. 'I'll fetch a proper torch from the butler's pantry and take a look. I'm afraid the maintenance team are in no fit state to be messing around in the electric system.'

'Thanks. Be careful.'

'I will.' He walked into the darkness, his phone screen lighting his way.

Lottie guided Fiona back to the ballroom where many of the guests had also turned on their phones, illuminating dozens of faces with an eerie light. Even without the lights, the buzz of voices would have led them there anyway, and the sound of Keegan shouting. 'Oh my God! What's happened?'

Lottie called for attention. 'Ladies and gentlemen. Apologies for the temporary power failure. Our generator should cut in any time soon with some emergency lighting and our maintenance team are on their way to fix it. Until then, can I ask that you stay exactly where you are to avoid anyone tripping or falling in the darkness? Please, bear with us and we'll have the party started again very soon.'

Lottie spotted Connor and Keegan, who was sitting on the dais, her face lit up by Shayla's torch.

'Can I help?' Shayla asked, taking Lottie aside.

'Yes, please. Could you make sure that everyone is OK for me? Let me know if you're concerned about anyone?'

'Will do.'

'Any ETA for the lights to be back on?' her boss asked.

Lottie decided to be honest with Shayla. 'They should have already kicked in,' she said discreetly. 'Jay's on his way to the generator now. If you could help me keep people calm in the meantime, I'd be grateful.'

'Let's hope it's sorted soonest. Keep me posted.' Although Shayla was calm, there was a distinct edge to her voice.

Lottie turned her attention to Keegan.

'Should we light the candles or something?' Connor suggested.

'At least that would be romantic,' Keegan said.

Lottie was a bit worried about the fire risk but relented, thinking anything that kept Keegan happy was a good thing and it really would be romantic . . . 'OK. It shouldn't be too long before we have power. Jay's gone to sort some emergency lighting.'

She asked the catering staff to bring in some tealights for the tables from the store room and soon the ballroom was lit by flickering candlelight. It was all very Christmassy and the delighted photographer took his chance to get some photos of a very happy couple by the tree. With the holly, ivy, decorations and romantic lighting, the room looked stunning and would make a wonderful showcase for future weddings.

Lottie's relief that Keegan was happy was undercut by her growing concern that the generator hadn't kicked in. Any moment now, the lights would flare into life and the disco ball glitter again but the minutes ticked by and the ripple of unease among the guests grew louder.

Just as Lottie was beginning to worry, the emergency lights came on to a collective murmur of thanks. A sea of relieved faces materialised in the low-level lighting, including the band, looking very pissed off that their set had been cut off.

'Thank goodness for that,' Fiona murmured.

Even though the lights made it safe for people to move around, they were hardly festive and there was still no power for the band or disco. With people at least able to see each other and visit the bar, Lottie went into the hall to take a call from Jay who was in the facilities room at the rear of the house.

It wasn't what she'd had hoped for.

'The diesel generator isn't working. I've no idea why so I've called the generator company and they're sending an emergency team but they're twenty minutes away. It's lucky the snow's melting but even in the best case it could be an hour before the power can be restored.'

'It's only seven,' she said in dismay. 'The party's barely started but I'll have to ask everyone to be patient.'

'The band could still play unplugged, and they can manage without the mikes,' Jay said. 'Why not ask them to do that?'

'Do you think they would?' Lottie said.

'I don't see why not. That's what I'd do. Do you want me to have a word? I recognised the guy on the bass guitar from the local gig circuit.'

'That would be great, thanks. I'll update Keegan and Connor.'

Jay was back in a couple of minutes and spoke to the band, while Lottie attempted to placate her bride and groom.

The novelty of the candlelight was already wearing off. 'What else is going to go wrong?' Keegan said. 'We've paid a fortune to have the perfect wedding here and so far, it's been one disaster after another.'

'Now, Keegan, that's not exactly fair, is it?' her mother said, obviously used to her daughter's tantrums. 'If this snow hadn't come down, you'd never have arrived by sleigh. You must be the only bride who's ever done that. And this candlelight is gorgeous.'

'I suppose so,' Keegan said grudgingly. 'But this *is* your responsibility,' she flung at Lottie.

'The power failure is due to the weather,' Lottie said

patiently. 'And while we couldn't have foreseen the generator problem, please accept my sincere apologies. The engineer is on his way and I'm confident we'll have it up and running soon.' She crossed her fingers mentally.

'Lottie's right. The power will soon be back on, nutkin,' Connor said.

In the nick of time, Jay came up. 'The band are going to carry on until we get the power restored. Don't worry, I'll watch out for the generator engineer and stress how urgent it is.'

After a short delay, the music started up again and Lottie was relieved to have an excuse to escape into the vestibule where Jay delivered the good news that the generator engineers were only moments away. The warm front had brought drizzle and a thaw, which must make it easier for them to get there.

A minute later, the lights of a van wavered on the driveway and pulled up outside.

'There they are,' Jay said. 'I'll take them to the facilities room.'

'I want to hear how long they think it will take,' Lottie said, pulling on her coat and following him, not adding that she'd like to get away from Keegan's moaning.

The engineer climbed out and Jay approached. From the way both men suddenly stopped and kept their distance from each other, she knew in an instant it was Ben.

They faced each other, Ben with a toolbox, Jay with a torch, like two gunfighters ready to draw, except it wasn't funny.

Lottie intercepted them both, standing between them.

'You're not going to make a thing of this, are you? I need this generator fixing now, or I'll have a furious bride and groom demanding their money back. Jay, you go back inside and make sure everyone's OK. I'll take you up to the generator, Ben.'

He glanced from Jay and back to Lottie. 'Thanks.'

'No, I'll take Ben to the generator room,' he said.

'Suit yourself but I'm coming too. No arguments. Now, get a move on.'

It didn't come naturally to boss two grown men around like a headmistress, but Lottie wasn't in the mood to mess around.

They caught up with her, one on either side. Lottie opened the door.

'It's in here.'

Lottie let him inside and he examined the generator.

'I was expecting a team. Didn't know you worked for Parsons,' Jay muttered.

'I don't. I'm self-employed now but I'm one of their on-call contractors. Believe me, I don't relish being out here in this bloody weather on a Saturday night but I'm the only team you're going to get.' He nodded to Lottie. 'Excuse me for being blunt. Obviously, it's my job to help customers out, but Jay did ask.'

Jay was stony-faced.

'None of us wants to be here,' Lottie said coolly. 'Can you fix it?'

'Fortunately, yes. It's a simple job. The transfer switch has gone, which was what I thought it might be when the message came through from head office. It's one of the most common reasons for this type of kit to fail and so I always keep spares.'

'Will it take long?' Lottie asked, relieved that one of her problems might be easily sorted out.

'Ten minutes. Fifteen tops.'

'Good because there's no chance of the mains power being restored anytime soon.'

'I heard it could be off until morning,' Ben said.

Jay lurked nearby, showing no signs of leaving. Lottie decided to let him stew and called Shayla with an update.

She waited while Ben replaced the switch, refusing to leave them alone.

He straightened up. 'There. It's done.'

'Thank you,' Lottie said.

'It's my job, you're very welcome and I'm happy to help. I'm sorry I said I hadn't wanted to come out.'

'It's OK.' Lottie was aware of Jay standing by, with a face like thunder.

Ben picked up his toolbox. 'Goodnight, then.'

'You too, safe journey home,' Lottie said, all too aware that 'home' meant the one he shared with Nadia and Seb. It was so frustrating to be constantly treading on eggshells with Jay, where Ben was concerned.

'Thanks,' he said. As he walked past Jay he said, 'Jay, I get that you're still angry with me but I can't stand seeing you like this – like a wounded animal who won't let people close. I am so very sorry that things turned out like they did.'

He held out his hand.

Jay stayed resolutely silent.

'OK. Don't take my hand, or even forgive me but ask yourself why – be honest with yourself – if you really want to let this fester and spoil all the good things you have now. I can't wish I'd never met Nadia. But sooner or later it would have happened anyway.'

Lottie despaired. She was embarrassed and upset at the level of enmity he'd nursed all this time. What did Ben mean, that he and Nadia would have got together anyway? She thought Jay and Nadia had had a happy relationship . . . but she couldn't afford to deal with it now.

'I'll walk with you down to the drive,' she said to Ben.

'I can find my way but thanks, anyway. You'd better get back to the wedding.'

With that, he let himself out of the building, leaving Jay and Lottie alone.

'I'm going back to the ballroom,' she said, waiting for him to say he'd join her.

'I suppose you think I should have thanked him?' Jay said.

She was about to deny it but was too worked up. 'I – it's none of my business and I can't deal with this now. I understand what it's like to cling on to love for someone – to try and hang on to something you can never get back.'

Jay tried to speak but Lottie wasn't to be silenced.

'I'm glad Connor turned up, no matter how hard it's been, because it's made me realise that we were never suited. That I didn't need him, or want him. Because of our break-up I moved to Firholme. Don't hate your brother. I've had rows with Steph – nothing like you have – but her illness has made me realise that it's never worth pushing away someone you love.'

Chapter Thirty-Nine

Lottie finally shut the door on the world just after two a.m. The generator powered the house and at midnight, the rest of the site was restored to the mains. The rain had turned to a full Lakeland downpour, sluicing through the snow, leaving the roads passable for the guests to leave in taxis or be picked up by the riding-school volunteers.

The bride and groom went up to their room along with the rest of the wedding party and the reception had wound up.

At one time, the thought of Connor spending his wedding night at Firholme, with another woman, would have broken Lottie's heart. Now, she was relieved that he was spending it with Keegan, and not her. She'd escaped from a marriage that would never have given her the contentment and joy she craved.

Jay's comment from earlier in the day wouldn't go away: he said he'd made all the effort for *her*. He'd pulled out all the stops and everything had been so promising until Ben had turned up. They worked as a team, he was kind, and she fancied him way more than she'd ever fancied Connor. He was exciting, complex and – she realised – a challenge. Was she attracted to him because of that? She mustn't let herself think of him as a lost cause that she could save.

Yet she was still unsettled by his lack of trust – and the scars of the breakdown in his relationship with his brother and Nadia had affected him. Could he ever trust someone again – especially after she'd lied to him about Connor?

Lottie didn't know but she wasn't sure they could move their relationship forward until she was sure.

With that on her mind, and after her rollercoaster of a day, she didn't think she'd be able to sleep but she also hadn't reckoned on how exhausted she was. The next thing she knew, it was morning and daylight was peeping through the curtains where she'd been too tired to shut them properly.

She woke and threw back the curtains on a world of melting snow, muddy fields and leaden clouds reaching down to the lake. It was such a contrast to the fairy-tale Narnia that had greeted her yesterday and it cast a pall over her mood.

Over breakfast, she sent a video of the reindeer arrival to Steph and the girls, smiling at the excitement with which it would probably be greeted. She only hoped the twins didn't expect a sleigh pulled by reindeer to arrive at their own front door on Christmas Eve.

What a pleasure it was to see the girls for Sunday lunch, while she and Steph ran the reindeer video over and over and looked at the latest photos emailed by their parents. Lottie didn't think she'd ever missed them more and plans were made for their visit in the early spring.

It was also a relief to tell Steph about the wedding and a real treat to put her feet up and throw herself into family life. The girls were a tonic for any ailment or worry. After lunch, they cosied up next to her on the sofa, brimming with excitement.

'We've bought you a present!' they trilled in unison.

Lottie raised an enquiring eyebrow. 'Oh, lovely but it's a bit early, isn't it?'

Myra folded her arms. 'You need this present *now*.'

'Open it!' Jodie ordered.

They handed Lottie a paper bag with several smaller parcels inside, wrapped in tissue paper.

'OK. If you insist.'

She opened the first and took out a wooden owl with huge yellow eyes. 'Wow. An owl. I love owls. I can hear them outside my window at Firholme.'

'He's for your tree!' Myra said. 'I chose him from the Christmas fair.'

Jodie tugged at her sleeve. 'Open mine next, Auntie Lottie!'

'I am. I want to make it last.'

'No, open them now!' they chorused.

Steph grinned. 'You'd better do as you're told, Auntie Lottie.'

The next parcel contained a wooden reindeer with a red ribbon to hang it from the tree. 'That is beautiful . . .' she held the decoration by the ribbon, brimful of emotion. 'Just like Cush's reindeer.'

'I chose that,' Jodie said. 'And Mummy chose this one.'

Steph smiled as Lottie took the largest of the parcels out of the bag. Inside the tissue was a globe containing something sparkly and pink. 'Wow, a snow globe,' she said. 'How pretty.'

'No, silly!' Myra giggled. 'It's gin.'

Jodie sniggered. 'Mummy got it from the fair. She said you wouldn't be able to wait until Christmas to drink it.'

'Mummy's right.' She gave Steph a look. 'Thanks. I will try and hang it on the tree, at least until Christmas Eve.'

Steph laughed. 'It's some kind of pink grapefruit flavour with edible glitter. Couldn't resist it.'

Lottie dangled the gin in front of her. 'It's way better than a snow globe.'

The twins were still jigging and Myra plucked another bag from behind a cushion. 'We got something else,' she said.

'For Jay.' Jodie took the bag and thrust it at Lottie.

'Jay?'

'It's a thank you for the tree,' Steph said. 'Sorry, but the girls insisted, even if he doesn't celebrate Christmas.'

'Open it!' the twins declared.

'No, it's for Jay to open,' Steph said. 'I'm sure Auntie Lottie will let us know what he thinks . . .' She exchanged a knowing glance with Lottie. 'And now, it is bedtime and no arguments!'

Steph flopped onto the sofa. 'How are you?' Lottie asked.

'I'm OK . . .'

'Any word from Kerr?'

'He sent me a WhatsApp message asking how I am. Did you give him my number?'

'Might have done,' Lottie said. 'I hope it was OK?'

349

'Definitely but don't get too excited. I replied saying I was fine, but I haven't heard anything since.'

'Maybe you need to make the first move. Kerr's a quiet kind of guy. He might be waiting for a hint.'

'You could be right but I'm too worried about this scan to take things further. Much as I fancy him, I need to know I'm going to have a future before I can start planning it.'

'Oh, hon. I'm so sorry I'd forgotten it was racing up so soon, with all the wedding chaos.'

'It's OK. You have to have a life of your own. I'll be fine.'

Despite this, Lottie knew Steph must be terrified of the cancer coming back. She'd have given up everything for her sister to be well but life didn't work like that; and all she could do was hug her and reassure her that she'd always be there for her, no matter what life threw their way.

It was ten o'clock when she arrived home, and made up the fire. After the laughter and excitement at Steph's, the Bothy felt very empty. However, the glowing hearth warmed her spirits and she made herself a hot chocolate and started to arrange the cards on the mantelpiece.

She added the new decorations from the tree to her own, wondering what to do with Jay's present. She had no idea when, if ever, would be the right opportunity to give it to him.

Since the adrenaline of the wedding she'd had more time to reflect on what had happened with Ben. Jay was obviously still hung up about Nadia, and Lottie wanted a fresh start. No matter how much she wanted it to be with Jay, it was never going to work for them.

With Steph's future uncertain and her hopes for Jay at rock bottom, no sparkle from the Christmas tree or music on the TV could lift her mood. Rain hammered against the windows and she could hear the beck rushing down past the end of the garden. She was mulling over whether to have a Baileys to cheer herself up when there was a knock at the door.

Her first thought was that it might be Shayla popping by but when she opened the door, she found Jay, standing in the rain in only a T-shirt and jeans.

'Jay!'

He leaned against the doorframe, white as a sheet and held his head in his hands. 'What's the matter?'

'It's Seb. He's in intensive care. It's meningitis and they're not sure he'll make it.'

Chapter Forty

Lottie virtually dragged him into the hall. 'Oh God, I'm so sorry. Come in, out of the rain.'

It was then Jay realised that his face wasn't wet because of rain but from tears of shock. He rubbed his hand over his eyes. 'Sorry. Dad only called a few minutes ago. I ignored all of Ben's calls . . . That's why my dad had to phone me. Oh God, Lottie, what have I done?'

She didn't hesitate. 'Nothing, but you *can* do something now. I'll drive you to the hospital in the truck. Get your coat.'

'I – do you really think they'll want me there?' Jay seemed frozen. 'I'm desperate to go but he's not my little boy. Jesus they must be out of their minds. They might lose him.'

'Would you want them at your side?'

'Yes. Yes. Of course!'

'Then you have your answer. I'll take you now.' She held his arms, looking into his face. 'Come on, let's go.'

Grabbing her own coat, she herded him out of the door

and into his cottage where Trevor was watching them from his blanket on the carpet. Trevor sat up with a hopeful whine.

'Not this time, Trevor,' Lottie said, ruffling his ears. She found Jay's jacket, 'Put it on,' she ordered.

Minutes later, Jay was hunched in the passenger seat, staring zombie-like out of the front window.

'Do you know when Seb was taken ill? Ben didn't say anything last night,' she said, steering the truck smoothly out of the gates and onto the public road.

'No . . .' Jay was crushed by the story his dad had told him. 'Apparently Seb was a bit under the weather last night though Nadia thought it was just a cold.'

'Oh no.' Lottie's knuckles whitened on the wheel.

'Seb seemed better this morning but then he went downhill after dinner and developed a rash this afternoon. They called an ambulance and it rushed him off to hospital. They must be out of their minds with worry.'

'He's in the best hands.' She steered the truck between the dry-stone walls of a narrow lane that was a short cut to the A road. The wipers swished furiously, barely coping with the rain.

'What if it's not enough?'

'You have to hope it will be. They'll be doing absolutely everything to save him.'

'But they might not be able to. You know that, Lottie.'

'Try not to think the worst. Ben needs you to be strong and positive for him. If something terrible happens, then he's going to need you to be even stronger.'

'Poor Nadia,' he murmured, thinking of the agony his ex must be going through. 'No one deserves this . . . and oh God, my mum and dad will be beside themselves with worry.'

'All the more reason for you to be there to support them.'

It was an agonising journey, made worse by the roads being so wet. Lottie did brilliantly with the strange vehicle, but they couldn't risk rushing too much and at one point, she had to negotiate through a flooded section.

On the journey, Jay texted his parents and received a reply from his father, saying they were 'hoping for the best', whatever that meant. He guessed his dad was putting on a brave face for the rest of the family. Seb was their first and only grand-child, unexpected – and his arrival had split the family apart – but he was also Jay's flesh and blood, and precious.

Lottie offered to stay, but Jay thought she might be there all night and he persuaded her to go home and get some sleep. He knew he'd have none. When Lottie dropped him off outside the hospital, he took a few moments to steel himself. He didn't even know if his little nephew was still alive but he tried to hold on to Lottie's words: his family needed someone to offer hope and strength, and if, God forbid, the worst happened, Lottie was right, they'd need him even more.

When she'd asked him if he'd want Ben with him, if he'd been in the same situation, he hadn't hesitated. No matter what had happened, he loved them. He always had even if that love had lain buried under an avalanche of disappoint-ment and bitterness.

None of it mattered now. He'd go through it a thousand times again if Seb could live.

Even as he thought it, he realised that bargains like that were futile.

He gave his name at the desk and was sent up to the paediatric ICU where a nurse told him Seb was still critical and showed him into a side room. His parents leapt up from their chairs and his mum flew into his arms and sobbed. His dad stood by, grim-faced, while Jay attempted to soothe his mother, although all he could do was let her cry, and keep saying, 'He'll be OK. I know he will,' while his mother cried herself out.

A couple of hours later, Jay went to get everyone a cup of tea but before he reached the machine, Ben emerged from the ICU. He looked like a broken man, grey-faced, and exhausted.

Jay experienced the worst moment of his life: one that eclipsed the moment he'd found out Seb wasn't his. One far darker and more terrifying than he had ever known.

He froze before meeting his brother. 'Ben?' was the only word he could squeeze from his paralysed throat.

'He's turned the c-corner,' Ben said. 'He's not out of danger but he's responding well.'

Ben's arms hung by his sides but Jay didn't hesitate. He flung his arms around his brother and held him more tightly than he'd ever held him before. Ben sobbed like a baby, and Jay let his own tears flow.

'Mate,' he said softly, releasing Ben. 'I'm more relieved than

355

you can ever know but for God's sake don't let Mum and Dad see us like this. Go and tell them now, put them out of their misery, eh?'

'Will you come with me? Nadia's still with Seb.'

'Course I will, if you want me to.'

Ben hugged him again, so hard, it took Jay's breath away. 'Thank you for coming. Thank you so much.'

It was early morning before his parents went home for a few hours' rest. Seb had continued to improve and was out of immediate danger. Jay had texted Lottie with an update on Seb's progress and asked her to look after Trevor for him.

Now morning was breaking, he decided it would be safe to go home himself. He was exhausted and in desperate need of a shower. He headed down the corridor. He could call Ben and Nadia later.

Ben saw him. 'Jay, wait!'

Ben thudded up behind him. 'Please don't rush off.'

'Seb's out of danger.'

'Thank you for being here for us. It means so much to me. To us – Nadia and me.'

'You don't have to thank me. You're family. All of you.'

Ben patted his back. 'That means the world to us. This is probably not the time but please hear me out. When I told you to move on, I didn't understand why you wouldn't forgive me. Well, I've tried to understand and I don't blame you. I came to accept you'd never see or speak to me again, that I've hurt you in the worst way I possibly could. I'm sorry. I can't undo the past.' He paused for breath. 'Like you said, I don't

356

wish to undo anything I did because that would mean I wouldn't have Seb. I would die for him, Jay.'

'I know you would,' Jay said. 'I would for you too – and for him if it would have helped. He's my family.'

Ben was on the verge of tears again. 'I don't deserve a brother like you.'

'C'mon,' Jay said. 'I'm only human, mate, and it's time we both put all of that behind us. I want to start my life again.'

Ben nodded and that 'big brother' glint appeared in his eyes, signalling he'd winkled out one of Jay's secrets. 'Does this fresh start involve Lottie by any chance?'

There was no point hiding. 'I don't know if she'll have me after the way I've treated her. I've probably blown my chances, letting all this . . . crap between us fester and blind me to any kind of future.'

With mock solemnity, Ben laid his hand on Jay's shoulder. 'Bro, don't you think you should be telling her this, not me?'

'Yes. I probably should.'

Ben hugged him, slapping his back. Jay held him, and his heart soared at the return of some of the warmth and love he used to feel for his brother. He'd spent a long, lonely time in the cold wilderness but he was home now. Almost home . . .

He thought of Lottie, waiting for his call to say he needed a lift from the hospital – but Jay had other plans.

Chapter Forty-One

Lottie's heart missed several beats when she saw Jay standing on her doorstep in the pouring rain, until she spotted the smile beneath the dark eyes and pallor.

She let him in, desperate for an update. She'd been waiting for his call but had only received texts saying things were going well and Jay had decided to get a taxi home.

She took him straight into the kitchen, which was warm from the Aga. 'Any more news of Seb?' she asked.

'He's still doing well and out of ICU. I got back a couple of hours ago and just had a kip and a shower.'

'Have you had anything to eat?'

He shook his head. 'Not yet. I wanted to let you know how Seb was and to thank you for taking me to the hospital. I wouldn't have been safe to drive.'

'It was the least I could do. Let me make you some breakfast.'

'Great. Thanks.'

After sitting him down at the kitchen table with a coffee, she got a pack of bacon from the fridge. She guessed he might want to talk about more than Seb but that could come in his own good time.

She turned on the gas under the frying pan, thinking of something undemanding to talk about while Jay collected his thoughts. He looked absolutely done in. 'I sent the video of Keegan and her reindeer to the twins,' she said, laying rashers in the pan.

'Were they impressed?'

'Of course. They loved it.'

She leaned against the work top while the rashers sizzled, filling the air with a sweet tang.

'I'm glad.' He wrinkled his nose. 'God, that smells good. I'm starving.'

'No wonder. You've had a hellish night.'

He shuddered. 'I never want to go through anything like that again.'

Lottie added another rasher to the pan for good measure.

'Is there anything I can do?' he asked above the hiss of frying bacon.

'You could slice some bread from the loaf. I've had some toast so just do yourself some.'

A few minutes later, she piled crispy bacon onto doorsteps of sourdough and found him a bottle of Daddies sauce. After making herself a fresh coffee, she joined him at the table. It gave her a lot of pleasure to watch him devour the sandwich, and to see the colour returning to his cheeks.

He'd had a massive shock, and coming on top of his row

with Ben, it had drained him. The worry had kept her awake much of the night too, waiting on, yet dreading, any news. She'd also wondered how Jay had managed with Ben during the crisis – and what would happen now between the family. Not to mention between her and Jay.

Once every crumb had gone from his plate, and been washed down with a second mug of coffee, he sat back with a sigh. He still looked tired but the tension had been replaced by a softer weariness.

'Thanks for that. It was exactly what I needed. Thanks for everything, Lottie. I don't know how I'd have coped without you. I was a complete mess last night.'

'That's understandable.'

'I don't mean at the hospital.' He swallowed. 'I mean after the wedding, with Ben and – and how I spoke to you. That was unforgivable. I want to tell you what happened between us.'

She wanted to hold him, soothe him, but felt he wasn't ready yet. 'Of course, I'll listen.'

'Nadia and me. Our relationship was on the rocks. In fact, I'm not sure we'd have stayed together if we hadn't found out the baby was on the way.'

'What?'

'It wasn't the perfect story that I let you think – or that I wanted to cling on to. Ben admitted to me that he'd been in love with her since I first introduced her to the family. They didn't do anything about it until one night when Nadia and I had had a row about something trivial that blew up out of all proportion. I drove off up to the fells and Ben came round while I was out. He found her and I suppose he comforted her.

That's when they slept together . . . It doesn't make what he did any easier but it makes it more understandable, I suppose.'

She waited for him to continue, unwilling to break the thread now he'd started.

'In other ways it made it harder for me – that they were in love for so long and she must have been thinking of leaving. I just wish that we could all have been honest with each other and split up. She did only sleep with him once, I think. She told me she kept trying to put it behind her and hoped we could still make a go of it with Seb. But when we were in that scan, the baby became so real, and she had to be honest with me.'

'Last Christmas, after I found out the baby wasn't mine, and I stormed out of the hospital, I drove around for hours. Eventually, I went over to Ben's flat and had it out with him. He was as shocked as I was – or so he claimed. Nadia hadn't told him that Seb might be his. He had no way of knowing that she and I hadn't had sex for a long time.'

Lottie thought that still didn't excuse Ben, but she kept quiet.

'We didn't come to blows but I said some really horrible stuff to him. I meant it at the time but now, I wish I hadn't blown up, no matter how upset I was.'

'So how did Nadia feel about it all?' Lottie asked.

'Devastated – not that I cared. I didn't go back home because I didn't want to see her. I tried to pretend she didn't exist, and directed all my hurt at Ben. I checked into the only hotel with a vacancy because I couldn't bear to see her or Ben or my mum and dad.' He glanced down at his hands. 'So, I basically spent last Christmas Day in a motorway service area, with Trevor, feeling sorry for myself. When I went back to the flat on Boxing Day, Nadia had gone. She'd packed up and left for Ben's place and she's stayed there ever since.'

'Oh, Jay. You can't beat yourself up for being so upset. What happened after Christmas?'

'I gave up the flat when the lease was up and applied for the job at Firholme here because I knew it had accommodation. I thought it would be a way of hiding away from the world. I've wasted a whole year wallowing in misery.'

'Not the whole year.'

'No.' His fingers closed over hers. 'You're right. You showed me how precious families are and how I could trust and love someone else again if I let go of all the fears and bitterness. I wasn't as healed as I thought – then I go and make the same mistake again.' He grasped Lottie's hand. 'Ben and I, we've decided to bury the hatchet and at least be civil with each other.'

'I'm so pleased to hear that.' Their fingers were entwined, each seeking and finding the trust they'd missed for so long. 'I want to tell you something about Connor and me.'

He frowned, perhaps expecting a fresh shock. 'What?'

'It's about the engagement and why it hurt so much when it ended. You see, Connor proposed to me at the end of a holiday in Cornwall. On a beach at sunset. He even went down on one knee, produced a ring and went for the whole rom com movie scene.'

'He really is a piece of work,' Jay murmured.

'I bought into the fantasy too . . . and when he changed

his mind and wanted people to believe we'd split up amicably I went along with that too. I felt humiliated and stupid that I'd let myself be so easily . . . conned. The last thing I wanted was pity. I was ashamed at being jilted, even though I hadn't been the cause of the pain.'

He grasped her hand again. 'Ashamed? You shouldn't have felt ashamed and yet, I *do* know how it feels. Oh, Lottie . . .'

'There was another reason why I didn't want anyone to know what had really happened between Connor and me. I did phone Steph to break the news, but I never got to tell her and I don't regret that. She'd only received her diagnosis that day. She didn't need any extra worry about me, so I lied and said it was a mutual decision and that I was fine with it.'

'Lottie, Lottie . . .' he kept saying, rubbing her hand. 'I'm so sorry for what you've been through.'

She was on the verge of tears. 'You're a good man, Jay, and you're the only person in the world who knows all the details, apart from Connor and me. You must promise me that things will stay that way.'

'Of course I will, but the man's more of an arse that I even dreamed. How have you been able to arrange the man's wedding, after what he did to you?'

'Gritted my teeth and got on with it, but . . . when he walked in, I was shocked. I was – jealous. I did think "what if" and I thought, for a few weeks, that I might still be in love with him. Gradually I realised I wasn't and that our time had gone – and most of all, that I didn't want our time to come again. Connor wasn't the man I'd once loved any more. He hadn't changed. I had . . . and I'd met you.'

His eyes shone with something like delight. She'd thought he was handsome from the start, but now he was literally making her go weak at the knees. She'd given up all hope of that ever happening to her – and yet it was. She also knew that it was a sincere, deep-rooted feeling, from a man whose heart wasn't given lightly.

There were no guarantees in life, but she was as sure as she could be that, this time, this love would not be snatched away again.

The chair scraped as he rose from the table.

'Please,' he said, reaching out his hand.

She allowed him to pull her to her feet, draw her into his arms and hold her close. 'Last Christmas, I vowed I'd never trust someone, or love someone, or risk my heart ever again. And yet . . .' He held her tighter. 'Here you are, against all the odds. I think I've loved you for a long time now, but I refused to allow myself to accept it. I built my walls higher and higher and tried to keep you out. I gave myself excuses, I searched for any reason not to trust you or open myself up again.'

He stroked her hair.

'Jay. I wish I'd been honest with you from the start.'

'You had no obligation to. I was so . . . thorny. Why would you share anything with me at all? Still, I couldn't keep you out or fight against how I feel for you.'

She had to smile. 'You make me sound like some kind of invader, crashing into your life.'

He laughed. 'No, you've done nothing – nothing except be *you*. And being you is more than enough and way more than I deserve.' He held her face in his hands. 'Can we start again?'

'I'd rather build on what we have.'

She wasn't sure who kissed who, only that it was the deepest, sweetest kiss she wanted to last forever. A little breathless afterwards, she said, 'I don't think there's any point you going all that way home in this terrible weather, is there?'

Jay nodded enthusiastically. 'No, I agree.'

She nodded her head. 'It might be safer for us to huddle together for warmth on my sofa before you venture outside.'

The next morning was Tuesday and Lottie was awake early. With Jay, all her worries had been set aside for a few hours. However, now, her thoughts were all for Steph.

'I'm afraid I have to go.'

'Work?'

'No. It's Steph. She's getting the results of her scan today and I promised I'd go with her to see the consultant. We're hoping it shows the all clear.'

Jay held her. 'I hope so too. Please let me know how it goes?'

'I will. What will you do today?'

'Me?' He smiled. 'Oh, I think I'll find something.'

With that mysterious statement, and another kiss, he let her go.

While she drove to pick up Steph, Lottie debated with herself whether to tell her sister she and Jay had finally got together. On the one hand it would distract her sister, on the other, was it something that should wait for a happier moment? *If* that happier moment came. Lottie fought down panic. What if she there was bad news? More aggressive treatment? No treatment? How would they help the girls to understand? How would they tell their parents?

The joy of her time with Jay evaporated, but at least she now had someone she could share her own worries with. Someone to support her, who understood her fears and who, she sensed, would always be there for her and never run out.

That thought gave her the renewed strength to be positive for Steph's sake.

An hour later, Lottie found herself sitting on a chair outside the consultant's office, waiting for the door to open and find out the answer. Would Steph be smiling or grim-faced? Lottie would know in an instant.

The time stretched on. Ten minutes, twenty, half an hour and just when Lottie felt she might scream with tension, Steph emerged.

Oh God, she had tears on her cheeks. Lottie could see them glistening. She jumped up, grabbing her bag as the door shut behind Steph and she walked slowly forward.

Lottie hurried over to her. 'Love . . .' she murmured.

'I-I'm OK. It's gone. They can't find anything . . .'

'Oh God.'

'Can w-we get out of here?'

'Mmm . . .' Lottie let out a breath and found her eyes full of tears. Her shoulders shook and she grabbed a handful of tissues from her bag.

It wasn't until they reached the car park that they both gave in, hugging each other and sobbing with relief.

'I am so so happy. I'm so relieved.'

Steph lifted her face to the sky. 'I am going to be OK!' she shouted.

'This calls for champagne!' Lottie said. 'For you, anyway. I'm driving so maybe I'd better bring it over on Christmas Day.'

'Look what happened the last time I had some! I put my foot in it with you and Jay!'

'Ah – I have news about that.' Lottie remembered that she'd also intended to tell Steph about Nadia and Jay. With all the chaos, and worry and excitement of the past few days, she hadn't got round to it. Although it was her own relationship with Jay she wanted to focus on from now on, she didn't think Jay would mind her explaining what had happened to Steph.

Steph wiped her eyes and they widened. 'What news?'

Lottie grinned. 'Jump in the car. I'll tell you on the way home.'

After she'd taken Steph home and they'd had a cuppa and given the twins the good news, Lottie went back to the Bothy and she and Jay headed up to the fells with Trevor. It was a crisp winter afternoon, the fell tops were covered in snow, the setting sun turning them pink as the day drew to a close. Nearing Firholme, lights began to pop on in the windows of the villages around the lake, and smoke spiralled from the chimneys. Sharing the place they both loved, Lottie was filled with a sense of excitement and joy she hadn't felt before, even with Connor.

The next morning, she had the very happy experience of waking up to a man beside her. A naked man, at that – Connor had favoured discreet grey shorts and T-shirt. Already awake, Jay got out of her bed, and crossed to the window, treating her to a pretty fabulous rear view. Lottie was in no mood to cut short her admiration so simply ran with it, drinking in his broad shoulders, toned thighs and bottom.

'Sun's out,' he said, peering around the side of the curtain. He turned back to her, with a front view that was equally impressive. 'I wish I could stay in bed with you all day but I have to get to work. The tree sales centre closes today and we need to start winding things up.'

'I have another day off. Do you have time for breakfast?'

'Yes, but . . .' He sat next to her and pulled the duvet back. 'There are better uses of that time.'

'What about Trevor?'

With a smile, he climbed back into bed. 'He'll forgive me, just this once.'

Jay eventually left, crunching down a piece of toast on the run. Five minutes later, she watched him jog towards the forest with Trevor lolloping alongside him. She stood in the middle of her sitting room, trying to adjust – to even believe – that finally, she and Jay had got together. Instead of feeling exhausted after a night with little sleep, she was fizzing with energy.

Connor and Keegan were far away on honeymoon. They were a memory, already receding into the distance, and all she had to do was enjoy the moment.

Anything was possible.

Jay messaged her several times during the morning and

called her at lunchtime, asking if she'd like to share dinner with him in his cottage.

Lottie went round, taking a bottle of wine.

He met her at the door, accompanied by Trevor, who could hardly contain himself at another human entering the house.

After the briefest of kisses and a pat for Trevor, Jay assumed a stern expression that made Lottie wonder what was coming.

'Wait here,' he ordered, taking the bottle bag from her hand. 'Close your eyes.'

She squeezed them shut, wondering what on earth he could be up to. Trevor's tail thumped against her leg as if he was as excited about the surprise as Jay was.

Jay guided her into his sitting room. 'Don't peep,' he warned. Her nose twitched as she smelled woodsmoke mingled with a fresh familiar scent. Pine . . .

She was gently manoeuvred into position, until he declared, 'OK. You can look now!'

She blinked. In the corner of the room was a small but beautiful spruce tree, its branches lush and green – and very bare.

'You got a tree . . .' Lottie said, stating the bleedin' obvious, as Steph might say.

'It is a tree,' he said. 'But not as we know it.'

Lottie burst out laughing.

'I brought it home this evening. It was practically the only one left and I didn't like to leave it lying there, all abandoned and lonely. We'd sold out of decs but I'll nip out for some tomorrow.'

Lottie put her arms around him. 'It's absolutely gorgeous.'

'So are you.' He kissed her and the thrill travelled all the way to her toes. 'You'll help me decorate it? I'm out of practice.'

'I can do better than that. Wait here. I promise I'll be back.'

'Sounds mysterious!' he called after but she was already halfway out of the door. A few minutes later, she was back with the twins' gift bag. 'I'd forgotten this. It's from the girls and while I don't know exactly what it is, I've a very good idea.'

He took the bag. 'I didn't expect anything from them.'

'They insisted on getting something for you from one of the stalls at the Christmas fair.'

He unwrapped the tissue and a broad grin spread across his face. 'Wow. It's a reindeer,' he said, holding up the wooden figure by its red ribbon.

'I thought so. I had one almost the same. Steph tried to hint that you didn't do Christmas, but it was impossible.'

'I can understand that . . . and it's beautiful. Thank them for me.' There was genuine delight in his voice and he looped the ribbon around a branch and stood back. 'It's a start but Rudolph's going to be a bit lonely.'

'We'll sort it out tomorrow. I can even set the girls to work making some home-made paper chains, if you like. They'd love to.'

'You do that.' He went quiet and then said, 'Lottie, I have a big favour to ask. I'd like you to come with me to my parents'. You'll want to be with Steph and the girls on Christmas Day for lunch but if you'd like to come with me for tea, I'd love that. Ben, Nadia and Seb will be there and I'd like to surprise my mum . . .'

Lottie was taken aback. 'I'd love to – but they won't be expecting me.'

'That's exactly why I'd like you to come and if you were by my side, I'd feel a lot better. Mum and Dad will be delighted to see me with . . .' his grin was sheepish '. . . with someone new, and looking happy. I'm sure Ben and Nadia will be relieved too.'

Still amazed to be asked, Lottie couldn't refuse him. 'If you want me to, then of course I'll come.'

'Good.' He heaved a sigh of relief. 'So, I have a tree, I'm ready to spread some festive cheer. I'm no longer an official Scrooge.'

She laughed. 'All you need do now is to rush out and buy the biggest turkey in the shop.'

He took her in his arms. 'That'll have to wait. I can think of far more exciting ways of celebrating the new reformed me.'

'In that case,' she said, 'let's open the fizz and take it to bed. Dinner – and the tree – will still be here.'

Chapter Forty-Two

Christmas Eve

Christmas Eve dawned dry but dull. No floods, no snow, just a grey dishcloth of a sky, but Lottie didn't care about the weather. Her mood was as bright as if she were standing on top of a fell, on a glorious day, gazing down at the lake, with the green fields and bluest of skies stretching on forever. It was the happiness that comes from having climbed a mountain, in the roughest weather, and against all the odds reached the peak.

It seemed Jay had caught her mood too, because she could hear him whistling in the kitchen below, and smell the coffee brewing. They'd spent the past three nights together in either her bed or Jay's, and it had been pure bliss. She went downstairs to find Trevor wolfing down his breakfast, while her own was laid out on the table.

'Any update on Seb?' she asked, thinking of the little boy first.

'He's doing incredibly well. The antibiotics are working and they plan to discharge him later today.' Jay smiled. 'Ben called to tell me. He'll be home for Christmas Day.'

'I'm so pleased. That's typical of children. They can go downhill fast but they bounce back too.'

'Thank goodness.' He put a plate in front of her. 'It's an unusual breakfast. I didn't have much in.'

'Christmas-tree-shaped crumpets? Wow. Where did you get these?'

'Petrol station store in the village. They're cheesy, but hey, it is Christmas Eve.'

They ate them with butter from a farm in the valley and jam made from local damsons, while planning their day.

'I've been thinking,' he said, suddenly serious. 'That I can't possibly take you away from Steph and the twins tomorrow. It's not fair to leave her alone.'

'I've already thought of it. She honestly won't mind if I come with you after lunch. We could always go back to hers later, if you like, once the twins are in bed.'

'Are you sure?'

'Yes. She'll enjoy some grown-up company and besides, I'm going to be there most of the day.'

He leaned over the table and kissed her. 'I'm really glad you're coming with me.'

'I want to,' Lottie said, though she already had a flutter of nerves as to how Jay's family might react.

'I spoke to Ben about tomorrow so he's already forewarned. Nadia's OK with it so it's only Mum and Dad who aren't in the know. We talked for a long time . . .'

'I'm so glad.'

'I'm not sure things can be exactly the same as before. Not yet, anyway, but we've made a good start.'

She was choked up by the promising news. 'That's all that matters.'

After breakfast, they took Trevor for a walk in the forest, and saw the squirrels again before Lottie left for Steph's and Jay left for Keswick to do some last-minute shopping. Very last-minute, thought Lottie, driving along the lanes to her sister's. She had finished hers and wrapped most of it. She also had some of 'Santa's' presents in the boot of the car, ready to sneak them into the shed while the girls were distracted.

The sun had finally broken through the clouds, and shadows were scudding along the lake. Sheep grazed peacefully in the fields. They would already be expecting their lambs, she thought, thinking of them romping on the fells by March. For now, she had a proper Christmas break to look forward to before the new season started at Firholme. So many new things to look forward to . . . fresh hope, new love and Jay by her side.

Steph must have been waiting for her because the door opened the moment she parked on the road outside. Mindful that the twins would likely be watching too, Lottie decided to leave the secret gifts and go straight in.

Steph seemed a bit flustered, with flushed cheeks and a suspicious smudge of mascara under her eyes. 'Everything OK?' Lottie asked, stepping into the hallway. 'Is the video call set up?'

'Yes. Mum and Dad are ready.' She grinned. 'I think they'll be a bit bleary-eyed as it's late night over there.'

Lottie walked in to find the girls sitting on the sofa in their best dresses, ready for the video call.

'You look lovely!' she said and they grinned.

'OK. It's time. Let's go for it.' Steph and Lottie squashed onto the sofa either side of the twins and started the call. A few moments later, their parents appeared and there were the usual squeals of excitement on both sides.

'Wow, you look smart considering it's so late,' Lottie said, seeing her mum's dress and her father in a jacket. 'I thought it was pyjamas at this hour.'

Her mum exchanged a glance with her father. 'We thought we'd make an effort, didn't we?'

Lottie stared at the screen. 'Is that a new sofa?'

Her mum laughed. 'We did some redecorating.'

Steph grinned.

'Hang on a moment,' her mum said. 'There's someone at the door.'

She got up and left the room. A moment later they heard her calling 'Tim!' to their father. 'It's for you!'

He rolled his eyes. 'Won't be a sec,' he said and left with an indulgent smile on his face. 'Must be a delivery.'

'Where have they gone?' Myra asked.

'Typical. We wait all week for the call and they vanish,' Steph said. 'I may as well put the kettle on.'

Lottie watched the screen while the girls fidgeted and slipped off the sofa, running into the kitchen. Something was odd about her parents' house . . .

Before she had time to wonder any longer, there was a commotion outside the door then shrieks and . . .

'Oh my God!

Lottie's hands flew to her face.

'Santa has come early this year . . .'

The twins were bouncing up and down as if they were on springs and holding the hands of two tanned fifty-somethings who Lottie hadn't seen for many long months.

'M-mum! What are you doing here? Oh my God, Dad!'

She flew at her parents, every bit as excited as the girls, and hugged them as if she'd never let them go. Once tissues had been deployed and eyes wiped, they sat on the sofa with the twins on their laps, while Lottie interrogated them.

'When did you decide to do this? I had absolutely *no* clue.'

'It's been planned for a while,' her mum said. 'We told Steph a couple of days ago but asked her to keep it a secret until now.'

'How long are you staying? Where are you staying?'

'We rented a holiday cottage just down the street and we're staying for a couple of months,' her dad said, with Myra wriggling on his knee.

'What about work? Have you both taken unpaid leave?'

Her parents exchanged a glance. 'No . . . in fact, we have another surprise for you all. We're moving back home to the UK. We've had a wonderful ten years but we miss you – all of you – and so we're both taking early retirement and coming back to the Lake District. After all that's happened lately, we've realised that nothing matters like family.'

'So, we'll be house hunting while we're here,' her dad said.

Much to the twins' alarm, all the adults around them began to cry again.

'The Internet is great,' her father said, with a wobble in his voice. 'But nothing compares with a hug, and being able to see your family face to face and we've decided that is far too precious to miss. We're determined we're never going to be apart again.'

After Steph had made tea, and everyone had stopped crying, the twins went to watch *Frozen* on TV.

'So, we'll all be together for Christmas Day, and I think we can just about squeeze around the dining table,' said Steph. 'I might need you to bring an extra chair from the Bothy, Lottie.'

'No problem,' Lottie said, still amazed that her parents were here. She was also working out how she could possibly be in two places at once. She couldn't leave her family tomorrow but the prospect of letting down Jay was unthinkable too. There would have to be a compromise.

'I have a favour to ask,' she said. 'Could you spare me after lunch for Christmas tea?'

Steph scrutinised her. 'Would that have anything to do with the gorgeous Jay?'

Her mother also stared at her. 'Who's the gorgeous Jay?'

Her dad raised his eyebrows. 'Is this a new bloke?'

'Um. Well. Yes, I guess he is.'

Steph held her arms aloft. 'Well. Hoo-bloody-ray! About bloody time.'

Her parents exchanged looks. 'Has this been going on a while?'

'Far too long,' Steph said. 'I've had so many sleepless nights worrying about the pair of them. It's official, then, is it, if you've been invited to his for Christmas tea?'

'Well, I haven't been invited, technically. Jay wants to surprise his family by taking me with him.'

'In that case, you must go,' her mum said. 'We can spare you for a few hours.'

Lottie hugged her mother.

'As long as we hear all about this Jay and get to meet him.'

Steph was in, like a flash. 'He must come to lunch!'

'He'll want to be with his own family,' her dad said.

'I have a better idea,' Steph said. 'What about if we have our lunch at dinner time. That way, Lottie and Jay can go to his family early and then come here later.'

'Are you sure?' Lottie said, wondering how much family Christmas cheer Jay could actually handle.

'Totally. It makes no difference to us. Gives me longer to cook that massive turkey to be honest.'

She laughed. 'That's very kind of you but I'll have to ask him first. It's – um – complicated,' she said. 'And then there's Trevor . . .'

'Trevor's welcome too. The girls would love to have him.'

Her dad was utterly confused. 'Who's Trevor?'

'A dog,' Lottie said.

'Ah. OK,' her mum said, clearly itching to know what kind of 'complicated' but trying not to pry. 'Can we at least know how you met Jay? Where does he live? Can we see a picture of him?'

'And Trevor,' her father said wryly.

Smiling to herself, Lottie got out her phone, shared every

photo she had, happy to be interrogated on the subject of Jay and Trevor until the cows came home.

Later, Steph and Lottie were in the kitchen, while the twins were entertained by their grandparents.

'This year had ended a lot better than it started,' she said. 'I'm on the mend, Mum and Dad are staying, and you're with Jay.' She had a sly smile on her face. 'And I've got a date with Kerr.'

'Woo! That's great. When did it happen?'

'I called him and asked him. You were right. He was waiting for some encouragement and didn't want to put any pressure on me. We're going to go out for a meal over the Christmas holiday so I'm going to need a babysitter . . . not that I have to look far with Mum and Dad here. I'm guessing you'll be otherwise engaged.'

Lottie laughed. 'I might be. That's very exciting news. I really like Kerr and I promise to grill you as hard about him as you have me about Jay.'

Steph rolled her eyes. 'I'd expect nothing less.'

Lottie left, feeling more hopeful about Steph than she had for so many months, but wondering how the next day would go with Jay and his family. He'd taken a massive leap of faith by arranging to meet Ben and Nadia on Christmas Day but as Lottie was painfully aware, just when you thought everything was going well in your world, it could all come crashing down.

Chapter Forty-Three

Christmas Day

Standing outside his parents' place, Jay took Lottie's hand in his. Even though he'd made his peace with Ben and they'd sworn a pact to make the day a happy one, this would be the first time they would all be together for a very long time.

Steph had insisted on inviting him to Christmas evening dinner, despite his not very serious protests that she wouldn't have enough food and that Lottie's family would want to be together. He'd been nervous but, for Lottie's sake, had accepted readily. He already felt comfortable in Steph's company, the twins were a hoot and if Lottie's parents were anything like she was, he couldn't fail to have a good time.

He felt a squeeze on his hand. 'Ready?' Lottie said.

He let out a breath. 'As I'll ever be. Trevor! Come on, boy.'

The dog pulled his nose out of a hedge, and followed Jay

and Lottie down the garden path, wagging his tail. The three of them were the only living creatures in the street, although almost every window of every house had lights in it. Jay hoped all the people inside were happy, or at least content. It was too much to expect them to be as happy as he was.

He rang the bell and it was answered almost immediately by his father, wearing a comedy elf apron.

'Nice apron, Dad,' Jay said, trying to hide his nerves. 'This is Lottie, my girlfriend.'

His father smiled at Lottie. 'Hello . . . Thank you for bringing Jay to the hospital last week.'

'No problem,' she said. 'And sorry for landing on you un-announced . . .'

Jay rested his hand on the small of her back. Her physical presence, not to mention her support, gave him courage. Why had he waited so long to realise how much he needed her? What an indispensable part of his life she suddenly seemed.

'We wanted to surprise you,' he said.

'We weren't expecting you now . . .' He smiled broadly. 'But that doesn't matter. It's wonderful to see you both but . . .' The grin was replaced by an anxious frown. 'You do know Ben and Nadia are here with Seb?'

'Yes,' Jay replied gently. 'I do.'

His mum appeared behind her husband, her eyes wide in amazement. 'Jay! You're early!'

'Yes. I am and I know it's a bloody cheek and you won't have enough food but we don't care about that. Lottie and I – we wanted to share Christmas lunch with you like I used to. Ben knows too, and Nadia. We wanted to surprise you and

381

I wanted you to meet my new partner.' He slipped his arm around her. 'Someone very special to me. Lottie.'

Jay's mum threw her arms around him and started crying, but then invited him in. Ben shook hands with him.

'Good to see you, bro.'

'You too.'

'You must be Lottie,' Nadia said.

'Yes. I'm so happy to see Seb is better.'

'We are too. We all are.' She seemed genuinely happy for Jay. He could honestly say that he felt . . . nothing – nothing but relief that Nadia hadn't had to go through an imaginable loss. Nothing but regret that he hadn't let her go sooner, and then a quiet recognition that regret of any kind was wasted energy. That today was about enjoying every second, and being thankful that he was surrounded by so many people whom he loved and who loved him.

Their parents vanished into the kitchen, leaving Jay with Lottie, Nadia and Ben. He felt strange, and she was obviously nervous about his reaction but he tried to keep things light.

Nadia smiled. 'Would you like to hold Seb?'

Jay remembered the time he'd seen Seb at the school. That had been a huge shock and he hadn't known how to react but now, he felt far more at ease with holding his little nephew. 'Yes – but is it OK?'

'Yes. He'll be fine.' She handed the baby to him and he looked remarkably well for a little boy whose life had been in danger a few days previously. Jay wasn't quite sure how to hold a baby and Seb was a lively wriggler, who seemed none the worse for his ordeal.

'He's very excited with all the new people and presents,' Nadia said, watching him struggle with Seb who was grabbing at Jay's hair again.

Lottie caught his eye, obviously remembering Seb's fascination with Jay at the nativity play.

'I remember the first Christmas with my nieces,' she said, tickling one of Seb's feet to distract him.

'How old are they?' Nadia asked.

'Five, and they could hardly contain themselves this morning, according to my sister. We're going to see them later today so I've saved my own presents for them.'

'That reminds me,' Jay said, 'I bought Seb a present. It's only small but it's from Firholme.'

'Oh, thank you. Shall I take him?' Nadia said. 'He probably wants to go onto the carpet.'

Taking Trevor with him, Jay went out to the car and collected the gifts. When he returned, Nadia and Lottie were chatting about the twins, children and Christmas. He thanked his lucky stars for someone like her, willing to be sensible and tactful. Ben walked in with some fizz and soft drinks on a tray, and exchanged a tentative smile with him. It was a green shoot of reconciliation, one that would need to be nurtured, if it were to bloom. Jay was ready to do what it took.

With Trevor settled with a chew, Ben sat on the carpet with Jay, and helped Seb tear at the wrapping paper. Inside, there were some woodland animal stacking blocks, which Lottie had helped him choose from the Firholme café gift shop.

Seb picked one up and promptly threw it at his grandad. Everyone burst out laughing.

'Thanks, I think he likes them,' Nadia said and Ben nodded.

After Jay had given his parents their gifts, Lottie went to the car and fetched a Firholme gift hamper. 'We've landed on you unexpectedly and this is a small contribution.'

Jay's mum looked delighted and gave her a peck on the cheek by way of thanks.

She kissed Jay too. 'Now we've all landed on you for Christmas dinner, we were worried you might not have enough food, Mum.'

'Me not have enough food for Christmas?' She laughed in derision. 'Don't be ridiculous! I told you I'd ordered a turkey big enough to feed an army. Now, come on, let's drink to Seb's good health and to a very happy Christmas.'

Chapter Forty-Four

It was late before Lottie and Jay made it back to Firholme. Trevor flopped on the carpet in Jay's cottage, worn out by strange smells, strange people and too many treats.

Lottie sank onto the sofa herself and put her feet up. 'I know exactly how he feels.' She rubbed her stomach. 'Today has been like the *Vicar of Dibley*. I never want to see another sprout as long as I live.'

'I had far too much turkey,' Jay said, sitting beside her and lifting her feet onto his lap. 'Trevor, mate, we're going to go on some very long walks, starting tomorrow.'

Lottie laughed. 'Can you take me with you?'

'First thing in the morning.'

She smiled, struck by the happiness that seemed to have lit him up from the inside. It had taken a lot of courage to make his peace with Ben and face Nadia, but it had been worth it for everyone's sakes. Jay's mum had been in tears and dinner at Steph's had been equally emotional, with her own parents' unexpected arrival.

'Why are you looking at me like that?' Jay said, a little bemused.

'Like what?'

'As if I'm an alien who's landed?'

She laughed. 'I was only thinking that for a man who vowed he'd do anything to avoid Christmas, you seem to have enjoyed two of them on the same day.'

'Three. They all came at once. You're the third Christmas for me. Being with you makes up a hundred times for the one I didn't have last year.'

Lottie leaned in to kiss him but then remembered something. 'Oh my God.' She sprang up from the sofa, causing Trevor to let out a yip of alarm.

'What?'

'I almost forgot your present!'

Jay slapped his forehead. 'Me too, though I wasn't expecting one from you.'

'Wait. I need to go to the Bothy.'

'Okayyy . . .'

She was back within a minute, with a large box. 'I got this a couple of days ago before I knew about . . .'

Jay was waiting with a much smaller box.

'Wow,' he said. 'You first.'

'No, you.' She thrust the box into his arms.

Lottie could hardly contain herself, while Jay put it on the coffee table and ripped off the paper.

He opened the flaps and peered inside. 'Wow, it's full of little parcels.'

'Open one.'

It had taken her hours to choose the decorations and wrap each one in tissue paper, but it was worth it to see the look on his face, as he unwrapped each figure.

'A red squirrel . . . more reindeer!' He laughed. 'An octopus?'

Lottie smiled. 'The girls suggested that one. There's tinsel too and a box of fairy lights. I'm sorry I forgot to give it to you in all the excitement.'

He gave her a long lingering kiss. 'We'll dress the tree tomorrow. Together.'

'I hoped you'd say that. Now,' he said, picking up the smaller box again. 'Your turn.'

With slightly shaky fingers, Lottie pulled the ribbon from the small parcel and undid the silver wrapping paper. There was a small leather jewellery box inside.

'Open it,' Jay said.

She opened the box and nestling in the top was a gold chain with a tiny Christmas tree topped with a diamond star. It was the most exquisite thing she'd ever seen but she couldn't speak for happiness.

'Do you like it?' Jay said, his voice unsure. 'I could always change it?'

'No!' she cried. 'Oh, no. It's perfect. I want to wear it now.' She picked it up and fastened it around her neck. 'I don't want to ever take it off.'

Jay laughed and she kissed him. 'I don't want to ever let you go,' he said.

'I'd hoped this year would be better than the last,' Lottie said. 'I couldn't imagine how it would be worse.'

'What I never expected is that it would be the best Christmas ever, thanks to you, Lottie.' He kissed her until she thought she might soar with happiness.

Trevor let out a bark.

Coming up for air, Lottie laughed. 'He's overwhelmed by me doing far too much of this hugging and kissing thing.'

'He'll get used it,' said Jay. 'It's going to go on for a very very long time. Happy Christmas, Lottie. I love you.'

Lottie told him the same, but no more words were needed. Leaving Trevor dreaming by the fire, she took him up to bed to make the most of what was left of Christmas Day, knowing there would be many more to come.

THE END

Acknowledgements

I started writing this book at the beginning of January 2020, unaware, like all of us, of the storm that was about to hit. It may sound trite, but the one thing I learned from this tough time was that the people I love are infinitely more precious to me than I'd ever realised. I hope this story reflects how much I value them.

My thanks go out to all of the people helped with research and supported me while writing *A Surprise Christmas Wedding*. If I've accidentally overlooked you, please accept my apologies.

Firstly, I'm hugely grateful to Hayley for sharing her recent experience of cervical cancer and send her every good wish for her continued recovery. I'd also like to thank my agent, Broo Doherty, Moira Briggs, the Coffee Crew, the Party People, the Friday Floras, Janice Hume and all the book bloggers and readers in my Facebook group who share their passion for books far and wide.

My amazing editor, Rachel Faulkner-Willcocks, played a

massive role in helping me turn this story into the novel you have in front of you – she is awesome. I'd like to thank Tilda McDonald for commissioning the book last year and Helena for her copy editing skills. There's no way my books would be on so many shelves or e readers without the wizardry and tireless enthusiasm of the Avon sales, marketing and publicity team, particularly Sabah and Ellie. Keep up the good work, guys!

Finally, to John, to my parents and Charles, and to Charlotte and James, you mean more to me than I can ever say.

**Escape to Cornwall with Phillipa Ashley's
bestselling Porthmellow series . . .**

Phillipa Ashley

*A Perfect
Cornish
Summer*

'Warm, funny and feel-good'
KATIE FFORDE

Christmas in Cornwall is just around the corner . . .

'Sparkling and festive – loved it!'
MILLY JOHNSON

A Perfect Cornish Christmas

Phillipa Ashley

The perfect getaway . . .

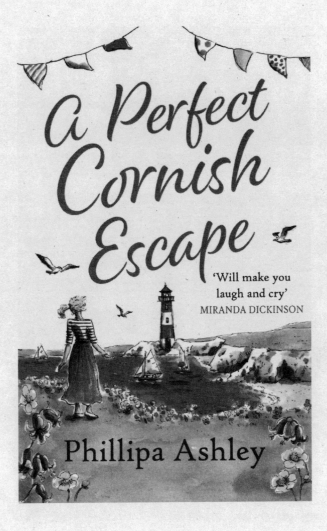

A Perfect Cornish Escape

'Will make you
laugh and cry'
MIRANDA DICKINSON

Phillipa Ashley